About the author

Sophie Hannah is the internationally bestselling author of ten psychological thrillers, as well as *The Monogram Murders*, the first Hercule Poirot mystery to be published since Agatha Christie's death and approved by her estate. Sophie is also an award-winning short story writer and poet. Her fifth collection of poetry, *Pessimism for Beginners*, was shortlisted for the 2007 TS Eliot Award and she won first prize in the Daphne du Maurier Festival Short Story Competition for 'The Octopus Nest'. Her psychological thriller *The Carrier* won the Crime Thriller of the Year award at the 2013 Specsavers National Book Awards, and *The Point of Rescue* and *The Other Half Lives* have both been adapted for television as *Case Sensitive*. Sophie lives in Cambridge with her husband and two children, where she is a Fellow Commoner at Lucy Cavendish College.

SOPHIE
HANNAH

hurting distance

HODDER

First published in Great Britain in 2007 by Hodder & Stoughton

An Hachette UK company

This edition published 2015

1

A CIP catalogue record for this title
is available from the British Library

B format paperback ISBN 978 0 340 84034 4

Typeset in Sabon by Hewer Text UK Ltd, Edinburgh
Printed and bound by Clays Ltd, St Ives plc

Hodder Headline's policy is to use papers that are natural, renewable
and recyclable products and made from wood grown in sustainable
forests. The logging and manufacturing processes are expected to
conform to the environmental regulations of the country of origin.

Hodder & Stoughton Ltd
Carmelite House
50 Victoria Embankment
London EC4Y 0DZ

www.hodder.co.uk

For Lisanne with love

From: *NJ <nj239@hotmail.com>*
To: *Speak Out and Survive*
   <survivorsstories@speakoutandsurvive.org.uk>
Subject: *This is not my story*
Date: *Mon, 18 May 2003 13:28:07 +0100*

This is not my story. I'm not sure I want to share that, or my feelings, with strangers, on a website. It would seem phoney, somehow – phoney and attention-seeking. This is just something I want to say, and your website gives no address for submitting letters.

Did you ever stop to wonder, when you were thinking of a name for your organisation, whether speaking out is always the best thing to do? Once you tell somebody something, it makes it more real. Why take what you wish had never happened and make it happen again and again in the minds of everyone you know? I will never tell anybody my so-called story, which means there will be no justice, no punishment for those who deserve it. Sometimes that thought is pretty hard to take. Still, it's a small price to pay for not having to spend the rest of my life being thought of as a victim.

Sorry, a survivor. Though that word makes me feel uneasy. At no point did anybody try to kill me. It makes sense to talk about survivors in the context of a plane crash or a nuclear explosion: situations in which it might be expected that everyone involved would die.

I

But in most cases rape is not a life-threatening event, so the sense of rare achievement that the word 'survivor' conveys seems patronising – a sort of false consolation.

When I first logged on to your site, I hoped that something I read there would make me feel better, but the opposite has happened. Why do so many of your correspondents use the same cloying vocabulary: thriving, telling and healing, smiling through tears, rising from the ashes, etc.? It reminds me of the lyrics of a bad heavy-metal album. Nobody says that they do not ever expect to get over what happened to them.

This will sound terrible, but I am actually jealous of many of the people whose stories are posted on your site: the ones with insensitive, demanding boyfriends, the ones who drank too much on first dates. At least they can make sense of their ordeals. My attacker was someone I had never seen before and have not seen since, someone who kidnapped me in broad daylight and knew every detail about me: my name, my job, where I lived. I don't know how he knew. I don't know why he chose me, where he took me or who all the other people were. I will not go into any more detail than that. Perhaps if I did, you'd understand why I feel so strongly about what I'm going to say next.

On the 'What Is Rape?' page of your site, you list a number of definitions, the last of which is 'any sexually intimidating behaviour'. You go on to say, 'No physical contact needs to have taken place – sometimes an inappropriate look or comment is enough to make a woman feel violated.' When I read that, I wanted to hit whoever wrote it.

I know you'll disapprove of this letter and me and everything I've said, but I'm sending it anyway. I think it's important to point out that not all rape victims have the same mindset, vocabulary and attitudes.

N.J.

2006

Part I

I

Monday 3 April

I could explain, if you were here to listen. I am breaking my promise to you, the only one you ever asked me to make. I'm sure you remember. There was nothing casual about your voice when you said, 'I want you to promise me something.'

'What?' I asked, propping myself up on one elbow, burning my skin on the yellow nylon sheet in my eagerness to be upright, attentive. I was desperate to please you. You ask for so little, and I'm always looking for small, subtle ways to give you more. 'Anything!' I said, laughing, deliberately extravagant. A promise is the same as a vow, and I wanted there to be vows between us, binding us.

My exuberance made you smile, but not for long. You're so grave when we're in bed together. You think it's a tragedy that you'll soon have to leave and that is how you always look: like a man preparing for calamity. I usually cry after you've gone (no, I've never told you, because I'm damned if I'm going to encourage your mournful streak), but while we're together in our room I'm as high as if I were on strong, mind-altering drugs. It seems impossible that we will ever be apart, that the moment will end. And in some ways it doesn't. When I go home, when I'm making pasta in my kitchen or chiselling Roman numerals in my workshop, I'm not there really. I'm still in room eleven at the Travel-tel, with its hard, synthetic, rust-coloured carpet that feels like the bristles of a toothbrush under your feet and its pushed-together twin beds with mattresses that aren't mattresses at all but thick, orange foam mats, the sort that used to cover the floor of the gymnasium at my secondary school.

Our room. I knew for sure that I loved you, that it wasn't just infatuation or physical attraction, when I heard you say to the receptionist, 'No, it has to be room eleven, same as last time. We need the same room every time.' Need, not want. Everything is urgent for you; nothing is casual. You never sprawl on the faded, bobbly sofa, or take your shoes off and put your feet up. You sit upright, fully clothed, until we're about to get into bed.

Later, when we were alone, you said, 'I'm worried it's going to be sordid, meeting in a shitty motel. At least if we stick to one room, it'll feel more homely.' Then you spent the next fifteen minutes apologising because you couldn't afford to take me somewhere grander. Even then (how long had we known each other? Three weeks?) I knew better than to offer to share the cost.

I remember nearly everything you've said to me over the past year. Maybe if I could bring to mind the right phrase, the crucial line, it would lead me straight to you. I do not really believe this, but I keep going through it all in my mind, just in case.

'Well?' I prodded your shoulder with my finger. 'Here I am, a naked woman offering to promise you anything, and you're ignoring me?'

'This isn't a joke, Naomi.'

'I know. I'm sorry.'

You like to do everything slowly, even speaking. It makes you angry if you're rushed. I don't think I've ever made you laugh, or even seen you laugh properly, though you often talk about laughing – in the pub with Sean and Tony. 'I laughed till I cried,' you say. 'I laughed till the tears were pouring down my face.'

You turned to me and asked, 'Do you know where I live?'

I blushed. Damn, I'd been rumbled. You'd spotted that I was obsessed with you, collecting any fact or detail I could get my hands on. All week I had been chanting your address in my head, sometimes even saying it or singing it aloud while I was working.

'You saw me writing it down last time, didn't you? On that form for the receptionist. I noticed you looking.'

'Three Chapel Lane, Spilling. Sorry. Would you rather I didn't know?'

'In a way,' you said. 'Because this has to be completely safe. I've told you that.' You sat up then too, and put on your glasses. 'I don't want it to end. I want it to last for a long time, for as long as I last. It has to be a hundred per cent safe, completely separate from the rest of my life.'

I understood at once, and nodded. 'But . . . now the Traveltel receptionist knows your address too,' I said. 'What if they send a bill or something?'

'Why would they? I always pay when I leave.'

Does it make it easier, having an administrative ritual to complete before you go, a small ceremony that takes place on the boundary of our life and your other life? I wish I had an equivalent task to perform before leaving. I always stay the night (though I allow you to think it's only sometimes, not every time) and march briskly out of the Traveltel the next morning, barely stopping to smile at the receptionist. It feels too informal, somehow, too quick and easy.

'There's no paperwork to send,' you said. 'Anyway, Juliet doesn't even open her own post, let alone mine.' I

7

noticed a slight vibration in your lower jaw, a tightening around your mouth. It always happens when you mention Juliet. I am collecting details about her, too, though I wish I weren't. Many of them involve a 'let alone': she doesn't know how to turn on a computer, let alone use the Internet. She never answers the phone, let alone rings anyone herself.

She sounds like a freak, I have wanted to say so often, and stopped myself. I shouldn't allow my envy of her to make me cruel.

You kissed me lightly before saying, 'You mustn't ever come to the house, or ring me there. If Juliet saw you, if she found out in that way, it'd break her.' I love the way you use words. Your speech is more poetic, grander than mine. Everything I say is heavy with mundane detail. You were staring past me, and I turned, half expecting, from your expression, to see a misty grey-and-purple mountain range wreathed in white cloud instead of a beige plastic kettle labelled 'Rawndesley East Services Traveltel', one that regularly contributes little granules of limescale to our hot drinks.

What are you staring at now? Where *are* you?

I wanted to ask for more details. What did you mean, about Juliet breaking? Would she collapse, sobbing, on the floor, lose her memory, become violent? People can break in a range of ways, and I have never been able to work out if you are frightened of your wife or frightened for her. But your tone was solemn and I knew you had more to say. I didn't want to interrupt you.

'It's not just that,' you muttered, scrunching up the diamond-patterned coverlet in your hands. 'It's her. I can't bear the thought of you seeing her.'

'Why?' I felt it would be tactless to tell you that you had nothing to worry about on that score. Did you imagine I was curious, desperate to know who you were married to? Even now, I have a horror of seeing Juliet. I wish I didn't know her name. I would like to keep her as unreal as possible in my mind. Ideally, I would know her only as 'she' and there would be less for my jealousy to latch on to. But I could hardly have said that, could I, when we first met? 'Don't tell me your wife's name, because I think I might be in love with you and I can't stand to know anything about her.'

I doubt you could imagine the anguish I've felt, climbing into bed every night this past year and thinking: Juliet will be lying next to Robert in their bed at this moment. It isn't the thought of her sleeping beside you that makes my face twist in pain and my insides clench, it's the idea that she regards it as ordinary, routine. I don't torment myself with the image of the two of you kissing or making love; instead, I imagine Juliet on her side of the bed, reading a book – something boring about a member of the Royal Family or how to look after houseplants – and barely looking up when you come into the room. She doesn't notice you undressing, getting into bed beside her. Do you wear pyjamas? I can't picture it, somehow. Anyway, whatever you wear, Juliet is used to it, after years of marriage. This is not special for her; it's just another boring, unremarkable night at home. There is nothing she particularly wants or needs to say to you. She is perfectly able to concentrate on the details of Prince Andrew and Fergie's divorce or how to pot a cactus. When her eyelids start to droop, she tosses her book down on the floor and turns on her side, away from you, without even saying goodnight.

I want the opportunity to take you for granted. Although I never would.

'Why don't you want me to see her, Robert?' I asked,

because you seemed to be stuck in a thought, trapped somewhere in your head. You had that look you always get: a frown, your lower jaw jutting out. 'Is there something . . . wrong with her?' If I'd been someone else, I might have added, 'Are you ashamed of her?' but for the past three years I have been unable to use the word 'ashamed'. You won't understand this, because of what I haven't told you. There are things I too like to keep separate.

'Juliet's not had an easy life,' you said. Your tone was defensive, as if I'd insulted her. 'I want you to think of me as I am when I'm with you, here. Not in that house, with her. I hate that fucking house! When we get married, I'll buy us somewhere new.' I remember giggling when you said this, because I'd recently seen a film in which a husband takes his new wife to see the house he has designed and built for her. It is huge and beautiful and has a big red bow wrapped round it. When he removes his hands from her eyes and says, 'Surprise!' the wife storms off in a huff; she is angry that he hasn't consulted her, has presented her with a fait accompli.

I love it when you make decisions for me. I want you to feel proprietorial towards me. I want things because you want them. Except Juliet. You say you don't want her, but you're not yet ready to leave. It's not if, it's when, you say. But not yet. I find that hard to understand.

I stroked your arm. I cannot and never have been able to touch you without feeling faint and tingly, and I felt guilty then because I was supposed to be having a serious conversation, not thinking about sex. 'I promise I'll keep my distance,' I said, knowing you need to be in control, cannot bear to feel events slipping away from you. If we are ever married – *when* we are married – I will call you a control freak affectionately and you will laugh. 'Don't worry.' I held up my hand. 'Scout's honour. I won't suddenly turn up at your house.'

Yet here I am, parked directly opposite. You tell me, though: what choice do I have? If you are here, I will apologise and explain how worried I've been, and I know you'll forgive me. If you are here, maybe I won't care if you forgive me or not; at least I'll know you're all right. It's been more than three days, Robert. I'm starting to go slowly crazy.

When I turned into your road, the first thing I saw was your red lorry, parked right at the bottom on the grass verge, beyond the few houses and before the road narrows to become a country path. I felt a surge in my chest, as if someone had given me a shot of helium, when I read your name on the side of the van. (You're always telling me not to call it a van, aren't you? You wouldn't accept 'Red Van Man' as a nickname, though I tried several times.) Robert Haworth, in big black letters. I adore your name.

The lorry is the same size it's always been, but it looks enormous here, at an angle on the grassy slope, crammed in between the houses and the fields; there is barely enough space for it. My first thought was that this isn't a very convenient place for a lorry driver to live. It must be a nightmare, reversing out on to the main road.

My second thought is that it's Monday. Your lorry shouldn't be here. You should be out in it, on a job. I am getting really worried now, too worried to be intimidated – by the sight of your house, yours and *hers*, Juliet's – into scurrying home to pretend everything is probably okay.

I knew your house was number three, and I suppose I imagined that the numbers would go up to twenty or thirty as they do on most streets, but yours is the third and last house. The first two are opposite one another, nearer to the main road and the Old Chapel Brasserie on the corner. Your house stands alone further down, towards the fields at the end of the lane, and all I can see of it from the road is a bit of slate roof and a long, rectangular slab of beige stone wall, broken up only by a small square window on the top right-hand side: a bathroom, perhaps, or a box room.

I have learned something new about you. You chose to buy the sort of house I'd never buy, one where the back is front-facing and the front is concealed, not visible to passers-by. It gives an unwelcoming impression. I know it's for the sake of privacy, and it makes sense to have the front overlooking the best views, but I've always found houses like yours disconcerting all the same, as if they have rudely turned their backs on the world. Yvon agrees; I know, because we drive past another back-turned house on our regular route to the supermarket. 'Houses like that are for recluses who live on their hermity own and say, "Bah, humbug," a lot,' Yvon said the first time we passed it.

I know what she'd say about 3 Chapel Lane if she were here: 'It looks like the house of someone who might say, "You mustn't ever come to the house." As indeed it is!' I used to talk to you about Yvon, but I stopped after you frowned and said she sounded sarcastic and chippy. That was the only time something you said really upset me. I told you she was my best friend and had been since school. And, yes, she is sarcastic, but only in a good way, only in a way that cheers you up, somehow. She's blunt and irreverent and she firmly believes we should all poke fun at everything, even bad things. Even agonising love for a married man you can't have; Yvon thinks that, especially, is something we ought to poke fun at, and half the time her levity is the only thing that keeps me sane.

When you saw that I was hurt by your criticism of her, you kissed me and said, 'I'll tell you something I read in a book once that's made life easier for me ever since: we do as much harm to ourselves and others when we take offence as when we give offence. Do you see what I'm saying?' I nodded, although I wasn't sure I did.

I never told you, but I repeated your aphorism to Yvon, though of course I didn't tell her the context. I pretended you'd made some other hurtful remark, one that was unconnected to her. 'How astonishingly convenient,' she said, giggling. 'So let's get this straight: you're as guilty when you love a tosser as when you *are* a tosser. Thank you, oh great enlightened one, for sharing that with us.'

I have worried endlessly about what will happen at our wedding, when we eventually get married. I can't imagine you and Yvon having a conversation that doesn't descend rapidly into silence on your part and uproarious ridicule on hers.

She phoned your house last night. I made her, begged her, ruined her evening until she agreed. It makes me feel slightly sick, the idea that she has heard your wife's voice. It's one step closer to something I don't want to face up to, the physical reality of Juliet in the world. She exists. If she didn't, you and I would already be living together. I would know where you were.

Juliet sounded as if she was lying. That's what Yvon said.

In front of the back of your house, there is a stone wall with a brown wooden gate set into it. Nowhere is there a number three; I am able to identify your house only by a process of elimination. I climb out of my car and stagger slightly, as if my limbs are unused to movement. It is a windy, blustery day, but bright – almost spectacularly so. It makes me squint. I feel as if your street has been high-lighted, nature's way of saying, 'This is where Robert lives.'

The gate is high, level with my shoulders. It opens with a creak and I slip on to your property. I find myself standing on a twig-strewn dirt path, staring at your garden. In one corner, there is an old bathtub with two bicycle wheels in it, beside a pile of flattened cardboard boxes. The grass is patchy. I can see many more weeds than plants. It's clear that there were once flowerbeds here, distinct from the scruffy lawn, but now everything is merging into a matted green-and-brown chaos. The sight makes me furious. With Juliet. You work every day, often seven days a week. You haven't got time to tend the garden, but she has. She hasn't had a job since she married you, and the two of you have no children. What does she do all day?

I head for the front door, passing the side of the house and another small, high window. Oh, God, I mustn't think of you trapped inside. But of course you can't be. You're a broad-shouldered, heavy, six-foot-two man. Juliet couldn't confine you anywhere. Unless . . . But I mustn't allow myself to start being ridiculous.

I have decided to be bold and efficient. I vowed to myself three years ago that I would never be scared of anything or anyone again. I will go straight to the front door, ring the bell and ask the questions that need to be asked. Your house, I realise once I get round the front, is a cottage, long and low. From the outside it looks as if nothing has been done to it for several decades. The door is a faded green, and all the windows are square and small, their panes divided into diamonds by lines of lead. You have one big tree. Four straggly lengths of rope dangle from its thickest branch. Was there once a swing? The lawn here at the front slopes down, and beyond it, the view is the kind that landscape painters would fight over. At least four church towers are visible. Now I know what attracted you to the back-turned cottage. I can see right up the Culver Valley, with the river snaking its way along as far as Rawndesley. I wonder if I could see my house, if I had a pair of binoculars.

I cannot pass the window without looking in. I feel elated, suddenly. This rooms is yours, with your things inside it. I put my face close to the glass and cup my hands around my eyes. A lounge. Empty. It's funny – I've always imagined dark colours on the walls, copies of traditional paintings in heavy wooden frames: Gainsborough, Constable, that sort of thing. But your lounge walls are white, uneven, and the only picture is of an unkempt old man in a brown hat watching a young boy play the flute. A plain red rug covers most of the floor, and beneath it is the sort of cheap wood-laminate that looks nothing like wood.

The room is tidy, which is a surprise after the garden. There are lots of ornaments, too many, in neat rows. They cover every surface. Most of them are pottery houses. How odd; I can't imagine you living in a house full of such twee knick-knacks. Is it a collection? When I was a teenager, my mother tried to encourage me to collect some hideous pottery creatures that I think were called 'Whimsies'. No thanks, I told her. I was far more interested in amassing posters of George Michael and Andrew Ridgeley.

I blame Juliet for turning your living room into a housing estate in miniature, just as I blame her for the laminate floor. Everything else in the room is acceptable: a navy-blue sofa and matching chair; wall lights, with semicircular cups of plaster around them so that you can't see the bulb; a wooden, leather-topped footstool; a tape measure; a small stand-up calendar. Yours, yours, yours. I know it is a lunatic thought, but I find I identify with these inanimate objects. I feel exhilarated. Against one wall there is a glass-fronted cabinet containing more pottery houses, a row of tiny ones, the smallest in the room. Below these, a fat, honey-coloured candle that looks as if it has never been lit . . .

The change happens quickly and without warning. It's as if something has exploded in my brain. I back away from the window, stumbling and nearly falling, pulling at the neck of my shirt in case it's that that's restricting my breathing. With my other hand I shield my eyes. My whole body is shaking. I feel as if I might be sick if I can't suck in some air soon. I need oxygen, badly.

I wait for it to pass, but it gets worse. Dark dots burst and dissolve in front of my eyes. I hear myself moaning. I can't stay upright; it is too much effort. I fall down on to my hands and knees, panting, sweating. No more thoughts of you, or of Juliet. The grass feels unbearably cold. I have to stop touching it. I move my hands and slump forward. For a few seconds I just lie there, unable to understand what has sent my body into this state of emergency.

I don't know how long I spend paralysed and breathless, in this undignified position – seconds or minutes. I don't think it can be more than a few minutes. As soon as I feel able to move, I scramble to my feet and run towards the gate without looking back into the room. I couldn't turn my head in that direction if I tried. I don't know how I know this, but I do. The police. I must go to the police.

I dart round the side of the house, reaching out both my hands for the gate, desperate to get there as soon as I can. Something terrible, I think. I saw something terrible through the window, something so unimaginably terrifying that I know I did not imagine it. Yet I can't for the life of me say what it was.

A voice stops me, a woman's voice. 'Naomi!' it calls out. 'Naomi Jenkins.' I gasp. There is something shocking about having my full name yelled at me.

I turn. I am on the other side of the house now. There is no danger that I will see your lounge window from here. I am far more frightened of that than I am of this woman, who I suppose must be your wife.

But she doesn't know my name. She doesn't know I exist. You keep your two lives completely separate.

She is walking towards me. 'Juliet,' I say, and her mouth twists, briefly, as if she is swallowing a bitter laugh. I examine her closely, just as I did the tape measure, the candle, the picture of the old man and the boy. She is something else that belongs to you. Without your income, how would she survive? She'd probably find another man to support her.

I feel drained, ineffectual, as I ask, 'How do you know who I am?'

How can this woman be Juliet? From everything you've told me about her, I have built up a picture of a timid, unworldly housewife, whereas the person I'm looking at has neatly braided blond hair and is wearing a black suit and sheer black tights. Her eyes are blazing as she walks slowly towards me, deliberately taking her time, trying to intimidate me. No, this can't be your wife, the one who doesn't answer the phone and can't turn on a computer. Why is she dressed so smartly?

The words rush into my head before I can stop them: for a funeral. Juliet is dressed for a funeral.

I take a step back. 'Where's Robert?' I shout. I have to try. I came here determined to find you.

'Was it you who phoned last night?' she says. Each word embeds itself in my brain, like an arrow fired at close range. I want to shy away from her voice, her face, everything about her. I can't bear it that I will now be able to picture scenes and conjure conversations between the two of you. I have lost forever that comforting shadowy gap in what I could imagine.

'How do you know my name?' I say, wincing as she comes closer. 'Have you done something to Robert?'

'I think we both do the same thing to Robert, don't we?' Her smile is smug. I have the sense that she might be enjoying herself. She is wholly in control.

'Where is he?' I say again.

She walks right up to me until our faces are only inches apart. 'You know what an agony aunt would say, don't you?'

I jerk my head back, away from her warm breath. Fumbling for the gate, I grab the bolt and pull it free. I can leave whenever I want to. What can she do to me?

'She'd say you're better off without him. Think of it as a favour from me that you don't deserve.' Barely raising her hand, she gives me a small wave, an almost imperceptible flutter of her fingers, before turning to go back to the house.

I can't look at where she's walking. I can't even think about it.

2

3/4/06

'Liv? Are you there?' Detective Sergeant Charlie Zailer spoke quietly into her mobile phone, tapping her fingernails on the desk. She looked over her shoulder to check no one was listening. 'You're supposed to be packing. Pick up the phone!' Charlie swore under her breath. Olivia was probably doing some last-minute shopping. She refused to buy things like aftersun lotion and toothpaste in a foreign supermarket. She spent weeks working on a list of everything she would need, and bought it all beforehand. 'Once I leave the house, I'm on holiday,' she said, 'which means no errands, no practicalities, just lounging on the beach.'

Charlie heard Colin Sellers' voice behind her. He and Chris Gibbs were back, had stopped only to trade insults with two detectives from another team. She lowered her voice and hissed into her phone, 'Look, I've done something really stupid. I'm about to go into an interview that might last a while, but I'll ring you as soon as I'm free, okay? So just be there.'

'Something really stupid, Sarge? Surely not.' It would never occur to Sellers to pretend he hadn't overheard a private conversation, but Charlie knew he was only teasing. He wouldn't push his luck or use it against her. He'd already forgotten about it, was concentrating on the computer in front of him. 'Grab a chair,' he said to Gibbs, who ignored him.

Had she really said, 'Just be there,' to her sister, in such an imperious tone? She closed her eyes, regretting it. Anxiety made her bossier, which was a direction in which she definitely didn't need to go. She wondered if she could delete the message from Olivia's voicemail somehow. It'd be a good excuse to keep Simon waiting a bit longer. She knew he'd already be wondering what was keeping her. Good. Let him stew.

'Here we go,' said Sellers, nodding at the screen. 'Might as well print this lot now. Do you think?' Clearly he assumed he was not working alone. Gibbs wasn't even looking at the screen. He dawdled, some distance behind Sellers, chewing his fingernails. He reminded Charlie of a teenager determined to look bored in front of the grown-ups. If he hadn't been so obviously depressed about it, Charlie would have suspected Gibbs of lying about his forthcoming wedding. Who on earth would marry such a morose bastard? 'Gibbs,' said Charlie sharply. 'Do your meditation practice in your own time. Get back to work.'

'Same to you. I'm not the one phoning my sister.' The words came out in a torrent, spat in Charlie's direction. She stared at him in disbelief.

Sellers was shaking his head. '*How to Make Life Easier*, by Christopher Gibbs,' he muttered, fiddling with his tie. As usual it was too loose round his neck and the knot was too tight, dangling low like a pendant. He reminded Charlie of a dishevelled bear. How was it, she wondered, that Sellers, who was larger, fatter, louder and physically stronger than Gibbs, appeared entirely benign? Gibbs was short and thin, but there was a condensed ferocity about him, one that had been packed into too small a container. Charlie used him to scare people when she needed to. She'd worked hard not to be scared of him herself.

Gibbs turned on Sellers. 'Shut the fuck up.'

Charlie switched her phone off and threw it into her bag. Olivia would try to ring while she was busy with this interview, and by the time Charlie could call her back, her sister would have gone out again – wasn't that the way it always worked? 'To be continued,' she said coldly to Gibbs. She couldn't deal with him now.

'Hols tomorrow, Sarge!' Sellers called out cheerfully as she left the room. It was code for 'Go easy on Gibbs, won't you?' No, she bloody well would not.

In the corridor, at a safe distance from the CID room, she stopped, pulled her hand-mirror out of her bag and opened it. People talked about bad hair days, but they never mentioned bad face days, and that was what Charlie appeared to be having. Her skin looked worn, her features ungainly. She needed to eat more, do something about the severity of those cheekbones, flesh out the hollows. And her new black-framed glasses did nothing to make her bleary eyes look better.

And – if you wanted to go beyond the face, which Charlie didn't – there were three strands of grey in her short, dark, wavy hair. Was that fair, when she was only thirty-six? And her bra didn't fit properly; none of her bras did. A few months ago she'd bought three in the size she thought she was, and they all turned out to be too big around her body, the cups too small. She didn't have time to do anything about it.

Feeling uncomfortable in her clothes and in her person, Charlie snapped the mirror shut and headed for the drinks machine. The corridors in the original part of the building, the part that used to be Spilling Swimming Baths, had walls of exposed red brick. As Charlie walked, she heard the sound of water travelling at speed beneath her feet. It was something to do with the pipework for the central-heating system, she knew, but it had the odd effect of making the police station sound as if its main function were still an aquatic one.

She bought a cup of café mocha from the machine outside the canteen, recently installed for the benefit of those who didn't have time to go in, though the irony was that the drinks available from the buzzing box on the corridor were far more varied and appealing than the ones made by real people with alleged expertise in the field of catering. Charlie gulped down her drink, burning her mouth and throat, and went to find Simon.

He looked relieved when she opened the door of interview room one. Relieved, then embarrassed. Simon had the most expressive eyes of anyone Charlie knew. Without them, he might have had the face of a thug. His nose was large and uneven, and he had a wide, prominent lower jaw that gave him a determined look, like a man intent on winning every fight. Or afraid he might lose and trying to hide it. Charlie gave herself a mental shake. *Don't go all soft about him, he's a shit. When are you going to realise that it takes effort and planning to be as irritating as Simon Waterhouse is?* But Charlie didn't really believe that. If only she could.

'Sorry. Got held up,' she said.

Simon nodded. Opposite him sat a slim, pale, sharp-eyed woman wearing a long black denim skirt, brown suede clogs and a green V-necked jumper that looked like cashmere. Her hair was wavy, shiny reddish brown – a colour that made Charlie think of the conkers she used to fight Olivia for as a child – and she wore it in a shoulder-length bob. At her feet was a green-and-blue Lulu Guinness handbag, which Charlie guessed must have set her back a few hundred quid.

The woman pursed her lips as she listened to Charlie's apology, and folded her arms more tightly. Irritation or anxiety? It was hard to tell.

'This is Detective Sergeant Zailer,' said Simon.

'And you're Naomi Jenkins.' Again, Charlie smiled apologetically. She'd made a resolution to be more soothing, less abrasive, in interviews. Had Simon noticed? 'Let me have a look at what we've got so far,' she said, picking up the sheet of A4 paper that was covered with Simon's tiny, neat handwriting. She'd once teased him about it, asking if his mother had forced him to invent a fictional country when he was a kid and fill leather-bound notebooks with tales of his made-up land, like the Brontë sisters. The joke hadn't gone down well. Simon was touchy about his television-free childhood, his parents' insistence on mind-improving activities.

Once she'd skim-read what he'd written, Charlie turned her attention to the other set of notes on the table. These had been taken by PC Grace Squires, who had interviewed Naomi Jenkins briefly before passing her on to CID. She'd insisted on speaking to a detective, the notes said. 'I'll summarise what I take the situation to be,' said Charlie. 'You're here to report a man missing. Robert Haworth. He's been your lover for the past year?'

Naomi Jenkins nodded. 'We met on the twenty-fourth of March 2005. Thursday the twenty-fourth of March.' Her voice was low-pitched, gravelly.

'Okay.' Charlie tried to sound firm rather than abrupt. Too much information could be as obstructive as too little, particularly in a straightforward case. It would have been easy to leap to the conclusion that there was no case here at all: plenty of married men left their lovers without adequate explanation. Charlie reminded herself that she had to give it a chance. She couldn't afford to close her mind against a woman who said she needed help; she'd done that before, and still felt terrible about it, still thought every day about the chilling violence she might have prevented if only she hadn't leaped to the easiest conclusion.

Today she would listen properly. Naomi Jenkins looked serious and intelligent. She was certainly alert. Charlie had the impression that she'd have answered the questions before they'd been asked if she could.

'Robert is forty, a lorry driver. He's married to Juliet Haworth. She doesn't work. They have no children. You and Robert have been in the habit of meeting every Thursday at the Rawndesley East Services Traveltel, between four o'clock and seven o'clock.' Charlie looked up. 'Every Thursday for a year?'

'We haven't missed one since we started.' Naomi sat forward and tucked her hair behind her ear. 'And we're always in room eleven. It's a regular booking. Robert always pays.'

Charlie cringed. She could have been imagining it, but it seemed to her that Naomi Jenkins was imitating her – Charlie's – way of speaking: summarising the facts briskly and efficiently. Trying too hard.

'What do you do if room eleven's not available?' asked Simon.

'It always is. They know to expect us now, so they keep it free. They're never very busy.'

'So last Thursday you set off to meet Mr Haworth as usual, except he didn't arrive. And he hasn't been in touch to explain why. His mobile phone's been switched off and he hasn't replied to your messages,' Charlie summarised. 'Correct?'

Naomi nodded.

'That was as far as we got,' said Simon. Charlie skimmed the rest of his notes. Something caught her eye, struck her as unusual. 'You're a sundial-maker?'

'Yes,' said Naomi. 'Why is that important?'

'It isn't. It's an unusual job, that's all. You make sundials for people?'

'Yes.' She looked slightly impatient.

'For . . . companies, or . . . ?'

'The odd company, but usually private individuals with big gardens. A few schools, the odd Oxbridge college.'

Charlie nodded, thinking that it would be nice to have a sundial for her tiny front yard. Her house had no garden, thank God. Charlie hated the thought of having to mow or prune anything – what a waste of time. She wondered if Naomi did a petite range, like Marks & Spencer.

'Have you phoned Mr Haworth's home number?'

'My friend Yvon – she's also my lodger – she phoned last night. His wife, Juliet, answered. She said Robert was in Kent, but his lorry's parked outside his house.'

'You've been there?' Charlie asked, at exactly the same time as Simon was saying, 'What kind of lorry is it?' The difference between men and women, thought Charlie.

'A big red one. I don't know anything about lorries,' said Naomi, 'but Robert calls it a forty-four-tonner. You'll see it when you go to the house.'

Charlie ignored this last comment, avoided catching Simon's eye. 'You went to Robert's home?' she prompted.

'Yes. Earlier this afternoon. I came straight here from there—' Her words cut off suddenly, and she looked down at her lap.

'Why?' asked Charlie.

Naomi Jenkins took a few seconds to compose herself. When she looked up, there was a defiant glint in her eyes.

'After I'd been to the house, I knew something was seriously wrong.'

'Wrong in what sense?' asked Simon.

'Juliet has done something to Robert. I don't know what.' Her face paled slightly. 'She's arranged it so that he can't contact me. If for some reason he couldn't get to the Traveltel last Thursday, he'd have rung me straight away. Unless he physically couldn't.' She flexed the fingers of both hands. Charlie had the sense that she was putting a lot of effort into appearing calm and in control. 'He isn't trying to give me the brush-off.' Naomi directed this comment to Simon, as if she expected him to contradict her. 'Robert and I have never been happier. Ever since we first met we've been inseparable.'

Charlie frowned. 'You're separable and separate six days out of every seven, aren't you?'

'You know what I mean,' Naomi snapped. 'Look, Robert can barely last from one Thursday to the next. I'm the same. We're desperate to see each other.'

'What happened when you went to Mr Haworth's house?' asked Simon, fiddling with his pen. Charlie knew he hated anything like this, anything emotionally messy. Though he'd never use that phrase.

'I opened the gate and went into the garden. I walked round the side of the house to the front – the front is at the back, if you're coming from the street. I was planning to be quite direct, just ring the bell and ask Juliet straight out: "Where's Robert?" '

'Did Mrs Haworth know you and her husband were having an affair?' Charlie interrupted.

'I didn't think so. He's desperate to leave her, but until he does, he doesn't want her to know anything about me. It'd make life too difficult . . .' Creases appeared on Naomi's forehead and her expression darkened. 'But later, when I was trying to get away and she ran after me . . . But that was afterwards. You asked me what happened. It's easier for me to tell it as it happened, in the right order, or else it'll make no sense.'

'Go ahead, Miss Jenkins,' said Charlie gently, wondering if this ticking-off was a prelude to uncontrollable hysteria. She'd seen it happen before.

'I'd rather you called me Naomi. "Miss" and "Ms" are both ridiculous in different ways. I was in the garden, heading for the front door. I . . . passed the lounge window and I couldn't resist looking in.' She swallowed hard. Charlie waited. 'I could see the room was empty, but I wanted to look at all Robert's things.' Her voice tailed off.

Charlie noticed Simon's shoulders stiffen. Naomi Jenkins had just alientated half her audience.

'Not in a sinister, stalker-ish way,' she said indignantly. Apparently the woman was a mind-reader. 'It's well known that if the person you love has a completely other life that doesn't involve you, you desperately miss those everyday details that couples who live together share. You start to crave them. I just . . . I'd imagined what his lounge might look like so often, and then there it was in front of me.'

Charlie wondered how many more times the word 'desperately' was going to make an appearance.

'Look, I'm not scared of the police,' said Naomi.

'Why would you be?' asked Simon.

She shook her head, as if he'd badly missed the point. 'Once you start looking into it, you'll find that Robert *is* missing. Or something else is very seriously wrong. I don't want you to take my word for it, Sergeant Waterhouse. I want you to look into it and find out for yourself.'

'DC Waterhouse,' Charlie corrected her. 'Detective

Constable.' She wondered how she'd feel if Simon were to take and pass his sergeant's exams, if she were no longer higher than him in rank. It would happen eventually. It shouldn't bother her, she decided. 'Does Mr Haworth have a car? Might he have taken that to Kent?'

'He's a lorry driver. He needs his lorry for work, and he works every minute that he can when he's not with me. He has to, because Juliet doesn't earn anything – it's all down to him.'

'But does he also own a car?'

'I don't know.' Naomi blushed. 'I've never asked.' Defensively, she added, 'We hardly have any time together, and we don't waste what little we have on trivialities.'

'So, you were looking through Mr Haworth's lounge window—' Charlie began.

'The Traveltel has a cancellation policy,' Naomi talked over her. 'If you cancel before noon on the day you're due to arrive, they don't charge you. I asked the receptionist and Robert hadn't cancelled, which he definitely would have if he'd been planning to stand me up. He would never waste money like that.' There was something hectoring – punitive, almost – about the way she spoke. You try to be tolerant and patient and look what happens, thought Charlie. She guessed Naomi Jenkins would remain in this mode for the rest of the interview.

'But Mr Haworth didn't turn up last Thursday,' Simon pointed out, 'so presumably you paid.' Charlie had been about to make exactly the same objection. Once again Simon had echoed her thoughts in a way that no one else ever did.

Naomi's face crumpled. 'Yes,' she admitted eventually. 'I paid. It's the only time I have. Robert's quite romantic and old-fashioned in some ways. I'm sure I earn a lot more than him, but I've always pretended I earn hardly anything.'

'Can't he tell from your clothes, your house?' asked Charlie, who had known as soon as she'd walked into the interview room that she was looking at a woman who spent considerably more on clothes than she did.

'Robert's not interested in clothes, and he's never seen my house.'

'Why not?'

'I don't know!' Naomi looked tearful. 'It's quite big. I didn't want him to think . . . but mainly because of Yvon.'

'Your lodger.'

'She's my best friend, and she's lived with me for the past eighteen months. I knew she and Robert wouldn't like each other from the second I met him, and I didn't want to have to deal with them not getting on.'

Interesting, thought Charlie. You meet the man of your dreams and instantly know that your best friend would hate him.

'Look, if Robert had decided to end our relationship, he would have turned up as planned and told me face to face,' Naomi insisted. 'We talk about getting married every time we meet. At the very least he'd have phoned. He's the most reliable person I've ever known. It comes from a need to be in control. He'd have known that if he suddenly vanished, I'd look for him, that I'd go to his house. And then his two worlds would crash into one another, as they did this afternoon. There's nothing Robert would hate more. He'd do anything to make sure his wife and his . . . girlfriend never met, never talked. With him not there, we might start comparing notes. Robert would rather die than allow that to happen.'

A tear rolled down her cheek. 'He made me promise never to go to his house,' she whispered. 'He didn't want me to see Juliet. He made her sound as if . . . as if there was something wrong with her, like she was mad or sick in some way, like an invalid. And then when I saw her, she seemed so confident – superior, even. She was wearing a black suit.'

'Naomi, what happened at Mr Haworth's house this afternoon?' Charlie glanced at her watch. Olivia was sure to be back by now.

'I think I saw something.' Naomi sighed and rubbed her forehead. 'I had a panic attack, the worst I've ever had. I lost my footing and fell down on the grass. I felt as if I was suffocating. I got up as soon as I could and tried to run away. Look, I'm sure I saw something, okay?'

'Through the window?' asked Simon.

'Yes. I'm starting to feel clammy now just talking about it, even though Robert's house is miles away.'

Charlie frowned, leaning forward in her chair. Had she missed something? '*What* did you see?' she asked.

'I don't know! All I know is, I panicked and had to escape. My whole reason for being there was . . . obliterated suddenly, and I had to get away as quickly as possible. I couldn't stand to be anywhere near the house. I *must* have seen something. I was fine until that moment.'

It was all far too hazy for Charlie's liking. People either saw things or they didn't. 'Did you see anything that led you to believe harm had come to Robert?' she asked. 'Any blood, anything broken, any evidence of a fight or struggle having taken place?'

'I don't *know*.' Naomi's voice was petulant. 'I can tell you all the things I remember seeing: a red rug, a wood-laminate floor, loads of not very tasteful pottery houses in all shapes and sizes, a candle, a tape measure, a cabinet with glass doors, a television, a sofa, a chair—'

'Naomi!' Charlie interrupted the woman's agitated

chanting. 'Do you think you might be assuming – mistakenly – that this sudden reaction must have been an immediate one to some mysterious, unidentified stimulus, something you saw through the window? Couldn't it have been an eruption of stress that had been mounting for a while?'

'No. I don't think so,' she said flatly. 'Go to Robert's house. You'll find something. I know you will. If I'm wrong, I'll apologise for wasting your time. But I'm not wrong.'

'What happened after the panic attack?' asked Charlie. 'You say you tried to run away . . .'

'Juliet came after me. She called me by my name. She knew my surname as well. How did she know?' Naomi looked utterly bewildered for a moment, like a lost child. 'Robert made sure to keep his two lives absolutely separate.'

Women are such idiots, Charlie thought, including herself in the insult. 'Perhaps she found out. Wives often do.'

'She said to me "You're better off without him. I've done you a favour." Or words to that effect. That's as good as admitting that she's done something to him, isn't it?'

'Not really,' said Simon. 'She could have meant that she's persuaded him to end his relationship with you.'

Naomi flattened her lips into a line. 'You didn't hear her tone. She wanted me to think she'd done something much worse than that. She wanted me to fear the worst.'

'Maybe she did,' Charlie reasoned aloud, 'but that doesn't mean the worst has happened. She's bound to be angry with you, isn't she?'

Naomi looked offended. Or perhaps disgusted. 'Doesn't either of you know anybody who always turns up half an hour early for everything because they think the world will end if they're a second late?' she demanded. 'Someone who phones if they're only going to be five minutes early to apologise for being "almost late"?'

Simon's mother, thought Charlie. She could tell from the way he hunched over his notes that he was thinking the same thing.

'I'll take that as a yes,' said Naomi. 'Imagine one day you go to meet them and they don't turn up. And they don't phone. You'd know, wouldn't you, as soon as they were five minutes late, even one minute late, that something bad had happened? Well? Wouldn't you?'

'Leave it with us,' said Charlie, standing up. Robert Haworth was probably sleeping on a mate's floor, moaning over a pint at this very moment about how he couldn't believe he'd been rumbled, the latest in a long line of men to leave his credit-card bill lying around for his wife to find.

'Is that it?' Naomi snapped. 'Is that all you can say?'

'Leave it with us,' Charlie repeated firmly. 'You've been very informative, and we'll certainly follow it up. As soon as there's some news, we'll be in touch. How can we contact you?'

Naomi tutted, fumbling with her handbag. Her hair fell in front of her eyes and she yanked it behind one ear, hissing an obscenity under her breath. Charlie was impressed: most middle-class people tried not to swear in front of the police, and if they slipped up, they quickly said sorry. Ironic, since most cops swore all the time. Detective Inspector Giles Proust was the only one Charlie knew who didn't.

Naomi threw down a business card on the table, as well as a photograph of herself and a man with dark-brown hair and frameless glasses. The lenses were thin rectangles that barely covered his eyes. He was handsome, in a chunky sort of way, and looked as if he was trying to outstare the camera. 'There! And if you're not in touch very soon, I will be. What am I supposed to do, sit and twiddle my thumbs, not knowing if Robert's dead or alive?'

'Assume he's alive until you've good reason to think he isn't,' said Charlie dryly. God, this woman was a drama queen. She picked up the business card and frowned. '"Silver Brae Luxury Chalets? Proprietor: G. Angilley"?'

Naomi winced and drew back slightly, shaking her head. 'I thought you made sundials.'

'I gave you the wrong card. Just . . . just . . .' Naomi rummaged in her bag again, red in the face.

'Did you go to one of these chalets with Mr Haworth?' Charlie was curious. Nosey, really.

'I told you where I went with Robert, to the Traveltel. Here!' The card she thrust at Charlie this time was the correct one. There was a colour picture on it of a sundial – a tilted half-sphere of greenish stone with gold Roman numerals and a large gold butterfly wing protruding from the middle. There was a Latin phrase too, in gold letters, but only part of it was visible: '*Horas non*'.

Charlie was impressed. 'This one of yours?' she asked.

'No. I wanted my business card to advertise my competitors' merchandise.' Naomi glared at her.

Okay, so it had been a daft question. Competitors? How many sundial-makers could there be? 'What's "*Horas non*"?'

Naomi sighed, put out by the question. '*Horas non numero nisi aestivas*. I only count the sunny hours.' She spoke quickly, as if she wanted to get it over with. Sunny hours made Charlie think of her holiday, and Olivia. She nodded at Simon to wind things up and left the interview room, letting the door bang shut behind her.

In the corridor, she switched on her phone and pressed the redial button. Thankfully, her sister answered after the second ring.

'Well?' Olivia said, her mouth full of food. Smoked-salmon and cream-cheese parcels, Charlie guessed. Or a chocolate-filled brioche – something that could be taken out of the packet and eaten without any preparation. Charlie heard no suspense in her sister's voice as she asked, 'What new and unsurprising feat of idiocy do you have to report?'

Charlie laughed convincingly, filing away the unflattering implications of Olivia's question for inspection at some later date, and launched into her confession.

'Gnomons,' said Simon. 'Interesting word.' He had the home page of Naomi Jenkins' website up on the screen in front of him. The CID room had an abandoned air: papers scattered over unpopulated desks, broken Styrofoam cups on the floor, quiet apart from the faint hum of computers and striplights. There was no sign of Sellers, or Gibbs, the arsehole. DI Proust's glass cubicle in the corner was empty.

Charlie read over Simon's shoulder. ' "A gnomon is a shadow-caster." Isn't that how sundials work? The way the shadow falls tells you what time it is? Oh, look, it says she does miniature ones too. I could get one for my window-sill.'

'I wouldn't ask her if I were you,' said Simon. 'You'd probably get your teeth kicked in. Look, she does all sorts: wall-mounted, plinth-mounted, vertical, horizontal, brass, stone, fibreglass. Impressive, aren't they?'

'I love them. Except that one.' Charlie pointed to a picture of a plain stone cube with triangular iron gnomons attached to two of its sides. 'I'd prefer a Latin motto. Does she carve the letters herself, do you think? It says they're hand-carved . . .'

' "Time is a shadow," ' Simon read aloud. 'Why would anyone commission a sundial with that on it? Imagine: sunbathing, gardening, next to a reminder of your own rapidly approaching death.'

'Charmingly put,' said Charlie, wondering if Simon knew she was pissed off with him. Pissed off, upset, whatever. She was trying as hard as she could to hide it. 'What did you make of *Miss* Jenkins?'

Simon abandoned the keyboard and turned to face her. 'She's overreacting. A bit unstable. She implied she's had panic attacks before.'

Charlie nodded. 'Why do you think she was so angry and resentful? I thought we gave her a fair hearing, didn't you? And why did she say, "I'm not scared of the police"? That was out of the blue, wasn't it?' She nodded at the computer screen. 'Is there a page about her on the website, personal information, anything like that?'

'If this Haworth guy's avoiding her, I don't blame him,' said Simon. 'It might be the coward's way out and all that, but would you fancy trying to end a relationship with her?'

'He'd promised her marriage as well, so it would have been quite a let-down. Why are men such dicks?'

A photograph of Naomi Jenkins filled the screen. She was smiling, sitting on a large black semicircular sundial, leaning against its silver cone-shaped shadow-caster, its gnomon. That word would take some getting used to, thought Charlie. Naomi's auburn hair was tied back and she was wearing red cords and a faded blue sweatshirt.

'She looks normal enough there,' said Simon. 'A happy, successful woman.'

'It's her website,' said Charlie. 'She'll have designed it herself.'

'No, look, it says "Summerhouse Web Design" at the bottom.'

Charlie tutted impatiently. 'I don't mean literally. I mean she'll have supplied all the information and the photographs herself. Any freelancer having a website designed to promote their business is going to think very carefully about what sort of image they want to project.'

'Do you think she's lying to us?' asked Simon.

'Not sure.' Charlie chewed her thumbnail. 'Not necessarily, but . . . I don't know. I'm only guessing, but I doubt that mislaying her lover was the beginning of her problems. Anyway, find Haworth, check he's okay, and that'll be the end of that. Meanwhile, I'll . . . go and lie on the beach in Andalucia.' She grinned. It was over a year since she'd been able to have five consecutive days off. And now she was about to take a proper week's holiday, like a normal person. Could it be true?

'Here's the Shadow-caster's business card,' she said. 'I certainly won't need to contact her on my holi-jollies. Do you want one for Silver Brae Luxury Chalets as well, by any chance? *Ms* Jenkins lied to me about that. When I said, "Silver Brae Luxury Chalets," she looked like I'd hit her. I bet she and Haworth *did* go there.' Charlie turned the card over. 'I forgot to give it back to her. Hm. They do transfers from Edinburgh Airport. Home-cooked meals provided if you want them, spa facilities, all the beds super-king size . . . Maybe you and Alice could go.' *Damn.* Why had she said that?

Simon ignored the comment. 'What did you make of that window business?' he asked. 'Think she saw something?'

'Oh, please! That was a load of utter shite. She was stressed and she lost it – simple as that.'

Simon nodded. 'She said Haworth likes to be in control of everything, but she seemed like the control freak to me. Insisting on telling the story chronologically, ordering us to go to Haworth's house.' He picked up the photograph of Naomi with Robert Haworth and studied it. There was a Burger King sign in the background, above a row of cars. 'Looks like it was taken outside the Traveltel,' he said.

'Scenic.'

'It's a bit sad, isn't it? He's never been to her house and they've been together a year.'

'Their relationship's the real mystery in all of this,' said Charlie. 'What's wrong with him that she doesn't want her best friend to meet him?'

'Maybe the friend's the one she's ashamed of,' Simon suggested.

'What could an arty sundial-maker with a designer handbag and a skint lorry driver possibly have in common?'

'Physical attraction?' Simon looked as if he didn't want to dwell on this for too long.

Charlie nearly said, 'You mean sex?' but she stopped herself in time. 'He doesn't look like a lorry driver, does he?' She frowned. 'How many lorry drivers do you know who wear collarless shirts and trendy square glasses?'

'I don't know any lorry drivers,' said Simon rather glumly, as if it had just occurred to him that he might like to.

'Well . . .' Charlie slapped him on the back. 'All that's about to change. Send us a text once you've found him, won't you? It'll brighten up my holiday no end to find out he's emigrated to Australia to avoid the Shadow-caster. On second thoughts, don't. Last time I went on holiday Proust rang me at least once a day, the bastard. It can wait till I get back.'

Charlie slung her bag over her shoulder and started to gather her things together. Everything to do with work could wait for a week. What couldn't wait was the explanation Olivia had demanded. Charlie was going straight from the police station to meet her sister at the airport, and she'd have to do better than she had on the phone. Why did she feel the irresistible urge to reveal all to Olivia the moment she fucked up? Until she'd confessed, she felt panicky and out of control; it had been that way ever since they were teenagers. At least she'd succeeded in shocking Olivia into silence for three or four seconds; that hadn't happened before. 'I've no idea why I did it,' she'd said, which was true.

'Well, you've got three hours to think about it and reach a plausible conclusion,' Olivia had retorted once she'd rediscovered her voice. 'I'll ask you again at Heathrow.'

And whatever I say then to shut you up, I'll still have no idea, thought Charlie.

3

Tuesday 4 April

There is only one person behind the bar at the Star Inn: a short, skinny man with a long face and a large nose. He whistles, polishing beer glasses with a frayed green towel. It is just after midday. Yvon and I are his first customers. He looks up and smiles at us. I notice that his teeth are long, like horses' teeth, and there is a slight dip on either side of his head, above each ear, as if his face has been squeezed by a large pair of tweezers.

Do you think that's a fair description? You never describe things. I don't think you want to inflict the way you see the world on other people, so you stick to simple nouns: lorry, house, pub. No, that's wrong. I have never heard you use the word 'pub'. You say 'local', which I suppose is a sort of description.

I don't know why I am so disappointed to find the Star empty apart from this peculiar-looking barman. It's not as if I expected you to be here. If I had even the tiniest hope then I must have been deluding myself. If you were able to go out drinking, you'd be able to contact me. Yvon squeezes my arm, noticing my desolate expression.

At least I know I'm in the right place. As soon as I walked across the threshold, all my doubts vanished. This is where you mean when you talk about the Star. It doesn't surprise me that you chose an out-of-the-way place, tucked into the valley, right on the river. It is in the centre of town, but you can't see it from Spilling Main Street. You have to take the road between the picture-framer's and the Centre for Alternative Medicine, and follow it all the way down past Blantyre Park.

The pub is one long room, with the bar at one end. There is a damp, yeasty smell and a haze of smoke in the air, trapped since last night.

The barman is still grinning. 'Morning, ladies. Afternoon, rather. What can I get you?' From this I guess that he is the sort of young man who is in the habit of speaking as an old man might. In a way, I am glad not to have a choice about who to talk to. Now I can concentrate on what I ought to say.

The walls are covered with framed pages of old newspapers: the *Rawndesley Telegraph*, the *Rawndesley Evening Post*. I glance at the one nearest to me. In one column is the story of an execution that took place in Spilling in 1903. There is a picture of a noose and, beside it, another of the unfortunate criminal. The second column has the headline 'Silsford farmer wins prize for best pig', and a sketch of the animal and its owner, both looking proud. The pig is called Snorter.

I blink away tears. Finally, I am seeing all the things you have seen, your world. Yesterday it was your house, today this pub. I feel as if I'm taking a guided tour of your life. I hoped it might bring me closer to you, but it has the opposite effect. It's horrible. I feel as if I'm looking at your past, not your present, and certainly not anything I could ever share. It's as if I'm trapped behind a glass screen or a cordon of red rope and I can't reach you. I want to scream out your name.

'I'll have a double gin and tonic,' says Yvon loudly. She is trying to sound jolly for my sake, as if we're here for a fun day out. 'Naomi?'

'Half a lager shandy,' I hear myself say. I haven't had this drink for years. When I'm with you, I only ever drink the Pinot Grigio you bring, or the tea that's in our Traveltel room.

The barman nods. 'Coming right up,' he says. He has a broad Rawndesley accent.

'Do you know Robert Haworth?' I blurt out, too frantic to waste time thinking about the best way to approach the subject. Yvon looks worried: I told her I'd be subtle.

'Nope. Should I?'

'He's a regular. He comes here all the time.'

'Well, we think he does,' Yvon corrects me. She is my more moderate shadow, here to dilute whatever effect I might have. With me, in private, she's sarcastic and opinionated, but in public she is keen to obey social norms. Perhaps you'd understand this better than I do. I often think, when you look troubled and remote, that there's a struggle going on inside you, forces pulling in opposite directions. I've never been like that, not even before I met you. I've always been an all-one-way sort of person. And ever since the first time I saw you, I've been pulled entirely towards you. Nothing else stands a chance.

'He does,' I say firmly. When Yvon looked in the Yellow Pages this morning, she found what she called 'three contenders': the Star Inn in Spilling, the Star and Garter in Combingham and Star Bar in Silsford. I ruled out the last two immediately. Combingham is miles away and grim, and I know Star Bar. I sometimes pop in, if I'm visiting a customer nearby, and have a pot of organic mint tea. The idea of you sitting on those low leather banquettes reading the infusions menu nearly made me laugh out loud.

'I've got a photo of him on my phone,' I tell the barman. 'You'll know him when you see him.'

He nods amiably. 'Could be,' he says, putting our drinks on the bar. 'That'll be seven pounds twenty-five, please. There are lots of faces I can't put names to.'

I pull my phone out of my bag, trying to prepare myself for the worst, as I do every time. It doesn't get easier. If anything it gets harder. I want to howl when I see that there is no small envelope icon on the screen. Still no message from you. A fresh burst of pain and fear mixed with sheer disbelief makes my chest contract. I think about DS Zailer and DC Waterhouse, and want to smash their dense, unresponsive heads together. They as good as admitted that they planned to do nothing.

'What about Sean and Tony?' I snap at the barman, scrolling through the photographs on my phone while Yvon pays for our drinks. 'Do you know them?'

My question elicits a throaty laugh. 'Sean and Tony? You're having me on, right?'

'No.' I stop fiddling with my phone and look up. My heart is racing. The names mean something to him.

'No? Well, I'm Sean. And Tony also works here, behind the bar. He'll be in this evening.'

'But . . .' I am at a loss for words. 'Robert talked about you as if . . .' I assumed that you, Sean and Tony came here together. Thinking about it now, you never actually said that was what happened. I must have made it up, leaped to the wrong conclusion.

You come here alone. Sean and Tony are here already because they work here.

I turn back to my phone. I don't want Yvon to see that I am confused. How can this development by anything but good? I have found Sean and Tony. They know you, they're your friends. All I need to do is show Sean a photograph and he'll recognise you. I choose the one of you standing in front of your lorry outside the Traveltel, and pass my phone across the bar.

I see instant recognition in Sean's eyes and allow myself to breathe again.

'Elvis!' He chuckles. 'Tony and me call him Elvis. To his face, like. He doesn't mind.'

I nearly burst into tears. Sean *is* your friend. He even has a nickname for you.

'Why do you call him that?' asks Yvon.

'Isn't it obvious?'

Yvon and I shake our heads.

'He looks like a bigger version of Elvis Costello, doesn't he? Elvis Costello after he's eaten all the pies.' Sean laughs at his witticism. 'We said that to him an' all.'

'You didn't know his name was Robert Haworth?' says Yvon. Out of the corner of my eye I can see that she is looking at me, not at Sean.

'I don't think he ever told us his name. He's just always been Elvis. Is he okay? Tony and me were saying last night we haven't seen Elvis for a while.'

'When?' I say sharply. 'When did you last see him?'

Sean frowns. I must have sounded too fraught. I've put him off. *Idiot.* 'Who are you, anyway?' he says.

'I'm Robert's girlfriend.' I have never said this before. I wish I could say it over and over again. I wish I could say wife instead of girlfriend.

'Did he ever mention a Naomi?' asks Yvon.

'Nope.'

'What about Juliet?'

Sean shakes his head. He is starting to look wary.

'Look, this is really important,' I say. This time I make sure my voice is calm and not too loud. 'Robert's been missing since last Thursday . . .'

'Hang on . . .' Yvon touches my arm. 'We don't know that.'

'I know it.' I shake her off. 'When did you last see him?' I ask Sean.

He is nodding. 'Would've been around then,' he said. 'Thursday, Wednesday, something like that. But he's normally in most nights for a sly pint and a chat, so after a few nights of him not turning up, me and Tony started wondering. Not that it doesn't happen, mind. We get loads of punters like that: regular as clockwork for years and then suddenly, boof! They're gone and you never clap eyes on them again.'

'And he didn't say anything about going away?' I ask, though I already know the answer. 'He didn't mention any plans to go on holiday or anything?'

'Did he say anything about Kent?' Yvon chips in.

Sean shakes his head. 'Nothing like that. He said, "See you tomorrow," same as always.' He laughs. 'Sometimes he said, "See you tomorrow, Sean, if we're spared." If we're spared! Bit of a gloomy sod, isn't he?'

I stare at the dark wooden floorboards, blood pounding in my ears. I've never heard you use that expression. What if you said it to Sean for a reason? What if, this time, you have not been spared?

Yvon is thanking Sean for his help, as if the conversation is over. 'Wait,' I say, dragging myself out of the haze of dread that temporarily silenced me. 'What's your surname? What's Tony's?'

'Naomi . . .' Yvon sounds alarmed.

'Is it all right if I give your names to the police? You can tell them what you've just told us, that you agree that Robert's missing.'

'He didn't say that,' says Yvon.

'I don't mind. Like I say, me and Tony did think it was a bit funny. Mine's Hennage, Sean Hennage. Tony's is Willder.'

'Wait here,' I say to Yvon, and I'm outside with my bag and my phone before she has a chance to object.

I sit at one of the white-painted metal tables and pull my coat tight around me, tugging my sleeves down over my hands. It'll be a while before people are drinking outside. It is spring in name only. I watch three swans glide down the river in a line as I dial the number I spent an hour tracking down this morning, the one that will get me straight through to CID at Spilling Police Station. I wanted to phone immediately to ask what exactly Detective Sergeant Zailer and Detective Constable Waterhouse were doing about trying to find you, but Yvon said it was too soon, I had to give them a chance.

I am certain that they are doing nothing. I don't think they will lift a finger to help you. They believe you've left me by choice, that you've chosen Juliet over me and you're too scared to tell me this directly. Only you and I know how ridiculous that idea is.

A Detective Constable Gibbs answers the phone. He tells me that Zailer and Waterhouse are both out. His manner is offhand, verging on rude. Does he so resent speaking to me that he is trying to use as few words as possible in response to my questions? That's the impression I get. He has probably heard all about me and thinks I'm some kind of bunny-boiler, hounding you when you'd rather be left alone, sending the police to do my dirty work. When I tell him that I want to leave a message, he pretends he has a pen, pretends he is writing down Sean and Tony's names, but he can't be. He growls, 'Got it,' too quickly. I can tell when someone is really making a note of something – there are long pauses, and sometimes they repeat bits under their breath, or check spellings.

Detective Constable Gibbs does none of these things. He puts the phone down while I am still talking to him.

I walk over to the white-painted iron railings that separate the pub's terrace from the river. I ought to ring the police station again, demand to speak to the most senior person in the building – a chief constable or chief super-intendent – and complain about the way I've been treated. I am brilliant at complaining. It is what I was doing the first time you saw me, and it's why you fell in love with me – you always tell me that. I had no idea you were watching, listening, otherwise I'm sure I would have toned it down a bit. Thank God I didn't. Beautifully savage: that's how you describe the way I was that day.

It would never occur to you to protest about anything – on your own behalf, I mean; you would always stick up for me. But that's why you admire my fighting spirit, my conviction that misery and shoddiness do not have to be part of life. You're impressed that I have the nerve to aim absurdly high.

I can't go back into the pub, not yet. I am too churned up. Tears of rage fill my eyes, blurring the cold, slow-moving water in front of me. I hate myself when I cry, really loathe myself. It doesn't do any good. What's the point of resolving never to be weak and helpless again if all you can do when your lover vanishes into thin air is stand beside a river and weep? It's pathetic.

Yvon will tell me again to give the police a chance, but why should I? Why aren't Detective Sergeant Zailer and Detective Constable Waterhouse here at the Star, asking Sean when he last saw you? Will they bother to go to your house and speak to Juliet? Unaccounted-for married lovers

46

must be bottom of their list of priorities. Especially now, when all over the country, it sometimes seems, networks of maniacs are planning to blow themselves up and take train-loads of innocent men, women and children with them. Dangerous criminals – those are the people the police care about finding.

My heart jolts as an impossible idea begins to take shape in my mind. I try to push it down but it won't go away; it advances from the shadows slowly, gradually, like a figure emerging from a dark cave. I wipe my eyes. No, I can't do it. Even to think about it feels like a terrible betrayal. I'm sorry, Robert. I must be going properly mad. Nobody would do that. Besides, it would be a physical impossibility. I wouldn't be able to utter the words.

What kind of a person does that? Nobody! That's what Yvon said when I told her about how we met, how you drew yourself to my attention. I told you she'd said it, remember? You smiled and said, 'Tell her I'm the person who does the things nobody would do.' I did tell her. She mimed sticking her finger down her throat.

I clutch the railings for support, feeling wrung out, as if this new fear that has suddenly saturated me might dissolve my bones and muscles. 'I can't do it, Robert,' I whisper, knowing it's pointless. I had this exact same sensation when we first met: an unwavering certainty that everything that was going to happen had been laid down long ago by an authority far more powerful than me, one that owed me nothing, entered into no contract with me, yet compelled me entirely. I couldn't have tampered with it, however hard I'd tried.

It's the same this time. The decision has already been made.

* * *

Sean smiles at me as I walk back into the pub – a bland, cartoon smile, as if he hasn't met me before, as if we haven't just agreed that you are missing, that there is cause for serious concern. Yvon sits at the table furthest from the bar, playing with her mobile phone. She's got a new game on it that she's addicted to. It's clear that, in my absence, she and Sean have not been talking to one another. It makes me angry. Why am I always the one who has to drive everything?

'We've got to go,' I say to Yvon.

Her name has not always been Yvon. I've never told you this. There's a lot I haven't told you about her. I stopped mentioning her after it occurred to me that you might be jealous. I am not married, and apart from you Yvon is the most important person in my life. I am closer to her than I am to any of my family. She has lived with me ever since her divorce, which is another thing I haven't told you about.

She's tiny and skinny – five feet tall, seven and a half stone – and has long, straight brown hair that reaches her waist. Usually she wears it in a ponytail that she twists round her arm when she's working, or playing games on her computer. Every few months she chain-smokes Consulate menthol cigarettes for between a week and a fortnight, but then she gives up again. I'm never allowed to mention these lapses from healthy living once they're over.

She was christened Eleanor – Eleanor Rosamund Newman – but when she was twelve she decided that she wanted to be called Yvon instead. She asked her parents if she could change her name, and the fools agreed. They're both classicists at Oxford, strict about education but nothing else. They believe it's important to let children express their personalities, as long as it doesn't interfere with their getting straight 'A's all the way through school.

'They're a pair of numbskulls,' Yvon often says. 'I was twelve! I thought "Too Shy" by Kajagoogoo was the best song ever written. I wanted to marry Limahl. They should have locked me in a cupboard until I grew out of it.'

When Yvon married Ben Cotchin, she took his surname. Her friends and family, including me, were mystified when she decided to keep it after the divorce. 'Every time I change my name, I make it a little bit worse,' she explained. 'I'm not risking it again. Anyway, I *like* having a shit, wrongly spelled first name and the surname of a spoiled, lazy alcoholic. It's a fantastic exercise in humility. Whenever I pick up an envelope addressed to me, or fill in the electoral register form, I remember how stupid I am. It keeps the old ego in check.'

'Are we going home?' she asks now.

'No. To the police station.'

I so badly want to tell her. Yvon is the person whose opinions I use to test my own. Often I don't know what I think about something until I've heard what she thinks. But I can't risk it this time. Besides, there's no point. I know all the reasons why it's wrong and bad and crazy, and I'm going to do it anyway.

'The police station?' Yvon begins to protest. 'But—'

'I know, I should give them a chance,' I say bitterly. 'But this isn't about that. This is something different.' I feel stunned by my own outrageous nerve, but calmer, also, now that I have decided on a course of action. No one can accuse me of being a coward if I do this.

'Let's talk outside,' Yvon says. 'I don't like this place at all. It's too close to the river, the water's too loud. Even inside there's a damp, waterlogged atmosphere. I'm starting to feel like a creature from *Wind In the Willows*.' She stands up, pulls her purple shawl around her shoulders.

'I don't want to talk. I just need a lift. You don't have to come in with me, you can drop me off and go home. I'll make my own way back.' I start to march towards the car park.

'Naomi, wait!' Yvon runs after me. 'What's going on?'

Saying nothing is not so hard after all. This isn't the first secret I've kept from her. I've had three years to practise.

Yvon waves her car keys in the air, leaning against her red Fiat Punto. 'Tell me or I'm not driving you anywhere.'

'You don't believe me, do you? You don't believe that Juliet's done something to Robert. You think he's dumped me and hasn't got the guts to tell me.'

There is an echoey squawk of birds above our heads. It's as if they're trying to join in our conversation. I look up at the grey sky, half expecting to see a committee of gulls staring down at me. But they are oblivious, going about their business as usual.

Yvon groans. 'Can I refer you to my forty-seven previous answers to the same question? I don't know where Robert is, or why he hasn't been in touch. And neither do you. It's very, very unlikely that Juliet's chopped him into small pieces and buried him under the floorboards, okay?'

'She knew my name. She'd found out about the affair.'

'It's still unlikely.' Yvon relents and unlocks the car. I am disappointed. She could have persuaded me to tell her, if she'd pushed a bit harder. Most people are not as persistent as I am. 'Naomi, I'm worried about you.'

'It's Robert you should worry about. Something's happened to him. He's in trouble.' I wonder why I am the only person to whom this is obvious.

'When did you last eat?' Yvon asks, once we're in the car. 'When did you last get a good night's sleep?' Every question she asks me I think of in relation to you. Are you hungry and tired somewhere, gradually giving up hope, wondering why I'm not trying harder to find you? Yvon thinks I'm being melodramatic, but I know you. Only something that paralysed or confined you, or took away your memory, would prevent you from making contact with me. A lot of tragedies are unlikely, but they still happen. Most people do not fall off bridges, or die in house fires, but some do.

I want to say to Yvon that statistics are irrelevant and unhelpful, but I can't spare the words. I need all my energy to steel myself for my next step. It's obvious, anyway. Even if the odds are one in a million, that one could be you. It has to be somebody, doesn't it?

Yvon is on Juliet's side; she too believes I'm better off without you. She thinks you're repressed and sexist, and that the way you talk is grandiose and pretentious, that you say lots of things that sound deep and meaningful but are actually meaningless and trite. You present clichés as if they are profound, newly discovered truths, she says. Once, she accused me of trying to mould my personality to suit what I imagine you want, although she took that back the following morning. I could tell from the look on her face that she had meant it, but thought she'd gone too far.

I wasn't offended. Meeting you did change me. That was the best thing about it. Knowing I had a future with you helped me to bury everything I hated about the past. How I wish I could leave it buried.

We drive up the steep tree-lined road, the sound of the river fading behind us. There are no leaves yet on these trees, which throw their bare arms up towards the sky.

Yvon doesn't ask again why I want to go to the police station. She tries a new tactic. 'Are you sure I wouldn't be better off driving you to Robert's house? If you're so sure you saw something through the window . . .'

'No.' The dread I feel at the mention of it is like a hand closing round my throat.

'It's one mystery we could easily get to the bottom of,' Yvon points out. I understand why she thinks it's a reasonable suggestion. 'All you need to do is go and look again. I'll come with you.'

'No.' The police will go, as soon as they've heard what I'm about to tell them. If there's something to be found, they'll find it.

'What could you possibly have seen, for God's sake? It can't have been Robert, handcuffed to a radiator and covered in bruises. I mean, you'd remember that, wouldn't you?'

'Don't joke about it.'

'What *do* you remember seeing in the room? You still haven't told me.'

I haven't because I can't. Describing your lounge to DS Zailer and DC Waterhouse was bad enough; some reflex in my brain kept springing back, away from the image.

Yvon sighs when I fail to answer. She turns on her car radio and jabs one button after another, finding nothing she wants to listen to. In the end she chooses the station that's playing one of Madonna's old songs, and turns the volume down so that it's barely audible.

'You thought Sean and Tony were Robert's best mates, didn't you? That's how he talked about them. He misled you. They're just two guys who work behind the bar at his local pub.'

'Which is how they met Robert. Obviously they became friends.'

'They don't even know his real name. And how come he's in the Star every night? How come he's in *Spilling* every night? I thought he was a lorry driver.'

'He doesn't do overnights any more.'

'So what does he do? Who does he work for?'

She is picking up speed, and I raise both my hands to stop the flow. 'Give me a chance,' I say. 'There's nothing mysterious about it. He's self-employed, but mainly he works for supermarkets – Asda, Sainsbury's. Tesco.'

'I understand the concept of supermarkets,' Yvon mutters. 'You don't have to list them all.'

'He stopped doing overnights because Juliet didn't like being left on her own. So most days he loads up out of Spilling, drives to Tilbury, where he loads up again. Or sometimes he loads up out of Dartford . . .'

'Listen to yourself,' says Yvon, shooting a puzzled look at me. 'You're talking like him. "He loads up out of Dartford"! Do you even know what that means?'

This is becoming irritating. I say sharply, 'I assume it means that, in Dartford, he puts some things in his lorry which he then transports back to Spilling.'

Yvon shakes her head. 'You don't get it. I knew you wouldn't. It's like he's taken you over, and what have you got in exchange? He gives you nothing but empty promises. Why can't he ever stay the night with you? Why can't Juliet be left on her own?'

I stare at the road ahead.

'You don't know, do you? Have you ever said to him, "What exactly is wrong with your wife?"'

'If he wants to tell me, that's up to him. I don't want to interrogate him. He'd feel disloyal discussing her problems with me.'

'Very noble of him. Funny, he doesn't feel disloyal fucking you.' Yvon sighs. 'Sorry.' I hear a trace of something in her voice: scorn, perhaps, or a weary kindness. 'Look, you saw Juliet yesterday. She appeared to be a

53

self-sufficient, able-bodied grown-up. Not at all the poor, frail thing Robert's described . . .'

'He hasn't described her. He's never said anything specific.' I am starting to feel a little bit angry. I need all my energy to look for you, to stay positive, to stop myself going crazy with worry and fear. It is too much to have to defend you at the same time. Too preposterous, as well, when the attack comes from someone who's never met you.

'Why can't you pin him down? If he can't leave Juliet now, when will he be able to? What will change between now and then?'

I want to protect you against the sting of Yvon's hostility, so I say nothing. You could have lied about why you won't leave Juliet immediately; many men would have. You could have made up a story that would have kept me at bay: a sick mother, an illness. The truth is harder to accept, but I'm glad you told me. 'It's nothing to do with Juliet,' you said. 'She won't change. She'll never change.' I heard what sounded like determination in your voice, but perhaps it was a sort of furious resignation, anger filling the gap where hope once was. Your eyes narrowed as you spoke, as if in response to a sudden sharp pain. 'If I left her now, it'd be the same as if I leave her in a year, or five years, from her point of view.'

'Then why not leave her now?' I asked. Yvon isn't the only one who has wondered.

'It's me,' you admitted. 'This won't make sense, but . . . I've thought about leaving her for so long. Planning it, looking forward to it. I've probably thought about it too much, in a way. It's turned into this . . . legendary thing in my mind. I'm paralysed. It's become too big for me. I get too preoccupied about the details – how and when to do it.

In my mind, I'm already caught up in the process of leaving her. The grand finale – what I've been working towards for so long.' You smiled sadly. 'Trouble is, the process hasn't yet manifested itself in the world outside my head.'

You took a long time to say all this, taking care to choose exactly the right words, the ones that most accurately described your feelings. I've noticed you don't like to talk about yourself unless it's to say how much you love me, or that you only feel truly alive when you're with me. You're the opposite of a self-absorbed, oblivious man. Yvon thinks I'm obsessed with you, and she's right, but she's never seen you in action. Nobody but me knows how you stare at me hungrily, as if you might never see me again. Nobody has ever felt the way you kiss me. My obsession is dwarfed by yours.

How can I explain all this to Yvon? I don't entirely understand it myself.

'What if leaving Juliet always seems too big?' I asked you. 'What if you always feel paralysed?' I'm not a total fool. I've seen the same films Yvon has about women who waste their whole lives waiting for their married lovers to get divorced and commit to them properly. Though I will never regard you as a waste of time, no matter what happens. Even if you never leave Juliet, even if all I can ever have of you is three hours a week, I don't care.

'I *will* always feel paralysed,' you said. It wasn't what I wanted to hear, and I turned my face away so that you wouldn't see my disappointment. 'I'll always feel the way I do now: hovering on the verge, not ready to throw myself over the edge. But I will do it. I'll make myself do it. Once, I really wanted to marry Juliet. And I did marry her. Now you're the one I'm desperate to marry. I look forward to it every minute of every day.'

When I replay things you've said and hear your voice so clearly in my mind, I feel like a dying animal. It can't be over. I have to be able to see you again. There are two days to go until Thursday. I will be at the Traveltel at four o'clock. As usual.

Yvon nudges me with her elbow. 'Probably I should keep my big gob shut,' she says. 'What do I know about anything? I married a lazy alcoholic because I fell in love with the summerhouse in his back garden and thought it'd be ideal for my business. Got what I deserved, didn't I?'

Yvon lies about her romantic history all the time, making herself sound worse than she is. She married Ben Cotchin because she loved him. Still does, I suspect, despite his aimlessness and his drinking. Yvon and her business, Summerhouse Web Design, now live in the converted basement of my house, and Ben's summerhouse, if Yvon's spies are to be believed, is used primarily as an extra-large drinks cabinet.

We are nearly there. I can see the police station, a blur of red bricks in the distance, getting closer. There is a large obstruction in my throat. I can't swallow.

'Why don't we go away for a couple of days?' says Yvon. 'You need to relax, detach a bit from all this stress. We could drive up to Silver Brae Chalets. Did I show you their card? I could get us a chalet for next to nothing, being well connected, you know how it is. After you've done whatever you need to do at the police station, we could—'

'No,' I snap. Why is everybody talking about bloody Silver Brae Chalets? Detective Sergeant Zailer quizzed me about it, after I stupidly gave her the card by mistake. She asked if you and I had ever been there.

I don't want to be reminded of the only time you've ever been really angry with me, not now you're missing. It's funny, it never bothered me before. I forgot it almost as soon as it had happened. I'm sure you did too. But this one bad memory seems to have taken on a sudden significance, and my mind swerves away from it.

It can't possibly have anything to do with you being missing. Why would it make you decide to leave me now, four months after it happened? And everything has been fine since then. Better than fine: perfect.

Yvon had a pile of those wretched cards lying around her office and I picked one up. I thought you needed a proper break, far away from Juliet and her leech-like demands, so I booked us a chalet as a surprise. Not even for a whole week, just for a weekend. I had to negotiate a special rate on the phone, with a rather ungracious woman who sounded as if she actively didn't want me to boost her profits by staying in one of her cottages.

I know you don't like being away overnight as a rule, but I thought that if it was just a one-off, it'd be okay. You looked at me as if I'd betrayed you. For two hours you didn't speak – not one single word. Even after that, you wouldn't get into bed with me. 'You shouldn't have done it,' you kept saying. 'You should never have done it.' You withdrew into yourself, drawing your knees up to your chest, not even reacting when I shook you by the shoulders, hysterical with guilt and regret. It's the only time you've been close to crying. What were you thinking? What was going on in your head that you couldn't or didn't want to tell me?

I was distraught all week, thinking it might be over between us, loathing and cursing myself for my presumptuousness. But the following Thursday, to my amazement, you were your usual self. You didn't refer to it at all. When I tried to apologise, you shrugged and said, 'You know I can't go away. I'm really sorry, sweetheart. I'd love to, but I can't.' I didn't understand why you hadn't just said that straight away.

I never told Yvon, and can't tell her now. How can I expect her to understand? 'I'm sorry,' I say. 'I didn't mean to snap at you.'

'You've got to get a grip,' she says sternly. 'I honestly believe Robert's absolutely fine, wherever he is. It's you who's cracking up. And, yes, I *know* I'm in no position to lecture you. I'm the proud owner of the shortest marriage on record, *and* I'm extremely precocious when it comes to ballsing up my life. I got divorced while most of my friends were taking their A levels . . .'

I smile at the exaggeration. Yvon is obsessed with the fact that she is divorced at thirty-three. She thinks there's a stigma attached to having a failed marriage behind you at such a young age. I once asked her what was an okay age to get divorced and she said, 'Forty-six,' without a moment's hesitation.

'Naomi, are you listening? I'm not talking about since Robert did a runner. If you ask me, you were cracking up long before then.'

'What do you mean?' All my defensive impulses kick in at once. 'That's bullshit. Before Thursday I was fine. I was happy.'

Yvon shakes her head. 'You were staying every Thursday night at the Traveltel on your own while Robert went home to his wife! There's something sick about that. How can he let you do it? And since he's gone on the dot of seven, why don't you just come home? Shit, I'm ranting. So much for being diplomatic.'

She turns left into the police-station car park. No running away, I tell myself. No last-minute changes of mind.

'Robert doesn't know I always stay the night.' It might be crazy, my Thursday-night routine, but you are not implicated.

'He doesn't?'

'I've never told him. He'd be upset, thinking of me there on my own. As for why I do it . . . it'll sound mad, but the Traveltel is *our* place. Even if he can't stay, I want to. I feel closer to him there than I do at home.'

Yvon is nodding. 'I know you do, but . . . God, Naomi, can't you see that's part of the problem?' I don't know what she's talking about. She carries on, her voice agitated. 'You feeling close to him in some grotty, anonymous room while he's at home with his feet up watching telly with his wife. The things you don't tell him, the things he doesn't tell you, this strange world the two of you have created that exists only in one room, only for three hours a week. Can't you see?' We are driving up and down rows of parked cars. Yvon cranes her neck, looking for a space.

I might one day tell you that I stay at the Traveltel alone every Thursday. I've only kept it from you out of mild embarrassment – what if you would think it's too extreme? There may be other things that I happen not to have told you about myself, but there is only one thing I really want to hide from you, from everyone. And I'm about to make that impossible. I cannot believe that I have ended up in this situation, that what I am about to do has become necessary, unavoidable.

Yvon swears under her breath. The Punto jerks to a standstill. 'You'll have to get out here,' she says. 'There are no spaces.'

I nod, open the passenger door. The sharp wind on my skin feels like total exposure. This can't be happening. After three years of meticulous secrecy, I am about to tear down the barrier I've built between me and the world. I am going to blow my own cover.

4

4/4/06

On his way to the Haworths' front door, Simon stopped in front of what he assumed was the window Naomi Jenkins had been looking through when she had her panic attack. The curtains were closed, but there was a small gap between them, through which Simon could see the room Naomi had talked about. She'd been remarkably precise about the detail, he realised. Navy-blue sofa and chair, glass-fronted cabinet, a perplexing number of tacky ornamental houses, a picture of a seedy old man watching a half-dressed boy play the flute – it was all there, exactly as she'd described. Simon saw nothing untoward, nothing that could explain Naomi's sudden extreme reaction.

He made his way round to the front door, noticing the untidy garden, which was more of a junk yard than anything else, and pressed the bell, hearing nothing. Were the walls too thick, or was the bell broken? He pressed again, and once more just to be on the safe side. Nothing. He was about to knock when a woman's voice shouted, 'Coming!' in a tone that implied she had not been given a fair chance.

If Charlie had been here, she would have held up her badge and ID card, ready to greet whoever opened the door. Simon would have had to follow her lead and do the same or he'd have stood out in a way he didn't like to. Alone, he only showed people his ID if they asked to see it. He felt self-conscious, almost parodic, whipping it out straight away, shoving it in people's faces as soon as he met them. He felt as if he was acting.

The woman who stood in front of him with an expectant look on her face was young and attractive, with shoulder-length blond hair, brown eyes and a few faint freckles on her nose and cheeks. Her eyebrows were two thin, perfect arches; she had evidently spent a lot of time doing something to them that must have hurt. To Simon they looked unpleasant and unnatural. He remembered Naomi Jenkins had mentioned a suit. Today Juliet Haworth was wearing black jeans and a thin black V-necked jumper. She smelled of a sharp citrusy perfume.

'Hello?' she said briskly, making it a question.

'Mrs Juliet Haworth?'

She nodded.

'Is Robert Haworth in, your husband? I wanted a quick word with him.'

'And you are . . . ?'

Simon hated introducing himself, hated the sound of his voice saying his own name. It was a hang-up he'd had since school, one he was determined no one would ever get wind of. 'Detective Constable Simon—'

Juliet Haworth interrupted him with a loud guffaw. 'Robert's away. You're a policeman? A detective? Bloody hell!'

'Do you know where he is?'

'In Kent, staying with friends.' She shook her head. 'Naomi's reported him missing, hasn't she? That's why you're here.'

'How long's Mr Haworth been in Kent?'

'A few days. Look, that slut Naomi's several ciabattas short of a picnic. She's a bloody—'

'When will he be back?' Simon interrupted her.

'Next Monday. Do you want me to bring him into the police station? Prove that he's still alive, that I haven't clubbed him to death in a jealous rage?' Juliet Haworth's mouth twitched. Was she admitting to jealousy, Simon wondered, or mocking the idea?

'It'd be helpful if he could come in and see me when he gets back, yes. Where in Kent is he?'

'Sissinghurst. Do you want the address?'

'That'd be useful, yes.'

Juliet appeared irritated by his answer. 'Twenty-two Dunnisher Road,' she said tersely.

Simon wrote it down.

'You know that woman's bonkers? If you've met her, you must know. Robert's been trying to cool things off for months, but she won't take the hint. In fact, this is good, you turning up like this. I should have been the one to get the police involved, not her. Is there anything I can do to stop her coming here all the time? Can I get an injunction?'

'How many times has she been here, uninvited?'

'She was here yesterday,' said Juliet, as if it were an answer to Simon's question. 'I looked out of my bedroom window and saw her in the garden, trying to run away before I got downstairs.'

'So she's only been here once. No court would issue an injunction.'

'I'm thinking ahead.' Juliet seemed now to be attempting a conspiratorial tone. She narrowed one eye as she spoke, a gesture that was halfway to a wink. 'She'll be back. If Robert doesn't make any overtures towards her, which he won't, it'll be no time at all before Naomi Jenkins is living in a tent in my garden.' She laughed, as if this were an amusing rather than a worrying prospect.

At no point had she taken a step back into the house. She

stood right on the threshold. Behind her, in the hall, Simon could see a light-brown ribbed carpet, a red telephone on a wooden table, a scattering of shoes, trainers and boots. There was a mirror, its glass smeared with some sort of grease in the middle, propped up against the wall, which was marked and scratched. To the right of the mirror, a long, thin calendar hung from a drawing pin. There was a picture of Silsford Castle at the top and a line for every day of the month, but no handwriting. Neither Robert nor Juliet had made a note of any appointments.

'Mr Haworth's lorry's parked outside,' said Simon.

'I know.' Juliet made no attempt to hide her impatience. 'I said Robert was in Kent. I didn't say his lorry was.'

'Does he have another car?'

'Yes, a Volvo V40. Which – I'll tell you now, to save you some unnecessary detective work – is parked out there as well. Robert went to Sissinghurst by train. Driving's his job. When he's not working, he tries to avoid it.'

'Do you have a phone number for where he is?'

'No.' Her face closed down. 'He's got his mobile with him.'

This sounded wrong to Simon. 'I thought you said he was staying with friends. You haven't got their number?'

'They're Robert's friends, not mine.' Juliet's curled lip suggested she wouldn't have wanted to share them, even if her husband had offered.

'When did you last speak to Robert?' Simon asked. His contrary streak had kicked in. Because Juliet Haworth was impatient for him to leave, he felt inclined to linger.

'I don't mean to be rude, but why is that any of your business? Last night, okay? He rang me last night.'

'Naomi Jenkins says he isn't answering his mobile phone.'

Juliet seemed to find this news invigorating. Her features became animated and she smiled. 'She must be spitting feathers. Reliable Robert not returning her calls – whatever next!'

Simon hated the way jealousy turned people turned into savages. He'd been that sort of savage himself, more than once; humanity disappeared, was replaced with beasthood. An image of Juliet as a predator, licking her lips while her prey bled to death in front of her, flared in his mind. But perhaps that was unfair, since Naomi Jenkins had admitted she wanted Haworth to leave Juliet and marry her.

Naomi had written down Robert Haworth's mobile number yesterday. Simon would leave a message later, ask Haworth to call him back. He'd make sure to inject some man-of-the-world levity into his tone. I'll pretend I'm Colin Sellers, he thought.

'Do me a favour, will you?' said Juliet. 'Tell Naomi that Robert's got his mobile with him and it's working fine. I want her to know that he's got all her messages and is ignoring them.' She pulled the front door closer to her, restricting Simon's view of the inside of her house. All he could see now was the small semicircular telephone table immediately behind her.

He gave her his card. 'When your husband gets back, tell him to contact me straight away.'

'I've already said I will. Now, can I go? Or rather, please can you go?'

Simon could imagine her bursting into tears as soon as she'd closed the door on him. Her manner, he decided, was too brittle, slightly artificial. An act. He wondered if Robert Haworth had gone to Kent in order to make his final decision: Juliet or Naomi. If so, it was no surprise that his wife was on edge.

Simon pictured Naomi sitting tensely at home, trying to apply logic to the problem of why Haworth had abandoned her. Love and lust had no respect for logic, that was the trouble. But why was Naomi Jenkins the one Simon suddenly felt sorry for? Why not the wronged wife?

'Naomi thought I didn't know about her,' said Juliet, with a snide grin. 'Stupid bitch. Of course I knew. I found a photograph of her on Robert's phone. Not just her. A picture of them together, with their arms round each other, at some service station. Very romantic. I wasn't looking – I found it by accident. Robert had left his phone on the floor. I was putting up Christmas decorations and I trod on it by mistake. There I was, pressing buttons at random, panicking because I thought I'd broken it, and suddenly I was staring at this photo. Talk about a shock,' she muttered, more to herself than to Simon. Her eyes had started to look glassy. 'And now I've got the police on my doorstep. If you ask me, Naomi Jenkins wants shooting.'

Simon stepped away from her. He wondered how Robert Haworth had managed to keep up his weekly meetings with Naomi, if Juliet had known about the affair since before Christmas. If she'd only found out last week, that might have explained Haworth's hasty departure to stay with friends in Kent.

There was a half-formed question lurking in the recesses of Simon's mind, but before he had a chance to knock it into shape, Juliet Haworth said, 'I've had enough of this,' and closed the door in his face.

She wasn't the only one. Simon raised his hand to ring the bell again, then decided against it. To ask any more questions at this stage would be prying. He returned to his car with much relief, turned on the engine, and Radio 4, and had forgotten about Robert Haworth's sordid little love triangle by the time he reached the end of the street.

Charlie marched into the bar of the Hotel Playa Verde and slung her handbag down on a bar stool next to her sister's. At least Olivia had followed her instructions and waited, instead of rushing to the airport and booking a first-class flight to New York as she'd threatened to. God, she looked out of place in that black off-the-shoulder dress. What had Liv expected? This was a four-hundred-pound, last-minute deal.

'There's nothing,' Charlie said. She took off her glasses and wiped the rain off them with the hem of her shirt.

'How can there be nothing? There must be a million hotels in Spain. I can't believe they aren't *all* better than this one, every man Jack of them.' Olivia examined her wine glass to make sure it was clean before taking a sip.

Neither she nor Charlie spoke more quietly than usual; neither cared if the barman heard. He was an elderly man from Swansea with two large, navy-blue butterflies tattooed on his forearms. He'd moved here, Charlie had heard him telling a customer earlier, after working for twenty years as a driving instructor. 'I don't miss Britain,' he'd said. 'It's gone to shit.' His sole concession to his new country of residence was to tell everyone who approached the bar that a jug of sangria was half price and would be until the end of the week.

Charlie and Olivia were his only customers this evening, apart from an overweight, orange-skinned couple with a huddle of suitcases around them. They hunched over six peanuts in a silver dish, occasionally poking at them with their thick fingers, as if hoping to roll one over and find something remarkable beneath it. 'You Wear It Well' by

Rod Stewart was playing very faintly in the background, but you'd have had to strain to hear it properly.

All four walls of the Bar Arena were covered with green, red and navy tartan wallpaper. The ceiling was nicotine-stained Artex. Still, it was the only place to be if you were unfortunate enough to be in the Hotel Playa Verde, since at least it served alcohol. There was no minibar in the tiny room Charlie and Olivia were sharing. This came as a shock to Olivia, who opened every drawer in the cupboard and bent to peer inside it, insisting, 'It must be here somewhere.'

A net curtain that stank of old cigarettes and grease hung at the bedroom's narrow window. It couldn't have been washed for years. The bed Olivia chose because it was closer to the en-suite bathroom was so close that it actually blocked the doorway. If Charlie needed to go to the loo in the night, she would have to climb across the bottom of her sister's bed. She'd made the effort this afternoon and found dried toothpaste stuck to one of the two plastic glasses by the basin, and a stranger's soggy hair clogging the bath's plughole. So far the fire alarm had gone off twice for no noticeable reason. Each time it had been over half an hour before someone had had the gumption to turn it off.

'Did you look on the Internet?' asked Olivia

'Where do you think I've been for the past two hours?' Charlie took a deep breath and ordered a brandy and dry ginger, once more refusing the barman's offer of half-price sangria, moulding her face into a false smile when he mentioned that she had until the end of the week to take advantage of this one-off special rate. She lit a cigarette, thinking that smoking couldn't possibly be bad for your health in situations like this, even if it was the rest of the time. The end of the week seemed very, very far away.

Plenty of time to kill herself, then, if things didn't get any better. Perhaps she ought to suicide-bomb the shitty hotel.

'Trust me, there was nothing you'd have approved of,' she told Olivia.

'So there *were* places with availability?'

'A few. But either they didn't have pools or they weren't right on a beach or they had no air conditioning or only a buffet in the evenings . . .'

Olivia was shaking her head. 'We're hardly going to need air conditioning or a pool at this rate,' she said. 'It's cold and rainy. I told you it was too early in the year for Spain.'

A tight ball of heat began to expand in Charlie's chest. 'You also said you didn't want a long-haul flight.' Olivia had suggested going away in June, to avoid what she called 'hot-weather anxiety'. Charlie had thought it a good idea; the last thing she wanted was to have to watch her sister leap out of bed every morning at six, run to the window and howl, 'I can't see any sun yet!' But Detective Inspector Proust had put the kaibosh on the plan. Too many people were going to be away in June, he'd said. There was Gibbs's honeymoon, for a start. And before that Sellers had booked an illicit holiday with his girlfriend, Suki. The official story was that he was going away with CID on a residential team-building trip. Meanwhile his wife Stacey would be in Spilling, not unlikely to bump into Charlie, Simon, Gibbs, Proust – the people Sellers had told her he'd be swinging on ropes and crawling through mud with in the depths of the countryside. Charlie was amazed Sellers' double life had lasted as long as it had, given that his lies were so ill-thought-out.

'So you wouldn't mind somewhere with no pool and no air conditioning?' said Charlie, suspicious of what appeared to be an easy solution. There had to be a catch.

'I mind that it's not sunny and I mind that it's colder than it is in London.' Olivia sat straight-backed on her bar stool, legs crossed. She looked elegant and disappointed, like a jilted spinster from one of those long, boring films Charlie hated, full of hats and sullied reputations. 'But there's nothing I can do about it, and I'm certainly not going to sit by an outdoor pool in the pissing rain.' Her eyes lit up suddenly. 'Was there anywhere with a nice indoor pool? And a spa? A spa'd be great! I fancy one of those dry floatation treatments.'

Charlie's heart plummeted. Why couldn't everything have been perfect, just this one time? Was that too much to ask? No one was more fun to be with than Olivia, if the conditions were right.

'I didn't look,' she said. 'But I think it's unlikely, unless you want to spend a small fortune.'

'I don't care about money,' Olivia was quick to say.

Charlie felt as if there was a coiled spring inside her, one she had to keep pushing down or else it'd leap up and destroy everything. 'Well, unfortunately, I have to care about money. So unless you want me to look for two separate hotels . . .'

Olivia was less well off than Charlie. She was a freelance journalist and had a colossal mortgage on a flat in London's Muswell Hill. Seven years ago she'd been diagnosed with ovarian cancer. The operation to remove both ovaries and her womb had been immediate, and had saved her life. Ever since, she'd been throwing money around like the spoiled child of aristocrats. She drove a BMW Z5 and took taxis from one side of London to another as a matter of course. Getting the Tube was one of the many things she claimed to have given up forever, along with compromising, ironing and wrapping presents. Sometimes, when she couldn't sleep, Charlie worried about her sister's financial situation. It had to involve a lot of debt – an idea Charlie hated.

'If we can't do the hotel thing properly, I'd rather do something completely different,' said Olivia, after mulling it over for a while.

'Different?' Charlie was surprised. Olivia had vetoed, quite unambiguously, any form of self-catering on the grounds that it was too much effort, even after Charlie had said she'd do any shopping and cooking that was required. As far as Charlie was concerned, making some toast in the morning and a salad at lunchtime was not hard work. Olivia ought to try doing Charlie's job for a day or two.

'Yes. Camping, or something.'

'*Camping?* This from the woman who wouldn't go to Glastonbury because the toilet paper isn't folded into a point by a maid?'

'Look, it's not my preferred option. A nice hotel in Spain in June, in the heat, was what I wanted. If I can't have that, I'd rather not have some sad mockery of my ideal. At least camping's meant to be shit. You go there expecting to sleep on some mud, under some cloth, and eat packets of dried food . . .'

'I'm sure you'd dissolve like the Wicked Witch of the West from *The Wizard of Oz* if you ever tried to go camping.'

'What about Mum and Dad's, then? We haven't been there together for ages. Mum'd wait on us hand and foot. And they're always asking me when I'm next coming, with just a trace of disinheritance in their voices.'

Charlie pulled a face. Her and Olivia's parents had recently retired to Fenwick, a small village on the Northumberland coast, and developed an obsession with golf that was at odds with the game's leisurely image. They behaved as if golf were their full-time job, one they might be fired from if they weren't diligent enough. Olivia had been to their club with them once, and she'd reported to Charlie afterwards that Mum and Dad had been about as relaxed as drugs mules in front of airport customs officials.

Charlie didn't think she had the stamina to cope with all three members of her immediate family at the same time. She could not reconcile the concept of parents with the concept of holiday. Still, it was ages since she'd last made the trip up north. Perhaps Olivia was right.

The barman turned up the volume of the music. It was still Rod Stewart, but a different song: 'The First Cut Is the Deepest'. 'I love this one,' he said, winking at Charlie. 'I've got a "Rod is God" T-shirt, me. I normally wear it, but I'm not wearing it today.' He looked down at his chest, apparently bemused.

The combination of Rod Stewart and the tartan wall-paper gave Charlie an idea. 'I know where we can go,' she said. 'How do you feel about flying to Scotland?'

'I'll fly anywhere that's got a nice holiday to offer. But why Scotland?'

'We'd be near enough to Mum and Dad to go to theirs for a lunch or two, but we wouldn't have to stay with them. We could down our roast dinners and escape . . .'

'To where?' asked Olivia.

'Someone at work gave me this card for a holiday chalet place . . .'

'Oh, for God's sake . . .'

'No, listen. It sounded good.'

'It'll be self-catering.' Olivia made a squeamish face.

'The card said home-cooked meals are available if you want them.'

'Three times a day? Breakfast, lunch and dinner?'

How was it possible to need a stiff drink even while you held one in your hand, even as you were throwing it down your neck in large gulps? Charlie lit another cigarette. 'Why don't I phone and ask? Honestly, Liv, it sounded really good. All beds super-king size, that sort of thing. Luxury chalets, the card said.'

Olivia laughed. 'You're a marketing man's dream, you are. Everything calls itself "luxury" these days. Every flea-bitten B&B, every—'

'I'm pretty sure it said spa facilities too,' Charlie cut her off.

'That'll mean a derelict shed with a cold puddle in it. I doubt they offer dry-floatation treatments.'

'You want to dry-float? Why don't we go upstairs and I'll hurl you off our balcony?' Didn't they say that all the best jokes had an undertone of seriousness?

'You can't blame me for being a bit cautious.' Olivia looked Charlie up and down as if she'd just met her for the first time. 'Why should I trust you when you're quite plainly mad?' She lowered her voice to a fierce whisper. 'You made up a boyfriend!'

Charlie looked away, blew a smoke ring into the air. Why did she feel a compulsion to tell her sister everything she did, even knowing perfectly well the flak she'd get?

'Did you give him a name?' asked Olivia.

'I don't want to talk about it. Graham.'

'*Graham?* Jesus!'

'I'd had a bowl of Golden Grahams for breakfast that morning. I was too knackered to be imaginative.'

'If I adopted the same approach, I'd be going out with apple-and-cinnamon Danish. Did Simon believe you?'

'I don't know. I think so. He didn't seem very interested one way or the other.'

'Does Graham have a surname? Semi-skimmed Milk, perhaps?'

Charlie shook her head, smiling half-heartedly. The ability to laugh at oneself was supposed to be a virtue. It was one Olivia expected Charlie to practise rather too often.

'Nip it in the bud as soon as you get back,' Olivia advised. 'Tell Simon it's over with Graham. Rejoin the world of the sane.'

Charlie wondered if Simon had said anything to Sellers and Gibbs. Or, God forbid, to Inspector Proust. Everybody in CID saw her as a romantic disaster area. They all knew how she felt about Simon, and that he'd rejected her. They knew she'd slept with more people in the past three years than most of them had in their lives.

Charlie was already attached to her lie, to the new status and dignity it afforded her. She wanted Simon to think she had a proper boyfriend. Not just another of her hopeless one-night stands – a relationship that might last. Like a grown-up.

She hadn't told Olivia about Alice Fancourt and Simon. It depressed her too much. Why was Simon thinking about Alice suddenly, after nearly two years of no contact? What good could come of seeing her again now? Charlie had assumed he had forgotten about Alice, or was in the process of doing so. It wasn't as if anything had even happened between them.

He'd told Charlie solemnly that he was planning to ring Alice, as if expecting her to remonstrate with him. He'd known she would care. When she'd dropped her non-existent Graham into the conversation a few days later, it had been obvious that Simon didn't.

Olivia kept saying as much, as if Charlie were in danger of forgetting. 'Simon doesn't care if you've got a boyfriend or not. I don't know why you think you can make him jealous. If he wanted you, he could have had you long ago.'

Was it possible for Simon to find out that she'd invented Graham? Charlie didn't think she could stand that. 'Do you want me to ring Silver Brae Charlets or not?' she said wearily.

'It cannae be worse than this dump.' Olivia faked a Scottish accent. 'Och, aye, lassie, why not?'

5

Tuesday 4 April

'I want to report a rape,' I tell Detective Constable Waterhouse.

He frowns, looking at the sheet of paper in his hand as if it might tell him what to ask next. 'Who was raped?'

'I was.'

'When?'

I doubt he'd be so brusque if he believed me.

'Three years ago,' I say. His eyes widen. Clearly, he was expecting a different answer. 'The thirtieth of March 2003.' I hope I won't have to say the date again. DC Waterhouse stands by the door as if guarding it, makes no move to sit down.

The interview room we are in is not much bigger than my bathroom at home. The pale-blue walls are covered with posters about solvent abuse, domestic violence, benefit cheats and video piracy. I cannot believe anybody really cares about people making illegal copies of films and selling them, but I suppose the police have to deal with all crimes, whether they care about them or not. All the posters have the police logo in the bottom right-hand corner, which makes me wonder if there is a design department some-where in this building, someone whose job it is to decide what colour background a poster about Social Security fraud ought to have.

Designing is my favourite part of what I do. My heart

always sinks when a customer has too specific an idea of what they want. I prefer the ones who are happy to leave it to me. I love choosing the Latin motto, deciding what kind of stone to use, what colour paint, what furniture. Dial furniture is anything on a sundial that isn't directly to do with time-telling, any ornamental touches.

I've hardly told you anything about my work, have I? You never mention yours, and I don't want to give the impression that I think mine is more important. I once made the mistake of asking you why you chose to become a lorry driver. 'You mean I should be doing something better,' you said immediately. I couldn't work out if you were offended, or if you were projecting your own feelings about your job on to me.

'I don't mean that at all,' I said. I really didn't. Once I thought about it, I could see all sorts of advantages to doing what you do. Being self-employed, for a start. Being able to listen to CDs or the radio all day. I started to think that perhaps our jobs weren't so dissimilar after all. I suppose there must be some ingrained snobbery in me that made me assume all lorry drivers were stupid and coarse, men with pot bellies and crew cuts who become violent at the prospect of rising petrol prices.

'I like to be on my own and I like driving.' You shrugged; to you, the answer was simple and obvious. You added, 'I'm not thick.' As if I would ever have thought you were. You're the most intelligent person I've ever met. I'm not talking about qualifications. I don't know if you've got O levels and A levels; I suspect you haven't. And you don't show off in conversation like some clever people do – quite the opposite. I have to drag opinions out of you. You offer your views and preferences apologetically, as if reluctant to have any sort of impact. The only thing you're expansive about is how much you love me. 'I'm my own man,' you said. 'Just me and the lorry. It's better than being a Commie.' In all the time we've known one another, this is the only reference you've ever made to politics. I wanted to ask what you meant, but I didn't because our time together was running out; it was nearly seven o'clock.

'Why did you ask for me or Sergeant Zailer?' says DC Waterhouse. 'I assumed you wanted to talk about Robert Haworth.'

'I do. Robert is the person who raped me.' The lie slides off my tongue. I'm not nervous any more. My brazen streak has taken over. I have a crazy, powerful feeling that tells me I can write the rules from now on. Who's going to stop me? Who has enough imagination to understand what my imagination is capable of?

I'm the person who does the things nobody else would do.

A horrible thought occurs to me. 'Am I too late?' I ask.

'What do you mean?'

'Can I still report it even though it happened so long ago?'

'Robert Haworth raped you?' Waterhouse makes no effort to hide his disbelief.

'That's right.'

'The man you're in love with, and who's in love with you. The man you meet every week at the Rawndesley East Services Traveltel.'

'I lied yesterday. I'm sorry.'

'Everything you said was a lie? You and Mr Haworth aren't in a relationship together?'

I know from reading rape websites that some women remain romantically or sexually involved with their rapists afterwards, but I could never pretend to be the sort of fucked-in-the-head fool who might do that. Which means there's only one thing I can say. 'Everything I told you yesterday was a lie, yes.'

Waterhouse doesn't believe me. He probably thinks I'm too composed. I hate the way everybody expects you to emote in public. 'Why tell such a lie?' He says it in the way he might to a suspect.

'I wasn't sure I wanted to report the rape at first.' I keep using it, the word I've avoided for three years. It gets easier with each repetition. 'I wanted to scare him – Robert Haworth. I thought a visit from the police, with my name mentioned, would terrify the life out of him.'

Waterhouse stares at me in silence. He is waiting for me to crumble. 'So why the change of plan?' he asks eventually.

'I realised all my other ideas were stupid. Taking the law into my own hands . . .'

'The thirtieth of March 2003 was a long time ago. Why wait until yesterday?'

'Three years is nothing. Ask anyone who's been raped. I was in shock for a long time. I was in no fit state to make decisions.' I answer each question quickly, like a robot, and accept my own congratulations for having had the sense not to put myself through this ordeal three years ago.

Reluctantly, Waterhouse pulls a chair out from under the table and sits down opposite me. 'You were more convincing yesterday than you are now,' he says. 'Has Mr Haworth given you the brush-off, is that it? Is this your way of punishing him?'

'No. I—'

'Are you aware that falsely accusing someone of rape is a serious criminal offence?' He keeps his eyes on his sheet of paper. It is covered in writing, the smallest handwriting I've ever seen. I can't read any of it.

I am about to answer him, but I stop myself. Why should I let him fire question after question at me? He's got into a rhythm now, like someone throwing a tennis ball at a wall. I'm entitled to more respect and sensitivity. I am lying about one detail only. If I removed you from my rape story and put in a man whose name I don't know, a man whose face I still see clearly in body-jolting, sweat-soaked nightmares, it would be a hundred per cent true. Which means I deserve better treatment than this.

'Yes, I'm aware,' I tell him. 'And you should be aware that I'm going to make a complaint about you if you don't stop looking at me and talking to me like I'm shit on your shoe. I'm doing my best to be straight with you. I've apologised for lying yesterday and I've explained why I did it. I'm here to report a *more* serious crime than falsely accusing someone of rape, since we all know there's a pecking order, and I think you should start concentrating on that instead of whatever prejudices you've got against me.'

He looks up. I can't tell if he's angry, daunted, startled.

'Why don't I make life easier for both of us?' I say. 'I can prove I'm telling the truth. There's an organisation called Speak Out and Survive – they've got a website: speak-outandsurvive – all one word – dot org dot uk. On the page called "Survivors' Stories", there's a letter I wrote, dated May the eighteenth 2003. The stories are numbered. Mine's number seventy-two. I signed it only with my initials: N.J.'

Waterhouse is writing all this down. When he's finished, he says, 'Wait here,' and leaves the room, letting the door bang shut. I am alone in the small blue cage.

In the silence, my head fills with your words. DC Waterhouse is nothing to me. He's a stranger. I remember what you said about strangers, on the day we met, after you'd taken my side in an argument between me and a man named Bruce Doherty – another stranger, an idiot. 'You don't know him and he doesn't know you,' you said. 'Therefore he can't hurt you. It's the people we're closest to who can hurt us the most.' You looked disturbed, as if you were trying to shut something out of your mind, something unwelcome. I didn't know you well enough then to ask if you'd been badly hurt, and by whom. 'Believe me, I know,' you said. 'The people you love are within hurting distance, close range. Strangers aren't.'

Thinking of my own experience, I said vehemently, 'You're telling me a stranger can't hurt me?'

'If the pain isn't personal, it isn't as bad. It's not about you, or the other person, or the relationship between the two of you. It's more like a natural disaster, an earthquake or a flood. If I was drowning in a flood, I'd call it bad luck, but it wouldn't be a betrayal. Chance and circumstance have no free will. They can't betray you.'

Now, for the first time, I see what you mean. DC Waterhouse is behaving in the way he is because he has to, because it's his job to doubt everything I tell him. It's not about me. He doesn't know me at all.

I wonder what you would say about strangers who are kind, who smile at me in the street and say, 'Sorry, love,' when they bump into me by accident. To anyone who's experienced deliberate brutality, the slightest kind word comes as a shock forever after. I'm so pathetically grateful even for the small, meaningless kindnesses that cost people nothing; grovellingly thankful that someone thought me worth a smile or a 'sorry'. I think it's the shock of the contrast; I'm amazed that offhand generosity and offhand evil can exist in the same world and barely be aware of one another.

If the police find you safe and well, they will tell you what I've accused you of, all the sordid details. Will you believe me if I say I made it up? Will you understand that I only blackened your name in desperation, because I was so worried about you?

I wonder, not for the first time, if I ought to change all the specifics of the attack, so that the story I tell DC Waterhouse, if he ever lets me, is completely different from what really happened. I decide I can't. I can only be confident if I have a bedrock of fact to support me. I haven't slept properly for days. All my joints ache and my brain feels as if it's been grated. I haven't got the energy to invent rapes that never happened.

And no made-up story could be worse than my real one. If I can only persuade DC Waterhouse that I'm telling the truth, looking for you will leap straight to the top of his to-do list.

After about ten minutes the door opens. He edges back into the room, carrying several sheets of paper. Eyeing me warily, he asks, 'Would you like a cup of tea?'

I am encouraged by this, but pretend to be annoyed. 'I see. So now that I've proved myself, I get offered refreshments. Is there a sliding scale? Tea for rape, sparkling water for sexual assault, tap water for a mugging?'

His expression hardens. 'I've read what you wrote. What you say you wrote.'

'You don't believe me?' He's more stubborn than I thought. I prepare to go into battle. I like a good fight, especially when I know I can win. 'How would I know it was there if I hadn't written it? You think women who haven't been raped cruise rape websites for fun, and then when they find a story that happens to have their initials at the bottom—'

' "My attacker was someone I had never seen before and have not seen since," ' Waterhouse reads aloud from one of the pages in his hand. He's printed out my letter. I baulk, uncomfortable with the idea that it's in the room with us.

I speak quickly, before he can read me any more of my own words. 'I didn't know who he was at the time. I found out later. I saw him again. Like I told you, I bumped into him at Rawndesley East Services on Thursday the twenty-fourth of March last year.'

Waterhouse is shaking his head, flicking through his papers. 'You didn't say that,' he contradicts me flatly. 'You said you first met Mr Haworth on that date, but not where you met him.'

'Well, that's where I met him. At the service station. But it wasn't the first time. The first time was when he raped me.'

'Rawndesley East Services. At the Traveltel?'

I picture Waterhouse's brain as a computer. Everything I tell him is a new piece of data to enter. 'No. In the food-court bit. What I said about the Traveltel was a lie. I know there's a Traveltel at Rawndesley East Services, and I wanted to keep my lie as close to the truth as possible.'

'What about room eleven? The same room every time?' He says this more quietly and sensitively than he's said anything else. It's a bad sign. He watches me carefully.

'I made that up. I've never been inside the Traveltel or any of its rooms.'

Once he's heard my story, he will be in no doubt that I'm telling the truth; he won't bother to talk to staff at the Traveltel. And he knows I know this is something he could easily check. So why, he will think, would I tell such a risky lie?

'So you met Mr Haworth, your rapist, for the second

time on the twenty-fourth of March last year, in the food court of Rawndesley East Services?'

'Yes. I saw him. He didn't see me.'

Waterhouse leans back in his chair, throws his pen down on the desk. 'It must have been a shock, seeing him like that.'

I say nothing.

'How did you find out his name and where he lived?'

'I followed him out to his van. It's got his name and phone number on it. I got his address from the phone book.' He can ask me anything. I will have my answer ready – a good, plausible answer – within seconds. Every time he draws my attention to a detail that he hopes will trip me up, I find a way to work it into my story. Everything can be reconciled. All I have to do is approach it methodically: this must be the case, and this must also be the case. What story will make that possible?

'I can't see it,' says Waterhouse. 'You know his name, you know where he lives. You said you were thinking about taking things into your own hands. Why didn't you?'

'Because if I'd ended up with a criminal record, that'd be another victory for him, wouldn't it? I told you, I wanted the police to turn up at his house and give him the fright of his life. I didn't want to have to . . . be face to face with him myself.'

'So you cooked up a whole story about an affair, room eleven every Thursday night, your friend ringing up and speaking to Mr Haworth's wife?'

'Yes.'

He consults his notes. 'Do you have a friend and lodger called Yvon?'

I hesitate. 'Yes. Yvon Cotchin.'

'So not everything you said yesterday was a lie. That's at

least one lie you've told today, then. What about the panic attack, going to his house? Meeting Mrs Haworth?'

'That was all true,' I tell him. 'I did go there. That was what made me think I couldn't handle it myself. So I came to you.'

Waterhouse says, 'Yesterday you gave me and Sergeant Zailer a photograph of you with Mr Haworth. How do you explain that?'

I try not to let surprise and annoyance show on my face. I should have thought about this, and I haven't. I completely forgot about the photo. Calmly, I say, 'It was a fake.'

'Really? How did you do it, exactly?'

'I didn't. I took a photograph of Robert Haworth, and a photograph of me, and a friend did the rest.'

'Where did you get the one of Mr Haworth?'

I sigh, as if this should be obvious. 'I took it myself, in the service-station car park. On the twenty-fourth of March last year.'

'I don't think so,' says Waterhouse. 'He didn't see you, standing right in front of him? And how come you had a camera with you?'

'I wasn't standing right in front of him. I took the picture from a distance, on my digital camera. My friend enlarged it on a computer and zoomed in on his head and shoulders, to make it look like a close-up . . .'

'What friend? Miss Cotchin again?'

'No. I'm not going to give you his name. Sorry. And, to answer your other question, I always have a camera with me when I'm on my way to see a prospective client, as I was that day. I take photographs of their gardens, or their walls, wherever it is they want the sundial. It helps me to work if I've got a picture of the location to refer to.'

Waterhouse looks uncomfortable. I see a flicker of doubt

in his eyes. 'If the story you're telling me now is true, then the way your mind works is very strange,' he says. 'If it isn't, I can prove that you're lying.'

'Perhaps you ought to let me tell you what I came here to tell you. Once you've heard what happened to me, you'll see how it might mess with anybody's head. And if you still don't believe me after I've told you what I went through, I'll make sure never to say another word to you ever again, if you think I'd lie about something like that!'

I know it doesn't help to endear me to him that I am furious instead of weepy, but I am so used to anger. I'm good at it.

Waterhouse says, 'As soon as I take your statement, this becomes official. Do you understand?'

A small spasm of panic shakes my heart. How will I begin? *Once upon a time* . . . But I am not confessing or revealing. I am lying through my teeth – that's the way to look at it. The truth will only be there to serve the lie, which means I don't have to feel the feelings.

'I understand,' I say. 'Let's make it official.'

6

4/4/06

STATEMENT OF NAOMI JENKINS of 14 Argyll Square, Rawndesley.
Occupation: self-employed, freelance sundial-maker. Age: 35 years.

This statement is true to the best of my knowledge and belief, and I
make it knowing that, if it is tendered in evidence, I shall be liable to
prosecution if I have wilfully stated anything in it which I know to be
false or do not believe to be true.

Signature: Naomi Jenkins Date: 4 April 2006

On the morning of Monday, 30 March 2003, I left my house at 0940 and
went to collect some Hopton Wood stone that I needed for my work from a
local stonemason, James Flowton of Crossfield Farm House, Hamblesford.
Mr Flowton told me that the stone had not yet arrived from the quarry, so I
left immediately and walked back up the track to the main road, Thornton
Road, where I'd parked my car.

A man I had never seen before was standing beside my car. He was tall,
with short, dark-brown hair. He was wearing a light-brown corduroy jacket
with what looked like a sheepskin lining, black jeans and Timberland
boots. As I approached, he called out, 'Naomi!' and waved. His other hand
was in his pocket. Even though I didn't recognise him, I assumed he knew
me and was waiting for me. (I now know the man to be Robert Haworth, of
3 Chapel Lane, Spilling, but I did not know this at the time.)

I walked right up to him. He grabbed my arm and produced a knife from his jacket pocket. I screamed. The knife had a hard, black handle about three inches long and a blade that was about five inches long. He pulled me towards him, so that we were standing chest to chest, and pushed the tip of the knife against my stomach. Throughout all this he kept smiling at me. In a quiet voice, he told me to stop screaming. He said, 'Shut up or I'll cut your guts out. I'll cut your heart out. You know I mean it.' I stopped screaming. Mr Haworth said, 'Do exactly what you're told and you won't end up with a knife inside you, all right?' I nodded. He seemed angry that I hadn't answered him. 'All right?' he repeated.

This time I replied by saying, 'All right.'

He put the knife back in his pocket, linked his arm through mine and told me to walk to his car, which was parked approximately two hundred metres further up Thornton Road in the direction of Spilling, outside a shop called Snowy Joe's, which sells sports equipment. His car was black. I think it was a hatchback. I was too frightened to notice the make, model or registration.

He unlocked the car as we walked towards it, using a key fob that came from the same pocket as the knife. When we got to the car, he opened the back door and told me to get in. I climbed on to the back seat. He slammed the door, then went round to the other side of the car and got in next to me. He took my handbag, removed my mobile phone from it and threw the bag out of the car window. He threw the phone on to the front passenger seat of the car. There was a shelf in the car, running the full length of the top of the back seats. He reached behind me and pulled something off the shelf. It was an eye mask made of blue padded fabric, with a black elastic strap. He put it on me, covering my eyes, and told me that if I took it off, he would use the knife on me. He said, 'If you don't want to bleed to death slowly, you'll do what I say.'

I heard the car door slam. From what I heard next, I could tell that he'd got into the driver's seat. He said, 'I'm adjusting the rear-view mirror so I can see you all the time. Don't try anything.' The car began to move. I don't know how long we were in the car. It felt like hours, but I was so frightened that I was not able to assess this accurately. I estimate that we were driving for at least two hours and possibly much longer. At first I tried to persuade Mr Haworth to let me go. I offered him money in exchange for releasing me. I asked him how he knew my name, and what he intended to do with me. He laughed at me whenever I asked a question, and didn't answer. Eventually, he seemed to get irritated and he told me to shut up. I kept quiet after that, because he again threatened me with the knife. He told me he'd locked all the car doors, and that if I tried to escape, I'd regret it. He said, 'All you have to do is what I tell you and you won't be hurt.'

For the whole journey, Radio 5 Live was playing in the car. I did not notice which programmes were on, just the station. After a while, during which there was no verbal exchange between us, Mr Haworth started to tell me things about myself. He knew my home address and that I was a sundial-maker. He asked me questions about sundials and insisted I answer them. He said that if I got one wrong, he'd pull over and get his knife out. It was clear from his questions that he knew a reasonable amount about sundials. He mentioned scaphe dials, and he knew what an analemma was. These are both technical terms that those unfamiliar with sundials might not know. He knew that I was born in Folkestone, that I'd studied typography at Reading University and that I'd started my sundial business using a substantial sum of money I'd made when I sold a typographical font I created in my final year at university to Adobe, the word-processing software company. He asked me, 'How does it feel to be a successful businesswoman?' The tone of his questions was mocking. I had the impression that he wanted to taunt me with how much he knew about me. I asked him how he knew all this information. He stopped the car at that point, and I felt something sharp against my nose. I assumed this was the knife. Mr Haworth reminded me that I wasn't allowed to ask questions and made me apologise. Then he started driving again.

Some time later the car stopped. Mr Haworth opened my door and pulled me out. He linked his arm through mine again and told me to walk slowly. He steered me in the direction he wanted me to go. Eventually, I could tell from the feel of the ground beneath my feet that we were entering a building. I was led up some steps. Mr Haworth grabbed me and pulled my coat off. He told me to take my shoes off, which I did. It was very cold inside whatever building we were in, colder than outside. He turned me round and told me to sit down. I sat. He told me to lie down. I thought that I was probably on a bed. He tied ropes round my ankles and wrists and pulled my body into an X-shape as he tied each of my limbs to something. Then he took the eye mask off my face.

I saw that we were in a small theatre. I was tied to a bed on the stage. The bed was made of some kind of dark wood – perhaps mahogany – and had a carved acorn sticking up from each of the four corners of its frame. The mattress that I was lying on had some sort of plastic cover over it. I noticed that there were steps leading down on one side of the stage and assumed these were the steps I'd just walked up. The curtains were open in front of me, so I could see the rest of the theatre. Instead of rows of seats for the audience, there was a large, long dinner table made of what looked like the same dark wood as the bed, and lots of dark wood chairs with white cushion seats. Every place at the table was set with several knives and forks.

Mr Haworth said, 'Do you want to warm up before the show?' He put his hand on my breast and squeezed it. I begged him to let me go. He laughed and took his knife out of his pocket. He began, very slowly, to cut my clothes off. I panicked and again begged him to let me go. He ignored me and continued to cut. I was unsure how long he took to cut my clothes off, but there was a small window that I could see from where I lay, and I noticed it was getting darker outside. I estimate that it took him at least an hour.

Once I was completely naked, he left me alone for a few minutes. I think he left the theatre. I called for help as loudly as I could. I was freezing cold and my teeth were chattering.

After a few minutes Mr Haworth returned. 'You'll be glad to hear I've turned the heating on,' he said. 'The audience'll be here soon. Can't have them freezing their balls off, can we?'

I saw that he was holding my mobile phone. He asked me if it was one that could take photographs. I was too scared to lie, so I told him it was. He asked me what he needed to do if he wanted to take a picture. I told him. He took a photograph of me lying on the bed and showed it to me. 'A souvenir,' he said. 'Your first main part.' He asked me how to send the photo to another mobile phone. I told him. He said he was sending the picture to his own mobile phone. He threatened to send it to all the numbers stored on my phone if I didn't obey his orders, or if I ever went to the police. Then he sat on the edge of the bed for a while and began to touch my private parts, laughing at me when I cried and recoiled.

I don't know how much time passed, but a while later, there was a knock at the door and Mr Haworth left me alone again, disappearing down the steps and then behind me and out of sight. I heard the sound of lots of people's footsteps. The theatre had a wooden floor, so the noise was loud. I heard Mr Haworth greeting what sounded like lots of other men, but no names were mentioned. Then I saw several men, all wearing the sort of dinner dress that is known as 'black tie', approach the table and sit down at it. There were at least ten men present, excluding Mr Haworth. Most of them were Caucasians, but at least two were black. Mr Haworth poured wine for them and welcomed them. They exchanged a few comments about the weather and the conditions on the roads.

I screamed and begged the men to help me, but they all laughed at me. They stared at my body and made lewd remarks. One of them said to Mr Haworth, 'When do we get a closer look?' and he replied, 'All in good time.' Then he disappeared into a room at the back of the theatre, on the opposite side of the room to the stage. He emerged a couple of minutes later holding a tray, and put down a small plate in front of each man at the table. Each plate had smoked salmon and a slice of lemon on it, and a globule of something white with green flecks in it.

As the men began to eat and drink, Mr Haworth came back on to the stage. He proceeded to rape me, first orally and then vaginally. While this was going on, the men cheered, laughed, clapped and made lewd comments. After he had finished raping me, Mr Haworth began to clear the plates away, taking them back into the small room behind where the men were sitting. He left the door to this room open, and I became aware of a range of sounds typical of a kitchen, noises I associated with cooking and washing up. I realised there were people in the kitchen.

Mr Haworth came back on to the stage and untied me. He told me to walk down the steps and reminded me that if I disobeyed him in any way, he would 'gut' me. I did what he said. He led me to the table, where there was one chair still unoccupied. He pushed me down on to it and began to tie me up again. He pulled my arms behind my back and behind the back of the chair and tied my wrists together. Then he pushed my legs as far apart as they would go and told me to put my ankles together underneath the chair. He then tied my ankles. The other men continued to clap and cheer.

Mr Haworth then served three more courses to the men, one that was a slab of some sort of meat with some vegetables, a tiramisu and then cheeses. None of the other men apart from Mr Haworth touched me at all, but while they were eating, they mocked and taunted me. From time to time, one of them asked me a question – for example, I was asked what my favourite sexual fantasy was, and my favourite sexual position. Mr Haworth ordered me to answer. 'And you'd better make it good,' he said. I said the sorts of things I thought he wanted me to say.

After the men had finished their last course, Mr Haworth cleared away all the things from the table. He brought a bottle of port and some glasses from the kitchen, then a box of cigars, then some ashtrays and matches. Then he untied me and told me to lie face down on the table. I did so. Some of the men lit cigars. Mr Haworth climbed on top of me and raped me anally.

When he'd finished, he said, 'Does anyone want a go?'

One of the men replied, 'We're all too pissed, mate.'

A few of the men, including Mr Haworth, then tried to encourage a man named Paul to rape me. They said things like, 'What about you, Paul?' and, 'Go on, Paul, you've got to do her.' This made me think that the men all knew each other quite well, that they were an established group of friends and perhaps Paul was the leader, or known as some sort of character within the group. I couldn't see which of the men was Paul, but I heard him say, 'No, watching's enough for me.'

Mr Haworth told me to stand up. He handed me my coat and my shoes and told me to put them on. Once I was dressed, he put the mask over my eyes again and made me walk outside with him, leaving the men inside the room. He pushed me into the car and slammed the door. Mr Haworth didn't speak to me at all during this second car journey. I think I must have fainted or blacked out for much of the journey, because I lost all track of time. Some time later, while it was still pitch dark, the car stopped and I was pulled out. I fell down to the ground. Mr Haworth did not give me back my mobile phone. I heard the car drive away and assumed he had gone. After a few seconds I plucked up the courage to pull off the mask and I saw that I was just down the road from my own car, on Thornton Road in Hamblesford. My car keys were in my coat pocket, so I got into my car and drove home.

I told no one about what happened to me and did not report my abduction and attack to the police. I later encountered Mr Haworth again by chance, on 24 March 2005 at Rawndesley East Services, and was able to identify him by following him to his lorry in the car park, which had his name painted on it.

Statement taken by: DC 124 Simon Waterhouse, Culver Valley CID
Station: Spilling
Time and place statement taken: 1610, 4.4.06 Spilling

7

5/4/06

'A rozzer?' The man who was showing Charlie and Olivia around their holiday chalet threw up his hands in alarm. 'I wouldn't have told you we had availability if I'd known you were one of the boys in blue. Girls in blue, rather.' He winked and turned to Olivia. 'You a rozzer as well?' He had the sort of polished accent Charlie thought of as 'public school'.

'No,' said Olivia. 'Why does everybody who meets us together always say that?' she asked Charlie. 'No one asks you if you're a journalist. It makes no sense. Is it meant to run in the family, the desire to enforce the law?' Anyone who knew Olivia would have known how ludicrous it was, the idea of her chasing a teenage thug down the street or breaking down the door of a crack house. 'Does your brother own a holiday-chalet business?' she enquired innocently.

The man wasn't offended, thank goodness. He laughed. 'This might come as a surprise, but, yes, my brother and I have been in business together for several years. So, you're a journalist, are you? Like whatsername? Kate Adie!'

Charlie wouldn't have put up with the man's prying if he had been any less handsome or if she had been any less thrilled with the chalet. She could tell Olivia loved it too. There was a bath big enough for two people, which stood on four gold feet in the centre of a large bathroom with a black slate floor. A straw basket beside the basin over-flowed with Molton Brown products and the large, flat, gleaming shower-head in the glass stall in the corner looked capable of unleashing a satisfying downpour.

Both beds in the chalet were wider than ordinary dou-bles. The frames were sleigh-shaped, cherry wood, with curved head- and footboards. Their friendly if slightly intrusive host – Mr Angilley, Charlie assumed, the one whose name was on the card – had given them a pillow menu when they'd first arrived. 'Duck down,' Olivia had said without a moment's hesitation. Charlie had thought, I wouldn't mind sharing my pillows with you, Mr Angilley, but she'd kept the thought to herself. He was the sort of good-looking that was unusual, verging on implausible – as if he'd been designed by a great artist or something. Almost too perfect.

A huge, flat-screened television was set into the wall in the living area, and although there wasn't a minibar, there was something called a 'larder' by the entrance to the kitchen that was stocked with every conceivable variety of alcohol and snack. 'Just tell us what you've had at the end of the week – we trust you!' Angilley had said, winking at Charlie. She didn't normally like to be winked at, but perhaps it wasn't sensible to be so rigid about things . . .

The kitchen was tiny, which Charlie knew had pleased her sister. Olivia was opposed to the big, sociable, island- and table-stuffed kitchens that most women loved. She thought cooking was a waste of time and that nobody who didn't have to do it professionally should do it at all.

'Not at all like Kate Adie,' she told Angilley. 'I'm an arts journalist.'

'Very sensible,' he said. 'Much better to get stuck at the Tate Modern than in downtown Baghdad.'

'It's a moot point,' Olivia muttered.

Charlie examined Angilley's big brown eyes, which had laughter lines round them. How old was he? Early forties, she guessed. His centre-parted floppy hair gave him an agreeably unkempt look. Charlie liked the greeny-grey tweed jacket he was wearing, and his scarf. He was stylish, in a country sort of way. And he wasn't wearing a wedding ring.

Much more attractive than Simon bloody Waterhouse.

'What's your name?' Charlie decided to do a bit of counter-prying.

'Oh, sorry. I'm Graham Angilley, the owner.'

'Graham?' She looked at Olivia and grinned. Her sister glared at her. 'What a coincidence.' Charlie moved automatically into flirtatious mode. She tilted her head and gave Angilley a mischievous look. 'My made-up boyfriend's called Graham.'

He seemed disproportionately pleased. Pink spots appeared on his cheeks. 'Made-up? Why would you want to make up a boyfriend? I'd have thought you'd have plenty of real ones.' He bit his lip and frowned. 'I don't mean *plenty*, I mean . . . well, you must have lots of admirers.'

Charlie laughed at his embarrassment. 'It's a long story,' she said.

'Sorry. I'm usually much more suave and cool than this.' He put his hands in his pockets and smiled sheepishly. He also knows how to flirt, thought Charlie; she didn't normally go for the shy, hapless approach.

Olivia said loudly, 'Are there any good restaurants nearby?'

'Well . . . Edinburgh's within reach, if you don't mind an hour or so's drive,' said Graham, 'and there's an excellent restaurant right here. Steph cooks for any guests who want top-notch home-cooked meals. All ingredients organic.'

'Who's Steph?' Charlie asked as nonchalantly as possible. She felt unaccountably irritated.

'Steph?' Graham grinned at her, letting her know that he'd understood the implications of her question. 'She's all my staff rolled into one: cook, maid, secretary, receptionist – take your pick. My dogsbody. Though I shouldn't malign our canine friends.' He laughed. 'No, to be fair, Steph's perfectly attractive if you like peasant girls. And I'd be lost without her, she's a darling. Shall I bring you over some menus later?' He was looking only at Charlie.

'That'd be great,' she said, feeling slightly giddy.

'And don't forget to check out the spa, which is in the old barn building. We've just had a tepidarium put in. Perfect place to relax and pamper yourself.'

Once he'd gone, Olivia said, 'That *is* a good sign. I'd choose a tepidarium over a sauna or sanarium any day.'

Charlie was mystified, but decided not to ask. She wondered if her sister ever did a full day's work.

'Not sure I want to risk Steph's cooking, though. We need to arm ourselves as soon as possible with a local taxi number, so that if we're starving and the food here is awful, we can get to Edinburgh before our ribs start to protrude.'

Charlie shook her head in mock despair. It would take months, possibly years, of deprivation before Olivia's ribs protruded. 'I assume you want the mezzanine?' she said, hauling her suitcase over to the other bed.

'Definitely. Otherwise I'll feel as if I'm sleeping in the lounge. You *will* be sleeping in the lounge.'

'It stops being the lounge there –' Charlie pointed '– and becomes my bedroom.'

'What's wrong with walls, that's what I want to know. What's wrong with doors? I hate all this open-plan nonsense. What if you snore and keep me awake?'

Charlie began to unpack, wishing she'd been on a proper shopping trip and bought some new, sexy clothes. She looked out of the open window, at the steep bank of tall trees on the other side of the stream that flowed right outside their chalet. There was no noise in this place, if you didn't include Olivia's loud voice: no rumble of traffic, no general hum of the world going about its business. The occasional exclamation from a bird was the only thing that interrupted the stillness. And Charlie loved the crisp, fresh air. Thank God Spain was a disaster. People said things always worked out for the best, but Charlie had always thought that was preposterous, a downright insult to anyone who'd ever experienced something tragic or horrific.

'Char? We are going to have a nice holiday, aren't we?' Olivia sounded uncharacteristically anxious. She was lying on her bed. Charlie looked up, saw her sister's bare feet through the wooden railings. Unpacking was another thing Olivia dismissed as being too much effort. She treated her large suitcase as a small cupboard.

'Of course.' Charlie guessed what was coming next.

'Promise you won't let your Tyrannosaurus Sex alter ego take over and wreck everything? I've been really looking forward to this week. I'm not having it ruined because of some man.'

Tyrannosaurus Sex. Charlie tried to bat the words away, but they had already embedded themselves in her brain. Was that how Olivia saw her, as a huge, ugly monster, a rampant sexual predator? She felt as if a series of doors were slamming inside her, in a futile attempt to protect her ego against damage that had already been done.

'Which man?' she said in a clipped voice. 'Angilley or Simon?'

Olivia sighed. 'That you need to ask that question neatly illustrates the seriousness of the problem,' she said.

'In other words, a mess,' said Inspector Giles Proust. 'Is that a fair assessment of the situation, would you say, Waterhouse? I'd call it a mess. What would you call it?'

Simon was inside Proust's transparent cubicle. The place not to be, unless you enjoyed feeling as if all your colleagues were watching you being ripped into ragged pieces by the small-framed, bald inspector: a silent but brutal movie, seen at a safe distance, through glass. Simon sat on a green armless chair that was spewing its stuffing, while the inspector stepped around him, occasionally spilling tea from the 'World's Greatest Granddad' mug he held in his hand. Simon ducked every now and then to avoid being scalded. If this were a film, he thought, any minute now Proust would whip out a razor and start slashing. But a razor wasn't Proust's preferred weapon; he was happy to make do with his toxic tongue and his distorted view both of the world and his place in it.

Simon had taken the foolhardy step of entering the inspector's lair without having been summoned. By choice, insofar as anyone in CID ever sought out the Snowman by choice. The nickname was a reference to Proust's ability to transmit whatever mood he happened to be in – especially the bad ones – to rooms full of innocent bystanders. If he switched from relaxed to tense, from sociable to dour, the whole of the CID room froze mid-breath. Words turned to stone in every mouth, and actions became self-conscious and stilted. Simon didn't know how Proust managed so wholly to cripple the general atmosphere. Was his skin porous? Did he have special psychic powers?

Just talk to him like he's a normal bloke.

Simon had a lot he needed to say, and he knew there was no point stalling. 'It's certainly a difficult and worrying situation, sir.' He would happily have agreed to 'mess' as a definition, were it not for the clear implication that he was in some way responsible. In some way? He chided himself for being naïve. Proust held him *entirely* responsible. What he couldn't work out was why.

'You should have been on to Kent police straight away, as soon as Mrs Haworth gave you an address. You should have faxed them the details and followed it up an hour later.'

Kent police would have loved that. Simon would have looked insane if he'd chased them after only an hour. 'That would have been unwarranted, sir. I didn't know then what I know now. Naomi Jenkins hadn't accused Haworth of rape at that point.'

'You'd know a damn sight more *now* if you'd contacted Kent police *then*.'

'Would you have done that, sir? In my position?' A direct challenge was risky. Sod it. 'Mrs Haworth told me she'd make sure Mr Haworth got in touch as soon as he got back. She said he was trying to end his relationship with Naomi Jenkins but Jenkins wasn't having any of it. I left a message on his mobile and I was waiting for him to get back to me. It seemed straightforward.'

'Straighforward,' said Proust quietly. Almost wistfully. 'Is that how you'd describe it?'

'Not *now*, no. It's not straighforward any more . . .'

'Indeed.'

'Sir, I followed correct procedure. I decided to put it to one side for the time being and chase it up early next week if I hadn't heard anything.'

'And what factors contributed to that decision?' Proust flashed a frightful false smile in Simon's direction.

'I did a standard risk assessment. Haworth's an adult, there's no indication he's unstable or suicidal . . .'

The Snowman unleashed a small tidal wave of tea as he whirled round, faster on his feet than Fred Astaire. Simon wished Charlie wasn't away on holiday. For some reason, life was always bad when she wasn't around. 'Robert Haworth has a wife and a mistress,' said Proust. 'More precisely, he has a wife who's found out about his mistress, and a mistress who won't allow him to call it a day. You're not married, Waterhouse, so you perhaps won't know this, but living with one woman who claims to be reasonably fond of you and whom you've never wronged in any appreciable way is hard enough. Take it from me, as a man who's done thirty-two years' hard labour in the matrimonial field. To have two to deal with, one at each ear, both blubbing about how *betrayed* they feel . . . well, I'd have gone a lot further than Kent if I were him.'

Hard labour in the matrimonial field? That was a classic. Simon would have to remember it, pass it on to Charlie. It was only thanks to the unstinting efforts of Lizzie Proust that the Snowman was able to appear to be a sane, functioning human being for even a fraction of the time.

If this conversation had taken place two years ago, or even last year, Simon would have been feeling hot and impatient by this stage, gritting his teeth and fast-forwarding, mentally, to the day when he would break Proust's nose with his forehead. Today, he felt weary from the effort of remaining in adult mode while talking to a man who was effectively a child. Oh, very good, Waterhouse, very *psychological*, Proust would have said.

Simon wondered whether it would be reasonable to start thinking of himself as someone who used to have a violent temper. Or was it too soon for that?

'What would you have done, sir? Are you saying that, on the basis of what we knew yesterday morning, you'd have chased it up with the Kent police?'

Proust never gave you the satisfaction of an answer. 'Risk assessment,' he said scornfully, though he was the person who had given Simon the ACPO 2005 guidelines on missing persons procedure and instructed him to commit every word to memory. 'Haworth's at risk, all right, and I shouldn't have to tell you why. He's at risk because he's involved, in some way that has yet to be determined, with this Naomi Jenkins woman. Risk assessment! She turns up one day and reports him missing, claiming he's been her lover for the past year and she's lost without him, and then the next day she's back saying forget all that, it was all a big lie, and accusing Haworth of a three-year-old abduction and rape?' He shook his head. 'This'll be a murder investigation by the end of the week, you watch.'

'I'm not sure, sir. I think it's premature to assume that.'

'I wouldn't need to assume anything if you'd taken control of the situation in a professional way!' Proust yelled at him. 'Why didn't you interview Naomi Jenkins properly on Monday, get the full story out of her then?'

'We did . . .'

'This woman's wrapping us round her little finger. She comes in whenever she feels like it, says whatever she fancies saying, and all you can do is nod and write down each new lie in great detail – a missing person report one minute, a rape statement the next. She's staging a pantomime, and she's cast you as the hind legs of the donkey!'

'Sergeant Zailer and I—'

'What, in the name of all things bright and beautiful, were you thinking of, taking a rape statement from her?

Clearly she's a rabid fantasist, and yet you choose to indulge her!'

Simon thought about Naomi Jenkins' account of her rape, what she said those men had done to her. It was the worst thing he'd ever heard. He considered telling Proust how he'd actually, honestly, felt when she'd told him. No chance. The physical proximity of the Snowman repelled any ideas he'd foolishly harboured about the possibility of genuine communication taking place; you only had to take one look at the man.

'If she's lying about the rape, how do you explain the letter, signed N.J., that she sent to that website in May 2003?'

'It's a fantasy she's had for years – since birth for all I know or care,' said Proust impatiently. 'Then she met Haworth and fleshed it out a little, added him to her absurd tale. Nothing she says can be relied upon.'

'I agree her behaviour's suspicious,' said Simon. 'Her instability's obviously cause for greater concern about Haworth's safety.' We don't disagree, he might have added. Pointless. 'Which is why, as soon as I'd finished taking her statement, I *did* get on to Kent police. And they've just got back to me.' *In other words, you narrow-minded shit, I've got some facts you might be interested in if you're willing to stop chucking blame at me for two seconds.* Simon had a sense of his words trickling back to him, having failed to get through, failed to permeate the rigid, invisible barrier that surrounded Proust at all times.

He persisted. 'The address Juliet Haworth gave me exists, but no one there knows anything about Robert Haworth.'

'She's unstable as well,' said the Snowman flatly, as if he suspected the two women in Robert Haworth's life of deliberately conspiring to create problems for him, Giles Proust. 'Well? Have you been back to the house and searched it? Have you searched Naomi Jenkins' house? If you'd read the new missing persons gubbins I gave you—'

'I have read it,' Simon cut in. The ACPO 2005 guidelines for the management of missing persons were hardly new. Proust was averse to change. For weeks after the clocks went forward or back, he made a distinction between 'old time' and 'new time'.

'—you'd know that under Section 17, part c – or is it d? – you can enter any premises if you have cause to believe someone's at risk—'

'I know all that, sir. I just wanted to check with you first, as Sergeant Zailer's away.'

'Well, what did you think I'd say? A man's missing. His bit on the side's a conniving lunatic, and his wife, far from being worried about his whereabouts, is actively trying to put you off the scent. What did you think I'd say? Put your feet up and forget all about it?'

'Of course not, sir.' *I have to consult you, you fucking wanker.* Did Proust think Simon enjoyed their little exchanges? It wasn't as bad when Charlie was around: she acted as a buffer, shielding her team from the inspector's bullying as much as she could. She also, more and more in recent months, made decisions that by rights were Proust's to make, in order to minimise his stress and allow him to have the sort of short, easy days he liked.

'Of course not, sir,' Proust mimicked. He sighed and swallowed a yawn – a sign that he'd run out of steam. 'Do the obvious things, Waterhouse. Search Jenkins' house, and Haworth's. Run the usual credit-card and telephony checks. Talk to everyone Haworth knows: friends, work contacts. You *know* what to do.'

'Yes, sir.'

'Oh, and while I'm underlining the absolutely elementary: bring in Naomi Jenkins' computer. We'll be able to tell, won't we, whether the letter she claims she sent to the rape website originated from her machine?'

'Yes, sir,' said Simon, thinking, Someone will, you won't. Proust was an expert on everything that required no expertise, that was his problem. 'If it's the same machine. She might have bought a new one since.'

'Get Sellers and Gibbs on to it too. As of today, it's our highest priority.'

You get them on to it, Simon nearly made the mistake of saying. Was Proust preparing for retirement, he wondered, handing out his responsibilities to anyone who'd have them?

'Grill Jenkins again. And go to the Traveltel—'

'I've just got off the phone with the receptionist.' Simon was pleased to be able to decapitate at least one of Proust's unnecessary instructions. Giving redundant advice was one of the Snowman's favourite hobbies, though he marginally preferred issuing completely uncalled-for warnings. He was forever telling Charlie and Simon and the rest of the team not to crash their cars or leave their front doors unlocked or fall off the sides of mountains if they went walking.

'A man and a woman fitting Haworth's and Jenkins' descriptions have spent every Thursday night at the Traveltel, in room eleven, for roughly a year. Exactly as Jenkins said on Monday. I'm waiting for the Traveltel receptionist to get back to me and confirm it's them. I've couriered a copy of the photo over to her—'

'Of course it's them!' Proust slammed his mug down on the desk.

'Sir, you're presumably not saying that I shouldn't have

bothered to check?' Such a basic failure – in a parallel universe in which Simon had still done lots of things wrong, but different things – would undoubtedly have resulted in a bollocking very similar to the one he was getting now.

The inspector looked thoroughly disgusted. Sounded it, too, as he said, 'Just get on with it, Waterhouse, all right? Anything else, or might you allow me a few minutes' calm in which to piece together the fragments of my shattered day?'

'The receptionist said the couple – Haworth and Jenkins, assuming it's them – seem very keen on one another.'

Proust threw up his hands. 'That's one mystery solved, then. That explains why they go to a roadside motel together every week. Sex, Waterhouse. What did you think: they both had a thing for eight-pound-ninety-nine platters?'

Simon ignored his sarcasm. The relationship between Robert Haworth and Naomi Jenkins was crucial, at the centre of this whole peculiar business, and the Traveltel receptionist, as far as Simon knew, was an objective, independent witness. He said firmly, 'She told me they always had their arms round each other. Stared into each other's eyes a lot, that sort of thing.'

'At reception?'

'Apparently.'

Proust snorted loudly.

'And the woman always stayed the night, left the next morning. Whereas the man left at about seven the same evening.'

'Always?'

'That's what she said.'

'What sort of nonsense relationship can that be, then?' said Proust, looking into his empty mug as if hoping to find that it had filled itself.

'Possibly an abusive one,' Simon suggested. 'Sir, I was thinking about Stockholm syndrome. You know, where women fall in love with men who abuse them . . .'

'Don't waste my time, Waterhouse. Get out there and do your perishing job.'

Simon stood up, turned to leave.

'Oh, and Waterhouse?'

'Sir?'

'You might buy me a book about sundials, while you're out and about. I've always found them fascinating. Did you know that sundial time is more accurate than clock time, than Greenwich Mean Time? I read that somewhere. If you're talking about measuring the precise position of the Earth in relation to the Sun – solar time – then a sundial's your man.' Proust smiled, startling Simon: happiness looked wrong on the inspector's face. 'Clocks would have us believe that all days are the same length, exactly twenty-four hours. Not true, Waterhouse. Not true. Some are a little bit shorter, and some a little bit longer. Did you know that?'

Simon did, only too well. The longer ones were the ones he was forced to spend in the company of Detective Inspector Giles Proust.

8

Wednesday 5 April

I hear my back door slam. This sound is followed by the sound of footsteps. They are coming from the house towards the shed, where I'm working. When I talk to customers I call it my workshop, but it's really just a medium-sized shed with a table, a wooden stool and all my tools in it. When I started up the business, I had two windows put in. I couldn't work in a place that had no windows, not even for one day. I have to be able to see.

There are too many footsteps for it to be Yvon on her own. Without turning to look, I know it's the police. I smile. A home visit. Finally I am being taken seriously. There are probably police officers on their way to your house as well, if they're not there already. Knowing I will soon have news of you makes the passing of time bearable. It won't be long. I try to focus only on getting the news, not on what it will be.

After days of blind, flailing panic, I feel as if I've scrambled up on to a small ledge. It's a relief to be able to rest on it for a while, knowing that while I am passive, others are active.

I continue to apply gold leaf with my badger-hair brush. The motto on the dial I'm working on at the moment is 'Better today than not at all'. It's a belated silver-wedding-anniversary present from a forgetful husband to his wife; he told me he hopes the gesture is grand enough to get him out of her bad books. He wanted a standing sculpture, for a particular spot in their back garden. I'm making him a pillar out of Hornton stone, with the dial part on its flat top surface.

I hear the door open behind me, feel the wind on my back, through my jumper.

'Naomi, two detectives are here to see you.' There is anxiety in Yvon's voice, as well as an eagerness to appear natural and relaxed.

I turn. A bulky man in a grey suit is smiling at me. It's a dubious sort of smile, as if he expects not to be wearing it for much longer. He has a fat stomach, straw-coloured hair that is spiky with gel on top, and a shaving rash. His colleague, short, dark and thin with small eyes and a low forehead, slips in between the fat man and Yvon, and begins to prowl around my workshop, uninvited. He picks up my bandsaw, looks at it and puts it down again, then does the same with my fretsaw.

'Get your hands off my things,' I say. 'Who are you? Where's DC Waterhouse?'

'I'm DC Sellers,' says the fat one. He is holding up a card in a plastic wallet. 'This is DC Gibbs.' I don't bother to check the ID. They're obviously police. They have a quality in common with Waterhouse and Sergeant Zailer, one that's hard to define. Inflexibility of manner, perhaps. Behaving as if there are charts and tables in their heads. A thin veneer of politeness masking a knee-jerk dismissiveness. They trust each other, but nobody else.

'We need to have a look round your house,' says DC Sellers. 'And the garden and any outbuildings. Which includes this shed. We'll cause as little disruption as we can.'

I smile. So the talking is over and there is going to be

action. Good. 'Don't you need a search warrant?' I say, though I have no intention of sending them away.

'If we believe a missing person to be at risk, we're entitled to search the premises,' says DC Gibbs stiffly.

'Are you looking for Robert Haworth? He isn't here, but search all you please.' Are they looking for you as a criminal or as a victim, I wonder. Perhaps both. I told DC Waterhouse that I'd considered taking the law into my own hands.

'We might need to take some things away with us,' says Sellers, smiling again now that he sees I'm not going to put up a fight. 'Your computer. How long have you had it?'

'Not long,' I say. 'A year or thereabouts.'

'Hang on a minute,' says Yvon. 'I live here too, and work here. If you're going to search the house, can you leave my office exactly as you found it?'

'What work do you do?' asks Sellers.

'I'm a website designer.'

'We'll need to take your computer as well. How long have you had it?'

'How long have you lived here?' says Gibbs, before Yvon's had a chance to answer the last question.

'Eighteen months,' she says shakily. 'Look, you can't take my computer, I'm afraid.'

'I'm afraid we can.' Gibbs smiles for the first time, a tight, gloating grin. He walks over to the windowsill, picks up a brass pocket sundial and tugs at the string. It's a sturdy little thing, which I can see disappoints him. He hoped he might break it. Sellers clears his throat, and I wonder if it's a reprimand.

'How will I work?' asks Yvon. 'When will I get it back?'

'We'll get it back to you as quickly as we can,' says Sellers. 'Sorry about the inconvenience. It's just routine, we have to do it.' She looks slightly reassured. 'Right, then.' He turns back to me. 'We'll start in the house.'

'Where's DC Waterhouse?' I ask again. The answer comes to me as I'm speaking. 'He's at Robert's house, isn't he?'

You are there somewhere, at 3 Chapel Lane. I know you are. I think of the panic attack I had outside your window, collapsing on the grass. Every blade was a cold brand on my skin, freezing its length into my flesh. My breath becomes jerky and I force myself to push the memory away before it overpowers me.

'Robert?' Sellers looks puzzled. 'You've accused this man of abducting and raping you. How come you're on first-name terms with him?'

Yvon's face has turned pale. I avoid her eye. Unless Sellers and Gibbs are completely incompetent, they will find several books about rape and its aftermath in the bottom drawer of my bedside cabinet, as well as a rape alarm and an aerosol spray. I've got the accessories to back up my story, all the depressing paraphernalia of victim-hood, hidden under a folded pillowcase.

'A woman can call her rapist whatever she wants,' I say angrily.

DC Gibbs leaves while I am still speaking, letting the door bang shut behind him. Sellers acknowledges my response with a very slight shift of his features. Then he too turns to go. I watch him as he rejoins his more malignant colleague outside on the path. The two of them set off towards the house.

Yvon doesn't follow them, even though I turn my back on her and pick up my brush. My back is stiff with tension, hard and flat, to repel what I know she is about to say.

'I'm sorry about your computer,' I mutter. 'I'm sure they won't keep it for long.'

'Robert abducted you and raped you?' she says in a tight voice.

'Of course he didn't. Close the door.'

She stands still, shaking her head.

In the end I get up and close it myself. 'I told a lie – a big one – to make the police think Robert's dangerous and needs to be found urgently.'

Yvon stares at me, aghast.

'What choice did I have?' I say. 'The police were doing sod all. I want to know what's happened to Robert. I know *something* has. I needed a way of making them look for him.'

'That's why you wanted me to take you to the police station yesterday.' Her voice is dull, toneless. 'What was the story? What exactly did you tell them?'

'I'm not going there, okay?'

'Why not?'

'Because . . . I've just told you, it was a lie, it was rubbish. Why are you looking at me like that?'

'You told the police that Robert – the man who according to you is your soul mate, the man you want to marry and spend the rest of your life with – you told the police he abducted you and raped you?' She is trying to shock me with the stark fact of what I've done. It won't work. I got over my shock a while ago. Now my lie, the extreme step I've taken, is simply part of my life like everything else: my love for you, my real ordeal at the hands of a man whose name I don't know, this stone sundial in front of me with a painted-on smiling sun at its centre.

'I've told you why,' I insist. 'The police didn't care about finding Robert when he was just my missing married boyfriend. I wanted to put a rocket under their arses, and it worked.' I gesture in the direction of the house. 'They're here, looking.'

'They must think you're insane. They're probably wondering if you've stabbed him or something.'

'I don't care what they think, as long as they look for him as hard as they can.'

'They know you're lying.' Yvon looks tearful. Her voice is laced with panic. 'If they don't already, they'll find out.' Deep down, she is still an obedient boarding-school girl. She is conventional in the way that almost everybody is. I realise that more people would agree with her about this than with me, which is a strange thought.

I say nothing. The police can't prove I wasn't abducted and raped, however hard they try, and they can't prove it wasn't you who did it until they find you.

Should I tell Yvon the truth about what happened to me? Yesterday I proved to myself that I could do it, tell the story. It wasn't as bad as I've spent three years imagining it would be. On the way home from the police station, I felt as if I'd clawed back a bit of dignity from the men who'd stolen it from me. I was no longer too frightened to speak.

No one will ever understand this – not even you, Robert – but it helps me to think that I told the story, eventually, in the way I did: as part of a deliberate strategy to manipulate the police. Not in good faith, not as a good girl humiliated. Maybe it even made it easier that Detective Constable Waterhouse spoke to me as if I were a criminal. Technically, I probably am one, now that I've made a false statement. I am no longer the prey of the man who attacked me. I am his equal; we are both law-breakers.

'You can't love Robert,' says Yvon in a choked voice. 'If you love him, how can you tell such an awful lie about him? He'll hate you.'

'I'll withdraw the accusation as soon as they've found him. I might get into trouble for lying to the police, but I don't care about that. Nothing bad can happen to Robert if I admit I was lying.'

'Are you sure? Can't the police pursue something like this irrespective of what you say? They'll still have a record of whatever story you told them yesterday, won't they? They can use that!'

'Yvon, there's no way that'd happen,' I say patiently, though my brain is starting to feel frayed at the edges. 'It's hard enough to get a conviction in a rape case at the best of times, even if the victim's a credible witness. There's no way the cops'll pursue this once Robert's been found and I've changed my story for the second time. It'd be laughed out of court.'

'You don't know that! What do you know about how the police and court systems work? Nothing!'

'Look, I've given them a date, okay?' I pause, unable to say March the thirtieth 2003 out loud. 'Since Robert didn't abduct me on that date, he'll be able to prove he didn't. He'll have been working – he works every day. He'll have an alibi, someone who saw him loading up or who took a delivery from him, someone who saw him at a service station or in a lorry park. Or he'll have been with Juliet.' I've been through this in my head dozens of times. 'There's no risk to Robert.'

'Bugger Robert!' Yvon's anxiety boils over into anger. 'You know what? I think he's fine, absolutely fine. Men like him always are!'

'What's that supposed to mean?'

'You could go to prison, Naomi. Isn't it perjury, what you've done?'

'Probably.'

'Probably? Is that all you can say? What's wrong with you? Have you gone mad? This is so crazy, it's . . .' She bursts into tears.

'There are worse things than going to prison for a bit,' I tell her calmly. 'They're hardly going to lock me up for life, are they? And I'll be able to say – truthfully – that I lied out of desperation. I've never been in trouble of any kind before. I've been a model citizen . . .'

'You can't even see what's wrong with it, can you?'

I consider this. 'On one level, yes. On another, no,' I say honestly. 'And the level on which it's right is the more important one.' I search my brain for things I could say that might help. How does a person like me get through to a person like Yvon? Her tolerance vanishes at the first hint of trouble and her mind shuts down. Like a country that has introduced strict emergency measures after a frightening and unforeseen attack. 'Look, by wrong, are you sure you don't just mean unusual?' I suggest.

'What the fuck are you talking about?'

'Well . . . most people wouldn't do what I'm doing. I know that. Most people would wait patiently, leave it in the hands of the proper authorities and hope for the best. Most people wouldn't inflame the situation by claiming their missing lover was a dangerous criminal in the hope that the police would look for him more efficiently.'

'That's right! Most people wouldn't!' Her concern for me has mutated into fully fledged anger. 'In fact, *nobody* would, except you!'

'That's what you object to, isn't it? Because ninety-nine out of a hundred women wouldn't do it, it has to be wrong, according to you!'

'Can't you hear how twisted that is? It's the other way round! Because it's wrong, ninety-nine out of a hundred women wouldn't do it!'

'No! Sometimes you have to be brave and do something that doesn't fit in with the general pattern, just to shake things up a bit, to make things happen. If everyone thought like you, women still wouldn't be allowed to vote!'

We stare at one another, both short of breath.

'I'm going to tell them.' Yvon takes a step back, as if she's about to run to the house. 'I'll tell the police everything you've just told me.'

I shrug. 'I'll say you're lying.'

Her face crumples. She amends her threat. 'If you don't tell them, I will. I mean it, Naomi. What the fuck's wrong with you? You've turned into some sort of sick weirdo!'

The last time I had such direct verbal insults thrown at me, I was tied by ropes – first to a bed, then to a chair – and couldn't do anything about it. There's no way I'm putting up with it now from my so-called best friend.

'I've done my best to explain it to you,' I say coldly. 'If you still don't understand, tough. And if you tell the police what I've just told you, you can start looking for somewhere else to live. In fact, you can leave right now.'

I have crossed another line. I seem to be doing it all the time these days. I wish I could erase my harsh words, swallow them back into my mouth, into non-existence, but I can't. I have to keep this defiant, set expression on my face. I will not be seen as weak.

Yvon turns to leave. 'God help you,' she says shakily. I want to scream after her that only a deeply conventional person would choose that as her last line before leaving.

9

5/4/06

Juliet Haworth was wearing a dressing gown today, a lilac satin one. There were sleep creases on one side of her face when she opened the door. It was three-thirty in the afternoon. She didn't look ill; neither did she apologise for her appearance, or seem embarrassed to be caught in her nightwear in the middle of the day, as Simon would have been.

'Mrs Haworth? DC Waterhouse again,' he said.

She smiled through a yawn. 'Can't get enough of me, can you?' she said. Yesterday she had been harsh and abrupt. Today she seemed to find Simon amusing.

'That address you gave me in Kent – you lied. Your husband's not there.'

'My husband's upstairs,' she said, bending her head forward and swaying slightly, one hand on the round brass doorknob. She eyed Simon provocatively through her fringe. Was she trying to imply that she and Robert Haworth had been having sex, that Simon had interrupted them?

'If that's true, I'd like a word with him. Once you've explained why you lied to me about Kent.'

Juliet's smile expanded. Was she determined to prove to Simon that nothing he said could worry her? He wondered why her mood had improved since yesterday. Because Robert was back?

She turned and shouted, 'Robert! Make yourself decent. A policeman's here who wants to see you.'

'Your husband was never at twenty-two Dunnisher Road in Sissinghurst. They don't know him at that address.'

'I grew up in that house. It was my childhood home.' Juliet Haworth looked pleased with herself.

'Why did you lie?' Simon asked again.

'If I tell you, you won't believe me.'

'Try it and we'll see.'

Juliet nodded. 'I had a sudden urge to lie. No reason – I just fancied it. See, I told you you wouldn't believe me and you don't. But it's the truth.' She undid the belt round her waist, pulled her dressing gown tighter around her, and retied it. 'When I first saw you, I thought I'd probably lie again today. I needn't have told you that Robert's upstairs. But then I changed my mind and thought, Why not?'

'You're aware that obstructing the police is an offence?'

Juliet giggled. 'Absolutely. It wouldn't be any fun otherwise, would it?'

Simon felt wooden and self-conscious. Something about this woman interfered with his ability to think straight. She made him feel as if she knew more than he did about his own thoughts and actions. Did she expect him to push past her and go upstairs in search of her husband, or to challenge her further about her flagrant lies? Naomi Jenkins had also calmly admitted to lying, when Simon had spoken to her yesterday. Did Robert Haworth have a thing for dishonest women?

Simon didn't believe Haworth was upstairs. He hadn't called out in response to his wife's instruction to make himself decent. Juliet was still lying. Simon was reluctant to enter the house and allow her to close the door behind him.

Something told him he might not emerge unscathed. He didn't think Juliet Haworth would attack him physically, but he was having trouble, nevertheless, making himself enter her home as he knew he had to. As she undoubtedly wanted him to, for whatever reason. Yesterday she had been equally determined to keep him outside.

Simon wished Charlie were with him. Seeing through other women was her speciality. He'd have given a lot to be able to talk to her about Naomi Jenkins too, the way she'd changed her story. But Charlie was on holiday. And she was pissed off with him, however carefully she was trying to hide it. Simon remembered this suddenly with a sort of perplexed irritation. All he'd said was that he might get in touch with Alice Fancourt, just to see how she was. Surely Charlie wouldn't mind, after all this time? Anyway, she had no right to mind. She wasn't his girlfriend, never had been. The same was true of Alice, Simon realised with a vague pang of regret.

'You might think this is funny now,' he told Juliet Haworth, 'but you won't when we get to the custody unit and I show you your cell.'

'You know what? I might. I think I really might.' She lolled in the doorway.

Simon put his hand on her shoulder and pushed her to one side. She didn't resist. He began to climb the stairs. The carpet beneath his feet was speckled with tiny white dots and patches that Simon couldn't identify. He bent to touch one; its texture was chalky.

'Stain-remover,' said Juliet. 'I can never be bothered to hoover it up, once it's dried. Still, white powder's better than a stain, isn't it?'

Simon didn't ask her to elaborate. He continued to climb the stairs, wanting to get away from her. Halfway up, he became aware of an unpleasant smell. By the time he'd reached the top landing, it was a stench. A familiar one: the meaty stew of blood, excrement and vomit. Simon felt a coldness in the pit of his stomach. The hairs on his arms prickled his skin. There was a closed door in front of him, and two other doors, half open, further along a narrow corridor.

'Did you find Robert?' Juliet called out in a sing-song voice. Simon shivered. He pictured her words as tentacles, wrapping around him, pulling him into the strange, depraved world she inhabited. He shut his eyes for a second. Then he tried the closed door. It was unlocked and opened easily. The awful smell hit Simon full in the face and he fought hard not to be sick. He saw a mess of colours and horror, grey skin, features twisted in pain. Proust had predicted this. *This'll be a murder investigation by the end of the week, you watch.*

The man was unmistakably Robert Haworth. He was nude, lying on his back on one side of a double bed. The blood from his head wound had soaked into the bedding beneath him and dried. One of his arms trailed on the floor. By his hand, Simon saw his glasses; one lens was missing, the other cracked.

Simon noticed a large stone doorstop, about the size of a rugby ball, in one corner of the room. Its top edge was dark and sticky with blood and matted hair; before he could stop himself, Simon thought of an evil child's hard, faceless doll, and shuddered. He placed his fingertips on Haworth's wrist because it was what you did, not because he held out any hope. At first he thought he'd imagined it, that small, insistent beating. He must have. The grey skin, the blood and the crusty filth around Haworth's body presented a clear image of death. A few more seconds convinced Simon he had imagined nothing. There was a pulse. Robert Haworth was still alive.

'Give us a snog, then, Sarge,' Graham whispered, kissing Charlie's neck. They were in her bed in the chalet, semi-clothed, the duvet pulled up over their heads. 'Do your underlings call you Sarge? Or ma'am? That's what they say on *Prime Suspect*.'

'Sh!' Charlie hissed at him. 'What if Olivia wakes up? Can't we go to your place?' She hadn't been groped in the same room as her sister since the two of them were fifteen and thirteen respectively. How weird those teenage parties were, in retrospect: dozens of couples dotted around somebody's dimly lit living room, necking and putting their hands inside one another's clothes while Ultravox or Curiosity Killed the Cat played in the background.

'My place? No chance,' Graham breathed in Charlie's ear. 'You're not setting foot over the threshold until the next time Steph gives the place a good spring clean. You'd be shocked by my slovenliness.'

'Steph cleans your house as well as the chalets?'

'Yep. She's my own personal waste-disposal system. She's my out-tray, at home and at work. Anyway, forget about the dogsbody. It's your body I'm interested in . . .'

It was strange, Charlie thought, to feel Graham and hear him but be hardly able to see him. The chalet was full of a deep, black darkness, reminding her that she really was in the countryside here. Even in Spilling, a rural market town, the night sky was a dark mushroom-skin colour, never pure black. She'd told Graham this as they'd stumbled tipsily back from the old barn building that housed the spa facilities and a small, cosy bar. 'We get proper nights here,' he'd said proudly. 'No light pollution at all.' Charlie had thought this was an interesting way to put it. She'd never thought of light as a pollutant before, but she could see what Graham meant.

She felt his bare chest against her skin, the thick hair on it. She wasn't sure she liked furry chests, but she could put up with it. Everything else about him was attractive. If they were a couple, people might say Graham was out of her league. She ordered herself to start thinking of him as a whole person, rather than as a composite of certain body parts: her imaginary boyfriend come to life. He had long muscly legs and a nice bum, though; Charlie couldn't help noticing that. Colin Sellers had once accused her of thinking like a man when it came to sex. That was a good thing, surely. Why shouldn't it be uncomplicated? It made more sense to have a purely physical relationship with someone who looked like Graham than to cry into your pillow every night over a non-relationship with someone like Simon Waterhouse, who put red wine in the fridge and couldn't even get himself a proper haircut.

Graham was tugging gently at Charlie's camisole, murmuring, 'No idea how to get this off at all . . .'

She giggled, aware that he had taken off more clothes than she had, that she was stalling. Graham had no doubts about what they were embarking upon, Charlie could tell. Which was nice. He reminded her – in attitude rather than appearance – of Folly, her parents' black Labrador, who leaped on top of Charlie and licked her enthusiastically whenever he could. She decided to keep the comparison to herself. Graham seemed fairly thick-skinned, but you could never be sure.

She helped him to remove her underwear. 'I don't think you're fully aware of how sexy you really are, ma'am,'

Graham whispered, running his fingers lightly over her body. 'Or is it guv?'

'No comment.'

'Your red lipstick and your jeans . . .'

'They're old, ordinary jeans.'

'Exactly.'

Charlie tried to kiss him, but he pulled away, saying, 'You're miles sexier than Helen Mirren . . .'

'Any particular reason why you're comparing me with her?'

'. . . and that wrinkly blonde bird from *The Bill*, and her from *Silent Witness*.'

'And Trevor Eve from *Waking the Dead*?' Charlie suggested.

'No, he's sexier than you,' said Graham with certainty. Charlie laughed and he put his hand over her mouth. 'Careful not to wake big sis.'

'Little sis, actually.'

'So why do you let her boss you around?'

Charlie's mobile phone began to ring. She'd chosen the opening bars of 'The Real Slim Shady' by Eminem as her ringtone. A mistake. The longer it went unanswered, the louder it got. 'Shit!' she hissed, fumbling in the darkness, pulling random objects out of her bag. She put her hand on the phone just as it stopped ringing.

Light filled the room. Charlie blinked, turned to look at Graham. She'd assumed he'd switched on a lamp to help her find her phone, but he was still lying down, almost completely covered by the duvet. He groaned, pulling it over his head. Great, thought Charlie. Just when I need a hero to rush to my rescue. Bracing herself, she turned and looked up.

Olivia had pulled the curtain aside and was squinting

down through the mezzanine's wooden railings. She was wearing her Bonsoir floral kimono pyjamas and looked tense and alert, not at all as if she had just been woken up. 'Yes, I've heard everything,' she said. 'Not that you two care.'

'Why didn't you say something?' said Charlie, pulling on first her knickers and then her shirt. Not again, she thought, as the painful memory of herself and Simon at Sellers' fortieth birthday party filled her head. She was furious with Olivia for making this like that, though Olivia knew nothing about the incident at the party. It was the one significant thing Charlie had never told her. 'Why were you pretending to be asleep?'

'Why didn't you check whether I was asleep or not before having sex in my bedroom?'

'It's not your bedroom! Your bedroom's up there. This is *my* bedroom.' Charlie felt anger rise and explode inside her like a firework display, blocking out everything else. For a moment she forgot Graham was there, until his head emerged from the bedding.

'Looks like I've overstayed my unwelcome,' he said. 'I'll leave you ladies in peace.'

'You're not going anywhere,' Charlie told him quietly.

'You stay.' Olivia was standing now, throwing clothes into her suitcase. 'You're the one Charlie wants to be with, not me. I'll go. One night of this shit's enough for me. I'm buggered if I'm spending a whole week being the odd one out, listening to you two shag each other senseless every night.' She pulled her long beige coat on over her pyjamas, looked as if she was on her way to a fancy-dress party.

'It's nearly midnight,' said Graham. 'Where are you going to go?'

'I'll get a taxi to Edinburgh. I don't care how much it

costs. I've got a number. I asked the barmaid, while you two were drooling all over each other this evening, ignoring me. I was planning my escape.'

'This is bound to be my fault,' said Graham. 'I'm an incorrigible leader-astray of people . . .'

'Let her go if she wants to,' said Charlie.

'No one's going to *let* me and no one's going to stop me,' said Olivia wearily. 'I'm going, that's all.'

'Hang on a sec,' said Graham. He reached for his jeans and pulled a mobile phone out of the back pocket. Charlie and Olivia watched him press buttons. 'Steph, one of the ladies in number three needs driving to Edinburgh. She'll be over at the lodge in a sec, okay?' His face darkened as he listened to the response. 'Well, get dressed. We've got a situation here.' Charlie had seen Steph briefly earlier in the evening. The dogsbody. Graham had called her that to her face and winked at her. She'd attempted a smile in response. Charlie had recognised it as a smile with a complicated history. Graham and Steph had slept together, she guessed.

She'd been surprised by Steph's appearance. This morning Graham had described her as peasant-like. Charlie had imagined someone with sun-beaten skin and thick calves and ankles. In fact, Steph was slim and pale-skinned, with layered brown hair that was highlighted gold, orange and red. 'Do you think she's working undercover for Dulux?' Olivia had whispered.

Charlie wasn't sure she wanted Steph to take her sister away. 'Liv, don't rush off into the night,' she said. 'It's late. Why don't we talk about this tomorrow?'

'Because you're too busy ingratiating yourself with anything that has a penis to talk to me, that's why.' Olivia clomped down the stairs in her high-heeled Manolo Blahnik sandals, carrying her suitcase.

'Olivia, the last thing I want to do is ruin your holiday,' said Graham.

She ignored him, looked at Charlie. 'How long are you going to carry on doing this? Fucking anything that moves, just to prove something to bloody Simon Waterhouse?'

Charlie felt the heat of shame spread across her face and down her neck.

'You've got a problem, Char. It's about time you dealt with it. Why don't you . . . stop trying to fill the wrong hole and go and see a shrink or something?'

Once Olivia had slammed the door, Charlie burst into tears, covering her face with her hands. Graham put his arms round her. 'I'm only crying because I'm so angry,' she told him.

'Don't be angry. Poor old Fat Girl Slim. It can't have been much fun for her, listening to us canoodling, can it?'

'Don't call my sister that!'

'What, even though she's just called you a slapper and me – now let me get this right – oh, yes, "anything that has a penis"?' He risked a small grin.

Charlie couldn't help laughing, though she was still crying. 'Do you have to give everything and everyone a nickname? I'm Ma'am, Steph's the dogsbody, now Olivia's Fat Girl Slim . . .'

'I'm sorry. Really. I was just trying to lighten the mood.' He stroked Charlie's back. 'Look, you'll sort it out. Steph'll tell us tomorrow which hotel she's gone to. I'll give you a lift into Edinburgh and you can kiss and make up properly. Okay?'

'Okay.' Charlie pulled her cigarettes and lighter out of her bag. 'If you tell me this chalet's non-smoking, I'll smash your head in.'

'Wouldn't dare. Ma'am. Guv.'

'All that stuff Liv said about me . . .'

'She was just lashing out because she felt exluded. I've forgotten it already.'

'Thank you.' Charlie squeezed Graham's hand. Thank God: a gentleman, she thought. Still, sleeping with him tonight was no longer a possibility, not with Olivia's words buzzing around her head. *Stop trying to fill the wrong hole.* Bitch.

'Charlie, stop worrying,' said Graham. 'You and Fat Girl Slim are solid, I can tell. You've got a better relationship than most siblings.'

'Are you taking the piss?'

'No. I'm dead serious. You yell at each other. That's a good sign. I haven't spoken to my brother properly for years.'

'You said you were in business with him.'

Graham looked unhappy suddenly. 'We are. Despite everything, we are, but he's done his best to ruin the business, that's the trouble. I'm the sensible, cautious one . . .'

'I find that hard to believe,' Charlie teased him.

'It's true. I don't take stupid risks we can't afford, because I want it to work. So I set it up and he pulls it down, or tries to.'

'How can you still work together if you don't talk?' Charlie asked.

Graham tried to smile, but his forehead didn't lose its worried creases. 'It's too absurd,' he said. 'You'll laugh if I tell you.'

'Go on.'

'We liaise via the dogsbody.' Graham shook his head. 'Anyway . . .' he leaned over and tried to pull Charlie back into bed '. . . let's not talk about our family probs any more. We've got the place to ourselves. Let's shag each other senseless, as your good sis suggested, then we'll be all contrite when we go and see her tomoz.'

'Graham . . .' said Charlie, pulling away from his kiss. 'I think these chalets are absolutely perfect. Dinner tonight was unbelievable and the spa's as good as any hotel's. I think the business will be just fine. Not even your incompetent brother could make a place like this unprofitable.'

'Is that so, Sarge? Hey, I've got a top idea. Since you liked dinner so much, I'm going to phone the dogsbody and order us some brekkie in bed for the morning.' He reached for his phone again.

'Don't!' Charlie yelped, grabbing his arm. 'She's with Olivia!'

'Oh, yeah. Fuck! We won't seem very contrite, will we, if we're already thinking about tomorrow's black pudding and hash browns. Yum.'

'Someone rang me,' Charlie remembered suddenly. She'd forgotten, in all the drama, that her phone had rung and started the row with Olivia. What if that hadn't happened? Would Olivia have lain awake, furious and resentful, listening to Charlie and Graham having sex?

'It can wait, can't it?' said Graham.

'Let me just see who it was.'

'You haven't got any other fat, scary sisters, have you, guv?'

'Don't call her that!'

Charlie pressed the unanswered calls button and saw Simon's number. Shit. He'd never ring her on holiday unless it was something serious. Simon was meticulous about respecting more privacy than any normal person could ever want or need. 'I've got to make a quick phone call,' said Charlie. 'I'm sorry, it's work. I'll go outside.' She pulled on her coat and pushed her feet into her trainers, squashing the backs with her heels. 'You wait here.'

'Think I will, as I've got no clothes on. And hurry up or I might be asleep when you get back. Like a tired, over-worked husband in a TV movie, when his wife spends too long beautifying herself in the bathroom. You can stand over me and smile fondly.'

'What are you talking about, you nutter?'

'There, see, you're smiling fondly already!'

Charlie shook her head, bemused, and took her cigarettes, lighter and phone outside. She liked Graham. Really liked him. He was funny. Maybe Olivia would have liked him too, if Charlie had handled things a bit more shrewdly. What a disaster of a night. And Simon had phoned, and she'd missed the call. Charlie felt more guilty about that than about Olivia. She lit a Marlboro Light, took a long drag. On the other side of the field was the lodge, which housed Graham's office. The light was still on, but the muddy car that was outside earlier had gone. The window's small square of gold-yellow, the pale-blue screen of Charlie's mobile phone and the tiny strip of fiery orange at the end of her cigarette were the only lights she could see. This place felt more foreign than Spain.

She looked at Simon's mobile number on the screen and pressed the call button, rehearsing what she would say as soon as he answered: 'I thought I made it clear I didn't want any interruptions on holiday.' She wouldn't say it too harshly, though.

10

Thursday 6 April

It is two in the morning. I am downstairs, curled in a tight ball on the sofa in front of the television, heavy and disorientated with tiredness but afraid to go to bed. I know I wouldn't sleep. I pick up the remote control and press the mute button. I could turn the TV off, but I'm superstitious. The flickering images on the screen are a link to something. They are all that's keeping me from slipping off the edge of the world.

All my cowardice comes out at night, all the weak and helpless feelings that I spend all day every day beating down.

My lounge window is a big square of black, with two gold globes of light reflected in it and, under those yellow discs, a washed-out counterpart of me. I look like a woman who is all alone. When I was little, I used to believe that if you let darkness into a well-lit room, it would become dark, just as it becomes light in the morning when you let the light in. My dad explained to me why it was different, but I wasn't convinced. Usually I close my curtains as soon as the sky starts to turn from blue to grey.

Tonight there's no point; the darkness is in the house already. It's in Yvon's absence, and the mess the police left, though I'm sure they think they tidied up after themselves, just as Yvon believes she's tidied up if she puts torn-up envelopes, squashed tea bags and sandwich crusts on the lid of the kitchen bin.

She's left most of her things here, which I am forcing myself to see as a good sign. All night I've wanted to ring her, but I've done nothing about it. Concealing what happened to me three years ago was easy. Walking into a police station and accusing an innocent man of rape was easy. So why is it so hard to phone my best friend and say sorry?

Yvon will think I don't care; that I might be scared would never occur to her. Of the two of us, I'm the frightening one. She teases me about it. It's true, I can be intimidating when I want to be. One pointed look from me is enough to make Yvon wipe up all the crumbs on the kitchen counter or put the lid back on the butter dish after she's used it. I like things to be tidy. I can't think straight if they're not. Tools are never left out in my workshop overnight; I always put them back in their proper place on the shelf: my dummy mallets next to my diamond whetstone, which lives next to my chisels.

You'd understand. At the Traveltel, you arrange your clothes neatly on the back of the sofa before getting into bed. I've never seen one of your socks on the floor. When I told Yvon this, she wrinkled her nose and said you sounded like a geek. I said it wasn't like that at all, she was imagining it wrongly if she thought that. You're cool about it, quick too. You must have practised, because you always make it seem as if you just happened to drop your clothes exactly parallel to the edge of the settee.

Do you remember, I once said to you that if Yvon ever disappeared, the police would be able to list everything she had recently eaten without too much trouble? To think of this now that you're missing makes the hairs on my arms stand up. But it's true. Dried pink flakes stuck to the underside of a frying pan would point clearly to salmon for dinner the previous night. A pan of congealed white fat with burned black bits in it would be evidence that she'd had sausages for lunch.

You told me I should insist that she clears up after herself. When I do, she accuses me of tyranny. 'You're turning into a monster,' she says, reluctantly removing a three-week-old empty milk carton from the fridge.

I'm so used to it now, my nobody's-going-to-get-away-with-anything attitude, I don't think I could change back. I have become – deliberately at first, though it soon stopped feeling like an effort – a person who makes an issue out of any small thing. 'Go with the flow,' Yvon is always telling me. But to me, going with the flow means marching obediently, at knifepoint, towards a stranger's car.

If I hadn't become a monster, you might never have noticed me that day in the service station. I don't know how much of the row you saw or heard. Nor have I ever managed to extract from you certain crucial pieces of information, such as whether you too were eating in the food court that day. Perhaps you were in the shop, on the other side of the covered walkway, and you only came over when you heard me shouting. I'd like to know, because I love the story of how we met and I want it to be complete.

I was on my way to see a possible customer, an elderly lady who wanted somebody to restore the cube sundial in her garden, which she said was eighteenth century and in bad condition. I'd told her I did mainly original commissions and very little restoration work, but she'd sounded so despondent that I'd relented and agreed to go and look at her dial. I realised I was hungry almost as soon as I set off, so I stopped at Rawndesley East Services.

No sane person expects decent food from a service station, and I was quite prepared for my chicken, chips and peas to be lukewarm, greasy and flavourless. I'm not like you; I don't mind mediocre food sometimes. It can be comforting to eat junk. But on this occasion, what was handed to me on a tray was offensive. Did you see it? Were you close enough, at that point, to get a proper look?

The chicken was grey and reeked of old dustbins that have never been washed. The smell made me retch. I told the man who was serving me that the meat was off. He rolled his eyes, as if I was being difficult, and said that I hadn't even tasted it yet. If it tasted bad, I could bring it back and he'd give me a new meal, he said, but he wasn't prepared to take it back when I hadn't even tried it. I asked to speak to the manager and he told me, sullenly, that he was in charge, the boss wasn't in yet.

'When will *she* be in?' I asked, hoping he was the sort of man who would hate to have a woman as a boss.

'It's a he,' he said. 'Not for another two hours.'

'Fine. Then I'll wait. And when your manager arrives, I'll advise him to fire you.'

'Suit yourself.' The man shrugged. His name was Bruce Doherty. He was wearing a badge.

'You only need to take one look at this chicken to know it's bad! It's rotting! You taste it if you don't believe me.'

'No thanks.' He smirked.

I took that as an acknowledgement that the meat was past its sell-by date and he knew it; he was gloating, showing me he didn't care. 'I'm going to make sure you get sacked, you wanker!' I yelled in his face. 'What'll you do then, hey? Brain surgeon? Rocket scientist? Or maybe something that's better suited to your talents: wiping shit off toilets, or selling your arse to visiting businessmen round the back of Rawndesley Station!'

He ignored me. There were people queuing behind me

and he turned to the first of these, saying, 'Sorry about that. What can I get you?'

'Look, I'm very busy,' I told him. 'All I want is a plate of food that isn't poisonous.'

A frumpily dressed middle-aged woman, waiting to be served, touched my arm. 'There are children here,' she said, pointing to a table across the room.

I shook her hand off me. 'That's right,' I said. 'Children who, if it was up to you and him and everyone else in here, would be fed rotting chicken and die of E. coli!'

Everybody left me alone after that. I phoned the woman that I was on my way to see about the cube dial and told her I'd been held up. Then I sat down at the table nearest to the serving counter, with my tray of stinking food in front of me, waiting for the boss to arrive. Rage bubbled inside me, but I think I did a pretty good job of appearing calm. I can't control everything, but I can make sure that no stranger is able to guess how I'm feeling simply by looking at me.

I caught Bruce Doherty's eye every now and then. It wasn't long before he started to look uncomfortable. Giving up didn't enter my head as a possibility. This was one small bit of justice I was determined to get. I'll vandalise the place, I thought. I'll walk round the room tipping people's trays of food on to the floor. I'll pick up my plate of hot poisonous slop and throw it in the manager's face.

After I'd waited for nearly an hour and a half, I saw you walking towards me. My anger had thickened and risen inside me so that it blocked out every other thought and feeling. That's why I didn't notice at first how odd you looked as you approached. You were wearing your grey collarless shirt and jeans, smiling at me, balancing a wooden tray on one hand, like a waiter. I saw your smile first. I was starving, dizzy, sustained only by my vindictive fantasies. My insides felt cold and hollow, and there was a sharp metallic taste in my mouth.

You walked a perfect straight line towards me, with your free arm behind your back. I only noticed you properly once you were standing beside my table. I was aware that the tray in your hand wasn't the same kind as the ones that were all over the food court – discarded on tables and in a tall pile in front of the counter where Doherty was still serving his lethal slop. Your tray was real wood, not wood-effect plastic.

On it was a knife and fork wrapped in a white cloth napkin, an empty glass and a bottle of white wine. Pinot Grigio: your favourite kind. This, like the coincidence of our meeting at the service station, sowed the seeds of a tradition. We have never shared a bottle of wine that wasn't Pinot Grigio; we meet at the Traveltel – even though you say it's not romantic enough, even though we could find somewhere much nicer for the same price – because Rawndesley East Services is where we first met. You have the mentality of an anxious collector, eager to preserve everything, to lose nothing we once had. Your love of tradition and ritual is one of the many things that has endeared you to me: the way you seize on anything pleasurable or good that happens by chance and try to make a custom out of it.

I tried to tell the police this – that a man who insists on drinking the same wine in the same room on the same day of every week would not suddenly break his own devout routine by disappearing without notice – but all they could do was look at me with stony indifference.

You picked up the tray Doherty had given me and placed it on the adjacent table. Then you put your tray down in front of me. Beside the napkin and cutlery was a china plate with a dome-shaped silver lid. You removed this without saying anything, smiling proudly. I was amazed, confused. As I told you later, I thought you were Doherty's boss; somehow you'd heard about what had happened, perhaps from another member of staff, and you were here to make amends.

But you weren't wearing the red-and-blue uniform or a name badge. And this was no ordinary amends. This was *Magret de Canard aux Poires*. You told me the name the next time we met. To me it looked like slices of tender duck breast – brown at the sides and pink in the middle – arranged in a neat circle around a peeled, cooked whole pear. It smelled as if it came from heaven. I was so ravenous I nearly burst into tears.

'You're supposed to drink red wine with duck,' you told me matter-of-factly. Those were the first words I heard you speak. 'But I thought white might be better, as it's the middle of the day.'

'Who are you?' I asked, preparing to be angry, hoping I wouldn't have to be, because I was desperate to eat the food you'd brought. Doherty was watching, as mystified as I was.

'Robert Haworth. I heard you yelling at that tosser.' You nodded in the direction of the hot-food counter. 'He's obviously never going to give you a lunch that's edible, so I thought I would.'

'Do I know you?' I asked, still mystified.

'You do now,' you said. 'I couldn't let you starve, could I?'

'Where did this meal come from?' There had to be a catch, I thought. 'Did you cook it yourself?' What sort of man, I was wondering, hears a stranger wrangling over a bad meal in a service station and rushes home to cook her something better?

'Not me. It's from the Bay Tree.' Spilling's most expensive bistro. My parents took me there once and our meal, including wine, cost nearly four hundred pounds.

'So . . .' I stared at you and waited, making it clear that further explanation was required.

You shrugged. 'I saw you were in trouble and I wanted to help. I rang the Bay Tree, explained the situation. Put in an order. Then I nipped down in my lorry and picked it up. I'm a lorry driver.'

I thought you must want something from me. I didn't know what, but I was on my guard. I wasn't prepared to eat a mouthful, even though my stomach hurt and my mouth was watering, until I'd worked out what your agenda was.

Doherty appeared beside us. There was a large fat stain on his shirt, roughly the shape of Portugal. 'I'm afraid you can't—'

'Leave the lady in peace to eat her lunch,' you said to him.

'You're not allowed to bring food—'

'*You're* not allowed to sell food that's inedible,' you corrected him. Your tone was quiet and polite throughout, but I wasn't fooled and neither was Bruce Doherty. We both knew you were going to do something. Astonished, I watched you pick up the plate with the chicken, chips and peas on it. You pulled open the neck of Doherty's shirt and tipped the food into the space between his uniform and his chest. He made a disgusted noise, halfway between a wail and a groan, looking down at himself. Then he walked unevenly out of the food court, spilling peas from his clothes. Some rolled on the floor in his wake, some he crushed with the soles of his black shoes. I'll never forget that sight as long as I live.

'Sorry,' you said once he'd gone. I had the impression that you'd lost some confidence. You spoke in a more stilted way, and seemed to hunch a little. 'Look, I just wanted to help,' you mumbled. You seemed embarrassed, as if you'd decided that bringing me a fancy duck dish from the nearest posh restaurant was a nerdy thing to do. 'Too many people stand by and do nothing to help people in trouble,' you said.

Those words changed everything.

'I know,' I said forcefully, thinking of the men in dinner suits who had applauded my rapist two years earlier. 'I'm grateful for your help. And this —' I pointed at the duck '— looks amazing.'

You smiled, reassured. 'Tuck in, then,' you said. 'I hope you enjoy it.' You turned to leave and I was surprised all over again. I'd assumed that at the very least, you'd stay and talk to me while I ate. But you'd said you were a lorry driver. You were bound to have an urgent delivery, a timetable. You couldn't afford to waste your whole day hanging around a service station with me. You'd done more than enough for me already.

I knew in that instant that I couldn't let you leave. This was the turning point in my life. I was going to make it the turning point. Instead of wasting all my energies reacting to the many bad things that happened to me, I would pursue one good thing.

You disappeared through the glass double doors at the front of the service station and soon you were no longer visible. That frightened me into action. I abandoned the food and ran outside as fast as I could. You were in the car park, about to get into your lorry. 'Wait!' I shouted, not caring how undignified I looked, sprinting wildly towards you.

'Problem?' You looked worried.

I was out of breath. 'Aren't you going to . . . have to take the tray and the plate back to the Bay Tree afterwards?' I said. Pathetic, I know, but it seemed like a reasonable pretext at the time.

You grinned. 'I hadn't thought of that. I probably ought to, yes.'

'Well . . . why don't you come back in, then?' I said, deliberately flirtatious.

'I suppose I could.' You frowned. 'But . . . maybe I should get moving, actually.'

I wasn't going to let you get away. Something amazing had happened, quite out of the blue, and I was determined not to let it slip from my grasp. 'Would you have done what you did – bringing that food and wine – for anybody?' I asked.

'You mean anybody who'd just been handed a plate of decaying chicken?'

I laughed. 'Yeah.'

'Probably not,' you admitted, looking away like a shy schoolboy. That was the happiest moment of my life. That was when I knew that I was special for you. You did something no one else would have done for me, and it set me free. It made me feel I could be as crazy as you, that I could do anything. There were no limits or rules. I saw your wedding ring and disregarded it entirely. You were married. So what? Bad luck, Mrs Robert Haworth, I thought, because I'm going to take your husband away from you. I was utterly ruthless.

For two years I hadn't considered getting involved with a man. The idea of sex had repulsed me. Not any more. I wanted to tear off my clothes right there in the car park and order you to make love to me. It had to happen; I had to have you. Meeting you enabled me to discard my whole history in an instant. You knew nothing about me, except that I was an attractive woman with a temper. That *Magret de Canard aux Poires* might as well have been a glass slipper from a prince. Everything was different now, all saved and redeemed. My life had changed from a nightmare to a fairy tale in the space of minutes.

An hour later we were booking room eleven at the Traveltel for the first time.

The doorbell rings. I run into the hall, thinking it's Yvon.

It isn't. It's DC Sellers, who was here this morning. 'Your curtains are open,' he says. 'I saw you were still up.'

'You just happened to be driving past my house at two in the morning?'

He looks at me as if it's a stupid question. 'Not quite.'

I wait for him to continue. I am as afraid to discover that you've abandoned me by choice as that something terrible has happened to you.

'Are you all right?' Sellers asks.

'No.'

'Can I come in for a minute?'

'Can I stop you?'

He follows me through to the lounge and perches on the edge of the sofa, his large stomach resting on his thighs.

I stand by the window. 'Do you expect me to offer you a drink? Ovaltine?' I cannot stop acting. It's a compulsion. I craft lines in my head and deliver them in a brittle voice.

'On Monday, you told DC Waterhouse and DS Zailer that if they went to Robert Haworth's house, they'd find something.'

'What have you found?' I snap. 'Have you found Robert? Is he all right?'

'On Tuesday, you told DC Waterhouse that Robert Haworth raped you. Now you're concerned for his welfare?'

'Is he all right? Tell me, you bastard!' I begin to sob, too exhausted to stop myself.

'What did you think we'd find in Mr Haworth's house?' Sellers asks. 'And how could you be so sure?'

'I told you! I told Waterhouse and Zailer: I saw something in Robert's lounge, through the window. It made me have a panic attack. I thought I was going to die.'

'What did you see?'

'I don't *know*.' There's still a huge black hole in the middle of my memory of that dreadful afternoon. But I'm sure I saw something. I'm surer of that than of anything else. I wait until I'm calm enough to speak. 'You must know that feeling. When you see an actor on television, and you know their name's buried in your brain somewhere, but your memory can't quite grasp it.' I'm so exhausted I can hardly focus. DC Sellers is a blur.

'Where were you last Wednesday night and last Thursday?' he says. 'Can you account for every minute of your time?'

'I don't see why I need to. Is Robert all right? Tell me!'

It's always worth fighting, no matter what the cost to yourself might be. This isn't a popular view any more. The world becomes more languidly callous by the day, and blanket condemnation of any and all wars, even wars of liberation, is the obvious symptom. Still, it's what I believe, passionately.

'How can you treat me like this?' I yell at Sellers. 'I'm a victim, not a criminal. I thought the police had polished up their act. I thought you were supposed to treat victims sensitively in this day and age!'

'Of what are you a victim?' he asks. 'Of rape? Or of your lover disappearing?'

'I'm the one who should be asking you: of what am I suspected?'

'You've lied to us, by your own admission. You can't expect us to trust you.'

'Is Robert alive? Just tell me that.' Three years ago I vowed that I would never beg again. Listen to me now.

'Robert Haworth never raped you, did he, Miss Jenkins? Your statement was a lie.' Sellers' rubbery face is mottled and pink; it makes me want to be sick.

'It was the truth,' I insist. With my defences down and my energy reserves drained to beyond empty, I resort to what's easiest: concealment.

It was the first thing I thought of after the rape, the only thing that mattered to me once I was certain that the attack, in all its phases, was over and I'd survived: how to hide from the world what had been done to me. I knew I'd cope with a private trauma better than I could cope with the shame of people knowing.

No one has ever felt sorry for me. I'm the most successful of all my friends, all my contemporaries. I've got a career that I love. I sold a typographical font to Adobe while I was still at university and used the money to set up a profitable business. To the world it must seem as if I have everything: rewarding, creative work, financial security, lots of friends, a great family, a beautiful house that I own outright. Until the attack, I had no shortage of boyfriends, and although I wasn't cold-hearted or anything, they mostly seemed to love me more than I loved them. Everyone I know envies me. They tell me all the time how lucky I am, that I am one of the blessed few.

That would all have changed if they'd found out what had happened to me. I'd have become Poor Naomi. I'd have been trapped for ever – in the thoughts of everyone I knew, everyone who mattered to me – in the state I was in when the man dumped me by the side of Thornton Road after he'd finished with me: naked apart from my coat and shoes, tears and snot all over my face, a stranger's semen leaking from my body.

No way was I going to let that happen. I pulled off the eye mask, checked no one was around. The road was empty. I told myself I was lucky that nobody had seen me. I walked briskly to my car and drove myself home. As I drove, I took control of the situation inside my head. I began to deliver a lecture to myself, thinking that it was important to impose some sort of order as quickly as possible. I told myself that it didn't matter how I felt – I'd worry about that later. For the time being, I would simply not allow myself to feel anything. I tried to make myself think like a soldier or an assassin. All that mattered was behaving as if I was fine, doing everything I would normally have done so that no one suspected a thing. I turned myself into a glossy robot, externally identical to my old self.

I did a brilliant job of it. Another achievement, something most people would never have been able to pull off. No one guessed, not even Yvon. The only part I couldn't manage was the boyfriends. I told everyone I wanted to focus on my career for a while without distractions, until I met someone special. Until I met you.

'Get dressed,' says DC Sellers.

My heart leaps up in my chest. 'Are you taking me to see Robert?'

'I'm taking you to the custody unit at Silsford Police Station. You can come voluntarily or I can arrest you. It's up to you.' Seeing my stricken expression, he adds, 'Some-body tried to murder Mr Haworth.'

'Tried? You mean failed?' My eyes lock on his, demand-ing an answer. After what seems like an eternity, he relents, nods.

Triumph surges through me. It's because of my lie that your house was searched, because I accused you of a terrible crime you didn't commit. I wonder what Yvon will say when I tell her I saved your life.

11

6/4/06

Charlie sat in front of Graham's computer, a trim Toshiba laptop, and typed the words 'Speak Out and Survive' into the Google search box on the screen. The first result that came up was the one she wanted – an organisation that offered practical and emotional support to women who had been raped. Once the website had loaded, Charlie clicked on 'Survivors' Stories'. They were listed by number. She clicked on number seventy-two.

Simon had described Naomi Jenkins' letter as acerbic. He believed Jenkins had written it, but wanted to know what Charlie thought. He's missing me, she thought. A mixture of pride and happiness swelled inside her. Did it matter if he was planning to meet up with Alice Fancourt? Charlie was the one he phoned in the middle of the night, when he was worried about something important.

She nodded as she read the letter 'N.J.' had sent to the website; it sounded like Naomi, from what little Charlie knew of the woman. Someone who objected to being called both 'Miss' and 'Ms' might well object to being labelled a rape 'survivor'. Charlie thought she made a good point about that, actually, but she was less impressed with Naomi's scorn for other rape victims – or survivors – and the way they expressed themselves. Charlie had only ever read official rape statements, which were always written very plainly; they had to be. Nothing at all like the lyrics of a bad heavy-metal album, which was the accusation Naomi made in her letter against the survivors' stories on the Speak Out and Survive website. Still, perhaps she had a point. A first-person account of a rape that was intended to be therapeutic would be very different from a police statement; the emphasis would presumably be on feelings as much as on facts, on sharing one's pain with others who had experienced something similar.

Charlie massaged her throbbing forehead. The positive effects of the four bottles of wine she'd drunk with Graham and Olivia the previous evening were starting to wear off, and a same-day hangover had lodged itself between her eyebrows, low down in the front of her head. Technically, it was a new day – Thursday morning – but it felt like the frayed end of a long, thin, washed-out Wednesday. Charlie was disgusted with herself. She'd been the one who kept insisting they needed more wine. She'd flirted brazenly with Graham, invited him back to the chalet, effectively forced her sister out. Nice one, Charlie. She'd driven the night forward relentlessly, cracking a whip behind it in her determination to have the best of all possible good times. *I'm the saddest of sad cows,* she thought.

Graham had been a sweetie. Understanding that it was urgent, he'd stopped making jokes, dressed quickly and unlocked the lodge so that Charlie could use his computer. His office was a small, chilly hut, just big enough for the two large desks that filled it. Behind each was a chair. At one end of the room was a dartboard, at the other a large water-cooler. Charlie had mentioned her headache, and Graham had rushed off to find painkillers. 'If Steph comes back and finds you in here, she'll give you a hard time,' he'd said. 'Just ignore her. Or threaten her with me.'

'Why would she mind?' Charlie had asked. 'You're the boss, aren't you?'

Graham had looked sheepish. 'Yes, but . . . the situation between me and Steph is complicated.'

Charlie knew all about complicated situations, after years of working with Simon. Never mix business with sex. Was that what Graham and Steph had done? Had it gone horribly wrong? At least Charlie and Simon still had a strong working relationship.

She thought back over what he'd told her on the phone. Naomi Jenkins had been proved right. Something bad had happened to Robert Haworth. Very bad; probably fatal. How had Naomi known? Was it a lover's intuition, Charlie wondered, or a would-be murderer's certain knowledge? If the latter, it was hard to imagine what Juliet Haworth's role might have been. She, after all, had been living in the same house as the blood-soaked, unconscious Haworth for nearly a week.

According to Simon, Haworth had been to the Star Inn in Spilling last Wednesday evening as usual. He didn't turn up to meet Naomi at the Traveltel on the Thursday, so he was probably attacked either on Wednesday after he got home from the pub, sometime during the night, or on Thursday morning, before whatever time he would have left the house to begin his day's work.

Simon had been at Culver Valley General Hospital when Charlie had called him back. Haworth was alive but unconscious, in intensive care. One more day without help and he'd have been dead, no question. The consultant was surprised he'd lasted as long as he had, given the severity of the trauma to his head. A series of heavy blows, Simon had explained, resulting in an acute subdural haemorrhage, a subarachnoid haemorrhage and cerebral contusions.

Haworth had had immediate surgery, had the haemor-
rhages drained to relieve the pressure on his brain, but the
doctors weren't optimistic. Neither was Simon. 'I don't
think we're going to be looking at an attempted murder for
long,' he'd said.

'Any sign of what caused the head injuries?' Charlie had
asked.

'Yeah, a bloody great stone. It was right there, on the
floor by the bed, no attempt made to hide it. It was covered
in hair and blood. Juliet Haworth said she and her husband
used it as a doorstop.' He broke off. 'She gives me the
creeps. She told me Haworth nicked the stone from the
River Culver one day when they were out walking. As soon
as I'd found Haworth, she came over all chatty. Almost as
if she was relieved, though she didn't really seem to care
one way or the other. She said that the previous owners of
their house had all the doors replaced with fire doors,
which wouldn't stay open . . .'

'Hence the need for a doorstop.'

'Yeah, there's one in every room, all big stones like the
one that caved in Haworth's head, but all from different
rivers. Haworth was keen on this idea, apparently. She
trotted out these little stories, all this irrelevant information
– she even listed the bloody rivers! But when I asked her if
she'd attacked her husband, she just grinned at me.
Wouldn't say a word.'

'Grinned?'

'She's refusing a lawyer. Doesn't seem to care what we
do with her. She gives a good impression of being determined to enjoy it, whatever we do.'

'Do you think she tried to kill Haworth?'

'I'm sure she did. Or I would be, if it wasn't for Naomi
Jenkins, who's also lied. We've brought her in too . . .'

'Have forensics finished with the house? What about cross-contamination?'

'No, Jenkins is at the custody unit at Silsford.'

'Good thinking.'

'She also doesn't want a lawyer. Do you think the two of them could be together on this?'

Charlie didn't, and she'd told Simon why not: it sounded too much like a Thelma-and-Louise-style feminist fantasy. In reality, the two women who loved an unfaithful man usually blamed and hated each other, while the two-timer emerged unscathed with both of them still wanting him.

Having read Naomi Jenkins' survivor's story, Charlie was curious about the others. While she waited for Graham to return with her painkillers, she thought she might as well look at a few of them. She clicked on numbers seventy-three, seventy-four and seventy-five in that order, and skim-read them. They were all descriptions of incestuous rapes. Number seventy-six was a stranger rape, but it was so lewdly described that Charlie was sure a male pervert had written it. Could Naomi Jenkins be a pervert? she wondered. That might explain why she'd lied about Haworth having raped her; Charlie was certain she *had* lied. But Naomi's letter to the website had contained no lurid details. She could easily have included some; there was no shortage of them in her statement, from what Simon had said, so if she was a fantasist, why not write up the full fantasy for inclusion on the website? Charlie wished she was at Silsford nick, able to ask Naomi Jenkins all these questions and watch her face as she replied.

The lodge door opened and Steph walked in. She was wearing a different outfit from the one Charlie had last seen her in, but this one also involved a pair of trousers, black ones this time, that stopped just below her jutting hipbones.

How did she keep them from sliding down her legs? It was a mystery. The jeans she'd been wearing yesterday morning were the same. You can practically see her pubic hair, thought Charlie. Then she amended the thought: a woman like Steph wouldn't have any, or if she did, it would be shaved into a heart shape or something gross like that.

Up close, Steph's multicoloured highlighted hair looked ridiculous – as if several birds, each one with a different stomach complaint, had emptied their bowels on her head at the same time. Her hair stuck out in strange, stiff tufts and irregular, gelled spikes, a style that was too much for any ordinary situation. It was the sort of thing you'd only really expect to see at a fashion show. And then it would be done much better.

Thick foundation covered what Charlie suspected was a poor complexion. Steph's lips, like her hair, were painted several different colours: pink and glossy in the middle with a thin red border inside an even thinner black line. As she walked into the lodge, she made a jangling noise, and Charlie noticed the gold bangles on her arms.

'That's our computer,' said Steph, immediately irate. 'You can't use it.'

'Graham said I could.'

Steph pouted. Charlie watched her glossy lips pull up and in. 'Where is he?'

'He's gone to find me some painkillers. I've got a headache. Look, a work emergency came up and Graham said it was fine for me to—'

'Well, it's not. Guests aren't allowed to use it.'

'Where did you take my sister?' asked Charlie. 'To a hotel?'

'She told me not to tell you.' Steph picked her teeth with a long fingernail that had what looked like a small diamond at its centre. 'Has Graham already fucked you, or what?' she said. 'You were all over each other earlier, in the bar.'

Charlie was too stunned to reply.

'He wouldn't have let you in here unless he'd fucked you or was planning to. Just to warn you: if he has, or if he does, he'll tell me all about it. Everything. He always does. You're not the first guest he's fucked, not by a long shot. There've been loads. He does impressions of the noises they make in bed. They're really funny!' Steph sniggered, hiding her mouth behind her hand.

If Graham hadn't reappeared at that moment, Charlie would have crossed the room and punched her in the face.

'What's up?' he asked Charlie. He had a packet of Nurofen in his hand. 'What's she said to you?'

'I just said she can't use the computer,' Steph answered before Charlie could.

'Yes, she can. Fuck off and get some sleep,' said Graham amiably. 'You've got a full day's skivvying tomorrow. Starting with breakfast in bed for me and the sarge, here. Full English. Her bed, that is. That's where we'll both be. Isn't that right, Sarge?'

Charlie stared at the computer screen, cringing.

Steph pushed past Graham. 'I'm going,' she said.

As she headed for the door, he started to sing loudly. 'White lines, going through my mind . . .' He clearly wanted Steph to hear. Charlie recognised the song as one that had been in the charts in the 1980s. She thought it was by Grandmaster Flash.

The lodge door banged shut.

'Sorry.' Graham looked shamefaced. 'She winds me up like you wouldn't believe.'

'Oh, I'd believe it,' said Charlie, still shocked by what Steph had said.

'Doesn't she know what a cliché she is? The stereotypical evil servant, like Mrs Danvers in *Rebecca* – have you seen it?'

'Read it.'

'Oh, very posh, guv!' Graham kissed Charlie's hair.

'Is Steph a coke-head?'

'No. Why, does she look like one?'

'You were singing "White Lines" at her – a song about drug abuse.'

Graham laughed. 'Private joke,' he said. 'Don't worry, we'll get our breakfast, you'll see. She's an obedient old mongrel.'

'Graham . . .'

'Now, a glass of water, so you can take your pills.' He turned to the water-cooler. 'No cups. Great. I'll have to get some from the storeroom. Won't be a sec. If the dogsbody comes back again, you know what song to sing.' He winked, then vanished, leaving the door wide open.

Charlie sighed. There was no way she was going to sleep with Graham now, and risk him sharing the details with his staff. She turned back to the Speak Out and Survive website. She would read Naomi Jenkins' letter once more, she decided, and then she'd go back to her chalet and collapse in bed. Alone.

Yawning loudly, she reached for the mouse. Her hand slipped, and instead of clicking on survivor story number seventy-two, she hit number thirty-one by mistake. 'Damn,' she muttered. She tried to go back to the previous screen, but Graham's computer had frozen. She pressed control, alt and delete, but nothing happened. Time to give up, she thought wearily. Graham could sort out the computer when he got back; she would leave it as it was – paralysed.

She was about to get up when she noticed something. A word, on the screen in front of her: 'theatre'. It took a while to reach her fuzzy brain. When it did, she jerked upright, inhaling sharply. She blinked a few times to check she wasn't hallucinating. No, it was really there, in survivor story number thirty-one. A little theatre. A stage. And a few lines further down, the word 'table'. It leaped off the screen, its black lines vibrating in front of Charlie's eyes. An audience eating dinner. They were all there, all the details from Naomi Jenkins' rape statement that Simon had mentioned on the phone. Charlie looked at the date – 3 July 2001. At the bottom, it said, 'Name and e-mail address withheld.'

She phoned Simon's mobile and got the engaged signal. *Damn.* She rang the CID room. *Please, please, somebody be there.*

After fourteen rings – she counted them – Gibbs answered. Charlie didn't bother with pleasantries, since he seemed to be a stranger to them these days. 'Get on to the National Crime Faculty at Bramshill,' she told him. 'Fax through Naomi Jenkins' rape statement and see if they've got any matches, anywhere in the UK.'

Gibbs grunted. 'Why?' he said truculently, as an afterthought.

'Because Naomi Jenkins *was* raped, and she wasn't the only one. This is a series,' Charlie uttered the words every detective dreaded. 'Tell Simon and Proust I'm on my way back.'

Part II

Speak Out and Survive
Survivor Story no. 31 (posted 3 July 2001)

This is so hard, forcing myself to write about what happened to me. It's only reading the pages of stories on this brilliant website and seeing how brave other women are willing to be that makes me want to try to do the same. I was raped three weeks ago, and the monster who did it told me that if I ever told anyone or went to the police, he would find me again and kill me.

I believed him then, and I still do. I know a lot of men who rape are inadequate or mentally ill, but this man seemed confident, not one of life's losers. He wouldn't have any trouble finding a girlfriend. He did not need to do what he did to me; he wanted to do it.

I was in Bristol city centre when he approached me. I had just come out of a meeting and had another one that evening, so I decided to look for something to eat. I am not from Bristol, so do not know its restaurants very well. I found a café that I liked the look of, called the One Stop Thali Shop. I was standing outside, looking through the window, on the point of going in, when the man approached me.

He called out my name as he walked over, and I thought I must know him. He came and stood beside me, and it was only then that I saw the knife. I was petrified. He made me walk to his car at knifepoint, telling me he'd cut my insides up if I screamed or alerted anyone. Once I was in the car, he put an eye mask over my eyes so that I couldn't see.

I'm not going to be able to write about everything that happened – it's too painful, and still too raw. He drove me somewhere – I don't know where – and only removed the mask once we were inside. It was a little theatre with a stage. He said to me, 'Do you want to warm up before the show?' but he wouldn't tell me what the show was going to be.

I knew I would find out soon, and I did. An audience arrived, all together in a group. Four men and three women. The women being there was one of the worst things about it. How can women enjoy seeing those things done to another woman? If that's their idea of a fun night out, I feel sorrier for them than I do for myself.

All seven of them were middle-aged verging on old. Two of the men had moustaches and beards. I hate men with facial hair. One had a proper bushy 'Santa' beard, but brown, and the other was one of those stupid beards that's like a circular plucked eyebrow around the mouth.

The chairs were not in rows like in normal theatres. They sat around a table, and while I was being attacked on stage, they ate dinner. Before he got started on me, the man served them their starters: small plates of Parma ham with rocket and Parmesan. I know this because he told them what it was.

This is so hard. I thought my suffering was over at one point, because I was taken off the stage, and I thought the man might be finished with me. He'd promised me that if I cooperated he wouldn't kill me, and I had cooperated. Even though he was a monster, I believed him about this. He didn't want to kill me. All he wanted was for me to help him put on his 'show'.

But it wasn't over. I can't write about what happened next, but it was worse than what happened on the stage. When the rapist had finally finished, he tried to persuade the man with the bushy beard – who was called Des – to rape me as well. Des climbed on top of me but, thank God, couldn't get an erection.

After they'd got as much entertainment out of me as they could, the mask was put over my eyes again and I was driven back to Bristol and pushed out on to the pavement outside the One Stop Thali Shop. My car keys and handbag were thrown on the pavement next to me. No one was around. I found my car, and although I was in no fit state, I drove all the way home. By the time I got back it was mid-morning. My neighbours were in their garden, and watched me walk from my car to the front door. That afternoon, one of them, the woman, rang my bell and asked if there was anything she could do. She asked me if I'd been to the police. I told her to mind her own business, and slammed the door on her. I knew I'd be killed if I said anything. The creature that attacked me knew my name and address and lots of other things about me.

I've hardly been out of the house since. I can't face my neighbours – I'm selling my house. I spend all my time having elaborate revenge fantasies, which is pathetic because that's all they will ever be – fantasies. Even if I mustered the courage to go to the police, it's probably too late by now. I've already done everything wrong – I had a bath as soon as I got home.

It would have been better if he hadn't known my name. As it is, I feel as if I've been singled out and I don't know why. Is it something I've done? I know the attack was not my fault, and I don't blame myself, but I would like to know what it was about me that made him choose me. I feel so alone now, so separate from the rest of the world. I just want to get back in somehow.

Thank you for taking the time to read this.

Name and email address withheld

SRISA (Survivors of Rape, Incest and Sexual Abuse)
MY STORY
Story no. 12 (posted 16 February 2001)
i can't believe there are so many of us, i was raped last year in the indian restarant where i worked, this is the first time ive told anyone, i stayed late that night because the

two men hadn't finished there curry and beers, i told the boss id lock up, that was the biggest mistake of my life. They were both drunk, drunk pigs, they wouldn't pay there bill, one pushed me down on the table and said my friends just the warm up im the main attraction. He called me the star of the show, he wanted to go last. They took turns, the first one couldnt get hard, the one who said he was the main attraction said use a beer bottle instead, the other man did, then the one who called himself main attraction turned me over so I was face down he forced himself on me that way, it hurt so much, the one who couldnt get hard had a camera and took photos of what the other one did, they made me tell them my name and where I live and where my family live. They said they would send the photos to my family if I went to the police, i have not been to the police yet but one day i will because I cant live with this if those pigs don't pay for what they did, and i am not going to let them ruin the rest of my life, i want to say to everyone whos been thru what I have, keep fighting.

Tanya, Cardiff
Email address withheld

12

6/4/06

Simon didn't like the way Juliet Haworth was looking at him. As if she was waiting for him to do something, and the longer he didn't do it, the more amusing she thought it was. Colin Sellers was asking the questions, but she wasn't interested in him. She addressed all her answers and her asides – of which there were plenty – to Simon. He couldn't work out why. Was it because he was the one she'd met first?

'It's unusual for a person in your situation not to want a lawyer present,' said Sellers conversationally.

'Is this interview going to be identical to the last one?' asked Juliet. 'How boring.' She was doing something with her hair as she spoke, hands behind her head.

'Did you get bored of your husband? Is that why you struck him repeatedly with a rock?'

'Robert's not talkative enough to bore anyone. He's quiet, but not in a dull way. He's very deep. I know it sounds corny.' Juliet's tone was chatty and conspiratorial. She sounded like a member of an in-crowd complimenting another person belonging to the same set. Simon thought of those '100 Greatest' programmes on Channel 4, the ones in which celebrities were always full of matey praise for one another.

'Robert's behaviour might be predictable, but his thoughts aren't. I'm sure Naomi's already told you all this.

I'm sure she's being much more helpful than I could ever be. Look.' Juliet turned round to show him that her hair was in a tight plait, sort of woven into the back of her head. 'A perfect braid, and I did it without mirrors or anything. Pretty impressive, no?'

'Has your husband ever been violent towards you?'

She frowned at Sellers as if irritated by his intrusion. 'Can you find me a hair bobble?' She pointed to the back of her neck. 'Otherwise it'll come loose again.'

'Was he habitually violent?'

Juliet laughed. 'Do I look like a victim to you? A minute ago you had me stoving Robert's head in with a rock. Make up your mind.'

'Was your husband physically or psychologically abusive towards you, Juliet?'

'You know what? I think it'll make your job more exciting if I don't tell you anything.' She nodded at the file in Simon's hands. 'Have you got a spare bit of paper?' she said in a softer voice. She was doing everything she could to make her preference clear. If she wanted Simon to play a more prominent role, he was determined to do as little as possible. Juliet didn't seem to give a damn about what happened to her; the only leverage he had at the moment was that she appeared to want something from him.

Sellers pulled a torn envelope out of his pocket and passed it across the table to Juliet, rolling a pen after it.

She leaned forward, spent a few seconds writing, then pushed the envelope towards Simon with a smile. He did nothing. Sellers picked it up and glanced at it briefly before holding it out behind him for Simon to take. Damn. Now he had no choice. Juliet's grin widened. Simon didn't like the way she was trying to communicate with him privately in a way that both used and excluded Sellers. He considered leaving the room, leaving Sellers to it. How would she react to that?

She'd written four lines on the envelope, either a poem or part of one:

> Human uncertainty is all
> That makes the human reason strong.
> We never know until we fall
> That every word we speak is wrong.

'What is this?' asked Simon, annoyed that he didn't know it. She couldn't have made it up, not so quickly.

'My thought for the day.'

'Tell me about your sexual relationship with your husband,' said Sellers.

'I don't think so.' She sniggered. 'Tell me about yours with your wife. I see you're wearing a wedding ring. Men didn't used to, did they?' she said to Simon. 'Sometimes it's hard to remember that things were ever different from how they are now, don't you think? The past vanishes, and it's as if the present state of affairs has always existed. You have to make a real effort to remember how things used to be.'

'Would you describe your sexual relationship as normal?' Sellers persisted. 'Do you still sleep together?'

'At the moment Robert's sleeping in the hospital. He may never wake up, according to DC Waterhouse.' Her tone implied that Simon might have lied about this simply to be mischievous.

'Before he was injured, would you say you and your husband had a normal sexual relationship?' Sellers sounded a lot more patient than Simon felt.

'I wouldn't say anything on that subject, I don't think,' said Juliet.

'If you had a lawyer here, or if you'd let us bring one in, he or she would advise you that if you don't want to answer a question, you say "no comment".'

'If I wanted to say "no comment", I'd have said it. My comment is that I'd prefer not to answer the question. Like Bartleby.'

'Who?'

'He's a fictional character,' Simon muttered. 'Bartleby the Scrivener. Whatever he was asked to do, he said, "I would prefer not to." '

'Except he wasn't being interviewed by the police,' said Juliet. 'He was just working in an office. Or, rather, not working. A bit like me. I suppose you know I've got no job, no career. And no kids. Just Robert. And now maybe not even him.' She stuck out her bottom lip, parodying a sad expression.

'Has your husband ever raped you?'

Juliet looked surprised, perhaps even a little bit angry. Then she laughed. 'What?'

'You heard the question.'

'Haven't you lot heard of Occam's razor? The simplest explanation and all that? You should hear yourselves! Has Robert ever raped me? Has he ever been violent? Has he psychologically abused me? The poor man's lying in hospital with a life-threatening injury, and you're—' She stopped suddenly.

'What?' said Sellers.

Her shrewd, knowing eyes had lost their sharpness. She appeared distracted as she said, 'Until quite recently it was legal for a man to rape his wife. Imagine that now, it hardly seems possible. I remember when I was a kid, walking through town with my mum and dad, and we saw a poster that said, "Rape in marriage – make it a crime." I had to ask my parents what it meant.' She was speaking automatically, and not about what was really on her mind.

'Juliet, if you didn't try to kill Robert, why don't you tell us who did?' said Sellers.

Her expression cleared instantly. Her focus had returned, but Simon sensed a change of mood. The flippancy had gone. 'Has Naomi told you that Robert raped her?'

Simon opened his mouth to answer, but he wasn't quick enough.

Juliet's eyes widened. 'She has, hasn't she? She's unbelievable!'

'You mean she's lying?' said Sellers.

'Yes. She's lying.' Juliet sounded deadly serious for the first time since the interview began. 'What exactly did she say he did?'

'I'll answer your questions when you answer mine,' said Sellers. 'Fair's fair.'

'There's no fairness involved,' said Juliet dismissively. 'Let me guess. She said there were men watching, eating dinner. Did she say Robert raped her on a stage? Was she tied to a bed? Bedposts with acorns on the top, by any chance?'

Something in Simon's head snapped. He was on his feet. 'How the fuck do you know all that?'

'I want to talk to Naomi,' said Juliet. Her smile had returned.

'You lied to us about your husband's whereabouts. You spent six days living in the house with him upstairs, beaten nearly to death, unconscious, lying in his own filth, and you didn't phone an ambulance. Your bloody fingerprints are on that doorstop, prints in Robert's blood. We've got enough to convict you several times over. It doesn't matter what you say to us or don't say.'

Juliet's face was impassive. Simon might as well have read her his shopping list instead, for all the difference it would have made. 'I want to speak to Naomi,' she repeated. 'In private. Just the two of us, nice and cosy.'

'Tough.'

'You must know that's a non-starter, so why bother asking?' said Sellers.

'You want to know what happened to Robert?'

'I know you tried to kill him, which is all I need to know,' said Simon. 'We're going to charge you with attempted murder, Juliet. Are you sure you don't want that solicitor?'

'Why would I try to kill my own husband?'

'Even without a motive, we'll get a conviction, which is all I care about.'

'That might be true of your friend —' Juliet nodded at Sellers '— but I don't think it's true of you. You want to know. And so does your boss. What's her name? DS Zailer. She's a woman, you see, and women like to have the whole story. Well, I'm the only person who knows it.' The pride in her voice was unmistakable. 'You tell your boss from me: if she doesn't let me talk to that bitch-cunt Naomi Jenkins, I'm the only person who'll ever know the truth. It's up to you.'

'We can't,' Simon said to Sellers as they walked back to the CID room. 'Charlie'll say it's out of the question, and it is. Jenkins and Juliet Haworth alone together in an interview room? We'd have another attempted murder on our hands. At the very least, Haworth'd taunt Jenkins with the details of her rape. Imagine the headlines: "Police allow murderess to taunt rape victim."'

Sellers wasn't paying attention. 'Why does Juliet

Haworth think I don't care about knowing the truth? Arrogant bitch. Why would you care more than I do?'

'I wouldn't worry about it.'

'Does she think I'm thick or something? Unimaginative? That's fucking ironic. She ought to hear the story I've told Stace to cover my week away with Suki. You know, I've even typed up a programme of activities for our team-building retreat, on police headed paper?'

'I don't want to know,' said Simon. 'I'm not lying to Stacey if I meet her while you're away and she asks me why I'm not with you in . . . wherever we're supposed to be.'

Sellers chuckled. 'You say that now, mate, but I know you *would* lie for me, if it came to it. Let's have less of the false modesty!'

Simon was keen to drop the subject. They'd discussed it before, too often. Sellers was always good-humoured in the face of criticism, which irritated Simon nearly as much as having his scruples treated as if they were some kind of endearing affection. Sellers *was* unimaginative, in this respect at least: he couldn't conceive of anyone genuinely, sincerely, disapproving of his ongoing infidelity. Why should anybody want to spoil his fun, when it was all gain and no pain, nobody was getting hurt? He was too optimistic, Simon thought. It was fun at the moment, and Sellers couldn't see that it had the potential to turn into anything else. Like losing his wife and kids, if Stacey Sellers ever found out. Until you've really suffered, thought Simon, you can't imagine what that level of pain might feel like.

'I had an idea for Gibbs' wedding present,' said Sellers. 'I know it's not for ages, but I want to get it sorted sooner rather than later. I've got more important things to think about.' He made a lewd gesture. 'Holiday preparations . . . lubrications . . . ejaculations . . .'

'Marital separations,' muttered Simon, thinking about the poem Juliet Haworth had written on the envelope. She wasn't a typical lorry driver's wife, any more than Naomi Jenkins was the average lorry driver's mistress. They've got more in common with each other than with him, thought Simon. Hard to know if he was right, with Haworth saying even less than the two women were. 'What's the idea?' he asked Sellers.

'A sundial.'

Simon laughed in his face. 'For Gibbs? Wouldn't he prefer a can of Special Brew? Or a porn video?'

'You know the Snowman's got a book about sundials?'

'Yeah. Do you know who bought him that book, and didn't get paid back?'

'I had a look at it. You can get this thing put on called a nodus.'

'You mean a gnomon?'

'No, all sundials have got those. A nodus is usually a round ball, although it doesn't have to be. It goes on the gnomon, so that there's like a blob that stands out on the edge of the shadow. Anyway, you can have a horizontal line put on the dial if you've got a special date or something – Gibbs and Debbie's wedding day for example. The horizontal date line crosses the downward time lines, the ones that mark out the hours and half-hours. And on that date every year, the shadow of the nodus follows the line all the way along. Do you get what I mean?'

'The specifics are irrelevant,' said Simon. 'In general, it's a bad idea. Gibbs wouldn't want a sundial. He'd perk up when he heard the words "date line", but ultimately he'd be disappointed.'

'Debbie might want one.' Sellers sounded hurt. 'They're nice, sundials. I'd like one. Proust said he would too.'

'Debbie wants to marry Gibbs. We can assume her taste's as bad as his.'

'All right, you fucking killjoy! I just wanted to get it sorted, that's all. When I get back from my week with Suki, the wedding'll only be a couple of days off. You lot'll have to sort it while I'm away, if you leave it till the last minute. God, talk about putting a dampener on things. I know Gibbs isn't exactly—'

'Exactly.'

'—but, you know, I just thought maybe we should aim high for a change.'

' "Look up in the sun's eye and give what the exultant heart calls good that some new day might breed the best, because you gave not what they would but the right twigs for an eagle's nest." ' Simon smiled. He wondered if Juliet Haworth would recognise the quote. Sellers didn't. 'W. B. Yeats. But he'd never met Chris Gibbs, and if he had, he'd have thought again.'

'Forget it,' said Sellers wearily.

'Which way round do you think it is?' Simon asked him. 'Did Robert Haworth rape Naomi Jenkins and tell his wife about it? Or was Jenkins raped by someone else, confided in her lover, and then he broke her confidence and told his wife?'

'Fuck knows,' said Sellers. 'In both scenarios you're assuming Haworth told Juliet about the rape. Maybe Naomi Jenkins told her. I can't get it out of my head that the two of them might be working together to mislead us. They're both cocky cows, and we know they've both lied. What if they aren't the enemies and rivals they seem to be?'

'What if anything?' said Simon despondently. 'With Haworth still unconscious and both women messing us around, we're getting fucking nowhere, aren't we?'

'I wouldn't say that,' said Charlie, coming up the corridor behind them. Simon and Sellers turned round. Her face was grim. She didn't sound pleased, as she normally did when progress was being made. 'Simon, I need a DNA sample from Haworth as soon as possible. And not one forensics took from the house, before you tell me we've already got it. I want one from the man himself. I'm not taking any chances.' Charlie was marching as she spoke; Simon heard Sellers panting behind him as they struggled to keep up with her.

'Sellers, get me background on Haworth, Juliet Haworth and Naomi Jenkins. Where's Gibbs?'

'Not sure,' said Sellers.

'Not good enough. I want Yvon Cotchin brought in for questioning, Jenkins's lodger. And get forensics on to Robert Haworth's lorry.'

'What was all that about?' asked Sellers, red in the face, once the sound of Charlie's high heels click-clacking along the corridor had faded.

Simon didn't want to guess, didn't want to speculate about what might constitute both progress and bad news. 'You can't keep covering for Gibbs,' he changed the subject. 'What's wrong with him, anyway? Is it the wedding?'

'He'll be fine,' said Sellers determinedly. Simon thought of the sundial on Naomi Jenkins' business card, its motto. He couldn't remember the Latin, but it translated as 'I only count the sunny hours.' That was Sellers to a tee.

13

Thursday 6 April

Sergeant Zailer unlocks the door of my cell. I try to stand up, and only realise how worn out I am when my knees buckle and a jangling noise starts up inside my head. Before I manage to convert the tangle of my thoughts into a coherent question, Sergeant Zailer says, 'Robert's doing well. The haemorrhaging's stopped and the swelling's going down.'

This news is all I need by way of an energy boost. 'You mean he's going to be okay? He'll wake up?'

'I don't know. The doctor I just spoke to said that with head injuries nothing is predictable. I'm sorry.'

I should have known: the ordeal is never over. It's like an endless race – the straight white finishing line dissolves into powder and scatters as I approach, and as it disappears, I glimpse a new line in the distance. And then I run towards that one, panting for my life, and the same thing happens. One wait comes to an end and another starts. It is this that is eroding me more than lack of sleep. I feel as if there's an animal trapped inside me, straining to get out, rocking back and forth. If only I could find a way to be still inside my head, I wouldn't mind lying awake all night.

'Take me to the hospital to see Robert,' I say, as Sergeant Zailer leads me out on to the corridor.

'I'm taking you to an interview room,' she says firmly. 'We've got some talking to do, Naomi – a lot of explaining and straightening out.' My body sags. I haven't got the energy for a lot of anything. 'Don't worry,' says Sergeant Zailer. 'You've got nothing to fear if you tell the truth.'

I could never be afraid of the police. They follow rules I understand and, apart from the odd exception, agree with.

'I know you wouldn't and didn't hurt Robert.'

Relief washes over me, sinking into my tired bones. Thank God. I want to ask if it was Juliet who hurt you, but there's been a power cut in the part of the brain that controls my speech, and my mouth will not open.

The interview room has pale coral walls and smells strongly of aniseed.

'Would you like a drink before we start?' Sergeant Zailer asks.

'Anything alcoholic.'

'Tea, coffee or water,' she says in a cooler voice.

'Just water, then.' I wasn't being facetious. I know the police are allowed to let people smoke. I've seen it on television, and there's an ashtray on the table in front of me. If tobacco and nicotine are permissible, why not alcohol? There's so much pointless inconsistency in the world, most of it the result of stupidity.

'Still or sparkling?' Sergeant Zailer mutters on her way out of the room. I can't tell if she's angry or joking.

As soon as I'm alone, my mind goes blank. I ought to be anticipating, preparing, but all I do is sit completely still while the thin fabric of my consciousness stretches to cover the chasm between this moment and the next.

You are alive.

Sergeant Zailer comes back with my water. She fiddles with the machine on the table, which looks more sophisticated than anything I would call a tape recorder, though that's clearly its function. Once it's recording, she says her name and mine, the date and the time. She asks me to state that I do not wish a solicitor to be present. Once I've done this, she leans back in her chair and says, 'I'm going to save us both a lot of time by skipping the question-and-answer rigmarole. I'll describe to you the situation as I understand it. You can tell me if I'm right. Okay?'

I nod.

'Robert Haworth didn't rape you. You lied about that, but for the best possible reason. You love Robert, and you believed something had happened to prevent him from meeting you at the Traveltel last Thursday, something serious. You reported your concerns to DC Waterhouse and myself, but you could see that we weren't as certain as you were that Robert had come to harm. You didn't think finding him would be a priority for us, so you tried a different tactic – you tried to make us believe Robert was violent and dangerous, and needed to be found quickly before he hurt anyone else. Right from the start, you planned to tell us the truth as soon as we found him. It was only going to be a temporary lie – you knew you'd redeem it with the truth eventually.' Sergeant Zailer pauses for breath. 'How am I doing so far?'

'It's all true, everything you've said.' I am slightly stunned that she has managed to work it out. Could she have spoken to Yvon?

'Naomi, your lie saved Robert's life. One more day and he'd have been dead for sure. The brain compression from his bleeds would have killed him.'

'I knew it was the right thing to do.'

'Naomi? You'd better make sure you never lie to me again. Just because you were right about Robert doesn't mean you can introduce a new set of rules whenever it suits you. Are we clear on that?'

'I've no reason to lie, now that you've found Robert and he's safe. Did . . . did Juliet try to kill him? What did she do to him?'

'We'll get to that in due course,' says Sergeant Zailer. She takes a packet of Marlboro Lights out of her bag and lights one. Her fingernails are long, painted a burgundy colour, the skin chewed and raw around the edges. 'So, if Robert Haworth didn't rape you, who did?'

Her words hit me like bullets. 'I . . . Nobody raped me. I made up the whole story.'

'A pretty elaborate story. The theatre, the table . . .'

'The whole thing was a lie.'

'Really?' Sergeant Zailer balances her cigarette on the edge of the ashtray and folds her arms, looking at me through the rising wisps of smoke. 'Well, it was a bloody imaginative lie. Why add so many weird elements – the dinner party, the acorn bedposts, the padded eye mask? Why not just say Haworth raped you one night at the Traveltel? You had a row, he got angry . . . et cetera. It would have been a lot simpler.'

'The more concrete details that go into a lie, the easier it is for people to believe,' I tell her. 'A fiction needs to contain as many specifics as a truth would contain, if it wants to disguise itself as a truth.' I take a deep breath. 'A row at the Traveltel wouldn't have been good enough – it's too personal to Robert and me. I needed you to believe Robert was a threat to women in general, that he was some kind of . . . ritualistic perverted monster. So I made up the worst rape story I could think of.'

Sergeant Zailer nods slowly. Then she says, 'I think you used that particular story because it was true.'

I say nothing.

She takes some papers out of her handbag, unfolds them

and spreads them out in front of me. One quick glance tells me exactly what they are. Their meaning rises to smother me, although I avoid looking at the words. There is a blockage in my throat.

'Very clever,' I say.

'You think these aren't real? Robert didn't rape you, Naomi, but you and I both know someone did. And whoever he is, he's done it to other women. *These* women. Why did you think you were the only one?'

Steeling myself, I look at the pieces of paper in front of me. They could be real. One of them is semi-literate. And the details are slightly different in each one. I don't think Sergeant Zailer would have done that. Why should she? It's like what she said about my story: it's too elaborate.

'Some women go to the police after they're raped,' she says in a conversational tone. 'Swabs are taken. Now that we've got Mr Haworth, we can take a sample of his DNA. If he's responsible for these rapes, we can prove it.' She watches me carefully.

'Robert?' This sudden about-turn confuses me. 'He could never hurt anyone. Take a sample of his DNA if you must. It won't match any . . . swabs.'

Sergeant Zailer smiles at me sympathetically. This time I'm determined not to fall for it. 'I think you could be a brilliant witness if you wanted to be, Naomi. If you start telling us the full truth, it'll help us to catch this evil shit who raped you and these other women. Don't you want that?'

'I was never raped. My statement was a lie.' Does she think I'm saying this to thwart her quest for justice, the stupid cow? It's because of me that I can't admit it. I'm the one who has to get through the rest of my life, and the only way I can do that is as a person it didn't happen to.

I've seen countless films in which people blurt out the truth they are desperate to hide after mild to moderate psychological prodding from a detective or shrink or lawyer. I've always thought those individuals must be pretty dim, or have a lot less stamina than I have. But maybe it's not stamina; maybe it's self-knowledge that enables me to resist Sergeant Zailer's appeals. I know how my mind works, so I know how to protect it.

Besides, I'm not the only liar in this room.

'These are stories from rape websites that you've printed out,' I say. 'You haven't got any swabs. You can't have.'

Sergeant Zailer smiles. She pulls some more papers out of her handbag. 'Have a look at these,' she says.

My chest feels tight. I have started to sweat. I don't want to take the pages from her hand, but she's holding them out. They're right under my chin. I have to take them.

I feel dizzy as I look down at the print. They are police statements, like the one I signed for DC Waterhouse on Tuesday. Rape statements, similar to mine in form and in content. In almost every ugly detail. There are two of them. Both were taken by a Detective Sergeant Sam Kombothekra from West Yorkshire CID. One is dated 2003, one 2004. If I weren't such a coward, if I'd reported what happened to me, I might have prevented the attacks on Prudence Kelvey and Sandra Freeguard. I can't help looking at the names, making it personal.

Two named women, one who chose to be anonymous, a waitress from Cardiff who gives only a first name – four other victims. At least.

I am not the only one.

For Sergeant Zailer, it's business as usual. 'How does Juliet Haworth know about what happened to you? She knows everything – all the things you claim you invented. Did Robert tell her? Did you tell him?'

I cannot answer. I am crying uncontrollably, like a pathetic baby. The ground is falling away and I am floating in the dark. 'Nothing happened to me,' I manage to say. 'Nothing.'

'Juliet wants to talk to you. She won't tell us if she attacked Robert, or whether she wanted to kill him. She won't say anything to us. You're the only person she'll talk to. What do you reckon?'

The words are recognisable as objects, but they make no sense to me.

'Will you do it? You can ask her how she knows you were raped.'

'You're lying! If she knows, it's because *you* told her.' My thighs are wet with sweat. I feel faint, as if I might throw up. 'I want to see Robert. I need to go to the hospital.'

Sergeant Zailer puts a photograph of you on the table in front of me. My heart jolts so violently it feels as I imagine whiplash would. I want to touch the picture. Your skin is grey. I cannot see your face because it's turned away from the camera. Most of the photo is blood, red around the edges, black and globular in the middle.

I'm glad she's shown it to me. Whatever's happened to you, I don't want to shy away from it. I want to be as close to you as I can be.

'Robert,' I whisper. Tears stream down my face. I have to get to that hospital. 'Did Juliet do this?'

'You tell me.'

I stare at Sergeant Zailer, wondering if we're taking part in two different conversations, two different realities. I don't know who did it. I have no idea. If I knew, I'd kill them. I can't think of anyone who might have attacked you apart from your wife.

'Perhaps it was you who hurt Robert. Did he tell you it was all over? Did he dare to fall out of love with you?'

This absurd proposition rouses me. 'Are all the detectives around here as dense as you?' I snap. 'Isn't there some kind of graduate-entry programme? I'm sure I read about one. Any chance I could talk to a graduate cop?'

'You're talking to a PhD.'

'In what? Imbecility?'

'We'll need a DNA sample from you, to put against the forensic findings from the scene where Mr Haworth was attacked. If you did it, we'll prove it.'

'Good. In that case, you'll soon know that I didn't. I'm glad we've more to rely on than your intuition, because that seems to be about as accurate as a—'

'Sundial in the dark?' Sergeant Zailer suggests. She is mocking me. 'Will you talk to Juliet Haworth? I'd be present throughout. There'd be no safety risk.'

'If you take me to see Robert, I'll speak to Juliet. If you don't, forget it.' I take a sip from my glass of water.

'You're something else,' she says under her breath. But she doesn't say no.

14

6/4/06

'Prue Kelvey and Sandy Freeguard.' Detective Sergeant Sam Kombothekra from West Yorkshire CID had brought photographs of both women with him, which were pinned to Charlie's whiteboard, alongside pictures of Robert Haworth, Juliet Haworth and Naomi Jenkins. Charlie had asked Kombothekra to tell the rest of the team what he'd already told her on the phone. 'Prue Kelvey was raped on the sixteenth of November 2003. Sandy Freeguard was raped nine months later, on the twentieth of August 2004. We took a full kit from Kelvey, but nothing from Freeguard, so no DNA there. She waited a week before reporting it, but the attack was identical to Kelvey's, so we were pretty certain we were dealing with the same man.'

Kombothekra paused to clear his throat. He was tall and thin, with shiny black hair, olive skin and a prominent Adam's apple that Charlie couldn't help looking at. It leaped up and down as he spoke. 'Both women were forced into a car at knifepoint by a man who knew their names and behaved as if he knew them until he got close enough to produce his weapon. Prue Kelvey just said a black car, but Sandy Freeguard was more specific: a hatchback, registration beginning with a 'Y'. Freeguard describes a corduroy jacket that sounds like the one Naomi Jenkins described. In all three cases the man was tall, Caucasian, with short dark-brown hair. Kelvey and Freeguard were both made to sit in the front passenger seat, not the back seat, so that's the first difference between our two cases and Naomi Jenkins' statement.'

'The first of many,' Charlie chipped in.

'That's right,' said Kombothekra. 'Once in the car, both women had eye masks put over their eyes – another point of similarity – but unlike Naomi Jenkins, at that point they were ordered to remove all their clothes from the waist down. Both did as instructed, fearing for their lives.'

Proust was shaking his head. 'So we've got three cases – three that we know of – of women being driven in broad daylight for, as far as we can tell, long distances, with masks over their eyes. Didn't anybody see the car and think it was suspicious? You'd think somebody passing on the street would have seen a passenger wearing an eye mask.'

'If I saw that, I'd assume they were trying to have a nap,' said Simon. Sellers nodded his agreement.

'Nobody came forward immediately,' said Kombothekra. 'After our television appeals, three witnesses made contact, but none of them could tell us much more than we already knew: a black hatchback, a passenger with something over their eyes, nothing at all about the driver.'

'So, front passenger seat rather than back seat, clothing removed en route rather than at destination,' Proust summarised.

'Kelvey and Freeguard were both continually sexually assaulted during the drive. Both said the rapist drove with one hand and used the other to touch their private parts. Both said he wasn't rough or violent. Sandy Freeguard said she thought he was doing it to show that he could more than anything else. It was about exercising power rather than inflicting pain. He made them sit with their legs wide apart. In both cases, he said something very similar to what

Naomi Jenkins claims her attacker said: "Don't you want to warm up before the show?"' Kombothekra consulted his notes. 'Kelvey's version was "I always like to warm up before a show, don't you?" She didn't know what show he was talking about at that point, of course. Freeguard was told, "Think of this as a little warm-up before the big show."'

'So it's the same man, no question,' said Proust.

'It seems very likely,' said Charlie. 'Although in each case, we're pretty sure it's a different audience, aren't we?'

Kombothekra nodded. 'We are. And a different audience again from survivor story number thirty-one on the Speak Out and Survive website. The writer of that described four men, two with beards, and three women. And she said they were middle-aged. Kelvey and Freeguard said their audiences were all young men.'

'What about the survivor story from the other website, Tanya from Cardiff?' asked Simon. 'If that's her real name. There was no audience for that rape, was there? That one seems the most different from the others. The only links are the star-of-the-show and warm-up references, and they could be a coincidence, two completely different attackers.'

Charlie was shaking her head. 'There was an audience of one. While each of the two men raped Tanya, the other watched. The words "show" and "warm-up" were used – that's enough of a link for the time being, until we prove it's unconnected. And photos were taken. Sam?'

'Sandy Freeguard said she was photographed naked and spread out on the mattress. The word "souvenir" was mentioned, as it was to Naomi Jenkins. Prue Kelvey says she thinks she was photographed. She heard clicks that she assumed came from a camera, but the crucial difference in her case was that the mask was never removed from her eyes, not at any point during the attack. The rapist worked that into his act. He seemed angry with her, she said, and kept saying that she was so ugly she had to have her face covered up or he wouldn't be able to perform sexually.'

'She's all right,' said Gibbs. It was the first time he'd spoken since the meeting began. 'Nothing special, but not a dog.'

Everyone but Charlie turned to the pictures on the board. She didn't need to: she'd already studied them in detail and been puzzled by the lack of physical similarities between the victims. Usually, in any crime series of a sexual nature, the scrote had a preferred type.

Prue Kelvey had a thin, pretty face with a small forehead and dark, shoulder-length hair. Naomi Jenkins had a similar hairstyle, though her hair was wavier and border-line auburn. Her face was fuller, and she was taller. Kombothekra had said Prue Kelvey was only five feet two inches tall, while Naomi Jenkins was five feet nine. Sandy Freeguard was a totally different physical type: a blonde with a square face, and about two stone overweight, whereas Kelvey was skinny and Jenkins was slim.

'Everyone else cares about what's happened to these women, even if you don't,' Charlie told Gibbs, feeling ashamed of him. Sam Kombothekra had frowned at the 'dog' comment. Charlie didn't blame him.

'Did I say that?' Gibbs challenged her. 'I'm just saying, Kelvey's not especially ugly. So there must have been another reason to leave the mask on throughout.'

'Just think before you speak,' Charlie snapped. 'There are better and worse ways to put things.'

'Oh, I'm thinking, all right,' Gibbs said ominously. 'I've been doing a lot of thinking. More than you lot.'

Charlie had no idea what he meant.

'Do we have to listen to you and Gibbs squabbling, Sergeant?' said Proust impatiently. 'Continue, Sergeant Kombothekra. I apologise on behalf of my detectives. They don't usually brawl like toddlers.'

Charlie made a mental note to forget to remind the Snowman of his wife's forthcoming birthday. Sam Kombothekra smiled apologetically at her, on Proust's behalf, she suspected. Instantly, he went up in her estimation. When he'd first arrived, she'd written him off as what, aged fifteen, she and her friends would have called a cuboid. She amended her snap judgement now; Sam Kombothekra was simply polite and well behaved. Later, if they got a moment alone, she would apologise to him for Proust's rudeness as well as Gibbs's callous remark.

'Prue Kelvey estimated that she was in the car for about an hour, give or take,' Kombothekra went on.

'She lives where?' asked Simon.

'Otley.'

Proust looked irritated. 'Is that a place?' he said. A bit bloody rich, thought Charlie, coming from a man who lived where he did. What did he think Silsford was, Manhattan?

'It is a place,' said Kombothekra. Another of his habits that had annoyed Charlie when she first met him: answering questions with 'It is' and 'I am', rather than simply saying, 'Yes.'

'It's near Leeds and Bradford, sir,' said Sellers, who was originally from Doncaster, or 'Donnie' as he called it.

Proust's slight nod indicated that the answer was acceptable, but barely.

'Sandy Freeguard said it could have been an hour or as much as two hours that she was in the car,' Kombothekra said. 'She lives in Huddersfield.'

'Which is near Wakefield,' Charlie couldn't resist adding. She kept her face totally straight; Proust would never be able to prove she wasn't being genuinely helpful.

'It sounds as if this theatre where the women were attacked is nearer to where Kelvey and Freeguard live than to Rawndesley, where Naomi Jenkins lives, then,' said Proust.

'We don't think Kelvey and Freeguard were attacked in the same place as Jenkins and survivor number thirty-one,' Simon told him. 'There was no stage or theatre mentioned in either Kelvey's statement or Freeguard's.' Kombothekra nodded at this. 'Both described a long, thin room with a mattress at one end and the audience standing at the other. No chairs, no dinner table. The spectators at Kelvey and Freeguard's rapes were drinking alcohol but not eating. Freeguard said champagne, didn't she?'

'A significant difference, then,' said Proust.

'There are more similarities than differences,' said Charlie. 'The line about warming up before the show – that's consistent across all three cases. Kelvey said the room she was in was freezing cold, and in Naomi Jenkins's statement, she says her rapist made a point of leaving the heating off until the audience arrived. He taunted her with it. Freeguard was attacked in August, so it's no surprise she didn't mention cold.'

'Sandy Freeguard and Prue Kelvey both said the room they were in had a strange acoustic.' Kombothekra consulted his notes again. 'Kelvey said she thought it might have been a garage. Freeguard also said the room didn't seem domestic. She thought it might have been an industrial unit of some kind. She said the walls didn't look real. The one she could see from the mattress wasn't solid – she said it was covered with some sort of material, thick material.

Oh – there were no windows in the room Freeguard described.'

'Jenkins mentioned a window in her statement,' said Charlie.

'You thought it was safe to assume Kelvey and Freeguard were attacked in the same place?' Proust asked Kombothekra.

'I did. The whole team did.'

'Jenkins was attacked somewhere different,' said Simon with certainty.

'If she was attacked at all,' said Proust. 'I still have my doubts. She's an habitual liar. She could have read those other two survivors' stories on the rape websites, both posted before hers, and decided to adopt a similar experience as a fantasy. Then later she met Haworth and wove him into the fantasy, first as rescuer, then later, when he understandably got fed up of her and dumped her, as rapist.'

'Very psychological, sir,' Charlie couldn't resist saying. Simon grinned and it made her want to cry. Sometimes the two of them shared a joke nobody else understood, and a sense of tragedy that they were not together and probably never would be overwhelmed Charlie. She thought about Graham Angilley, whom she'd left dissatisfied and confused in Scotland, promising to ring him. She still hadn't. Graham was too silly ever to make her cry. But perhaps that was a good thing, perhaps a less intense relationship was what she needed.

Kombothekra was shaking his head. 'There are details in Jenkins' statement that correspond with details in Kelvey's and Freeguard's, things she couldn't have known about from reading the stories on the Internet. For example, Jenkins says she was made to describe her sexual fantasies in detail and list her favourite sexual positions. Both Kelvey and Freeguard were ordered to do the same. And they were made to talk dirty, talk about how much they were enjoying the sex that was being forced on them while it was happening.'

Colin Sellers groaned in disgust. 'I know none of the rapists we meet are real charmers or anything, but this guy's about the worst I've heard of.' Everyone nodded. 'He's not doing it out of desperation, is he, because he's a sad, screwed-up fucker? He's planning it from a position of strength, like it's his favourite hobby or something.'

'He is. Albeit an imagined position of strength,' said Sam Kombothekra.

Simon agreed. 'He has no idea how sick he is. I bet he'd rather be labelled evil than sick.'

'It's not about sex for him,' said Charlie. 'It's about humiliating the women as much as possible.'

'It is about sex,' Gibbs contradicted her. 'Humiliating them's what turns him on. Or else why do it?'

'For the show,' said Simon. 'He wants to draw it out, doesn't he? Act One, Act Two, Act Three . . . making the women talk about sex in between the actual rapes, a verbal as well as a visual spectacle. It's all more stuff to pad out the performance. Are these paying audiences, or invited friends?'

'We don't know,' said Kombothekra. 'There's a lot we don't know. It's one of our biggest and most demoralising failures, not getting this guy. You can imagine how Prue Kelvey and Sandy Freeguard feel. If we can get him now . . .'

'I've got a theory,' said Sellers, looking brighter suddenly. 'What if Robert Haworth raped Prue Kelvey and Sandy Freeguard, then told both Juliet and Naomi that he'd done so. That'd explain how they both knew the MO.'

'Why did Jenkins lie, then, and say he'd raped her?'

'For the reason she admitted,' Charlie suggested. 'She didn't think we were looking for him hard enough. Once we found him, she planned to withdraw the accusation and she thought the whole thing'd go away. She didn't bank on us finding out about Kelvey and Freeguard.'

Simon shook his head vigorously. 'No way. Naomi Jenkins is in love with Haworth — there's no doubt in my mind about that. Juliet Haworth might be able to stay with a man who rapes other women, either for fun or profit, but Naomi Jenkins wouldn't.'

Proust sighed. 'You know nothing about the woman, Waterhouse. Don't be absurd. She's lied from the word go. Well? Hasn't she?'

'Yes, sir. But I think she's a fundamentally decent person, lying only in desperation . . . Whereas Juliet Haworth . . .'

'You're being contrary for the sake of it, Waterhouse! You know nothing about either of them.'

'We'll see what happens with Robert Haworth's DNA sample, whether it matches up,' Charlie intervened diplomatically. 'The lab are on it at the moment, so we should have a result by sometime tomorrow. And Sam's got a copy of the photo of Haworth to show the two West Yorkshire women.'

'Another similarity between Jenkins' account of her rape and Kelvey and Freeguard's accounts is the invitation to a member of the audience to join in,' said Kombothekra. 'A man called Paul, in the case of Jenkins. Kelvey said her rapist extended his invitation to join in to all the men present, but he was particularly keen for a man named Alan to get involved. He apparently kept saying, "Come on, Alan, surely you want a go?" And the other men encouraged this, also egging on this Alan character. Same story with Sandy Freeguard, except the man was called Jimmy.'

'And? Did Alan or Jimmy partake?' asked Proust.

'They didn't, neither one,' said Kombothekra. 'Free-guard told us that Jimmy said, "I'll play it safe, I think."'

'When you hear about men like these, you start to mourn the absence of the death penalty,' Proust muttered.

Charlie pulled a face behind his back. The last thing they needed was a diatribe from the Snowman about the good old days of hanging. He seized upon any excuse to lament the abolition of capital punishment: a theft of some CDs from HMV in town, nocturnal fly-posting. The inspector's readiness to wish death upon random civilians depressed Charlie, though she happened to agree with him about the man who had raped Naomi Jenkins, Kelvey and Freeguard, whoever he was.

'Why the differences, then?' she wondered aloud. 'It has to be the same man . . .'

'His method evolves with each rape?' Sellers suggested. 'He likes his basic routine, but maybe a bit of variety within that makes it more exciting for him.'

'So he made Kelvey and Freeguard undress in the car,' said Gibbs. 'To make the drive more fun.'

'Why the change of venue, for Freeguard and Kelvey, and why take the elaborate dinner out of the equation?' The Snowman barked impatiently. Charlie had been expecting his mood to deteriorate. When there were too many un-certainties, he usually grew ratty. She noticed that Sam Kombothekra was suddenly very still. He'd never met Proust before, never experienced one of his invisible ice installations, and was no doubt wondering why he felt unable to move or speak.

'Maybe the theatre became unavailable,' said Charlie.

'Maybe the panto season started and the stage was needed for *Jack and the Beanstalk*.' She spoke in a deliberately relaxed way, trying to diffuse the atmosphere; she knew from long experience that she was the only one of the team who could. Simon, Sellers and Gibbs seemed to accept it as inevitable that they would all congeal in the Snowman's disdain for hours, sometimes days. 'In Jenkins' statement, she says her attacker was serving the food as well, in between sexual assaults on her. Survivor number thirty-one alludes to the same thing.'

'So you're saying he decided to streamline his operation?' asked Simon.

'Maybe,' said Charlie. 'Think of what Naomi Jenkins described. That must have taken it out of him, don't you reckon? A kidnap followed by a long drive, multiple rapes, serving a posh dinner to more than ten guests, then a long drive back.'

'It's possible our man moved to West Yorkshire between the Jenkins rape and the Kelvey rape,' said Kombothekra. 'That could explain the change of venue.'

'Or he always lived in West Yorkshire, since Jenkins said her drive was much longer,' said Sellers.

'Maybe that was a red herring, though, and another part of what made this scrote's "act" too tiring to sustain long term,' said Charlie. 'Maybe he lived in Spilling – and that was how he knew Jenkins, or knew of her – and he drove her round and round in circles to make her think the site of the attack was at the other end of the country.'

'This is just pointless speculation,' Proust murmured in disgust.

'Has he got a day job?' asked Gibbs. 'Does he take time off to kidnap his victims?'

'There's one thing we haven't talked about yet,' said Charlie.

'That sounds unlikely,' Proust grumbled.

She ignored him. 'All the women say their kidnapper knew their names and numerous details about them. How? We need to find out if these women have got anything in common other than the obvious: they're all successful, middle-class, professional. Naomi Jenkins makes sundials. Sandy Freeguard is a writer – she writes children's books. Prue Kelvey's an asylum and immigration lawyer.'

'Was,' Sam Kombothekra corrected her. 'She hasn't worked since the attack.'

'We can't be sure in the case of survivor number thirty-one,' Charlie went on, 'but she writes like an educated person.'

'Jenkins, Kelvey and Freeguard all say that their rapists asked them how it felt to be successful career women, so we've got to assume that's a motivational link,' said Kombothekra.

'But then there's the survivor story from the SRISA website, Tanya from Cardiff,' Simon reminded him. 'She's a waitress, and her written English is poor. I'm not convinced her rape's part of the same series.'

'Chronologically, she was the first one,' said Sellers. 'Do you think she was the trial run, and then the rapist thought, That was great, but I'd prefer it with a posh bird and an audience?'

'Possibly,' said Charlie. 'Maybe—' She broke off, thinking.

Proust emitted a leaden sigh. 'Are we about to embark upon a flight of fancy?'

'The two men Tanya described were in the restaurant where she worked, having a curry. She was the only member of staff there, the men were both drunk, it was late. Maybe that was the first attack, a spontaneous, spur-of-the-moment one. One of the men forgot all about it, or saw it as a one-off, but the other found he'd acquired a taste—'

'Enough, Sergeant. You're not – what do they call it? – *pitching* to Steven Spielberg. Now, if there's nothing else . . .' He rubbed his hands together.

'Tanya from Cardiff's an odd one out, for whatever reason,' said Charlie. Let's pursue the professional-women angle. Gibbs, look into businesswomen's associations, anything like that.'

'There was something on Radio Four yesterday,' said Simon. 'Some organisation that brought self-employed people together. Jenkins and Freeguard are both self-employed. Maybe the rapist is too.'

'Kelvey isn't. Wasn't,' said Gibbs.

'Any progress on Yvon Cotchin?' Charlie asked him.

'I'll get on to it,' he said, looking bored. 'But we'll get nothing from her. She'll tell us exactly what Jenkins has told her to tell us.'

Charlie stared at him sharply. 'You should have spoken to her already. I told you to, and I'm now telling you again. Sellers, look for anything that might be someone trying to sell tickets to live rapes over the Internet, live sex shows, that sort of thing. And get on to SRISA and Speak Out and Survive, see if they've got contact details for Cardiff Tanya and survivor thirty-one. Name and address withheld is different from name and address not supplied.' Sellers stood up, already on his way.

'Simon, you explore the small theatre angle. Have I missed anything?'

'You have, I think.' Sam Kombothekra looked

embarrassed. 'The eye masks. Each of the three women was taken back, after the rape, to the spot where the attacker first approached her. Each was still wearing her eye mask when he drove away. Might he work for an airline? A pilot or steward would have easy access to as many masks as he needed, presumably.'

'Good thinking,' said Charlie diplomatically. 'Although . . . well, it's easy enough to buy eye masks at any branch of Boots.'

'Oh.' Kombothekra blushed. 'I never go to Boots,' he mumbled, and Charlie wished she'd kept her mouth shut. Out of the corner of her eye, she saw Proust edging towards his office. 'Sir, I need a word,' she said, holding her breath. The inspector hated it when one thing followed on immediately from another without a proper interval in between.

'A word? Would that it were only one. I'm going to make myself a cup of green tea, if I'm permitted,' the Snowman growled. He'd recently given up all things dairy without offering an explanation to any of his colleagues. 'All right, Sergeant, all right. I'll be in my office. Inflict yourself upon me without delay or hesitation.'

'Crikey! Is he always like that?' Sam Kombothekra asked after Proust had slammed the door to his glass Tardis. The room shook.

'He is.' Charlie grinned. Kombothekra would never guess she was taking the piss.

'Absolutely not. If it was your own terrible idea, I might try to make you feel better about it – though I dare say I wouldn't – but this is someone *else*'s terrible idea. You're usually good at demolishing those.' Proust stopped to slurp his drink. He'd always been a loud sipper, even when his drink of choice was PG Tips with lots of milk and three sugars. Charlie thought he had to be the least spiritually enlightened of all green-tea-drinkers.

'I agree with you, sir,' she said. 'I just wanted to check I wasn't being too rigid. Juliet Haworth told me unambiguously that if she was allowed to talk to Naomi Jenkins alone, she might reveal the truth. I didn't want to rule out that avenue and that chance without consulting you.'

Proust waved his hand dismissively. 'She wouldn't tell us anything, even if we agreed to her request. She just wants to torture Jenkins. One of them'd end up dead, or in hospital, alongside Robert Haworth. This is enough of a mess as it is.'

'Fair enough,' said Charlie. 'Then what about an interview between Juliet Haworth and Jenkins with me sitting in? I could interrupt if I thought things were turning nasty. If Juliet Haworth'd agree to that—'

'Why would she? She's already specified: alone with Jenkins. And why would Jenkins agree?'

'She already has. On one condition.'

Proust stood up, shaking his head in agitation. 'Everybody has a condition! Juliet Haworth has one, Naomi Jenkins has one. If Robert Haworth survives, no doubt he'll have one too. What are you doing wrong, Sergeant, that makes them think they can all put in these special applications?'

Why do I always have to be wrong? Charlie wanted to scream. In Proust's eyes, in Olivia's . . . Not being on good terms with her sister made Charlie feel insubstantial. She had to sort it out, soon. Why had she been so stupid? She'd heard the name Graham and that was it: the coincidence had made her lose all sense of proportion. Her fictional boyfriend made real. She'd allowed herself to get caught up in it. She would explain all this to Olivia. She'd ring her tonight – no more putting it off.

Tyrannosaurus Sex. Charlie pushed Olivia's insult out of her mind and, wearily, began to defend herself to Proust. 'Sir, I've approached this matter in exactly the same way that— '

'Do you know what Amanda told me the other day?'

Charlie sighed. Amanda was the Snowman's daughter. She was studying sociology at Essex University. Her birthday wasn't too far off either; Charlie made a mental note to circle it on Proust's desk calendar later.

'Twelve students in her year, doing the same subject – *twelve!* – are having some sort of special circumstances taken into account when it comes to the exam. They're all claiming to be dyslexic or . . . what's that other thing?'

'Naomi Jenkins will talk to Juliet Haworth if, in return, we take her to the hospital to see Robert Haworth.' Seeing the inspector's furious expression, Charlie added, 'And she hasn't asked to see him alone. I'd be there the whole time, supervising her.'

'Don't be a spastic, Sergeant!' Proust bellowed. 'She's a suspect in his attempted murder. How would that look, if the press got hold of it? We'd all be stacking shelves in Waitrose by the end of the week!'

'I'd agree with you if Haworth were conscious, sir, but for as long as he isn't, for as long as we're not sure if he'll even live—'

'No, Sergeant! No!'

'Sir, you've got to be more flexible!'

Proust's eyebrows slid closer together. There was a long silence. 'Have I?' he said eventually.

'I think so, yes. There's something really disturbing going on here, and the crucial thing, the key to it all, is in the relationships. Between Haworth and Jenkins, Haworth and his wife, Juliet and Jenkins. If they're keen to see one another, in any combination, we should seize the chance. As long as we're with them at all times, the pros outweigh the cons, sir. We could pick up crucial information from seeing how Jenkins behaves at Haworth's bedside . . .'

'You mean if you see her pull a large rock out of her cardy pocket?'

'. . . and how Juliet Haworth and Jenkins relate to one another.'

'You've had my answer, Sergeant.'

'If it makes any difference, Simon agrees with me. He thinks we should say yes to both, with the proper level of supervision.'

'It makes a difference,' said Proust. 'It strengthens my opposition to everything you propose. Waterhouse!' Not that useless reprobate, the tone implied. Simon had closed more cases than any of the other detectives under Proust's supervision, including Charlie.

'On another matter . . .'

'Sir?'

'What's wrong with Gibbs?'

'I don't know.' Or care.

'Well, find out, and whatever's wrong, right it. I'm fed up of finding him skulking outside my office like the spectre at the feast. Has Sellers told you his idea?'

'Gibbs'?'

'Obviously not. Sellers' idea to buy Gibbs a sundial as a wedding present.'

Charlie couldn't help smiling. 'No, no one's mentioned it to me.'

'Sellers thinks a dial with a date line, the date of Gibbs' matrimonials, but I'm not sure. It's too messy. You can't have a date line that represents only one day of the year, Sergeant. I've been reading up on it. Any such line would have to represent two days, because each date has a twin, you see. There's another day, somewhere in the year, when the declination of the sun is the same as it is on the date of Gibbs' wedding. So the little gismo – the nodus, it's called – its shadow would fall on the date line on this other day as well.' Proust shook his head. 'I don't like it. It's too messy, too random.'

Charlie wasn't sure what he was talking about.

'But Sellers' idea gave me one of my own. What about a sundial for our humble nick, on the back wall outside, where the old clock used to be? Nothing's replaced the clock – there's just a big, empty space. How much do you reckon a sundial would cost?'

'I don't know, sir.' Charlie imagined Proust putting his proposal to Superintendent Barrow and nearly laughed out loud. 'I'll ask Naomi Jenkins if you like.'

The inspector tutted. 'Obviously we can't commission one from her. And I'd have to get approval from the higher-ups. But it shouldn't be too expensive, should it? What do you think, maybe five hundred quid for a nice big one?'

'I really have no idea, sir.'

Proust picked up a big black book that was on his desk and began to leaf through it. 'Waterhouse very kindly bought me this. There's a section here on wall-mounted sundials . . . where is it? There are also dials that can be fixed directly to a wall, without even a mount, you know.'

'Sir, do you want me to look into it? Prices, waiting time, all that? You're so busy.' She knew it was what he wanted her to say.

'Excellent, Sergeant. That's very thoughtful of you.' Proust beamed, and Charlie found, to her embarrassment, that she felt heartened by the unexpected gust of praise. Was it human nature always to crave the approval of the most disapproving people one knew? She turned to leave.

'Sergeant?'

'Mm?'

'You do see my point, don't you? We can't possibly let Juliet Haworth and Naomi Jenkins have a private interview without a police presence. And we equally can't afford to leave Jenkins and Haworth unattended in his hospital room. The risks are too great.'

'If you say so, sir,' said Charlie tentatively.

'You tell Naomi Jenkins and Juliet Haworth that we're the ones who impose conditions around here. We run the show, not them! If these two . . . encounters are to take place, then there must be detectives present at all times. Not just detectives – I want *you* there, Sergeant. I don't care about your workload, or your *stress levels*.' He winced at the words. 'This isn't something to be delegated.'

Charlie faked a glum look, but inside she was rejoicing. 'If you insist, sir,' she said.

15

Friday 7 April

'What do you know about my husband?' Juliet asks me.

'That he loves me,' I tell her.

She laughs. 'That's about you, not him. What do you know about Robert? His family background, for example.'

DC Waterhouse picks up his pen. He and Sergeant Zailer exchange a look that I can't interpret.

'He doesn't see any of his family.'

'True.' Juliet makes a tick mark in the air with her index finger. With her other hand, she rubs her eyebrow, as if trying to smooth down the thin arc of hair, over and over again. A machine is recording our conversation. At the same time, my memory is recording all Juliet's mannerisms and expressions. This is your wife, the woman who often, I imagine, has spoken to you about everyday things – servicing the car, defrosting the fridge – while brushing her teeth, with a mouth full of toothpaste. That's how close she's been.

The more carefully I watch her, the longer I spend sitting here in this small grey room with her, the more ordinary she will seem. It's like when you can't bear to look at a picture of some gruesome deformity because you're too squeamish. When you eventually force yourself to stare at it and familiarise yourself with all its details, it soon becomes something mundane, nothing to be scared of at all.

It helps to remember that Juliet no longer shares something with you that I don't. People say marriage is no more than a piece of paper, and usually that's untrue, but not in this case. You and Juliet are as apart now as it's possible for a man and wife to be, separated not only by geography, by your respective incarcerations, but also by the fact that she did her best to kill you. If you wake up – no, *when* you wake up – there will be no question of your forgiving her.

'I know Robert's got three sisters, that one of them's called Lottie. Lottie Nicholls.' I had to drag this information out of you, and felt so guilty afterwards that I didn't ask for any more names.

Another shrill laugh from Juliet, for Waterhouse and Zailer to play back later. But they won't remember her cold, empty eyes in the way that I will. 'Why doesn't Robert ever speak to these sisters?' she asks me.

I remember your exact words, only have to paraphrase slightly. 'They think he's not good enough for them, and by thinking that, they proved *they* weren't good enough for him.'

'I was the cause of the big family feud,' Juliet says proudly. 'I bet Robert didn't tell you that. His nearest and dearest were horrified when they heard he'd got together with me. Which was bang out of order, considering I'd never done them any harm. The words "pot" and "kettle" spring to mind.'

I haven't a clue what she means.

'Has my husband ever said anything to you about any or all of his three sisters being – er, how shall I put this? – *dead*?' She leans forward, her pale blue eyes gleaming.

'What do you mean?'

Zailer and Waterhouse look as surprised and repulsed as I feel, but they say nothing. Your sisters, dead? *Any or all of them.* It's not possible. Juliet could easily be lying. She must be. Unless there was some sort of tragedy . . .

I've thought before that tragedy seems to be your element. You are passionate and sorrowful, like a condemned man, due to face the gallows any day, snatching a rare, precious moment with the woman he loves. When we first got together, once we'd established that the feeling was mutual, that neither one of us was more or less ardent than the other, I blurted out, like an idiot, 'This is so amazing. I can't believe there isn't a catch.'

You looked at me as if I were crazy. 'Oh, there's a catch, all right,' you said.

'So, I wonder who bashed Robert's brains in, then,' Juliet says matily, as if discussing the latest storyline in a soap opera. '*You* didn't do it, did you? You luurve Robert. You'd never hurt him.'

'That's right.' She can't mock me with something I'm proud of. 'You did it. Everyone knows you did it. Robert knows. When he wakes up, he'll tell the police it was you. Did you intend to kill him? Or was it a fight that got out of hand?'

Juliet grins at Sergeant Zailer. 'Have you trained her? She sounds like one of you lot.' She turns to me. 'Maybe you are. I don't know what you do for a living. Are you a cop?'

'No.'

'Good. There's only so much irony I can take.' Juliet leans forward. 'Why do you love my husband?'

'What do you mean?'

'It's a simple question. I suppose Robert's reasonably attractive, even now he's got a bit lardy. He was thinner when I met him. But is physical attractiveness enough? You must have noticed by now that he's a miserable sod and a tightarse.'

'I made a statement about a rape on Tuesday,' I tell her,

trying not to look at Sergeant Zailer or Waterhouse. 'I pretended Robert had raped me, to make the police look for him.'

'You really are off the rails, aren't you?' says Juliet.

'How did you know the details of what I put in my statement?'

She smiles. 'Why pretend he'd raped you? Rather than, say, beat you up or stolen your handbag?'

'Rape's the easiest crime to fake,' I answer eventually. It has often enraged me, the idea that there might be as many women pretending to have been raped as pretending not to have been. 'I had no bruises, so he could hardly have beaten me up.'

'You didn't pretend anything,' says Juliet. 'You *were* raped. Just not by Robert. I know exactly what happened to you. Scene by scene, frame by frame.' Juliet makes a loud clicking noise and mimes pushing the button of a camera.

'That's impossible,' I say, as soon as I am able to speak. 'Unless the police have shown you my statement.'

She looks suddenly impatient. 'No one's shown me any statements. Look, I might not answer all your questions, but I won't lie to you. If I give you an answer, it's an honest one.'

'Do you want to stop, Naomi?' Sergeant Zailer asks me. 'You can stop whenever you like.'

'I'm all right,' I say. This ice-cool woman, I remind myself, is the same Juliet who is too shy to answer the telephone, too spineless to learn how to use a computer, too frail to work, who made you stop doing overnight jobs because she couldn't bear to be in the house alone.

Remembering all the things you've said about her gives me my next line. 'You've changed. You used to be timid

199

and neurotic, scared of your own shadow, reliant on Robert for everything.'

'True.' She smiles. It's a game to her, one she's enjoying.

'You don't seem like that now,' I say.

'I've been – what's the word? Empowered.' She sniggers and looks at Sergeant Zailer, as if hoping to have impressed her.

'By what? By smashing Robert's head in with a brick?' I say.

'It was a stone acting as a doorstop that caused Robert's injuries. Haven't these nice officers told you the basic facts? My bloody fingerprints are all over it. But I could have picked it up after the attack, couldn't I? The distraught wife, on discovering her dying husband.'

'Someone who's been a frail wimp all her life doesn't suddenly turn into the cool, calculating, confident liar that you are now,' I say. 'Even if she does lose it and attack her husband for having an affair.'

Juliet looks bored and disappointed. 'I've known about Robert's affair with you since before Christmas,' she says. 'As you say, I was completely reliant on him. So I kept my mouth shut and put up with it. Pathetic or what?'

'So why did you attack Robert last week? Did he tell you he was leaving you for me? Was that what made you want to kill him?'

She examines her fingernails in silence. 'You're right,' she says. 'Someone who's been a feeble wimp all her life is unlikely to change her entire personality, even after a significant event takes place.'

'So what are you saying? That you *haven't* always been a wimp?'

'Ah.' Juliet closes her eyes. 'I wouldn't say you're getting warm, exactly, but you've stepped out of the Arctic region.'

'You faked your weakness,' I guess aloud. 'You're one of those women I hate, who are easily capable of looking after themselves but go all helpless the minute a man turns up. You made Robert believe you were needy and helpless because you knew he'd leave you otherwise!'

'Oh dear. I'm afraid you're back in the snow with Ernest Shackleton and Robert Falcon Scott. You may be gone for some time.' Juliet looks at DC Waterhouse. 'Did I get the quote right?'

'Was it that you didn't fancy working?' I stick to my guns, feeling as if I might finally be getting somewhere. 'Was it easier to stay at home and exploit Robert?'

'I used to love working, before I stopped,' Juliet says. Her face twists slightly.

'What did you do?'

'I was a potter. I made pottery cottages.'

Zailer and Waterhouse both write this down.

'I've seen them,' I say. 'They're all over your lounge. They're fucking hideous.' There is a loud roaring in my ears as I try hard not to picture Juliet's living room. Your living room.

'You wouldn't think that if I made one of your house,' Juliet says. 'That's what people did: commissioned me to make models of their homes. I used to love it – getting all the details right. I can do you one, if you like. I'm sure they'll let me work in prison. You will, won't you, Sergeant Zailer? I fancy starting again, actually. Tell you what: if all three of you bring me photographs of your houses, from all angles, in front, behind and the side-on view, I'll sort you all out.'

'Why did you give up work if you liked it so much?' I ask.

'Welcome home, Mr Shackleton.' She grins. 'You've lost a few toes to frostbite, but at least you're not dead. Pull up a chair by the fire, why don't you?'

'What the fuck are you talking about?'

She hoots with laughter at my anger. 'This is such fun. It's like being invisible. You can cause mayhem and there's nothing anyone can do.'

'Except leave you to rot in jail,' I point out.

'I'll be fine in jail, thank you very much.' She turns to Sergeant Zailer. 'Can I work in the prison library? Can I be the person who gets to push the trolley of books round the cell blocks? In the films, that position always has a certain amount of prestige attached to it.'

'Why are you doing this?' I ask her. 'If you really don't care about being locked up for the rest of your life, why not tell the police what they want to know: if you tried to kill Robert and why?'

Juliet raises her over-plucked eyebrows. 'Well, there's one I can answer easily: because of you. That's why I'm not revealing all like a good egg. You have no idea how much your existence, your place in Robert's life, changes everything.'

16

7/4/06

'I feel terrible,' said Yvon Cotchin. 'If I'd known Naomi was in prison, I'd have been there like a shot. Why didn't she ring me?' She sat with her knees pulled up to her chin, on a faded blue sofa in the middle of her ex-husband's messy living room in Cambridge's Great Shelford. Half-empty mugs, balled-up socks, remote controls, old newspapers and unopened junk mail littered the floor.

The house reeked of marijuana; the windowsill was covered with pieces of burned silver foil and empty plastic bottles with holes in their sides. Cotchin, who smelled of shampoo and a rich, sweet perfume, looked out of place in her tight red jumper and smart black trousers, clutching an unopened packet of Consulate cigarettes in one hand and a yellow plastic lighter in the other. More than out of place: marooned.

'Naomi wasn't in prison,' said Chris Gibbs. 'She came in to answer some questions.'

'And now she's bailed, she's back at home,' said Charlie, who had accompanied Gibbs to make sure he did a thorough job of questioning Naomi Jenkins' ex-lodger. He'd made it clear he didn't think they'd get anything useful from Yvon Cotchin, and Charlie didn't want it to be a self-fulfilling prophecy.

'Bailed? That sounds awful. Naomi hasn't done anything that bad, has she?'

'Has she done anything at all?'

Cotchin looked away. She fiddled with the cellophane on her cigarette packet.

'Yvon?' Charlie prompted. *Open the packet and light a fag, for fuck's sake.* She hated people who faffed around endlessly.

'I told Naomi I was going to tell you. It's not as if I ever said I'd go along with it, so I'm not betraying her by telling you.'

'Go along with what?' asked Gibbs.

'It's better if you know the truth before Robert . . . He's bound to be all right, isn't he? I mean, if he's survived this long . . .'

'You told us you'd never met Robert Haworth,' Charlie reminded her.

'That's true.'

'What did you tell Naomi Jenkins you wouldn't go along with?' Gibbs persisted.

'She lied. She pretended Robert had raped her. I couldn't believe she'd do something like that, but . . . she reckoned it was the only way to make you care about finding him.'

'Are you sure he didn't rape her?' asked Charlie.

'Very sure. Naomi worships the ground that man walks on.'

'It has been known for a woman to fall in love with her rapist.'

'Not Naomi.'

'How can you be certain?'

Cotchin considered the question. 'The way Naomi looks at the world. It's all black and white, all about justice. You'd have to know her to understand. She starts talking about revenge if someone nicks her parking space.' She sighed. 'Look, I've never been a huge fan of Robert

Haworth. I've not met him, but from what Naomi's told me
. . . But I *know* he didn't rape her. Hasn't she admitted to the
lie, now that Robert's been found? She said she would.'

'It's a bit more complicated than that.' Charlie opened
the file she was holding. On the sofa beside Yvon Cotchin,
she laid out copies of the three survivor stories: the one
from the SRISA website – Tanya's, the waitress from
Cardiff – and numbers thirty-one and seventy-two from
the Speak Out and Survive site. She pointed to number
seventy-two, the one by 'N.J.'. 'As you can see, this has got
Naomi's initials at the bottom and it's dated the eighteenth
of May 2003. When Naomi came in to tell her lie about
Robert Haworth, she directed one of my detectives to the
Speak Out and Survive website and told him how to find
her contribution.'

'But . . . I don't understand.' Cotchin's face had lost all
its colour. 'Naomi hadn't even met Robert in 2003.'

'Read the other two,' said Gibbs.

She didn't have the confidence, or a good enough reason,
to refuse. Wrapping one arm around her knees, she began
to read, narrowing her eyes, as if to block out some of the
words, or lessen their impact. 'What are these? What have
they got to do with Naomi?'

'The statement Naomi Jenkins signed on Tuesday –
Robert Haworth's fictional attack on her – shares many
details with these two accounts,' said Gibbs.

'How is that possible?' Cotchin sounded panicky. 'I'm
too stupid to understand this on my own. You'll have to tell
me what's going on.'

'There are also two cases in West Yorkshire that fit the
same pattern,' Charlie told her. 'You're not the only one
who wants to know what's going on, Yvon. We need to
find out if Robert Haworth raped Naomi Jenkins and these

other women, or if someone else did. We're hoping you can help us.'

Cotchin was squeezing her cigarette packet hard in the middle, crushing its contents. 'Naomi can't have been raped. She'd have told me. I'm her best friend.'

'Did you live with her then? Spring 2003?'

'No, but I'd still have known. Naomi and I have been best friends since school. We tell each other everything. And . . . she seemed fine in spring 2003, totally normal. Her usual strong self.'

'You can remember that far back?' said Charlie. 'I can't remember what sort of mood my friends were in three years ago.'

Cotchin looked wary. 'Ben and I were going through a bad patch,' she said eventually. 'The first of many. It was pretty serious. I was spending the night at Naomi's twice a week, if not more. She was fantastic. She cooked for me, emailed my clients and smoothed things over – I was too upset to work. She made me have showers and brush my teeth when all I wanted to do was neglect myself out of existence. Has either of you ever been through a marriage break-up?'

Charlie couldn't interpret the noise Gibbs made. 'No,' she said.

'Then you can't imagine how painful and destructive it is.'

'I find it a little unusual that you came here, after your fight with Naomi,' said Charlie. 'Most women don't run to their ex-husbands in times of trouble.'

Cotchin looked embarrassed. 'My parents are too pre-occupied with their work. They don't like people staying. And my siblings and all my friends apart from Naomi have got partners or kids. I was upset, all right?'

'There are hotels, B&Bs. Is a reconciliation with Ben on the cards?' Charlie prodded. 'Is that why you're here?'

'That's none of your business. We're not back together, if that's what you mean. I'm sleeping in the spare room.'

'Why did the two of you split up?' Might as well ask, thought Charlie even though it's probably irrelevant. Unless . . . A hypothesis began to take shape at the back of her mind. An unlikely one, but it was worth a try.

'I don't have to tell you that!' Cotchin protested. 'Why do you want to know?'

'Answer the question.' Gibbs' voice was full of unpleasant consequences.

'Ben drank too much, okay? And he refused to get a job.'

'This is a big place.' Charlie looked around. 'And that's an expensive telly and DVD player. How does Ben afford it all if he doesn't work?'

'It's all inherited.' Cotchin sounded bitter. 'Ben's never done a day's hard work in his life and he'll never have to.'

'You mentioned the first bad patch . . .'

'In January 2003 he slept with someone else while I was away visiting my brother and his family. When I got back, the woman had gone, but I found Ben fast asleep – or unconscious, more like – in bed with the used condom and one of her earrings. He'd been so drunk, he'd passed out and hadn't woken up in time to cover his tracks before I got home.'

She hasn't forgiven him, thought Charlie. If she had, she'd have said, 'He was unfaithful to me, but it was only a one-night stand. It meant nothing.'

Gibbs looked down at his notes. 'So you and Naomi Jenkins were together in her house on the night of Wednesday 29 March and all day on Thursday 30 March until she left to go and meet Haworth at the Traveltel?'

'That's right.' Yvon Cotchin looked relieved. She preferred to talk about the attempted murder of Robert Haworth than her love life.

'Could Naomi have left the house during Wednesday night or Thursday without you noticing?'

'I suppose she could have, in the middle of the night while I was asleep. But she *didn't*. She was asleep too. On Thursday, no. My office and bedroom are in the converted cellar of Naomi's house. Were,' Cotchin corrected herself. 'You've seen for yourself,' she said to Gibbs. 'My desk faces the window, with a clear view of the drive. If Naomi had left the house any time on Thursday, I'd have seen her.'

'You didn't leave your desk at all? To grab a sandwich or use the bathroom?'

'Well . . . yes, of course, but . . .'

'Can you see the drive from the basement window?' asked Charlie.

'Yes,' said Cotchin, with a trace of impatience in her voice. 'Ask him, he's been to the house.' She nodded at Gibbs. 'If you look up, you can see the drive, and the road. I'd have noticed if Naomi went out. And she didn't.'

'But she can't vouch for you in the same way, can she?' said Gibbs. 'If she was in that shed she works in, that's round the back of the house. She wouldn't have seen you if you'd gone out, would she?'

Cotchin turned to Charlie, an appeal in her eyes. 'Why would *I* want to attack Robert? I don't know him.'

'You disapprove of him,' said Charlie. 'Your marriage was destroyed – if only temporarily – by infidelity.' Cotchin blushed at the barbed aside. 'Robert Haworth was cheating on his wife with your best friend for a year. You must have disapproved.'

'Naomi gave me a home when Ben and I finally split up,'

said Cotchin angrily. 'I couldn't abandon her just because she was doing something I disagreed with.' She sighed. 'Anyway, as time went on, my disapproval got weaker and weaker.'

'Why was that?'

'Naomi adored Robert. She was so happy. I don't know how to describe it. It was like she was sort of lit up from the inside. And she said he felt the same. I thought, Maybe it's the real thing, they're destined to be together. I do believe in that, you know,' she said defensively. 'I saw that it was nothing like my situation with Ben. Ben's unfaithfulness wasn't about not loving me, or loving someone else more. I'm the person he's always wanted to be with, he was just too stupid and self-indulgent to treat me properly. He's changed now, though. He's given up booze, almost completely.'

And taken up drugs, thought Charlie, glancing at the paraphernalia on the windowsill. 'If Robert loved Naomi, why didn't he leave his wife to be with her?'

'Good question. I think he was stringing Naomi along, though she claimed he wasn't. He made out he couldn't leave Juliet, as if she was some sort of needy underdog type, but I always thought that was probably crap. If he was as unhappy with her as he told Naomi he was, he'd have left her. Men don't stay out of duty, not when they've got somewhere better to go. Only women are stupid enough to do that. And when Naomi went to Robert's house to look for him on Monday, she met Juliet and said herself that she was nothing like Robert had made out.'

The lounge door opened and a man Charlie assumed was Ben Cotchin came in wearing only a pair of long red-and-navy checked boxer shorts. He was tall, thin and unshaven, with long dark hair in a ponytail. Exactly like Yvon's hair, thought Charlie – same colour, same style. 'Anyone fancy a cuppa?' he said.

'No, thanks.' Charlie answered on behalf of herself, Gibbs and Yvon. If drinks were made, Ben would have to come back in and hand them out. Time would be wasted. As it was, Charlie had woken up this morning feeling crushed by the thought of everything she had to do before she would be able to climb back into bed tonight.

'Robert and Naomi only had one topic of conversation,' said Yvon, once her ex-husband had left the room. 'How much they loved each other and how unfair and sad it was that they couldn't be together. They created an alternative reality together that only existed for three hours a week, in one room. Why didn't he ever take her away for the weekend? He said he couldn't leave Juliet for that long . . .'

'What do you think the reason was?' asked Charlie.

'Robert's a control freak. He wanted Juliet and Naomi, and he wanted to keep Naomi inside a very definite box: four to seven on a Thursday. She can't see it. It's so frustrating. It's like she knows things about him that she doesn't know she knows, if that makes any sense. I mean, I only know he's a control freak from things she's told me. But I can see those things for what they are, and she can't.'

'What sort of things?'

The way Yvon rolled her eyes suggested she was spoilt for choice. 'He always brings a bottle of wine, when they meet. Once he knocked the bottle over while he was getting into bed. It was nearly full and most of the wine spilled on the carpet. Naomi said she'd go out and get another bottle, but he wouldn't let her. He got really upset when she suggested it.'

'If they only had three hours together—' Charlie began, but Yvon was shaking her head.

'No, it wasn't that. He explained it to Naomi. He was offended by her taking for granted that if you spill wine, you can just buy more to replace it. As far as he was concerned, it was his carelessness that had led to the wine being spilled, so he thought he should make do with no wine as a sort of penance. He didn't call it a penance, but that's what he meant. Naomi said he felt bad about knocking the bottle over and didn't want to let himself off the hook. "Casual vandalism", he called it. He came out with all sorts of rubbish, all the time, can't handle it at all if anything unexpected happens. I think he's a bit mental, actually. Screwed up.'

She turned to Gibbs. 'When am I going to get my computer back?'

'It's back,' he said. 'At Naomi Jenkins' house.'

'But . . . I'm staying here now. I need it to work.'

'I'm not a removals man. You'll have to fetch it yourself.'

Charlie decided it was time to air her theory. 'Yvon, is there any chance that it was you who was raped three years ago? Was that why you were in a state, and why your marriage started to fall apart? Did Naomi write to the Speak Out and Survive website on your behalf, and sign it with her initials to preserve your anonymity?'

It took a while for the suggestion to sink in. Yvon looked as if she was trying to assemble something inside her head, a machine with many complicated parts. Once she'd succeeded in doing so, she looked horrified. 'No,' she said. 'Of course not. What a terrible thing to say! How can you wish that on me?'

Charlie had little patience for emotional blackmail. 'All right,' she said, standing up. 'That'll do for now, but we'll probably want to talk to you again. You're not planning on going anywhere, are you?'

'I might be, yes,' said Yvon, like a child who'd been caught out.

'Where?'

'A place in Scotland. Ben said I need a break, and he's right.'

'He going too?'

'Yes. As a friend. I don't know why you're so interested in me and Ben.'

'I'm an all-rounder,' Charlie told her.

'We're nothing to do with this.'

'We'll need an address.'

Yvon reached for her small black handbag, which was beside the sofa, among the mugs and the newspapers. A few moments later she handed Charlie a card she recognised.

'Silver Brae Chalets?' Charlie kept her voice steady. 'You're going here? Why here?'

'I get a big discount, if you must know. I designed their website.'

'How did you come to do that?'

Yvon looked baffled by Charlie's interest. 'Graham, the owner, he's a friend of my dad's. Dad was his tutor at uni.'

'Which university?'

'Oxford. Graham got the highest first in classics in his year. My dad was disappointed that he didn't become a don. Why do you want to know all this?'

There was a question to avoid. Graham, a classics don. He'd teased Charlie for mentioning a book she'd read: *Rebecca* by Daphne Du Maurier. *Very posh, guv.* He was probably embarrassed by his cleverness. Modest. Stop it, Charlie told herself. You're not fond of him. You just fancied him in a fleeting, temporary sort of way. That's all.

'Has Naomi ever been to Silver Brae Chalets?' she asked. 'She had one of their cards.'

Yvon shook her head. 'I tried to persuade her, but . . . after she met Robert, she didn't ever want to go away. I think she thought that if she couldn't go with him, she'd rather not bother.'

Charlie was thinking fast. So that was why Naomi had the card. Graham knew Yvon Cotchin; now Charlie had no choice but to ring him. Naomi and Robert *might* have been to Silver Brae Chalets, whatever Yvon said.

'What do you care about Miss Minty Fags and her hippie husband?' Gibbs snapped, once they were back in the car. 'Arrogant cock-shite! There we were, staring at his bong collection on the windowsill, and he didn't give a toss!'

'I'm interested in other people's relationships,' Charlie told him.

'Apart from mine. Boring old Chris Gibbs and his boring girlfriend.'

Charlie massaged her temples with the balls of her hands. 'Gibbs, if you don't want to get married, for God's sake, don't. Tell Debbie you've changed your mind.'

Gibbs studied the road ahead. 'I bet you'd all like that, wouldn't you?' he said.

'I don't know,' said Prue Kelvey. She was sitting on her hands, looking at an enlarged photograph of Robert Haworth. Sam Kombothekra thought he was doing an excellent job of concealing his disappointment. 'When you first showed it to me, I was surprised – it's not the face I've been seeing in my mind since . . . since it happened. But memory and . . . feelings distort things, don't they? And this man is similar to the one in my head. It could be him. I just didn't . . . I can't say that I recognise him.' There was a long pause. Then she asked, 'Who is he?'

'I can't tell you that. I'm sorry.'

Kelvey accepted this without an argument. Sam decided not to tell her that the DNA profile taken from her rape kit was in the process of being compared with that of a man from the Culver Valley who'd been accused of a very similar crime. He sensed that Prue Kelvey didn't really want him to tell her anything; she was still reeling from the shock of finding Sam on her doorstep. He predicted it would be a few days before she got in touch to ask for more information.

She'd always been unsure of herself, tentative about everything she said apart from what was absolutely unequivocal. Sam hoped he'd have more luck with Sandy Freeguard. When he got up to leave, Prue Kelvey sagged with relief, and Sam felt awful when it occurred to him that, apart from her rapist's face, his own must be the one she associated most closely with her horrific ordeal.

It was an hour's drive, give or take, from Kelvey's house to Freeguard's. This wasn't the first time Sam had driven from one woman's house to the other's. He didn't mind the M62, unless it was nose to tail. The part he hated was the slog through Shipley and Bradford, past grimy, crumbling council flats and the shiny but equally depressing sprawl of the retail park and the new cinema with its multi-storey car park and chain restaurants. Big, grey, greedy blocks. Could architecture get any less imaginative?

The roads were mercifully empty, and Sam pulled up outside Sandy Freeguard's house forty-five minutes after leaving Otley. Freeguard was, in many ways, Prue Kelvey's polar opposite. She had made Sam feel at ease from the start, and he quickly stopped worrying about what he said to her. She always smiled when he turned up unannounced, always kept up a constant stream of comforting banter, barely allowing him to get a word in edgeways. If he lost concentration even for a moment, there was no hope of catching up. Sandy covered several dozen topics per minute. Sam liked her, and suspected her garrulousness was a deliberate strategy, to take the pressure off him. Did she guess how hard it was for him, dealing with women like herself, who had been through hell at the hands of men? It made him feel guilty and apprehensive. None of the men he knew were like that; the thought of knowing anyone who'd do what had been done to Prue Kelvey and to Sandy Freeguard made Sam want to be sick.

'. . . but, of course, it could have been that Peter and Sue were the ones who'd got the wrong end of the stick, and that's why Kavitha thought I'd mind.'

Sam hadn't a clue what she was talking about. Peter, Sue and Kavitha were his colleagues. Sandy Freeguard was on first-name terms with the whole team. She had given them all hope, even when it had started to look as if they might not catch the man who'd attacked her. She refused to be downcast. Instead, she set up a local victim-support group, trained as a counsellor, did voluntary work for Rape Crisis and the Samaritans. Last time Sam had seen her, she'd been talking about writing a book. 'Might as well,' she'd said, smiling ruefully. 'I'm a writer, after all, and this is a subject that isn't going to leave me alone. At first I thought it'd be exploitative to write about my experience, but . . . sod it, the only person I'd be exploiting is me, so if I don't mind, why should anyone else?'

Sam interrupted her chatter. 'I've got a photograph to show you, Sandy,' he said. 'We think it might be him.'

She stopped, mouth open. 'Good,' she said. 'You mean, you might have him?'

Sam nodded.

'Go on, then, show me,' she said. Her eyes were already

searching his clothing, looking at his hands to see if he was carrying anything. If he wasn't quick about producing the picture, she might frisk him.

He pulled the photograph out of his trouser pocket and passed it to her. She took a quick look, then inspected Sam curiously. 'Is this some kind of joke?' she said.

'Of course not. It's not him?'

'No. Definitely not.'

'I'm sorry . . .' Guilt swarmed in, clogging Sam's mind. He should have told her not to get her hopes up. He shouldn't have brought out the picture so quickly, whatever Sandy thought she wanted. Maybe she wasn't as tough as she seemed, maybe this would—

'Sam, I know this man.'

'What?' He looked up, shocked. 'But you said—'

'I said he wasn't the man who raped me.' Sandy Free-guard laughed at his astonished expression. 'This is Robert Haworth. What on earth made you think it was him?'

17

Friday 7 April

I am holding your hand. It's hard to convey the power of this feeling to anyone who hasn't experienced it. My body glows and crackles as you burn away the darkness inside me with a furious warmth. Something in me has been switched on by your touch and I feel the way I felt on that first day at the service station: alight, safe. I have scrambled back up on to the ledge. I was fading, and now, just in time, I have been plugged back into my source of life. Do you feel this too? I won't bother to ask the nurses. They would talk about probabilities and statistics. They would say, 'Studies have shown . . .'

I know you know I'm here. You don't have to move, or say anything; I can feel the energy of recognition flowing from your hand into mine.

Sergeant Zailer stands in the corner of your room, watching us. On the way here, she warned me that I might find the sight of you distressing, but she saw how wrong she was when we arrived and I ran to your bed, as eager to touch you as I always have been. I see you, Robert, not the bandages, not the tubes. Only you, and the screen that shows that your heart is pumping, alive. I don't need any doctors to tell me about your firm, steady heart.

Your bed has been adjusted so that the top part is at an angle, to support your back. You look comfortable, as if you've fallen asleep on a sunlounger, with a book on your lap. Peaceful.

'This is the first time,' I tell Sergeant Zailer. 'The first and only time he's managed to escape, in his whole life. That's why he isn't ready to wake up yet.'

She looks sceptical. 'Remember, we haven't got all day,' she says.

I grip your hand. 'Robert?' I begin tentatively. 'Everything's going to be fine. I love you.' I am determined to talk to you in exactly the way I would if we were alone; I don't want you to notice a difference in my manner and feel disorientated and scared. I am still me, and you're still you; the strange situation we're in hasn't changed us one bit, has it, Robert? We must think of Sergeant Zailer as part of the furniture, no different from the small black television on the high shelf opposite your bed, the green chair with wooden arms that I'm sitting on, or the small plastic round-edged table with the glass and jug of water on it.

They like round edges in this hospital. There are no right angles between the floor and the walls. Instead, the two are joined by a curved seal of grey rubber that runs all the way round the room. Seeing it makes me think of all the harmful things that must be kept outside, kept away from you.

Behind your bed, on the wall, there's a big red emergency button. My having to leave soon makes this an emergency.

'That's a bit daft,' I say, stroking your arm. 'They've put out water and a glass on the table, but how are you supposed to drink it? Someone in this hospital's got a strange sense of humour.' My tone is light, frivolous. I have always been the one who jollies us both along. I'm not going to sit beside you and wring my hands and weep. You've been through enough already and I don't want to make it worse.

'Actually, maybe it's a kind of bribe,' I say. 'Same with the telly on the wall. Do the doctors come in and tell you that if you wake up quickly, you can watch *Cash In the Attic* and have a drink of tap water? It's not great, is it, as incentives go? They should fill that jug with champagne instead.'

If you could smile, you would. You once told me that you love champagne, but only drink it in restaurants. I felt wounded, and thought it was tactless of you to mention it, since we have never been to a restaurant together and at the time I feared we never would. I pictured you and Juliet at the Bay Tree – where you went to get my *Magret de Canard aux Poires* – happy to chat endlessly to the chef when he emerged from the kitchen because you knew you'd have plenty of time to talk to one another later – the rest of your lives. I can still see that picture in my mind, and it stings my heart.

'I didn't think you'd have your own room,' I say. 'It's nice. Everything's so clean. Does a cleaner come in every day?'

I leave a pause before speaking again. I want you to know how much I hope you'll answer me.

'You've got a great view, too. A little square courtyard, covered with crazy paving. With benches around three sides and a knot garden in the middle.' I look at Sergeant Zailer. 'Is it called a knot garden?'

She shrugs. 'I'm the wrong person to ask about gardens. I hate the things. Haven't got one and don't want one.'

'It *is* called a knot garden. And on one side of the courtyard, there's a row of round bushes. If you turn your head to the right and open your eyes, you'll be able to see it.'

Sergeant Zailer's mobile begins to ring. The noise startles me and I drop your hand. I expect her to apologise and switch her phone off, but she takes the call. She says, 'Yep', several times, and then, 'Really?' I wonder if the call has anything to do with you or Juliet.

'Do you know what happened to you?' I whisper, leaning in closer. 'I don't, not exactly, but the police think Juliet attacked you. I think that's what happened. You very nearly died, but you didn't. Thanks to me, you were found in time. You had an operation—'

There is a knock at the door. I turn and see the nurse who showed us in, a plump young woman with blond hair scraped back into a short, high ponytail. I'm scared she's going to say I have to leave, but it is Sergeant Zailer she's glaring at. 'I've told you before, no mobile phones on the ward. It interferes with our machines. Switch it off.'

'Sorry.' Sergeant Zailer puts her phone back in her bag. Once the nurse has gone, she tells me, 'It's bollocks, that stuff about the machines. The doctors use their mobiles in here all the time. Stupid woman.'

'She's just doing her job,' I say. 'Like most people's, it involves the random application of nonsensical rules. You should understand, given what you do for a living.'

'Two more minutes and we're going,' she warns me. 'I've got work to do.'

I turn away from her, back to you. 'I don't think you mind being here, do you?' I say. 'A lot of people hate hospitals, but I don't think you do. We've never talked about it, but I bet if we did, you'd say you quite like them, for the same reason that you like service stations.'

'He likes service stations?' Sergeant Zailer's voice in-trudes. 'Sorry, but . . . I've never heard of that before. Everyone hates service stations.'

I've never hated them, and since you and I met I have loved them. Not just Rawndesley East – all motorway service stations. You're right: they are totally self-contained, places that could be nowhere or anywhere, free of what you once called the tyranny of geography. 'Each one's like a world that exists outside real space and real time,' you said. 'I like them because I've got an overactive imagination.'

'Do all lorry drivers feel that way about them?' I teased you. 'Is it a sort of vocation thing?'

You replied as if my question had been deadly serious: 'I don't know. Could be.'

Now, every time I drive past a sign that says 'Moto' or 'Welcome Break' and see a small picture of a bed, white lines against a blue background, I think of us and of room eleven.

'I went there last night,' I tell you. 'To our room. I thought . . . I couldn't bear to miss a week.'

'You were at the Traveltel last night?' Sergeant Zailer interrupts again.

I nod.

'But I collected you from home this morning.'

'I left the Traveltel at five-thirty and was home for six,' I tell her. 'I'm not sleeping much at the moment. I'm allowed to do that, aren't I?'

'If you really want to.'

Her phone rings again. This time I don't let go of your hand. 'Yep,' she says. 'What?' She looks at me in an odd way. 'Yeah. I'll ring you back.'

'What?' I ask, not caring if I'm overstepping the mark.

'Wait here,' she tells me. 'I'll be ten seconds.'

Once she's gone, I walk over to the table and pour myself a glass of water. 'She's not allowed to leave us alone,' I say. 'She told me on the way here. But she has. Which is good. It means she trusts me more than she did at first. Maybe seeing us together's made her realise . . .' I take a deep breath. 'Juliet tried to kill you, Robert. You can divorce her. And then we can get married. Will we still go to the Traveltel every Thursday once we're married? It wouldn't surprise me if you—' I stop. My heart springs up into my throat. I blink, to check I'm not hallucinating.

Your eyelids and lips are twitching. Your eyes are open.

I drop the water, run over to you, grab your hand. 'Robert?'

'Naomi.' It's more of an exhalation than a word spoken aloud.

'Oh, God. Robert. I . . .' I'm afraid to speak.

Your mouth is moving, as if you're trying to say something else. Your face contorts.

'Are you in pain?' I ask. 'Shall I call a nurse?'

'Go away. Leave me alone,' you whisper.

I stare at the dry white ridges of skin on your lips. Shake my head. It's impossible. There's no way. You don't know what you're saying. 'It's me, Robert. Not Juliet.'

'I know who you are. Leave me alone.'

Something inside me is falling, falling. This cannot be happening. You love me. I know you do. 'You love me,' I say aloud. 'And I love you.' I've felt it once before, this tearing feeling, the sensation of everything good in the world being ripped away from me. I know from experience that it's only a matter of seconds before it tears off completely and I'm adrift: every last link to safety and happiness has been destroyed and there is nothing to cling on to.

'Get out,' you say.

'Why?' I am too shocked and cold inside to cry. If you were in your right mind, you would not have said what you said, but I still have to ask for an explanation; what else can

I do? I want to pound your chest with my fists and make you be your real self again. This is my worst nightmare. Before the police found you, when my imagination was full of dreaded tragic endings, I never once thought of this.

'You know why,' you say, looking straight at me. But I don't. I am about to say this, to start pleading with you, when suddenly your back arches and you groan. Your eyes roll back and you begin to shake, as if there's an earthquake inside your body. White foam spills out of your mouth. It's a few seconds before I remember the emergency button and press it. I hear a faint, repetitive bleep coming from the corridor.

'Naomi?' Sergeant Zailer's voice is behind me. She looks at my finger on the button, at the glass and spilled water on the floor. 'Jesus Christ!' She drags me by my arm out into the ward corridor. 'What the fuck happened?' she yells. My body feels limp and icy, like a sponge that's been left in cold water. My mind searches frantically for an emergency exit, a way to undo the last few minutes of my life.

I don't care what you said. I would happily die if it meant you would live.

The last thing I see before I am pushed out of the intensive care unit is three nurses running into your room.

'I haven't told you the truth,' I confess to Sergeant Zailer. 'I lied. I'm sorry.' This morning I didn't care a damn what she thought. She has no idea how much I need from her now, how the power balance has shifted. For as long as I was sure you loved me, I was all-powerful.

We are nearly in Rawndesley. I don't want to be dropped off at my house, alone. I can't let Sergeant Zailer leave me there. I have to keep her talking. As she drives, I fight off vivid memory flashes – like movie stills – from what happened to me before, when I was kidnapped: the bed with acorn posts, the wooden table. The man. Your love for me was a padded layer that kept all that at bay, and now it's been peeled away. My soul is mangled and exposed.

'Lied?' says Sergeant Zailer. I feel as if I might suffocate in her indifference.

'My rape story was true, all of it. Except it wasn't Robert. I don't know who he was. I'm sorry for lying.' Yvon was right. This is all my fault, everything bad that's happened. I told a lie that blended the best thing in my life with the worst thing. Sacrilege. Casual vandalism, you would call it. And now I'm being punished.

'I could and should charge you with obstruction,' says Sergeant Zailer. 'What about the panic attack at Robert's window, last Monday, the terrible thing you claimed you saw but couldn't remember? Was that a lie too?'

Another bright flash, like a shutter being pulled back, and I can see your living room again. I am there, looking through the glass. I gasp, grabbing the seat, the dashboard. 'Stop,' I manage to say. 'Please!' I fumble with the catch that will release the door as if my life depends on it, like a person whose car is submerged in water. I can see that room, the glass cabinet. I am zooming in in my mind, speeding towards it. I have to get out.

Sergeant Zailer pulls over by the kerb. I open the car door and take off my seat belt. 'Put your head between your knees,' she says. I feel better with the belt off. The tight feeling in my chest gradually subsides and I gulp in as much air as I can. Sweat drips from my forehead on to my hands.

'Where did you find him?' I ask, panting. 'Robert. Was he in the lounge? Tell me!'

'He was in the bedroom, lying on the bed,' said Sergeant Zailer. 'We found nothing in the lounge.'

What I saw – the unbearable thing – was in the glass cabinet. I know that now, but I'm scared to tell Sergeant Zailer. A specific detail like that might make her suggest we go there, and I can't. I'd rather swallow poison than look through that window again.

'What's your first name?' I ask, once I've got my breath back.

She frowns, as if annoyed to be asked. 'Charlotte,' she says. 'Why?'

'Can I call you Charlotte?'

'No. I hate the name, makes me sound like a Victorian aunt. I'm Charlie, and no, you can't call me that either.'

'Phone the hospital again. Please.'

'Robert's still alive. If he wasn't, I'd have had a call.'

I am too weak to argue. 'Whatever I've said and done wrong, you've got to understand . . . I'm fighting for my life,' I tell her. 'That's how it feels.'

'Naomi, do you remember I left Robert's room to make a phone call?' Sergeant Zailer says gently.

I nod.

'DS Kombothekra from West Yorkshire CID showed Prue Kelvey and Sandy Freeguard a photograph of Robert earlier today. That's what the call was about.'

At first I can't place any of the names. Then I remember. I close my eyes, relieved. I hadn't even realised I'd been waiting for this news. 'Good,' I say. 'So you no longer suspect Robert of being a serial rapist.' The stupid, awful thing I did has been undone and we can all forget it ever happened.

'Prue Kelvey said she wasn't sure . . .'

'What? What do you mean?'

'She didn't make a positive identification, but she said he was the right type, it might have been him.'

'That's ridiculous. She can't remember. She probably thought it must be Robert, if a cop was showing her his photo, and she didn't want to ruin things by pointing out that it wasn't him!'

'I'm sure that's true,' says Sergeant Zailer. 'It's not her response I'm interested in. We've got a DNA profile to compare with Robert's in her case, so if he didn't do it, that'll soon prove it . . .'

'What do you mean, *if* he didn't do it? You *know* I made up that story. Don't you? The part about Robert.'

She nods. 'I think so. But when a person lies as easily as you did, it's hard to know what to believe. Would you recognise your assailant's face, do you think, after all this time?'

'Yes.'

'You're more confident than Prue Kelvey. Her response to the photograph wasn't very useful. It's Sandy Free-guard's response I'm more interested in. She said Robert definitely wasn't the man that raped her—'

'Thank goodness one of them's got a memory!'

'—but she also said she knew him. "That's Robert Haworth," she said.'

My mind tilts. Once again, everything familiar starts to spin, to rearrange itself into a new, random pattern. Nothing is where I think it is, or what I think it is. 'Tell me,' I say.

'Three months after she was raped, she met Robert. They started going out together.'

'Where did they meet? That's bollocks. No woman who's been through anything like what I went through would get herself a new boyfriend so quickly.'

'Sandy Freeguard did. They met in Huddersfield town centre. Her car collided with his.'

'You mean his lorry?' I am determined to fend off each new fact as it approaches. There must be some mistake. I don't know this DS Kombothekra, so why should I trust what he says?

'No, Robert was in his car, a Volvo. The accident was Freeguard's fault, she says, and she was upset about it. Robert was very understanding, apparently, and they ended up going for coffee. That was how the relationship started.'

'But . . . no! It's too much of a coincidence!'

'You're telling me,' Sergeant Zailer says caustically. 'I don't understand it either. You and Sandy Freeguard were attacked in the same way, probably by the same man, and you both went on to have relationships with Robert Haworth. How can that be?'

Her confusion scares me more than my own. 'When?' I ask. 'When did this Sandy woman go out with Robert?'

'November 2004. She was raped in the August of the same year.'

I have heard the word 'rape' so many times in the past week. I no longer dread hearing it. It has lost its power. 'I met Robert in March 2005. When did they split up?' I have a horrible premonition of what Sergeant Zailer will say next. 'Oh, God. They didn't split up, did they?'

'Yeah, they did. Just before Christmas 2004. You thought Robert was two-timing you with her?'

'No. Only because—'

'Would you care? He was two-timing you with his wife, wasn't he? It wasn't as if you thought he was faithful to you.'

'It's totally different. I knew about Juliet. Of course I'd care if I found out Robert had been lying to me all the time we were together, hiding a secret girlfriend.' I take a few deep breaths. 'Why did they split up, Robert and this Sandy Freeguard? Did she say?'

'DS Kombothekra asked her about the relationship in detail, including the break-up. Apparently Robert was the model boyfriend – very attentive and keen – until one day he told her it was all over, completely out of the blue. He just switched off, she said. Came over all dutiful and husbandly, said he didn't feel he was being fair to his wife and that was it. So . . .' She shrugged.

'So what?' I say angrily. 'So you're trying to make out he's unreliable, the sort of person who'd blow hot one minute and cold the next? No way. He's loved me for a year. There's no way he'd turn against me.'

'Sandy Freeguard couldn't understand it either,' Sergeant Zailer says patiently. 'Naomi, loads of men – especially married ones – declare undying love right up until the point when they want nothing more to do with you.'

'Robert's not like other men, and his motives are nothing like theirs. You wouldn't understand unless you knew him.'

Sergeant Zailer starts the car engine. 'Close your door,' she says. 'I've got to get back. We're not going to work this out just sitting here.' She lights a cigarette as she drives. I wish I smoked. 'Sandy Freeguard and Robert never had sex. I assume that's not true of you and Robert.'

'No. We had sex every Thursday, for three hours. I'm not surprised she didn't want to, though, if it was only three months after.'

'She wanted to. It was Robert who insisted on waiting, said she couldn't possibly be ready. She told him about what had happened to her.'

Wetness clouds my eyes. 'That sounds like him,' I say. 'He's really thoughtful.'

'Sandy Freeguard found it irritating. She wanted to be treated normally, and he kept telling her to take it slowly, not to do too much too soon. She said he discouraged her from setting up a support group and training as a counsellor and all the positive things she wanted to do. He said she wasn't ready and she wouldn't be able to cope if she took on too much.'

'He was probably right.' I defend you even though you've just smashed my heart up. One day we'll resolve the misunderstanding and you'll take back what you said today. Why were you in Huddersfield, in your car instead of your lorry? Why weren't you working that day?

Sergeant Zailer is shaking her head. 'From what Sam Kombothekra says, Freeguard's a bit of a dynamo. She copes by putting herself and her experiences out there and trying to turn them into something positive, for herself and for others. He says she's a real inspiration.'

'Well, bully for her,' I say pettily. I can't help it. How does she expect me to react to hearing that I've been beaten hands down in the Best Rape Victim Contest?

'I didn't mean it like that.' She sighs. 'Sandy Freeguard told Kombothekra that she didn't believe Robert's reason for ending the relationship. Let's face it, if he cared that much about saving his marriage he wouldn't have started an affair with you only a few months later, would he? I'm inclined to agree with Freeguard: he couldn't handle knowing about the rape, so in the end he left her. That'd explain why he didn't want to have sex, too.'

'That's a terrible thing to say! Robert would never be like that.'

'Are you sure? Maybe you feared he would be, and that's why you didn't tell him about what happened to you.'

'I didn't tell anyone.'

'And yet Juliet Haworth knows what happened to you. Who told her, if not Robert?'

'You're twisting everything to fit in with—'

'I'm trying to,' she agrees. 'But no matter how hard I try, I can't get my head round this one. You say Robert didn't rape you, and, for what it's worth, I believe you. But I don't believe in coincidences.'

'Neither do I,' I say quietly.

She grimaces. 'Then, whether you like it or not – whether *I* like it or not – we have to face facts. Robert Haworth's connected to these rapes somehow.'

18

7/4/06

'He's unconscious again?' Unreasonably, Sellers felt slighted, as if Robert Haworth might have done it to spite them.

'An epileptic fit, a rebleed, swollen brain tonsils. And he's been having small but regular epileptic fits ever since. It's not looking good.' Gibbs shook his jacket off his shoulders and took a sip of his pint. He and Sellers were in the Brown Cow, not the nearest pub to work, but the only one in Spilling that served seven different kinds of Timothy Taylor beer. The walls and ceiling were covered in dark wood panelling, and there was a no-smoking room to the left of the front door, with a framed portrait of the eponymous brown cow on the wall. No bobby or detective would risk sitting in there, even the ones who didn't smoke, in case someone saw them. The sarge, who did, thought it wasn't fair that the non-smokers got the picture of the cow in their room, the pub's only painting. 'All we get is the crappy menu boards,' she often complained. A sign to the right of the bar warned customers that, from Monday 17 April, the entire pub would be a smoke-free zone.

'*Status epilepticus*,' said Gibbs, in a hard, bitter voice. 'Just our fucking luck. What did you order me?' He took another large gulp of his pint, and belched.

'Steak pie and chips. I haven't ordered for Waterhouse.'

'He'll have a pint, no food. He's got some fucking weird

hang-up about eating in front of other people. Don't tell me you haven't noticed.'

When all was well, Sellers and Gibbs sometimes discussed Simon Waterhouse's peculiarities, but Sellers was reluctant to do so with Gibbs in this mood.

'I bet you're having chicken with something fancy stuffed up its arse, fruit or some shite like that.'

'Where's the sarge?' Sellers ignored the sneery tone. In fact, he had ordered a perfectly respectable haddock and chips.

'At the hospital, brushing up on boffin jargon.' Everything Gibbs said sounded like an excellent way to end a conversation.

Sellers tried again. 'I see we've got some extra bodies drafted in to help with the donkey work. How did Proust wangle that?'

'Waste of time. Half of them are on to the theatres, half are ploughing through rape porn sites on the Net, but so far, nothing. That cunt Juliet Haworth's still not talking, and we can't do a fucking thing about that, can we?'

'Meaning?'

'Meaning, she smashed her husband's head in with a rock. She's made it pretty clear our words will never hurt her, the cocky bitch. Time for some sticks and stones.'

'You want to start beating up women now? Look good on your CV, that will.'

'If it stops *innocent* women getting pulled off the street and raped . . .'

'How can that be down to Juliet Haworth?'

Gibbs shrugged. 'She knows something. She knew what had happened to Naomi Jenkins, didn't she? Know what I reckon? Haworth's our rapist, whatever Jenkins is saying now. And his cunt of a wife helped him.'

So why are you looking at me like it's my fault? Sellers wondered if he was getting paranoid in his old age.

'I spoke to the people at SRISA about Tanya from Cardiff,' said Gibbs. 'They had her details.'

'And?'

'Killed herself. Overdose.'

'Shit. When?'

'Last year. Want some more good news? Speak Out and Survive were a wash-out. They had nothing. New computers, very little paperwork. I've got someone on it, but I doubt we'll be talking to survivor thirty-one any time soon.'

'*Shit.*'

'Yeah. It is, really. Still, don't let it get you down.' Gibbs faked a sickly smile. 'You're off away with Suki soon, aren't you? Sun, fun and sex. You won't want to come back.'

'You're telling me,' Sellers murmured, ignoring the snide delivery. He was already getting worried about what he'd do when the holiday was over, when he no longer had it to look forward to. He was of the view that it was the anticipation of the sex more than the sex itself that made adultery and infidelity well worth the risk.

'If Stacey finds out where you are, you won't have the option of coming back, even if you want to. Maybe I could invite Suki to my wedding. That'd be a nice surprise for Stacey, wouldn't it?'

It took a lot to make Sellers lose his temper, but Gibbs had been putting in the hours recently. 'What the fuck's your problem? Are you jealous, is that it? You've got your honeymoon coming up. Where is it you're going? Seychelles?'

'Tunisia. My honeymoon. Of course – an age-old tradition. If you get married, you have a honeymoon.'

'What?' Sellers couldn't grasp the implication, if there was one.

'Traditions are important, aren't they? Wouldn't want to miss out,' said Gibbs. The last two words sounded clipped, exaggerated. Foam from his pint coated his upper lip.

Hearing the song that had begun to blare from the jukebox, Sellers realised that every day he liked Chris Gibbs less and less. 'Are you having second thoughts?' he asked.

'Second thoughts about what?' contributed a voice from behind them.

'Waterhouse! What are you . . . Oh, you've got one.' Sellers was pleased to see him. Anything to avoid a heavy conversation with Gibbs about feelings. Was Gibbs even capable of such a feat?

'Sorry I'm late,' said Simon. 'There've been some developments. I just got off the phone with forensics.'

'And?'

'The stain-remover on the Haworths' stair carpet. There's blood underneath it – Robert Haworth's.' Sellers opened his mouth, but Simon answered before he had a chance to ask. 'The stairs are visible from the front door. The master bedroom isn't. Anyway, there was too much blood in the bedroom. There'd have been no point even trying.'

'What other developments?' asked Sellers.

'Robert Haworth's lorry. Traces of semen all over the floor. Not his.'

'I bet loads of lorry drivers have a wank in the back of the van when they stop at services,' Gibbs mused.

'*Not* his?' Sellers echoed. 'Definitely?'

Simon nodded. 'That's not all. The keys to the lorry were in the house, and they've got Juliet Haworth's fingerprints on them as well as her husband's. That in itself might not be significant. All the keys in the Haworths' house live in a pottery bowl on the table in the kitchen, so Juliet could have touched the ones for the lorry when she was replacing her house keys, but . . .'

'The long, thin room Kelvey and Freeguard mentioned . . .' Sellers thought aloud. 'Haworth's lorry.'

'That was my first thought too,' said Simon. 'But where's the mattress? It wasn't in the lorry, and forensics got nothing from the one Robert Haworth was found lying on in his bedroom, just Haworth's DNA and Juliet's.'

'Naomi Jenkins mentioned a plastic cover on the mattress in her statement,' Sellers reminded him.

'Kelvey and Freeguard didn't,' said Simon. 'I rang Sam Kombothekra, asked him to check. There was no plastic cover in either case. Just a bare mattress. Which, let's face it, was probably taken to some tip and dumped.' He exhaled slowly. 'You're right, though. Kelvey and Freeguard were raped in Haworth's lorry. One of the long sides isn't metal – it's made of a sort of thick canvas. It's just a huge flap of material, basically, with ties all along the bottom to attach it to the side of the floor. Freeguard said something about a cloth wall. It's got to be the lorry.'

'I reckon Juliet Haworth's the driving force behind the rapes,' Gibbs tried his theory out on Simon. 'She's got a male accomplice, the one who's been dripping his cum all over the back of Haworth's lorry, but she's the brains behind it. She's been using hubby's lorry as a venue, selling tickets to live rapes. Nice little earner. So much for her not working.'

'Naomi Jenkins looks down on her for being a kept woman,' said Simon thoughtfully. 'She's always making jibes about it.'

'Kept, my arse.' Gibbs snorted. 'She probably makes more money from her little business than Haworth does from his driving.'

'I'm not sure,' said Sellers. 'We only know of four definites: Jenkins, Kelvey, Freeguard and survivor thirty-one. And only two of those were in the long, thin room. The others were in this theatre place, wherever the fuck.'

'Why the change from theatre to van?' said Simon.

'There might have been a lot more who didn't report it,' said Gibbs. 'Jenkins, Kelvey and Freeguard all said the rapist threatened to kill them. And if that wasn't enough of an incentive to keep quiet, let's face it, a lot of women wouldn't want to go public and be seen as damaged goods, and a lot of men *would* see them that way. Whatever they say.'

'All right,' said Sellers wearily. 'But assuming you're right about Juliet and her accomplice, did Robert Haworth know? Was he in on it?'

'My gut feeling is that he didn't. Maybe he found out, and that was why Juliet went for him with the doorstop,' said Simon. 'Here's something, though: when Charlie spoke to Yvon Cotchin, Cotchin told her that Naomi Jenkins had said Robert didn't do overnight jobs any more. Apparently Juliet didn't like him being away from home – that was the reason he gave Jenkins, anyway . . .'

'But you're thinking maybe she didn't like the lorry being away from home, because she needed it for her own work,' Sellers completed Simon's hypothesis for him. 'If you're right, it'd explain a few things. Robert Haworth started going out with both Sandy Freeguard and Naomi Jenkins *after* they were raped – three months after, in Freeguard's case and two years after in Jenkins'. Maybe Juliet fixed him up with them somehow.'

'Yeah, right,' Gibbs sneered. 'How exactly would she have managed that?'

'How, and why?' Simon chewed the inside of his lip, thinking. 'And even if she tried to, would Haworth really go along with it? I wondered about that, and decided it was impossible. Unlikely, at least.'

'I can answer the why,' said Gibbs. 'She's a pervert. She gets a sexual kick out of knowing her husband's knobbing these women who have already been knobbed by the rapist. Whoever he is.'

'But then Haworth'd have to contrive to meet them and strike up a relationship with them – it's too much effort. What's in it for him? Is he also a pervert? And who's to say the women'd want to get involved with him?'

'That's the kick, for both of them,' Gibbs persisted. 'Her arranging the rapes, then him fucking the victims. Spices up their sex life. *That*'s why Robert Haworth isn't doing the rapes himself. The women'd hardly go out with him if they recognised him as the man who raped them, would they?'

Sellers couldn't see it. 'Kombothekra said Sandy Freeguard never had sex with Haworth. She wanted to, he didn't. And he's been seeing Naomi Jenkins for a year. Why so long, if it's just so he and his wife can get their rocks off?'

'Is it possible for a couple to suffer, jointly, from Munchausen's syndrome by proxy?' Simon wondered aloud. He wasn't hopeful, but it was a theory. Sometimes the bad ones led on to good ones. 'If it is, perhaps the idea's that Juliet arranges the ordeal, then Robert comes along afterwards and looks after the women, helps them recover, rebuilds their confidence. Kombothekra said Sandy Freeguard complained about Haworth trying to mollycoddle her. He didn't want her to do too much too soon. Wouldn't have sex with her, for that reason.'

He frowned, seeing the flaw in what he was putting forward. 'But Naomi Jenkins didn't even tell him she was raped, and from what she's told us, it sounds as if he treated her completely differently, not like a victim at all. The two of them went to bed together within a couple of hours of meeting.'

'It's bollocks.' Gibbs yawned. 'I've never heard of couples having Munchausen's by proxy. It's an individual thing. You wouldn't talk about it, would you? How would they find out they both had it?'

'You're probably right,' said Simon. 'I might check with an expert, though.'

'Expert!' Gibbs scoffed.

'It's the weirdest thing I've ever come across,' said Sellers, his forehead creased with concentration. 'Robert Haworth's got to be the link – Juliet knew the MO for the rapes, and two of the victims went on to be Haworth's girlfriends . . . but that's it, isn't it? They *went on* to be his girlfriends. Does it make sense to say he's the link when he only met Freeguard and Jenkins *after* they'd been kidnapped and raped?'

Simon ran his finger around the circumference of his pint glass. ' "Human uncertainty is all that makes the human reason strong. We never know until we fall that every word we speak is wrong." '

'What the fuck's that?' Gibbs snapped.

'Juliet Haworth wrote it down for us,' said Sellers.

'It's by a C. H. Sisson,' said Simon. 'He died recently. The poem's called "Uncertainty".'

'Great. Let's set up a fucking reading group,' said Gibbs.

'Do you think it means anything?' asked Sellers. 'Was Juliet Haworth trying to give us some sort of message?'

'Loud and clear.' Gibbs looked disgusted. 'She's taking the piss. Give me ten minutes alone with her . . .'

'She's implying that we're wrong about everything.' Simon tried not to sound as depressed as he felt. 'That we'll only realise *how* wrong when it's too late.' Or perhaps that she herself had only realised, too late, that she was wrong about Robert, and that was why she tried to kill him? No, that was reading too much into it, surely.

Simon changed the subject. 'How did you do with the backgrounds? Is there anything in Juliet Haworth's that looks like it might lead us to her accomplice, assuming she's got one?'

'I've got a list of names of old friends, one or two business contacts,' said Sellers. 'Her parents were helpful.' And distraught to hear that their only child had been charged with attempted murder. Telling them that hadn't been a pleasant task.

'Business as in making and selling her pottery cottages?'

'Yeah. She did pretty well with it. Remmicks stocked some of her stuff for a while.'

'So she's got a head for business.' Gibbs looked pleased with himself. 'Tell him the interesting bit.'

'I was just about to.' Sellers turned back to Simon. 'She's not seen them for years, the names on the list. She's not seen anyone but her husband, basically, since she had a nervous breakdown in 2001 due to overwork.'

'She doesn't seem the nervous type,' said Simon, remembering Juliet Haworth's confident manner; regal, almost. 'The opposite. Are you sure?'

Sellers gave him a withering look. 'I've spoken to the woman who was her doctor at the time,' he said. 'Juliet Haworth didn't get out of bed for six months. She'd worked like a maniac for years, apparently, without a break, no holidays. She just . . . burned out.'

'Was she married to Robert then?'

'No. She lived alone before the breakdown, then moved back in with her parents after. She married Robert in 2002. I spoke to both her parents this morning, at length. Norman and Joan Heslehurst. Both say there's no way Juliet would harm Robert. But then they also insist she would want to speak to them and have them visit her, and we know she doesn't.'

'They won't be lying,' said Gibbs. 'They want to feel needed. Parents, aren't they?'

'Juliet and Robert met in a video shop,' Sellers continued to fill Simon in. 'In Sissinghurst, Kent. Blockbuster, on Stammers Road, near where the Heslehursts live. It was one of Juliet's first trips out, after the breakdown. She'd forgotten to take her purse and got upset when she got to the counter and realised. Robert Haworth was in the shop, in the queue behind her. He paid for her video and made sure she got home safely. Both parents seem to regard him as a bit of a saint. Joan Heslehurst's as upset about Robert as she is about Juliet. She says they've got him to thank for getting Juliet back on her feet. He was brilliant with her, apparently.'

Simon didn't like the sound of any of that, though he wasn't sure why. It sounded a bit too neat. He'd have to think about it. 'What was Haworth doing in a video shop in Kent? Where did he live at the time?'

'He bought the Spilling house just before his and Juliet's wedding,' said Gibbs. 'Before that, who knows. Fucking black hole's all the background we've got on him so far.'

'Was it something specific about Juliet Haworth's work that caused the breakdown?' asked Simon. 'Some change in her situation or circumstances?'

Gibbs leaned over to growl at a passing waitress about the food and why it was taking so long.

'She was becoming more and more successful,' said Sellers. 'Her mum said she was fine at the beginning, while the business was still struggling. It was when it started to do well that she fell apart.'

'Makes no sense,' said Gibbs.

'Yeah, it does,' said Simon. 'When things start to go right, that's when the pressure's really on. You've got to keep it up, haven't you?'

'Juliet's mum said she ran herself into the ground, worked day and night, stopped going out. She was completely driven. Always had been.'

'What do you mean?' said Simon.

'She was a high-flier all her life, before the breakdown. She was head girl at both her primary school and her secondary. An athlete too – she competed at county level, won bucket-loads of prizes. She was in the choir, got a music scholarship to King's College, Cambridge, which she turned down, went to art college instead . . .'

'She's still a high-flier,' said Gibbs, his face brightening at the sight of his steak pie emerging from the pub kitchen. 'Except now she's in the kidnap-and-sexual-assault business.'

'What sort of impression did you get of her personality?' asked Simon. The smell of Sellers' fish and chips was making his mouth water. He'd have to buy himself a sandwich on the way back. 'Manipulative? Devious? Defiant?'

'Not really. An extrovert, lively, sociable. A bit manic, though, her dad said, and when she was stressed about work she could get ratty and unreasonable. He did tell me she had a temper, before the breakdown. The mum was pissed off, as you can imagine. Thought he'd landed Juliet in it. I didn't point out how deep in it she was even before he opened his gob. The strangest thing was that both parents – everyone I've spoken to – talks as if there have been two Juliets, almost like two separate people.'

'Pre- and post-breakdown?' said Simon. 'That can happen, I suppose.'

'Her mum described the breakdown – what happened, you know.' Sellers rubbed his eyes and swallowed a yawn. 'Once she got going, I couldn't stop her.'

'What exactly did she say?' Simon ignored the dismissive grunt that came from Gibbs.

'One day Juliet was supposed to go round to her parents' place for dinner, and she didn't turn up. They phoned and phoned – nothing. So they went round. Juliet didn't answer the door, but they could tell she was in – her car was there, and loud music was playing. In the end her dad broke a window. They found her in her work room, looking like she hadn't eaten, slept or washed for days. She wouldn't speak to them, either – just looked through them, like they weren't there, and carried on working. All she said was, "I have to finish this." She kept saying it, over and over.'

'Finish what?' Simon asked.

'Whatever she was working on. Her mum said she used to get loads of commissions, and customers often wanted a fast turn around – presents, anniversaries. When it was done – in the early hours of the morning, after her mum and dad had sat and watched her half the night – they said, "You're coming home with us," and she didn't resist or anything. It was as if she didn't care what she did, her mum said.'

Gibbs nudged Sellers with his elbow. 'Waterhouse is starting to feel sorry for her. Aren't you?'

'Go on,' Simon said to Sellers. 'If there's more.'

'Not much, really. Her parents asked her who the model was for, the one she'd been working on until three in the morning – they thought, if it was that urgent, maybe they could deliver it, you know – but Juliet had no idea. All that frantic work, saying she had to finish it, and she couldn't even remember who it was for.'

'She'd flipped,' Gibbs summarised.

'After that night, though, she wanted nothing to do with work, couldn't even be in the same room as any of the stuff she'd made. She'd done a few for her parents, and they had to put them all in the cellar, so she didn't see them. And all the ones from her own house went in the parents' cellar too. And that was that – she's not worked since.'

'Yes, she has, she's just had a change of career,' said Gibbs. 'She's a workaholic, capable of driving herself mad – maybe that's what happened this time as well. The kidnap-and-rape business was a runaway success, she couldn't handle the pressure, so she lost it and went for her husband with a rock.'

'Her mum said she knew something was wrong,' Sellers spoke into his pint glass. 'Now, I mean. Before she found out what'd happened to Robert.'

'How come?' Simon asked.

'Juliet phoned out of the blue and said she wanted all the stuff back, all her pottery models.'

'When was this?' Simon did his best to conceal his annoyance. Sellers should have told him this first, the rest later.

'Last Saturday.'

'Two days after Haworth failed to show up for his meeting with Jenkins at the Traveltel,' said Simon thoughtfully.

'Right. Juliet didn't explain, just said she wanted it all back. She went and got it on the Sunday. She was in a good mood, according to her mum – better than she'd been for a long while. That's why her parents were so surprised when they heard—'

'So the little houses that Naomi Jenkins saw in the Haworths' lounge on the Monday . . . they'd been there less than twenty-four hours?'

'So what?' said Gibbs.

'I don't know. It's just interesting. The timing.'

'Maybe she was going to go back to it, making the models,' Sellers suggested. 'If she and Haworth had been involved in the rape thing together, and now he's in hospital, and maybe never coming out . . .'

'Yeah.' Gibbs nodded. 'She was planning to pretend all that never happened, and take up pottery again. She's a real charmer.'

'What about background on Haworth?' said Simon. 'And Naomi Jenkins?'

Sellers looked at Gibbs, who said, 'Nothing yet on Haworth. And nothing on his sister Lottie Nicholls. I've been busy with the websites this morning, but I'll chase it.'

'Naomi Jenkins is straightforward,' said Sellers. 'Born and grew up in Folkestone, Kent. Went to boarding school, did very well. Middle-class background, mother a history teacher, father an orthodontist. Studied typography and graphic communication at Reading University. Plenty of friends and boyfriends. Lively, an extrovert . . .'

'Just like Juliet Haworth,' said Simon. His stomach rumbled.

'Why don't you order something to eat?' Gibbs suggested. 'Is it some kind of Catholic guilt syndrome? Punish the flesh to purify the soul?'

The old Simon would have wanted to floor him. But personality could change, in response to a traumatic or significant event. For ever after, you saw your life as divided into two distinct time zones, pre and post. At one time everyone, Gibbs included, was wary of Simon's temper. Not any more. It had to be a good thing.

Simon had decided not to phone Alice Fancourt. It was too much of a risk. He'd be crazy to allow his feelings for her to destabilise him again. Avoid complication and trouble – that was the rule he tried to live by. His decision had nothing to do with Charlie. What did Simon care if she was pissed off with him? It wasn't as if it hadn't happened before.

He saw a fleeting panic in Sellers' eyes at the same time as he felt cold air on the back of his neck. He knew who had swung through the pub's double doors before he heard the voice.

'Steak pie and chips. Fish and chips. I remember what it felt like to be unconcerned about cholesterol.'

'Sir, what are you doing here?' Sellers pretended to be pleased to see him. 'You hate pubs.'

Simon turned round. Proust was staring at the food. 'Sir, did you . . . ?'

'I got your note, yes. Where's Sergeant Zailer?'

'On her way back from the hospital. I said so in the note,' Simon told him.

'I didn't read it *all*,' said Proust, as if this should have been obvious. He leaned his hands on the table, making it wobble. 'It's a shame the DNA from the lorry doesn't match Haworth's. It's another shame that Naomi Jenkins and Sandy Freeguard are insisting Haworth didn't rape them.'

'Sir?' Sellers provided the required prompt.

'We have a new complication. I like life when it's simple. And this isn't.' The inspector picked up one of Sellers' chips and put it in his mouth. 'Greasy,' was his verdict. He wiped his mouth on the back of his hand. 'I've been answering your phones like a secretary while you lot have all been draped over a pub jukebox swilling ale. Yorkshire rang.'

What, the whole county? Simon nearly said. The Snowman was scared of anything that constituted 'up north'. He liked to keep it vague, general.

'I don't know how much you all remember from past interludes of sobriety,' said Proust, 'but their lab's been comparing the DNA profile of Prue Kelvey's rapist with Robert Haworth's. Ring any bells?'

'Yes, sir,' said Simon. Sometimes, he thought, pessimists were pleasantly surprised. 'And?'

Proust took another chip from Sellers' plate. 'It's an exact match,' he said in a heavy voice. 'There's no room for ambiguity or interpretation, I'm afraid. Robert Haworth raped Prue Kelvey.'

'Will you ring Steph again if she doesn't ring you back?' asked Charlie.

It was ten o'clock and she was in bed already. Having a much-needed early night. With Graham, and the bottle of red wine he'd brought all the way from Scotland. 'We do have wine in England, you know,' she'd teased him. 'Even in a hick town like Spilling.'

It had a been a long, hard, confusing day at work, and Charlie had been pleased to get home and find Graham on her doorstep. More than pleased. Thrilled. He'd come all this way to see her. It would never occur to most men – Simon, for example – to do something like that. 'How did you know my address?' she'd grilled him.

'You booked one of my chalets, remember?' Graham had smiled nervously, as if worried his gesture, his pilgrimage, might be interpreted as over the top. 'You wrote it down for me then. Sorry. I know it's a bit stalker-ish to turn up unannounced, but, firstly, I've always admired the diligence of the stalker, and secondly . . .' He tilted his head forward, hiding his eyes behind a curtain of hair. Deliberately, Charlie suspected. ' . . . I . . . er . . . well, I wanted to see you again, and I thought—'

Charlie hadn't let him say anything else before she'd clamped her mouth on to his and dragged him inside. That was hours ago.

It felt comfortable having Graham in her bed. She liked the smell of his body; it reminded her of chopped wood and grass and air. He had a first in classics from Oxford, yet he smelled of outside. Charlie could imagine going to a funfair with him, to a performance of *Oedipus*, to a bonfire. An all-rounder. What – who – could be better, she asked herself rhetorically, making no space in her mind for an answer.

'I hope you're not going to cast me aside again, ma'am,' Graham had said, as they lay among their discarded clothes on Charlie's lounge floor. 'I've been feeling a bit like a male Madame Butterfly ever since you scarpered in the middle of the night. Mr Butterfly, that's me. It was pretty scary, I'll have you know, turning up here uninvited. I thought you'd be busy with work, and I'd end up feeling like one of those doe-eyed wives in Hollywood movies, the ones whose husbands have to drop everything to save the planet from immediate destruction by asteroid or meteorite or deadly virus.'

'Yeah, I've seen that film.' Charlie had grinned. 'All five hundred versions of it.'

'The wife, you'll have noticed, is always played by Sissy Spacek. Why does she never understand?' Graham had asked, twisting a strand of Charlie's hair round his finger, staring at it as if it were the most fascinating thing in the world. 'She always tries to persuade the hero to ignore the meteorite that threatens humanity in favour of the family picnic or the little league game. As forward planning goes, it's short-sighted. No understanding whatsoever of the principle of deferred gratification . . . unlike me . . .' Graham bent his head to kiss Charlie's breasts. 'What *is* little league, by the way?'

'No idea,' Charlie replied, closing her eyes. 'Baseball?' Graham chatted, she realised, in a way that Simon didn't. Simon said things he thought were important or else he said nothing at all.

Given what Graham had said about being ditched in favour of her work, Charlie had felt bad asking him the questions she needed to ask. She hadn't told him she'd been planning to phone him solely for that reason, instead of to suggest that they arrange to meet. What was wrong with her? Why hadn't she been bursting to see him again? He was sexy, funny, clever. Good in bed, albeit in a slightly over-eager-to-please sort of way.

When she'd finally plucked up the courage to ask him, Graham hadn't minded at all. He'd phoned Steph straight away. They were now waiting for her to ring back. 'You didn't tell her I wanted to know, did you?' asked Charlie. 'If you did, she'll never call.'

'You know I didn't. You were here when I rang her.'

'Yeah, but . . . didn't she know you were coming to see me?'

Graham chuckled. 'Course not. I never tell the dogsbody where I'm going.'

'She said you tell her about all the women you sleep with, in graphic detail. She also said a lot of them start out as customers.'

'The second part's not true. She meant you, that's all. She was trying to upset you. Most of my customers are fat middle-aged fishermen called Derek. Imagine the name Derek being moaned gently in the dark – it just doesn't work, does it?'

Charlie laughed. 'And the first part?' Did Graham think he could charm her into letting it drop?

He sighed. 'Once – and only because it was such an irresistible story – I told Steph about a woman I slept with. Static Sue.'

'Static Sue?' Charlie repeated slowly.

'I'm not kidding, this woman didn't move a muscle, just lay there, rigid, throughout. My stunning performance had no effect whatsoever. I kept wanting to stop and check her pulse, see if she was still with me.'

'I take it you didn't.'

'No. It would have been too embarrassing, wouldn't it? The funny thing was, the minute we disentangled ourselves, she started moving again, normally. She got up as if nothing had happened, smiled at me and asked me if I wanted a cup of tea. I tell you, I had a few worries about my technique after that little episode!'

Charlie smiled. 'Stop fishing for compliments. So . . . why would Steph want to upset me? Just because I used your computer, or . . . ?'

Graham gave her a wry look. 'You want to know what's going on with me and Steph, guv?'

'I wouldn't mind,' said Charlie.

'I wouldn't mind knowing what's going on with you and Simon Waterhouse.'

'How . . . ?'

'Your sister mentioned him, remember? Olivia. No nicknames from now on, I promise.'

'Oh, right.' Charlie had done her best to forget that awful moment: Olivia's outburst from the literal and moral highground of her mezzanine bedroom.

'Have you two patched things up yet?' Graham leaned on one elbow. 'She came back, you know.'

'She *what*?' He'd sounded a little too offhand for Charlie's liking. Anger rose inside her. If he meant what she thought he meant . . .

'To the chalet. The next day, after you'd gone. She seemed disappointed not to find you. I told her something important had come up at work . . . Why are you looking at me like that?'

'You should have told me this straight away!'

'That's not fair, guv. You've only just given me my mouth back. We've been busy, remember? It's not as if I've been twiddling my thumbs. Or, if I have, it was with the best possible intentions . . .'

'Graham, I'm serious.'

He shot her a knowing look. 'You haven't kissed and made up, have you? You thought your sis was still sulking, so you left her to it. Now you feel guilty and you're trying to pin it on me. An innocent bystander!' He stuck out his lower lip, curling it over in mock unhappiness.

Charlie was unwilling to acknowledge how right he was. 'You should have phoned me straight away. You've got my number. I gave it to Steph when I booked.'

Graham groaned and covered his eyes with his hands. 'Look, most people don't appreciate it when the proprietors of their holiday accommodation take an active interest in their family feuds. I know we almost—'

'Exactly.'

'—but we didn't, did we? So I was playing hard to get. Briefly, yes – I admit it, Officer – but at least I had a go. Anyway, I thought *she'd* phone you. She didn't seem annoyed any more. She apologised to me.'

Charlie's eyes narrowed. 'Are you sure? Are you sure this was my sister, not just someone who looked like her?'

'It was Fat Girl Slim as I live and breathe.' Graham rolled away so that she couldn't hit him. 'We had quite a nice chat, actually. She seemed to have revised her opinion of me.'

'Don't assume that, just because she wasn't laying into you.'

'I didn't. No initiative or guesswork was required. She told me. Said I'd be much better for you than Simon Waterhouse. Which reminds me: you didn't answer my question.'

Charlie was furious with her sister for interfering. She wondered if Olivia's new approach was a more subtle way of trying to ensure that Charlie and Graham didn't start a relationship. Was she relying on Charlie's rebellious streak to kick in?

'Nothing's going on with me and Simon,' she said. 'Absolutely nothing.'

Graham looked worried. 'Except you're in love with him.'

I could easily deny it, thought Charlie. 'Yes,' she said.

He bounced back quicker than most men would have. 'I'll grow on you, you'll see,' he said, chirpy again. Charlie thought he might be right. She could make him right if she tried, surely. She didn't have to be another Naomi Jenkins, falling apart because some bastard told her to leave him alone. A bigger bastard than Simon Waterhouse; Charlie was doing better than Naomi on every front. Robert Haworth. A rapist. Prue Kelvey's rapist. Charlie was still struggling to take in the implications.

Against Simon's advice, she'd given Naomi a full update on the phone this afternoon. She couldn't exactly say she'd grown to like the woman, and she certainly didn't trust her, but she thought she understood how Naomi's mind worked. A bit too well. An otherwise intelligent woman made foolish by the strength of her feelings.

Naomi had taken the news about the DNA match better than Charlie had expected her to. She'd gone silent for a while, but when she spoke, she sounded calm. She'd told Charlie that the only way she could deal with any of this was by finding out the truth, all of it. There wouldn't be any more lies from Naomi Jenkins – Charlie was convinced of that.

Naomi was due to talk to Juliet Haworth again tomorrow. If Juliet was involved in some kind of sick money-making scheme with the man who'd raped Naomi and Sandy Freeguard, Naomi was possibly the only person who could provoke her into letting something slip. For some reason that Charlie couldn't discern, Naomi was important to Juliet. Nobody else was, certainly not her husband – Juliet had made that abundantly clear. 'I'll *make* her tell me,' Naomi had said shakily on the phone. Charlie admired her determination, but warned her not to underestimate Juliet's.

'Well, I'm not in love with the dogsbody, you'll be glad to hear,' said Graham, yawning. 'Though I have . . . taken a dip, shall we say. Every now and then. But she's nothing compared to you, Sarge, however corny that sounds. I've had more than enough of her. You're the one I want, with your tyrannical charm and your impossibly high standards.'

'They are not!'

Graham snorted with laughter, folded his arms behind his head. 'Sarge, I can't even begin to understand what you require of me, let alone deliver it.'

'Yeah, well. Don't give up too easily.' Charlie feigned sulkiness. Graham had slept with Steph. *Taken a dip*. She could hardly complain, given what she'd just told him.

'Aha! I can prove that Steph means nothing to me. Wait till you hear this.' His eyes twinkled.

'You're a ruthless gossip, Graham Angilley!'

'Remember the song? Grandmaster Flash?' He began to sing. 'White lines, going through my mind . . .'

'Oh, yeah.'

'Steph, the dogsbod, has got a white line dividing her bum in half. Next time you come to the chalets, I'll get her to show you.'

'No thanks.'

'It looks as ridiculous as it sounds. Now, you *know* I could never be serious about a woman like that.'

'A white line?'

'Yeah. She spends hours on sunbeds, and as a result her arse is bright orange.' Graham smiled. 'But if you were to – how shall I put this? – separate one buttock from the other—'

'All right, I get the gist!'

'—you'd see a clear white stripe. You can see it a little bit even when she's just walking around.'

'Does she often walk around naked?'

'Actually, yes,' said Graham. 'She's got a bit of a thing for me.'

'Which you've done nothing to encourage, of course.'

'Of course not!' Graham faked outrage.

His mobile phone began to ring and he picked it up.

'Yup.' He mouthed, 'White line,' at Charlie, so that she didn't have to wonder who he was speaking to. 'Uh-huh. Okay. Okay. Great. Well done, mate. You've earned your stripes, as they say.' He nudged Charlie.

She couldn't help laughing. 'Well?'

'No Naomi Jenkins. Never been to the chalets.'

'Oh.'

'But she checked for any Naomis, being the thorough little terrier that she is. There was a Naomi Haworth – H, a, w, o, r, t, h – booked a chalet for a weekend last September. Naomi and Robert Haworth, but Steph said the wife made the booking. Is that any use to you?'

'Yes.' Charlie sat up, pushing Graham's hand off her. She needed to concentrate.

'Before you get your hopes up . . .'

'What?'

'She cancelled. The Haworths never turned up. Steph remembers her cancelling and says she sounded upset. Sounded like she was crying, in fact. Steph wondered if the husband had dumped her or died or something, and that was why she was having to cancel.'

'Right.' Charlie nodded. 'Right. That's . . . great, that's really helpful.'

'Are you going to tell me now what it's all about?' Graham tickled her.

'Stop it! No, I can't.'

'I bet you'd tell this Simon Waterhouse character all the details.'

'He already knows as much as I do.' Charlie grinned at his hurt look. 'He's one of my detectives.'

'So you see him every day?' Graham sighed, falling back on the bed. 'Just my luck.'

19

Friday 7 April

Yvon sits beside me on the sofa and places a small cake plate between us. There's a sandwich on it. She doesn't look at it, doesn't want to draw it to my attention in case that inspires me to reject it.

I stare at the television's blank grey screen. To embark upon eating anything, even this soft white bread, would be too much of an undertaking. Like setting off to run a marathon while you're still recovering from a general anaesthetic.

'You haven't eaten all day,' says Yvon.

'You haven't been with me all day.'

'You've eaten?'

'No,' I admit. I don't know how much of the day is left. It's dark outside, that's all I know. What does it matter? If Yvon hadn't turned up, I wouldn't have left my bedroom. There is only space in my head for you at the moment, nothing else. Thinking about what you said and what it meant. Hearing the coldness and the distance in your voice over and over. In a year, in ten years, I'll still be able to play it in my mind.

'Shall I turn on the TV?' Yvon asks.

'No.'

'There might be something light, something—'

'No.' I don't want to be distracted. If this enormous pain is all I have left of you, then I want to concentrate on it.

I prepare myself to say something more substantial. It takes a few seconds, and energy I don't feel I can spare. 'Look, I'm really glad you came and I'm glad we're friends again, but . . . you might as well go.'

'I'm staying.'

'Nothing's going to happen,' I tell her. 'If you're hoping for progress, forget it. There's not going to be any. I'm not going to start to feel better, or put it to one side and chat about something else. You can't take my mind off it. All I'm going to do is sit here and stare at the wall.' Somebody ought to paint a big black cross on my door, like they did during the Plague.

'Maybe we should talk about Robert. If you talk about it—'

'I won't feel better. Look, I know you're only trying to help, but you can't.' I long to let my grief pull me under. Fighting it, making an effort to appear civilised and in control, is too hard. I do not say this, in case it sounds melodramatic. You're only supposed to talk about grief when someone has died.

'You don't have to put on any kind of act for me,' says Yvon. 'Lie on the floor and howl if you want. I don't care. But I'm not leaving.' She curls up at the other end of the sofa. 'Have you thought about tomorrow?'

I shake my head.

'What time's Sergeant Zailer coming to get you?'

'First thing.'

Yvon swears under her breath. 'You can't speak or eat, you can barely summon the energy to move. How the hell are you going to get through another interview with Juliet Haworth?'

I don't know the answer to that. I'll get through it because I have to.

'You should ring Sergeant Zailer and tell her you've changed your mind. I'll do it for you, if you want.'

'No.'

'Naomi . . .'

'I have to speak to Juliet if I want to find out what she knows.'

'What about what *you* know?' Yvon's voice is loaded with frustration. 'I've never been Robert's greatest supporter, but . . . he *loves* you, Naomi. And he's not a rapist.'

'Tell that to the DNA experts,' I say bitterly.

'They've got it wrong. So-called experts make mistakes all the time.'

'Stop, please.' Her false consolations are making me feel even more wretched. 'The only way I can handle this is to face up to the worst possibility. I'm not going to let myself latch on to some unlikely theory, and be disappointed again.'

'Okay.' Yvon humours me. 'So what is the worst possibility?'

'Robert's involved in the rapes,' I say, in a dull, dead voice. 'He does some, the other man does some. Juliet's involved, maybe even in charge. They're a team of three. Robert knew all along that I was one of the other man's victims. Same with Sandy Freeguard. He went out of his way to meet us for that reason.'

'Why? That's crazy.'

'I don't know. Maybe to check we weren't going to go to the police. That's what spies do, isn't it? They infiltrate enemy territory, report back.'

'But you said Sandy Freeguard had already been to the police, before she started seeing Robert.'

I nod. 'The boyfriend of a rape victim would know how the investigation was progressing, wouldn't he? The police would keep the victim informed and the victim'd confide in her boyfriend. Maybe Juliet – or the other man, or Robert, or all three of them – wanted to be able to keep tabs on what the police were up to, in Sandy Freeguard's case. Haven't we always said Robert's a control freak?' I cannot stop the tears from escaping as I say this.

Do you know what the worst thing is? All the kind, loving, sweet things you've said and done have been so much more concrete and tangible in my mind since you rejected me in the hospital. It would help if I could make the bad times stand out, step forward into the spotlight. Then I might find a pattern I've overlooked until now and prove to my heart how wrong it has been about you. But all I can think of are your passionate words. *You have no idea how precious you are to me.* You said that at the end of every phone call, instead of goodbye.

My memory has turned against me, is trying to overwhelm me with the contrast between how you were this morning and how you have been in the past.

'Why did Juliet smash Robert's head in with a stone?' asks Yvon, picking up half of my sandwich and taking a bite. 'Why does she want to provoke you and taunt you?'

I can't answer either question.

'Because Robert *is* in love with you. It's the only possible explanation. He finally got round to telling her that he was leaving her for you. She's jealous – that's why she hates you.'

'Robert's not in love with me.' I am crushed by the weight of these words. 'He told me to go away and leave him alone.'

'He wasn't thinking straight. Naomi, she tried to kill him. If your brain had been bleeding and swelling, if you'd been unconscious for days, you wouldn't know what you were saying either.' Yvon brushes crumbs off the sofa on to the floor. It's her idea of cleaning. 'Robert loves you,' she insists. 'And he's going to get better, all right?'

'Great. I get to live happily ever after with a rapist.' I stare at the bread on the floor. For some reason it makes me think of the Hansel and Gretel fairy tale. Food is essential to any rescue mission. *Magret de Canard aux Poires* from the Bay Tree. There was food on the table in the little theatre where I was attacked, course after course.

'Put that sandwich down,' I tell Yvon. 'Are you hungry?'

She looks caught out, ashamed to be thinking of food at a time like this. I'm also thinking about it, though I don't think I could eat even a mouthful. 'What time is it? Will the Bay Tree still be taking orders?'

'The *Bay Tree*? You mean the most expensive restaurant in the county?' Yvon's expression changes; the agony aunt has been replaced by the strict headmistress. 'That's where Robert got that food from, wasn't it, the day you met him?'

'It's not what you think. I don't want to go there because I'm nostalgic for the good old days,' I say bitterly, mortified to think of what I used to believe in: the past, the future. The present. What you've done to me is worse than what the rapist did. He made me a victim for a night; thanks to you, I've been mocked, debased and humiliated for over a year without even knowing about it.

Yvon could see there was something wrong with our relationship from the start. Why didn't I see it? Why can I still not see it? I am determined to think the unthinkable about you, believe the unbelievable, because I have to kill the part of me that loves you in spite of everything I've been told. It should be small and ailing by now, but it isn't. It's huge. Rampant. It has spread inside me like a cancer, conquered too much territory. I don't know what'll be left of me if I succeed in wiping it out. Just scars, emptiness, a gaping hole. But I have to try. I must be as ruthless as a hired assassin.

Yvon doesn't understand why I suddenly want to go out, and I'm not ready to explain it to her. One horror at a time. 'If it's not nostalgia, then why the Bay Tree?' she says. 'Let's go somewhere else and not bankrupt ourselves.'

'I'm going to the Bay Tree,' I tell her, standing up. 'Are you coming or not?'

The building that houses the Bay Tree bistro is one of the oldest in Spilling. It's been standing since 1504. It has low ceilings, thick uneven walls and two real fires – one in the bar area and one in the restaurant itself. It resembles a well-turned-out grotto, though it's entirely above ground level. There are only eight tables, and normally you have to book at least a month in advance. Yvon and I were lucky; it's late, so we got a table somebody had booked weeks ago for seven-thirty. By the time we arrived, they were long gone – sated and not insignificantly poorer.

The restaurant has an outer door, which is always locked, and an inner door, to ensure that no cold air from the High Street dilutes the warmth inside. You have to ring a bell, and the waiter who comes to let you in always makes sure to close the first door before opening the second. Most of the staff are French.

I've been here once before, with my parents. We were celebrating my dad's sixtieth birthday. He banged his head on the way in. The Bay Tree's ceilings are a hazard, if you're tall. But I don't need to tell you that, do I, Robert? You know the place better than I do.

On that night, with my parents, we had a waiter who wasn't French, but my mother persisted in speaking to him in very slow simple English and in a quasi-continental accent: 'Can we av zee bill, pleez?' I restrained myself from pointing out that he was probably born and brought up in Rawndesley. It was a celebration, so no carping was allowed.

You've never met my parents. They don't even know about you. I thought I was protecting myself from their criticism and disapproval, but it turns out that they are the protected ones. It's an odd thought: that the large majority of people in the world – Mum and Dad, my customers, shoppers I pass on the street – have not had their lives devastated by you. They don't know you and never will.

And it's the same the other way round. The waiter who is looking after me and Yvon tonight – a little too atten-tively: he hovers too close to our table, his posture stiff and formal, one arm behind his back, surging forward to replenish our wine glasses each time one of us takes a sip – he has probably had his life shattered, at one time or another, by somebody whose name would mean nothing to me.

Only in a very minor, trivial sense do we inhabit the same world as others.

'How's your food?' asks Yvon.

I ordered only a starter, the foie gras, but she can see I haven't touched it. 'Is that some sort of trick question?' I say. 'Like, have you stopped beating your wife yet? Is the present king of France bald?'

'If you aren't planning to eat anything, what the hell are we doing here? Do you realise how much this meal's going to cost? The minute we walked in, I felt as if my bank account had turned into an hourglass. All my hard-earned money is sand, trickling away.'

'I'll pay,' I tell her, waving the waiter over. Three steps

and he's at our table. 'Could we have a bottle of champagne, please? The best one you've got.' He scuttles off. 'Anything to get rid of him,' I say to Yvon.

She stares at me, open-mouthed. 'The *best*? Are you crazy? It'll cost a million quid.'

'I don't care what it costs.'

'I don't understand you! Half an hour ago . . .'

'What?'

'Nothing. Forget it.'

'Would you rather I was back on my sofa, staring into space?'

'I'd rather you told me what's going on.'

I grin. 'Guess what?'

Yvon puts down her cutlery, steels herself for an unwelcome revelation.

'I don't even like champagne. It makes the inside of my nose itch and gives me really bad wind.'

'Jesus, Naomi!'

Once you accept that nobody is ever going to understand you, and overcome the enormous feeling of isolation, it's actually quite comforting. You're the only expert in your own little world, and you can do what you want. I bet that's how you feel, Robert. Isn't it? You picked the wrong woman when you picked me. Because I am capable of understanding how your mind works. Is that why you now want me to leave you alone?

The waiter returns with a dusty bottle, which he presents to me for inspection. 'That looks fine,' I tell him. He nods approvingly and disappears again.

'So why's he taken it away?' asks Yvon.

'He's gone to get one of those posh cooling buckets and special champagne glasses, probably.'

'Naomi, this is freaking me out.'

'Look, if it'll make you happy we can go to the drive-through Chickadee's tomorrow and you can buy a bucket full of birds' wings boiled in fat, okay? If you can't handle the high life.' I giggle, feeling as if I'm speaking lines written by someone else. Juliet, perhaps. Yes; I am aping her brittle, glib delivery.

'So, what's the deal with you and Ben?' I ask Yvon, remembering that her life has not ended even though mine has.

'Nothing!'

'Really? That big a nothing? Wow.' Ben Cotchin is not that bad. Or if he is, he's bad in a normal way. Which, the way I'm feeling at the moment, seems quite benign – perhaps the best anybody can hope for.

'Stop it,' says Yvon. 'I was uspet and I didn't have anywhere else to go, that's all. And . . . Ben's given up drinking.'

The waiter returns with our champagne in a silver bucket full of ice and water, a stand on wheels to support the bucket, and two glasses. 'Excuse me,' I say to him. Might as well do what I came here to do. 'Have you worked here long?'

'No,' says the waiter. 'Only three months.' He is too polite to ask me why, but there is an enquiry in his eyes.

'Who's been here the longest? What about the chef?'

'I think he has been here for a long time.' His English is meticulously correct. 'I could ask him, if you wish.'

'Yes, please,' I say.

'Shall I . . . ?' He nods at the champagne.

'Afterwards. Speak to the chef now.' Suddenly I can't wait.

'Naomi, this is insane,' Yvon hisses at me as soon as we're alone again. 'You're going to ask the chef if he remembers Robert coming in and ordering that meal for you, aren't you?'

I say nothing.

'What if he does? So what? What are you going to say then? Are you going to ask him what exactly Robert said? Did he look like a man who'd just fallen in love? This is *not* healthy, indulging your obsession like this!'

'Yvon,' I say quietly. 'Think about it. Look around you, look at this place.'

'What about it?'

'Eat your expensive food, it's going cold,' I remind her. 'Does this look like the sort of restaurant that'd let someone dash in off the street and order a takeaway? Can you see a takeaway menu anywhere? The sort of place that'd let a complete stranger walk out with not only food but also a tray and cutlery and an expensive cloth napkin? And just trust him to bring it back, when he was finished with it?'

Yvon considers this, chewing a mouthful of lamb. 'No. But . . . why would Robert lie?'

'I don't think he lied. I think he withheld certain crucial facts.'

Our waiter returns. 'I introduce you to our chef, Martin Gilligan,' he says. Behind him is a short, thin man with untidy ginger hair.

'How's your food?' Gilligan asks, in what sounds like a northern accent. I had a friend at university who was from Hull; this chef's voice reminds me of his.

'It's fantastic, thanks. Amazing.' Yvon smiles warmly. She says nothing about thinking it's overpriced.

'Etienne said you wanted to know how long I've worked here?'

'That's right.'

'I'm fixtures and fittings.' He looks apologetic, as if he

fears we might accuse him of being unadventurous for staying. 'I've been here since it opened in 1997.'

'Do you know Robert Haworth?' I ask him.

He nods, looks pleasantly surprised. 'Is he a friend of yours?'

I won't say yes to this, even if doing so would help the flow of the conversation. 'How do you know him?'

Yvon watches us as she might a tennis match, her head turning back and forth.

'He used to work here,' says Gilligan.

'When? For how long?'

'Oh . . . let's see, it must have been 2002, 2003, something like that. It was a good few years ago. He'd just got married when he started, I remember that. Told me he'd just got back off his honeymoon. And he left . . . ooh, about a year later. Went on to be a lorry driver. He said he preferred open roads to hot kitchens. We're still in touch, still have the odd bevvy now and then, at the Star. Though I've not seen him for a while.'

'Robert worked in the kitchen, then? He wasn't a waiter.'

'No, he was a chef. My second-in-command.'

I nod. That's how you were able to get your hands on your little surprise for me. They knew you at the Bay Tree – you'd worked here – so of course they trusted you. Naturally, they let you take a tray and cutlery and a napkin, and Martin Gilligan was only too happy to cook *Magret de Canard aux Poires* for you when you told him it was urgently needed to help a woman in distress.

I don't need to ask any more questions. I thank Gilligan, and he returns to the kitchen. Like Etienne, our waiter, he is too discreet to demand to know why I felt the need to interrogate him.

The same doesn't apply to Yvon. As soon as we're alone again, she orders me to explain. The temptation to be facetious and evasive is strong. Games are safer than reality. But I can't do it to Yvon; she's my best friend, and I'm not Juliet.

'Robert once said to me that being a lorry driver was better than being a commis,' I tell her. 'I didn't understand. I thought he meant Commie, Communist, which didn't seem to make much sense, but he didn't. He meant a commis chef – c, o, m, m, i, s. Because that's what he used to be.'

Yvon shrugs. 'So?'

'The man who raped me served a three-course meal to the men who watched,' I say. 'Every now and then he disappeared into a room at the back of the theatre and came out with more food. That room had to be a kitchen.'

Yvon is shaking her head. She can see where I'm going, and she doesn't want it to be true.

'I've never really thought about who cooked the food.'

'Oh, God, Naomi.'

'My rapist had his hands full. He had to entertain the men, clear each course, bring the next course. He was front of house.' I laugh bitterly. 'And we know he didn't operate alone, from what Charlie Zailer's said. At least two of the rapes took place in Robert's lorry, and it was Robert who raped Prue Kelvey.' I am making the agony worse, deliberately taking as long as I can to arrive at my conclusion. Like when you've got an elastic band round your wrist and you pull it back as far as it'll go, stretching it until it's taut and skinny, then letting it snap back against your skin. The further away it is, the more you know it will hurt you in the end. *Hurting distance.* Isn't that what you called it?

Yvon has stopped trying to defend you. 'While that man was attacking you, Robert was in the kitchen,' she says, giving up, letting me know I've convinced her. 'He cooked the meal.'

I jolt awake, with a scream trapped in my throat. I am soaked in sweat, my heart drumming fast. A bad dream. Worse than being awake, than real life? Yes. Even worse than that. Once I've waited long enough to check I'm not having a stroke or a heart attack, I turn to the radio alarm clock by my bed. I can only see the tops of the digits, small glowing red lines and curves poking out behind the tall pile of books on my bedside cabinet.

I knock the books on to the floor. It's three-thirteen in the morning. Three one three. The number terrifies me; the hammering in my chest speeds up. Yvon wouldn't hear me if I called her, even if I screamed. Her room is in the basement, and mine is on the top floor. I want to run downstairs to where she is, but there isn't time. I fall back; fear pins me to the bed. Something is about to happen. I must let it happen. I have no choice. Pushing it away only works for so long. Oh, God, please let it be over quickly. If I have to remember, then let me remember *now*.

I was Juliet. I pulled that certainty out of the nightmare with me. I've dreamed of being your wife for so long, but always while I'm awake. And the dream was that I, Naomi Jenkins, was your wife. I have never wanted to be Juliet Haworth. You talked about her as if she were weak, craven, pitiable.

In my dream, the worst I've ever had, I was Juliet. I was tied to the bed, to the acorn bedposts, on the stage. I had turned my head to the right, so that my cheek was flat against the mattress. My skin stuck to the plastic covering. It was uncomfortable, but I couldn't turn to look straight ahead, because then I'd have seen the man, seen the expression on his face. Hearing what he was saying was bad enough. The men in the audience were eating smoked salmon. I could smell it – a disgusting pink fishy smell.

So I kept my head where it was and stared straight ahead, at the edge of the curtain. The curtain was dark red. It was designed to go round three sides of the stage, every side apart from the back. Yes, that's how it looked. I didn't remember that before. And there was something else unusual about it. What? I can't remember.

Beyond the edge of the curtain was the theatre's inside wall. I looked down at a small window. That's right: the window wasn't at eye level, it was lower than that. It wasn't at eye level for the men around the table either.

I wipe sweat from my forehead with the corner of my duvet. I'm sure I'm right, the dream was accurate. That window was odd. It had no curtain. Most theatres don't have windows at all, not in the auditorium. I had to cast my eyes downwards to see it, and the men would have had to look up. It was between the two levels, in the middle. As it got darker, I stopped being able to see anything. But before, when I was Juliet in the dream and I was lying on the bed, and that man was cutting off my clothes with a pair of scissors, I could see what was outside. I fixed my eyes on it, trying not to think about what was happening, what was going to happen . . .

I throw the duvet off me, feel the chill night air rush in to cover me instead. I know what I saw through the small theatre window. And I know what I saw through the window of your living room, Robert. And why I had the dream I've just had; I know what it all means now. It changes everything. Nothing is as I thought it was.

Thought I *knew* it was. I cannot believe how wrong I've been.

Oh, God, Robert. I have to see you and tell you everything – how I worked it out, put it all together. I must persuade Sergeant Zailer to take me to the hospital again.

20

8/4/06

EDITED TRANSCRIPT OF AN INTERVIEW
SPILLING POLICE STATION, 8 APRIL 2006, 8.30 A.M.

Present: DS Charlotte Zailer (C.Z.), DC Simon Waterhouse (S.W.), Miss Naomi Jenkins (N.J.), Mrs Juliet Haworth (J.H.).

J.H.: Morning, Naomi. What is it they say? We must stop meeting like this. Did you and Robert ever say that to each other?

N.J.: No.

J.H.: I'm relying on you to help me talk some sense into these morons. They all woke up this morning convinced that I'm a porn magnate. [*Laughs.*] It's ridiculous.

N.J.: Is it true you first met Robert in a video shop?

J.H.: Why would a woman run a company that profited from other women being raped? [*Laughs.*] Though I suppose you might say that someone who tries to pulverise her husband's brain with an enormous stone is capable of anything. Do you think I did it, Naomi? Do you think I sold tickets to men who wanted to watch you being raped? Paper tickets, torn in two at the door, like when you go to the pictures? How much do you think you were worth?

S.W.: Cut it out.

N.J.: I know you didn't do that. Tell me about how you met Robert.

J.H.: Sounds like you already know.

N.J.: In a video shop?

J.H.: *Oui. Si.* Affirmative.

N.J.: Tell me.

J.H.: I just did. Have you got Alzheimer's?

N.J.: Did he approach you, or did you approach him?

J.H.: I bashed him over the head with a video, dragged him home and forced him to marry me. The funny thing was, all the time he was shouting. 'No, no, Naomi's the one I love.' Is that what you want to hear? [*Laughs.*] The story of how I met Robert. Picture poor little me in the queue for the till, clutching the video case in my sweaty paws, shaking with nerves. It was the first time I'd left the house in ages. I bet you can't see me as a nervous wreck, can you? Look at me now – I'm an inspiration to us all.

N.J.: I know you had a breakdown, and I know why.

[*Long pause.*]

J.H.: Really? Do share.

N.J.: Go on. You were in the queue.

J.H.: I got to the front and found I'd forgotten my purse. It felt like the end of the world. My first trip out – my parents were so proud – and I'd gone and ruined it by forgetting to bring any money. Nearly wet myself, I did. I knew I'd have to go home empty-handed and admit I'd failed, and I knew I wouldn't dare to go out again after that. [*Pause.*] I started mumbling to the woman behind the till – don't remember what, really. Actually, I think I just kept apologising over and over again. Everything's my fault, you see. Ask our good detectives here. I'm a wannabe murderess *and* a theatrical porn entrepreneur. But back to the story: next thing I know, someone's tapping me on the shoulder. Robert. My hero.

N.J.: He paid for the video.

J.H.: Paid for the film, scooped me up off the floor, walked me home, reassured me, reassured my parents. God, they were keen to get me off their hands. Why do you think I married Robert so quickly?

N.J.: I imagine it was a whirlwind romance.

J.H.: Yes, but what made the wind whirl? I'll tell you: my parents didn't want to look after me, and Robert did. It didn't scare him like it scared them. Madness in the family.

N.J.: Didn't you love him?

J.H.: Course I bloody did! I was a total wreck. I'd given up on myself, proved beyond a shadow of a doubt that I was comprehensively worthless, and Robert came along and told me I'd got it all wrong: I wasn't worthless at all, I'd just been through a bad patch and needed to be looked after for a while. He said that some people weren't cut out for working, that I'd already achieved more than most people did in a lifetime. He promised to look after me.

N.J.: This great achievement – he meant those ugly pottery houses of yours? I've seen them. In your lounge. In the cabinet with the glass doors.

J.H.: And?

N.J.: Nothing. I'm just telling you I've seen them. It's funny. Your work made you have a nervous breakdown, yet you've got those models all over your living room. Don't they remind you? Bring back memories you'd rather forget?

[*Long pause.*]

C.Z.: Mrs Haworth?

J.H.: Don't interrupt, Sergeant. [*Pause.*] My life's had its ups and downs, but do I want to erase it from my memory? No. Call me vain if you want to, but it's important to me to hang on to some sort of evidence that I've existed. If that's all right with all of you? So that I know I didn't imagine my entire fucking life?

N.J.: I can understand that.

J.H.: Oh, I'm so pleased. I'm not sure I want to be understood by someone who pulls her pants down for the first stranger she bumps into in a service station. A lot of rape victims go on to become promiscuous, I believe. It's because they feel worthless. They give themselves to anyone.

N.J.: Robert isn't anyone.

J.H.: [*Laughs.*] That's certainly true. Boy, is that true.

N.J.: Did you get to know him properly before you fell in love with him?

J.H.: No. But I know a lot about him now. I'm a real expert. I bet you don't even know where he grew up, do you? What do you know about his childhood?

N.J.: I told you before. I know he doesn't see his family, that he's got three sisters . . .

J.H.: He grew up in a small village called Oxenhope. Do you know it? It's in Yorkshire. Just down the road from Brontë country. Which is a greater masterpiece – *Jane Eyre* or *Wuthering Heights*?

N.J.: Robert raped a woman who lived in Yorkshire. Prue Kelvey.

J.H.: So I've been told.

N.J.: Did he do it?

J.H.: You should get Robert on the subject of the Brontës. Assuming he ever speaks to you again. Or anyone, for that matter. He thinks Branwell was the one with the real talent. Robert goes for the underdog every time. When he was growing up, he had a poster of a painting of Branwell Brontë on his wall – a feckless drunkard and a layabout. Odd, isn't it? With Robert being such a hard worker.

N.J.: What are you implying?

J.H.: He only told me all this after we were married. He saved it, he said, like people used to do with sex in ye olde days. I assume you've noticed my husband's addiction to deferred gratification. What else? His mum was the village bike, and his dad was involved with the National Front. Left the family for another woman, in the end. Robert was six. It really fucked him up. His mum never stopped loving his dad, even though he'd discarded her, even though he'd used her as a punchbag for most of their marriage. And she didn't give a shit about Robert, even though he adored her. She just ignored him, or criticised him. And because they were so poor after the dad left, she had to stop shagging everything in trousers and go out to work. Guess what line of work she chose?

N.J.: Did she make ridiculous pottery ornaments?

J.H.: [*Laughs.*] No, but she was a businesswoman. Started her own company, just like you and me. Except hers was telephone sex. She made a lot of money from it, enough to send the kids to a posh private school. Giggleswick. Heard of it?

N.J.: No.

J.H.: Robert's dad never loved him. He labelled Robert the thick one, and the difficult one, the second child he'd been tricked into having that he'd never wanted. So when he upped and left, the mum blamed Robert for driving him away. Robert became the official black sheep. He failed his exams, despite the expensive education, and ended up working in the kitchen at the Oxenhope Steak and Kebab House. Maybe that's why he identifies with Branwell Brontë.

N.J.: You could be making this up. Robert's never told me any of this. Why should I believe you?

J.H.: Do you have a choice? It's the information I give you or it's no information. Poor Naomi. My heart bleeds.

N.J.: Why do you hate me so much?

J.H.: Because you were going to steal my husband, and I didn't have anything else.

N.J.: If Robert dies, you'll have nothing.

J.H.: [*Laughs.*] Wrong. You'll notice I used the past tense: I *didn't have* anything else. I'm fine now. I've got something much more important than Robert.

N.J.: What's that?

J.H.: Work it out. It's something you ain't got, I'll tell you that much.

N.J.: Do you know who raped me?

J.H.: Yes. [*Laughs.*] But I'm not going to tell you his name.

21

8/4/06

'The Brontës came from Haworth,' said Simon. 'Robert's surname is Haworth.'

'I know.' Charlie had had the same thought.

'Know the name of the man Charlotte Brontë married?'

She shook her head. It was the sort of thing Simon knew and most normal people didn't.

'Arthur Bell Nicholls. Remember Robert Haworth's sister Lottie Nicholls, the one he told Naomi Jenkins about?'

'Jesus. The three sisters! Juliet hinted that they were dead.'

'Looks like Haworth took his identification with Branwell Brontë a bit too far,' said Simon grimly. 'What about his surname? Think it's a coincidence?'

Charlie told him what she'd told Naomi Jenkins the previous day: 'I don't believe in coincidences. Gibbs is pursuing the Giggleswick School and Oxenhope angles, so we should have something concrete soon. No wonder we got nothing from the Lottie fucking Nicholls connection.'

'I don't like these interviews.' Simon swirled an inch of lukewarm tea around the bottom of his Styrofoam cup. 'Robert Haworth's two crazy women. They give me the creeps.'

He and Charlie were in the police canteen, a bare-walled, windowless hall with a broken one-armed bandit machine in one corner. Neither was happy with the backdrop, or the tepid, weak tea. Normally, they would have had a conversation like this in the Brown Cow over a proper drink, but Proust had made a comment to Charlie about how in future he wanted his detectives to do their work *at* work, not slope off to sleazy lap-dancing clubs in the middle of shifts.

'Sir, the only thing you're likely to find in your lap at the Brown Cow is one of Muriel's red napkins, before she serves you your lunch,' Charlie had objected.

'We come to work to work,' Proust roared. 'Not to indulge our tastebuds. A quick dash to the canteen every day – that's the lunch I've had for twenty years and you don't see me complaining.'

Funny, that was exactly what Charlie saw. Nor was it an unfamiliar sight. The Snowman was in a foul mood at the moment. Charlie had got him some prices from the most economical sundial-maker she'd been able to find, an ex-stonemason based in Wiltshire, but even he had said the final price, for the sort of dial Proust was after, would be at least two thousand pounds. Superintendent Barrow had vetoed the plan. Funds were limited, and there were higher priorities. Like fixing the one-armed bandit machine.

'Do you know what the cretin told me to do?' Proust had ranted to Charlie. 'He said the garden centre near where he lives sells sundials for much less than two grand. I've got his permission to buy one from there if I want to. Never mind that those ones are free-standing and our nick's got no perishing garden! Never mind that they don't even attempt to tell the time! Oh, did I forget to mention that crucial fact, Sergeant? Yes, that's right: Barrow doesn't see the difference between an ornamental, garden-centre dial that's just for show and a real one made to keep solar time! The man's a liability.'

Charlie heard Simon say, 'Proust.'

She looked up. 'What?'

'I think what we're doing's unethical. Tossing Naomi Jenkins into Juliet Haworth's cage, using her as bait. I'm going to talk to the Snowman about it.'

'He approved it.'

'He doesn't know what's being said. Both women are lying to us. We're getting nowhere.'

'Don't you bloody dare, Simon!' Threats wouldn't work with him. He was a contrary bugger, prone to thinking he was the sole guardian of propriety and decency. Another thing to blame on his religious upbringing. Charlie softened her tone. 'Look, the best chance we've got of working out what the fuck's going on here is if we let those two keep going at each other and hope something comes out of it. Something already has: we know more about Robert Haworth's background than we did yesterday.'

Seeing Simon's sceptical expression, Charlie added, 'All right, Juliet might be lying. Everything she says might be a lie, but I don't think so. I think there *is* something she wants us to know, something she wants Naomi Jenkins to know. We've got to give it time to come out, Simon. And unless you've got a better plan, I'd appreciate it if you didn't run snivelling to Proust and try to persuade him to fuck up mine.'

'You think Naomi Jenkins is tougher than she is,' said Simon in a level voice. He didn't rise to the bait any more, Charlie had noticed. 'She could crack at any time, and when she does, you'll feel shit about it. I don't know what it is with you and her . . .'

'Don't be ridiculous . . .'

Sophie Hannah

'Okay, she's intelligent, she's not a scuzz like a lot of the people we deal with. But you're treating her like she's one of us, and she's not. You're expecting her to do too much, you're telling her too much . . .'

'Oh, come on!'

'You're telling her everything to arm her against Juliet because you're sure Juliet's the one who tried to kill Haworth, but what if she isn't? She hasn't confessed. Naomi Jenkins has lied to us from the get-go, and I say she's still lying.'

'She's withholding something,' Charlie admitted. She needed to get Naomi on her own. She was sure she'd be able to get the truth out of her if they were alone.

'She knows something about whatever Juliet's not telling us,' said Simon. 'And Juliet can see that, and doesn't like it one bit. She wants to be the one with all the knowledge, releasing it piece by piece. She's going to stop talking, I reckon. No more interviews. It's the only way she can exercise her power.'

Charlie decided to change the subject. 'How's Alice?' she said casually. The question she'd resolved never to ask. *Damn.* Too late now.

'Alice Fancourt?' Simon sounded surprised, as if he hadn't thought about her for a while.

'Do we know any others?'

'I don't know how she is. Why would I know?'

'You said you were going to meet her.'

'Oh, right. Well, I didn't.'

'You cancelled?'

Simon looked puzzled. 'No. I never arranged to see her.'

'But . . .'

'All I said is, I might get in touch, see if she fancied meeting up. But I decided not to, in the end.'

Charlie didn't know whether to laugh or throw cold tea in his face. Anger and relief struggled for dominance inside her, but relief was the weaker feeling and didn't stand a chance. 'You fucking arsehole,' she said.

'Hey?' Simon adopted his most innocent expression: the bewilderment of a man who has been randomly accosted by trouble he could not have foreseen. What made it even more bloody irritating was that it was genuine. About work, Simon could be arrogant and overbearing, but in any personal matter he was self-effacing. Dangerously humble, Charlie had often thought. His modesty made him assume that nothing he said or did was likely to have an impact on anyone.

'You told me you were going to meet her,' she said. 'I thought it was all fixed up. You must have known I'd think that.'

Simon shook his head. 'Sorry. I didn't mean to give that impression, if I did.'

Charlie didn't want to talk about it any more. She'd shown that she cared. Again.

Four years ago, at Sellers' fortieth birthday party, Simon had rejected Charlie in a particularly unforgettable way. Not before he'd raised her hopes, though. They'd found a quiet, dark bedroom and closed the door. Charlie was sitting astride Simon, and they were kissing. That they would end up having sex had seemed a foregone conclusion. Charlie's clothes were in a pile on the floor, though Simon hadn't removed any of his. She should have been suspicious then, but she wasn't.

Without explanation or apology, Simon had changed his mind and left the room without a word. In his hurry, he'd not bothered to shut the door. Charlie had dressed quickly, but not before at least nine or ten people had seen her.

She was still waiting for something to happen to her that would neutralise that moment in her memory, make it cease to matter. Graham, perhaps. So much better for the ego than Simon and more accessible too. Perhaps that was the problem. Why was that invisible barrier so attractive?

'Go and see how Gibbs is getting on,' she said. It was strange to think that if she hadn't got the wrong end of the stick about Alice, she would not have invented a fictional boyfriend called Graham. And if she hadn't done that, she might not have been so determined to make something happen with Graham Angilley when she met him. On the other hand, she might have. Wasn't she Tyrannosaurus Sex, man-eater and all-round freak?

Simon looked worried, as if he thought it might be unwise for him to get up and leave now, though it was clearly what he wanted to do. Charlie didn't return his tentative smile. *Why haven't you asked me a single question about Graham, you bastard? Not one, since I first mentioned him.*

Once Simon had gone, she pulled her mobile phone out of her handbag and dialled the number of Silver Brae Chalets, wishing she'd remembered to get Graham's mobile number. She didn't want to have to navigate her way through a stilted conversation with the dogsbody.

'Hello, Silver Brae Luxury Chalets, Steph speaking, how may I help you?'

Charlie smiled. Graham had answered the phone the only other time she'd rung, from Spain, and he hadn't gone through that whole spiel. It was typical of him to make the dogsbody do the full receptionist bit that he'd never dream of doing himself.

'Could I speak to Graham Angilley, please?' Charlie put on a strong Scottish accent. A purist might say she didn't sound Scottish, but she didn't sound like herself either, which was what mattered. The disguise was purely strategic. Charlie wasn't scared of a confrontation with Steph – in fact, she was looking forward to telling the silly tart what she thought of her the next time they met; she'd been too stunned to respond after Steph's tirade in the lodge – but now wasn't the time for a verbal scrap. Charlie had no doubt that the dogsbody would prevent her from talking to Graham if she could, so subterfuge was her best bet.

'I'm sorry, Graham's not here at the moment.' Steph tried to make her voice sound more refined than the one Charlie had heard her use earlier in the week. Pretentious cow.

'Do you have a mobile number for him at all?'

'May I ask what it's regarding?' An edge crept into Steph's voice.

Charlie wondered if her Scottish accent was more rubbish than she'd allowed for. Had the dogsbody guessed who she was? 'Oh, just a booking. It's not important,' she backtracked. 'I'll ring again later.'

'There's no need,' said Steph, sounding sure of herself again. The hostility had vanished from her voice. 'I can help you with that, even if you spoke to Graham originally. I'm Steph. I'm the general manager.'

You're the fucking dogsbody, you liar, thought Charlie. 'Oh, right,' she said. She couldn't be bothered to go through the rigmarole of making a fake booking, one that'd need to be cancelled later, but she couldn't think of a way out. Steph was keen to demonstrate her efficiency. 'Erm . . .' Charlie began tentatively, hoping she sounded like a busy, multitasking Scot who was leafing through her diary.

'Actually,' said Steph conspiratorially, filling the gap in

the conversation, 'don't tell him I told you this, but you're better off dealing with me, not Graham. My husband's not the most precise person when it comes to admin. His head's usually somewhere else. I've lost count of the number of times people have turned up and I've had no idea they were coming.'

Charlie gulped air as the shock blasted through her. She felt winded, as if someone had punched her in the stomach.

'Oh, it's never a problem,' Steph chattered on confidently. 'I always sort it out and everybody's happy. We only ever have satisfied customers.' She giggled.

'Husband,' said Charlie quietly. No Scottish accent.

Steph didn't seem to notice the change, of pronunciation or of mood. 'I know,' she said. 'I must be mad, living with him *and* working with him. Still, like I always tell my friends, at least I won't have that culture shock that a lot of women get when their husbands retire and suddenly they're around all the time. I'm used to having Graham under my feet.' As Steph spoke, Charlie felt herself slowly deflating.

She pressed the end call button on her phone and marched out of the canteen.

When Charlie got back to the CID room and found Gibbs waiting for her practically on the threshold, his face contorted with impatience, her first thought was that she couldn't do it, couldn't speak to him. Not now. Conversations with Chris Gibbs required stamina and a certain amount of hardiness. She needed an hour alone. Half an hour, at least. Tough. Hers wasn't the sort of job where that was possible.

It had been a mistake coming straight back here. She'd passed the ladies' toilets on the way back from the canteen and considered going in, hiding in there until she was ready to face the world again. But who the fuck knew when that would be? And if she locked herself in a cubicle, she would cry, and then she'd have to wait fifteen minutes or so until her face looked normal again. Whereas going straight back to the CID room meant crying wasn't an option. Good, she'd thought. She had known Graham Angilley less than a week, for Christ's sake. She'd seen him a total of three times. It ought to be easy to forget about him.

'Where have you been?' Gibbs demanded. 'I've got that background on Robert Haworth.'

'Great,' said Charlie weakly. She didn't want to ask him to tell her what he'd got until she was sure she'd be able to stay and listen. It wasn't out of the question that she'd need to run to the loo after all.

'Well worth the wait, I'd say.' There was triumph in Gibbs' eyes. 'Giggleswick School and Oxenhope – both true. Sarge?'

'Sorry. Go on.'

'You told me it was urgent. Do you want to hear it or not?' Gibbs jabbed his head in her direction as he spoke, like an angry turkey. The body language of a bully.

At that moment Charlie couldn't have cared less about Robert Haworth's village of origin or education. 'Give me five minutes, Chris,' she said. That startled him. She'd never called Gibbs by his first name before.

She left the room and went to stand in the corridor, leaning her back against the wall. The ladies' toilets were tempting, but she resisted. Crying wasn't the answer – she bloody well refused to cry – but she needed to allow the adjustment process to complete itself. She couldn't be around any of her team for as long as she could feel a weight sinking inside her, while this loop of thoughts was endlessly repeating in her head. Five minutes, she thought, that's all I need.

Steph hadn't known it was Charlie on the phone, so why would she lie? She wouldn't.

Steph knew Graham had spent part of Wednesday night in Charlie's chalet, in bed with Charlie. In the lodge, after the row about the computer, Graham had ordered Steph to bring him and Charlie a full English breakfast in bed in the morning. He'd been specific: Charlie's bed, he'd said. 'That's where we'll both be.' Flaunting his infidelity in front of his wife.

And Charlie wasn't the only one, or the only one Steph was party to. There had been Static Sue as well. And countless other chalet customers, if Steph was to be believed.

Had Graham lied? Not technically. He'd admitted he'd slept with Steph, more than once.

Yes, he'd fucking lied.

He not only called Steph 'the dogsbody'; he treated her like one. He treated her terribly. No wonder Steph had been so antagonistic towards Charlie. And yet she stayed with Graham, joked about him affectionately on the telephone. *My husband's not the most precise person when it comes to admin.* Why did she stay with him?

He'd told Charlie about Steph's white line, the skin the sunbeds couldn't reach.

What had he told Steph about Charlie's anatomy?

He'd persisted in calling Olivia Fat Girl Slim, despite Charlie's protests.

Fact after fact, truth after unpalatable truth, stood out from the haze of rage and confusion in Charlie's brain. She knew the way it went, had been through something similar after Simon pushed her off his lap at Sellers' party and disappeared into the night: first there was the explosion of the big shock, then the many smaller aftershocks, as associated, subsidiary grounds for pain and horror presented themselves. Hundreds of small incidents demanded to be reconsidered in the light of the new knowledge. Sometimes several occurred to you all in one go, and it was like being peppered with tiny, lethal bullets.

Only after you'd been thoroughly peppered and pierced, and once the tremors had subsided, could you see the whole picture. Eventually, the succession of blows, major and minor, came to an end and you were more stable; you settled into your misery as if it were an old jumper.

Charlie didn't love Graham. She'd had to struggle to keep Simon out of her mind, for Christ's sake, even when they were having sex. So it was hardly the romance of the century. If Graham had phoned her and suggested calling it a day, that would have been fine. It wasn't losing him that stung; it was being made a fool of. She felt utterly humiliated, more so when she thought that, by now, Steph must have realised who the mysterious Scottish caller had been. She and Graham were probably having a hearty laugh at her expense at this very moment.

It was too similar to what Simon had done to her, that was what Charlie couldn't take. Was everyone's life full of such indignities, or was it just hers?

She wanted to make Graham pay in some way, but if she did or said anything at all, he would know she cared. To respond to his humiliation of her would be to acknowledge it, and Charlie was damned if she'd give him the satisfaction, him or Steph.

Still leaning against the wall outside the CID room, she dialled Olivia's number. Please, please answer, she thought, trying to transmit the words telepathically to her sister.

Liv was out. Her answerphone message had changed. It still said, 'This is Olivia Zailer. I can't come to the phone at the moment, so you'll have to leave a message after the beep,' but a new bit had been added: 'I'm particularly keen to receive messages from anyone who wants to apologise profusely to me. Any such calls will definitely be returned.' The tone was acerbic, but it didn't detract from the reassuring message. Two tears slid down Charlie's cheeks and she wiped them away quickly.

'Here's that message you've been waiting for,' she said to her sister's answerphone. 'I apologise profusely and more than profusely. I'm an enormous pillock and a dickhead, and I deserve to be keel-hauled. Although I don't think people are keel-hauled any more—' She stopped abruptly, realising she sounded like Graham. It was the sort of joke he'd make: self-conscious, protracted. 'Ring me tonight, please. Once again, my head and life are totally fucked up – sorry, I know it's getting a bit tedious – and I might have to throw myself under a train if you don't come to my rescue. If you're free tonight and can be arsed slogging up to Spilling, please, please come round. I'll leave the key in the usual place.'

'Sarge, for fuck's sake!' Gibbs had materialised in the corridor.

Charlie whirled round to face him. 'If I ever catch you eavesdropping on a call of mine again, I'll cut your bollocks off with a steak knife, have you got that?'

'I wasn't—'

'And don't fucking swear at me, and don't fucking order me around! Clear?'

Gibbs nodded, red in the face.

'Right.' Charlie took a deep breath. 'Good. What have you got on Haworth, then?'

'You're going to love this.' Gibbs looked, for the first time in weeks, as if he wouldn't mind delivering some good news. Charlie would have put money on a deterioration in his attitude, not so swift an improvement. Maybe she ought to give him more regular tongue-lashings. 'What Juliet Haworth told you and Waterhouse was true: shag-happy mum with a phone-sex business, dad heavily involved in far-right politics, one older brother, parents divorced, Giggleswick School—'

'What about the surname?' Charlie interrupted him.

Gibbs nodded. 'That's the reason we weren't finding the background on him: he wasn't born Robert Haworth. He changed his name.'

'When?'

'This is interesting too. Three weeks after he met Juliet in the video shop. But I've spoken to her parents, the Heslehursts, and they always knew him as Robert Haworth. That's who he said he was.'

'So he'd been planning the change for a while,' Charlie deduced aloud. 'And this was all long before he raped Prue Kelvey. Did he have a criminal record he wanted to lose?'

'Nope. Not a sausage. Clean as they come.'

'Why the name change, then?' said Charlie thoughtfully. 'Because he idolised Branwell Brontë?'

'He grew up on Haworth Road. Number fifty-two. His new surname was his old road name. Anyway . . . criminal record or no criminal record, he must have had something to hide.'

'Why won't he fucking wake up so that we can interview him?' Charlie snapped.

'He might, Sarge.'

'He won't. He's still having epileptic fits. Every time I speak to the ward sister, she tells me something new and bad: cerebellar tonsillar herniation, tonsillar haemorrhagic necrosis. Layman's terms? He's on his way out.' She sighed. 'So he was born Robert? You said "his new surname".'

'Yeah,' said Gibbs. 'Born on the ninth of August 1965. Robert Arthur Angilley. Unusual name, isn't it? Sarge? What's—'

Gibbs stared after her as she ran along the corridor and through the double doors that led to reception. Should he follow her? After a few seconds, he decided he ought to. He hadn't liked the way she'd looked before she ran: white-faced. Scared, almost. What the fuck had he said? Perhaps it wasn't anything to do with him. He'd overheard the tail end of her phone call, and she'd said something about her head being fucked up.

He felt a bit low for having vented his frustration as much on the sarge as on Waterhouse and Sellers. Sellers, especially. He was the one who really deserved it. The sarge was a woman; women's minds worked differently. He ought to have let her off the hook.

Gibbs ran through reception and out on to the steps, but he was too late. Charlie was already in her car, pulling out of the car park on to the road.

Part III

22

Saturday 8 April

In films, following someone in a car is always made to look difficult. If the person ahead knows he or she is being pursued, there are sudden turns down hidden alleyways, sideways lurches on to fields, brief flights through air that end with metallic crashes and fires. If the prey is oblivious, there are other hurdles: traffic lights that change at the worst moment, large vans that overtake and block the follower's view.

I've been lucky so far. None of these things has happened to me. I am in my car, following Sergeant Zailer in her silver Audi. I passed her as I was driving towards the police station, on my way to see her. She was zooming off in the opposite direction, apparently in a hurry. I did a three-point turn in the middle of the street, blocking the traffic on both sides, and set off after her.

I don't think Charlie Zailer has seen me, and I've been right behind her all the way out of the town centre. Spilling isn't the sort of place where other drivers cut in front of you. Most people are probably chugging along to some local antique or craft fair. The only person on the road with a sense of urgency is Sergeant Zailer. And me, as I can't risk losing her. I am careful not to let a space open between my car and hers. If she overtakes somebody, I glide past in her wake.

At the second roundabout after the High Street ends, she takes the first left turn. This is the road that leads to

Silsford. It goes on for miles, winding through countryside, dark like a tunnel because of the overhanging trees on both sides. I am fiddling with the radio, distracted, searching for loud music so that I won't have to be alone with my thoughts, when she turns again. Right, this time. I do the same. We're on a small street of red-brick terraced houses, all of which are set back from the road, with tiny square yards at the front. Most of the houses look smart from the outside. Some have brightly coloured external paintwork: jade green, lilac, yellow.

Cars line both sides of the street, and there are few spaces. Sergeant Zailer parks unevenly about halfway down and gets out of her Audi. I catch a glimpse of her face and see that she has been crying. A lot. Instantly, I know that she is not here for any reason to do with work. This is where she lives; something's wrong and she's come home.

She slams the car door and opens the red wooden gate, not bothering to lock the Audi. I am in my car, in the middle of her street, only a few metres away from her, but she hasn't noticed me. She doesn't look as if she is aware of her surroundings at all.

Shit. I have no idea what to do now. If something bad's happened, if there's been some sort of family tragedy, she won't want to talk to me. But who else can I go to? DC Waterhouse? I would not be able to persuade him to take me to the hospital again to see you, no matter what information I could give him in exchange. I feel his antipathy towards me every time I'm in a room with him.

I am being ridiculous. Sergeant Zailer, however upset she might be, and for whatever reason, is the officer in charge of your case. I have new information that I know she'll want, whatever state she's in.

I park in one of the few available spaces by the side of the road and walk back to her house. It's smaller than mine, which makes me feel guilty in a peculiar sort of way. I'd assumed she must live somewhere much bigger and grander than where I live, because she's a figure of authority. Not that I've always accepted her authority. I won't accept it now, if she says she won't take me to see you. I don't change, Robert. All that matters to me is you, now as always.

I ring the bell and get no response. She doesn't know who I am, doesn't know I've seen her go in. I ring again, pressing for longer this time. 'Go away!' she shouts. 'Leave me the fuck alone, whoever you are.' I ring again. A few seconds later, through the stained-glass panel in the front door, I see the blurred shape of her walking towards me. She opens it and recoils. I'm the last person she wants to see. I don't care. From now on, I don't think I will let small things get to me. I will enjoy not caring. Like your wife. She and I have got more than you in common, haven't we, Robert?

'Naomi. What are you doing here?' Charlie Zailer's eyes are watery and puffy, her nose red and raw.

'I was on my way to see you. You were driving away, so I followed you.' I say nothing about her obvious distress, guessing that this is what she would prefer.

'I'm not at work now,' she says.

'I can see that.'

'No, I mean . . . I'm not working. So this'll have to wait.' She tries to close the door, but I push it open with my arm.

'It can't wait. It's important.'

'Then find DC Waterhouse and tell him.' She puts her full weight behind the door and tries again to push it shut. I take a step forward so that I'm inside her hall. 'Get out of my house, you crazy bitch,' she says.

'There are things I need to tell you. I know what I saw through Robert's lounge window, why I had the panic attack—'

'Tell Simon Waterhouse.'

'I also know why Juliet's acting the way she is. Why she's not cooperating, and why she doesn't care that you think she tried to murder Robert.'

'Naomi . . .' Sergeant Zailer lets go of the door. 'When I go back to work, whenever that is, I'm not going to be working on Robert Haworth's case. I'm really sorry, and I don't want you to take this personally, but I don't want to speak to you any more. I don't want to see you or speak to you again. Okay? Now, will you go?'

Dread tugs at my heart. 'What's happened? Is it Robert? Is he still alive?'

'Yes. He's the same. Please go. Simon Waterhouse'll—'

'Simon Waterhouse'll look at me as if I'm a Martian, like he always does! If you send me away, I won't tell him or anyone else anything. None of you will ever know the truth.'

Sergeant Zailer pushes me out on to the street and is about to slam the door in my face. 'Juliet isn't involved in the rapes,' I shout from her front yard. 'If it's a business, she's nothing to do with it. She never has been.'

She looks at me. Waits.

'The theatre – there was a window,' I say breathlessly, tripping over my words. 'I could see it, when I was tied to the bed. I saw what was right outside. It was so close, not more than a few metres away. I only remembered because of a nightmare I had last night, that I'd seen something through that window. I mean, I always knew I'd seen the window, but that was all. I wasn't aware I'd seen anything else, but I must have, it must have been in my subconscious . . .'

'What did you see?' Sergeant Zailer asks.

I want to howl with relief. 'A little house. A bungalow.' I stop to catch my breath.

'There are thousands of bungalows,' she says. 'The theatre could be anywhere.'

'Not like this one. It's very distinctive. But that's not the point.' I can't get the words out fast enough. 'I've seen that little house again since then, since the night I was attacked. I saw it through Robert's lounge window. One of Juliet's pottery houses, in the cabinet with the glass doors. It's the same one, the one I saw through the window while I was being raped. It's made of bricks that look like stone, if that makes sense. They're the same colour as stone – they're probably reconstituted stone. And they're not smooth. They look as if they'd feel abrasive if you touched them. It's hard to explain if you haven't seen it. Royal-blue paintwork, a blue front door with an arched top—'

'—and three windows above the door, also with arched tops?'

I nod. I don't bother asking, knowing she wouldn't answer.

Charlie Zailer pulls her jacket off a peg in the hall and takes her car keys out of her pocket. 'Let's go,' she says.

For a while we drive in silence, no questions and no answers. There is too much to say; where would we start? We are back on the High Street, turn left at the Old Chapel Brasserie, on to Chapel Lane.

I promise I will never come to your house.

This is not where I want to be. It's not where you are.

'I want you to take me to see Robert again, in hospital,' I say.

'Forget it,' says Sergeant Zailer.

'Did you get into trouble for taking me to see him? Is that why you're upset? Are you in trouble at work?'

She laughs.

Three Chapel Lane still has its back turned to the road. I allow myself to entertain a strange fantasy – that only a few moments ago your house was facing forward, welcoming and open; it swivelled round only when it saw me coming. *I know who you are. Leave me alone.*

Sergeant Zailer parks badly, the tyres of her Audi scraping the kerb. 'You need to show me this pottery house,' she says. 'We need to know if it's really there or if you were imagining things. Are you likely to have another panic attack?'

'No. I was afraid of realising what it was I'd seen – that was what my mind was resisting. I got the panic over with last night. You should have seen my bedsheets – you'd think they'd fallen in a swimming pool.'

'Come on, then.'

We walk round the side of your house. Everything is the same as it was on Monday – the neglected rubbish dump of a garden, the impressive panoramic view. How often did you stand here, in the dead and dying grass, surrounded by the detritus of your life with Juliet, and wish you could escape to the beauty that was clearly visible but just out of reach?

I lead the way to the window. When Sergeant Zailer joins me, I point to the cabinet against the wall. The model of the bungalow with the blue arched door is there, on the second shelf down. 'It's the one next to the candle,' I say, feeling as shocked as I would have felt if it had been absent. But I suppose it's easy to mistake a sudden awareness that something significant has happened for surprise.

Charlie Zailer nods. She leans against your back wall, takes a packet of cigarettes out of her pocket and lights one. Her cheeks and lips have turned pale. The pottery bungalow means something to her, but I'm not sure what, and am afraid to ask.

I am about to mention again the possibility of going to see you in hospital when she says, 'Naomi.' From her expression, I know that there's another shock coming. I prepare myself for the impact. 'I know where that house is,' she says. 'I'm going to get into my car and drive there now. The man who raped you will be there when I arrive. I'm going to get a confession out of him, even if it means tearing his fingernails out with pliers, one by one.'

I say nothing, fearing she may have gone mad.

'I'll drop you at the taxi rank,' she says.

'But how . . . what . . . ?'

She is walking towards your gate, towards the road. She will not stop to answer my questions.

'Wait,' I call after her, running to catch up. 'I'm coming with you.' I am standing where Juliet stood on Monday. Sergeant Zailer stands where I stood. The choreography is identical; the cast has changed.

'That'd be unwise, from both our points of view,' she says. 'Your well-being and safety, my career.'

If I do this, if I go with her to the place, wherever it is, and see the man, then whatever happens, I will never have to think of myself as a coward again. 'I don't care,' I tell her.

Charlie Zailer shrugs. 'Neither do I,' she says.

23

'Has either of you seen Charlie?' Simon was anxious enough to call out to Sellers and Gibbs, in a louder voice than he'd normally think of using, while they were still some metres away.

'We were just coming to find you.' Sellers stopped by the drinks machine outside the canteen. He reached into his pocket for change.

'Something's up with her,' said Gibbs. 'No idea what. I was talking to her before—'

'Did you tell her Robert Haworth's real name?'

'Yeah, I started telling her—'

'Shit!' Simon rubbed the bridge of his nose, thinking. This was a serious problem. How much should he tell Sellers and Gibbs? Laurel and fucking Hardy, he thought. But he had to tell them.

'. . . I'd got as far as telling her Haworth was born Robert Angilley, and she just walked off,' Gibbs was saying. 'Out of the building, got in her car and off she went. She didn't look good. What's going on?'

'I couldn't find her, couldn't find any of you,' said Simon. 'Her mobile's switched off. She never does that – you know Charlie, she's never out of touch, and she never goes off without telling me where. So I phoned her sister.'

'And?' said Sellers.

'It's not good. This holiday she cut short, Spain, it was supposed to be.'

'Supposed to be?' said Gibbs. As far as he knew, that was where the sarge had been, where she'd flown back from when the Robert Haworth case started to get more complicated.

'The hotel was no good, so she and Olivia sacked it and booked a new place: Silver Brae Chalets in Scotland.'

Sellers looked up, spilling hot chocolate on his fingers. 'Shit!' he said. 'Silver Brae Chalets? The same one that's run by Robert Haworth's brother? I just jotted down the name, ten minutes ago.'

'Same one,' said Simon grimly. 'Olivia reckons Charlie and Graham Angilley are . . . involved in some kind of relationship.'

'She can't have been there more than a day!'

'I know.' Simon saw no need to tell Sellers and Gibbs the rest of what Olivia Zailer had told him: that Charlie had invented a fictional boyfriend called Graham to make Simon jealous, that when she'd met a real Graham she'd leaped at the chance of making her lie true. All that was too much for him to think about right now.

He stuck to the relevant facts. 'Naomi Jenkins gave us the business card for Silver Brae Chalets by mistake when she came in on Monday to report Haworth missing. She thought she was handing over her own business card. Charlie still had it after she'd gone – she showed it to me, mentioned that they had some kind of special offer on. Obviously when the hotel in Spain turned out to be a dump, she thought of the chalets.'

'Hang on,' said Gibbs, holding out his hand for Sellers' drink. Sellers sighed, but gave it to him. 'So Naomi Jenkins had Haworth's brother's business card? Did Jenkins know Haworth's real name, then? Had she met his family?'

'She's not answering her mobile either,' said Simon. 'But I don't think so. She was desperate for us to look for Haworth, to find him as quickly as possible. If she'd known he had a brother – or that he'd changed his name, for that matter – she'd have told us when she came in on Monday. She gave us everything she could to help us find him.'

'She must have known,' said Sellers. 'It can't be a coincidence. What, she just happens to be carrying the business card of her lover's brother, even though she doesn't know that's who he is? Bullshit!'

Simon was nodding. 'It's not a coincidence. Far from it. I've just looked at the Silver Brae Chalets website. Guess who designed it?'

'No idea,' said Sellers.

Gibbs was quicker off the mark. 'Naomi Jenkins' best mate's a website designer, her lodger.'

'Got it in one,' said Simon. 'Yvon Cotchin. She did the Silver Brae Chalets website. She also designed one for Naomi Jenkins, for her sundial business.' He waited, expecting to see dawning awareness on their faces, but all he saw was bewilderment. They hadn't got there yet. They weren't conspiracy-minded in the way Simon was, that was why.

'Listen,' he said. 'Robert Haworth raped Prue Kelvey. We know that, it's been proved. We also know he didn't do all the rapes. He didn't rape Naomi Jenkins or Sandy Freeguard, but someone did, someone Haworth was very probably working with, since the MO was almost identical.'

'You're saying it's the brother, Graham Angilley?' asked Sellers. He still hadn't got his drink back.

'I fucking hope I'm wrong, but I don't think I am. If Angilley's the other rapist, that'd explain how he knew so much about Naomi Jenkins. There's personal information about her on her website, as well as her address, which is the same as her business's address. I'm sure that's how he chose her as a victim: from a list of Yvon Cotchin's previous clients. If Cotchin did Jenkins' website before she did Angilley's, she might well have told him to have a look at some others she'd designed, as a sort of reference.'

'Fuck,' said Sellers quietly.

'Prue Kelvey and Sandy Freeguard—' Gibbs began.

'Sandy Freeguard's a writer and has her own website, with personal information and photos, like Jenkins'. And the company Prue Kelvey worked for has an individual webpage for each member of staff, giving personal as well as professional information, and a photograph. That's how Angilley and Haworth knew so much about them.'

'Naomi Jenkins was raped before Kelvey and Freeguard,' said Gibbs.

'Exactly.' Simon had followed the same deductive trail himself, minutes earlier. 'She might have been the turning point for Angilley and Haworth. They've been selling tickets to live rapes since at least 2001. We know that from the date on survivor thirty-one's story. However they selected their victims in the early days, I reckon it all changed when Angilley had the website done for the chalets. If Yvon Cotchin *did* tell him to look at some of her other work, including Naomi Jenkins' site . . .'

'Pretty big if,' said Sellers. 'What if the chalets' site predated Jenkins'?'

'I'll check,' said Simon. 'But I don't think it did. And that's how Graham Angilley came to know about Naomi Jenkins. He must have realised that there were hundreds of other potential victims on the Internet, with their own websites. But he couldn't only rape women Yvon Cotchin had designed sites for, could he? That'd be too obvious, too risky. So they branched out, he and Haworth – they started to look for any websites belonging to professional women . . .'

'With photos, so they could check they fancied them,' said Gibbs. 'Sick cunts.'

Simon nodded. 'Sandy Freeguard's website was designed by Pegasus. And another company did the one for Kelvey's firm – I've just spoken to the MD's assistant on the phone.'

'How does the sarge fit into this?' asked Sellers. His fingers combed his pocket for more change, but found none. Gibbs had finished his drink and had a small, foamy, brown moustache to prove it.

'I'll get to that in a minute,' said Simon, keen to put off thinking about that side of things for as long as he could. 'Naomi Jenkins got the card for Silver Brae Chalets from Yvon Cotchin. She had no idea there was any connection to Robert Haworth.'

Sellers and Gibbs looked at him sceptically.

'Think about it. Cotchin's worked with Graham Angilley, effectively. She's helped him set up his business. He'd be bound to send her a bunch of cards, so she could give them to people. Naomi took one, and thought – as anyone would – that Silver Brae Chalets was just a holiday place that her mate had done a website for. She had no idea her married boyfriend's brother was the owner and manager . . .' Simon's words tailed off.

'Or that the same brother was the bloke who'd kidnapped and raped her,' said Gibbs.

'That's right. There have been no coincidences in this case, not a single one. Every part of the answer to this mess is connected to every other part: Jenkins, Haworth, Angilley, Cotchin, the business card . . .'

'And now our skipper.' Sellers looked worried.

'Yeah,' said Simon, speaking on a long out-breath. His chest felt as if it was full of concrete. 'Charlie got the chalets' card from Naomi Jenkins. She didn't know Graham Angilley was anything to do with Robert Haworth, not until you told her Haworth's real name.' He looked at Gibbs.

'Fucking hell. As soon as I told her, she must have thought what you did: that there's a strong chance Angilley's the other rapist. And if she's been screwing him . . .'

'That's why she took off in such a hurry,' said Simon. 'She must be in a right state.'

'I feel like shit now,' said Gibbs. 'I've been giving her a hard time.'

'Not only her.' Sellers raised his eyebrows at Simon.

'Yeah, well. You two deserve it. She doesn't.'

'Fuck off! I've done nothing,' said Sellers.

Simon had an active – some might say overactive – conscience. He knew when he'd done something wrong. There were no sins with Chris Gibbs' name on them, last time he looked. There was a big fat file under the name Charlie Zailer.

'I'm getting married in June. You're both invited. *He*'s my best man.' Gibbs jerked his head at Sellers. 'And he's off round the world with his secret shag the week before. I haven't heard anything about a stag night. I'll probably be sat in on my own the night before I sign my freedom away, watching Ant and fucking Dec, while he shakes the empty condom packets out of his suitcase . . .'

'Give me a chance.' Sellers looked sheepish. 'I haven't forgotten about your stag night. I've been busy, that's all.' Simon noticed his cheeks were slightly pink.

'Yeah – busy thinking about your cock, as usual,' Gibbs fired back.

'This can wait,' said Simon. 'We've got more important things to worry about than hiring strippers and tying you to a lamp post with no clothes on. We're in deep shit here.'

'So what do we do?' asked Sellers. 'Where's the sarge gone?'

'Olivia says Charlie left a message on her voicemail telling her to go round later, so she's obviously planning to be at home this evening, even if she isn't there now. I'll go round and talk to her. In the meantime . . .' Simon braced himself. They might both tell him to fuck off. He wouldn't blame them if they did. 'I know I shouldn't ask, but . . . any chance you could keep this well away from the Snowman?'

Sellers' eyes widened. 'Oh, shit. Proust's going to go ballistic when he . . . Oh, *shit*. The skipper and the prime suspect . . .'

'She'll have to be taken off the case,' said Simon. 'I'm going to try and persuade her to tell Proust herself. Shouldn't be hard. She's not stupid.' He said this more to reassure himself than anything else. 'She's probably in shock and needs to be on her own for a bit to get her head round it.' He didn't want to think about what would happen if Proust found out before Charlie told him.

'How can we keep it quiet?' asked Gibbs. 'Proust asks for the sarge every five minutes. What do we say?'

'You won't need to say anything, because you'll be on your way to Scotland.' To Simon's amazement, neither Sellers nor Gibbs questioned his authority. 'Bring Graham Angilley back with you, and Stephanie, his wife. I'll deal with Proust. I'll tell him Charlie's gone to Yorkshire to talk to Sandy Freeguard, now that we've got a possible ID for the man who raped her. Proust won't question it. You know what he's like – he does his most energetic fault-finding first thing in the morning.' Seeing their faces, he said, 'Have you got any better ideas? If we tell him Charlie's gone awol, we'll make things worse for her, and that's the last thing she needs.'

'What'll you be doing?' asked Gibbs suspiciously. 'While we're in haggis country chasing a pervert?'

'I'm going to talk to Yvon Cotchin, and then Naomi Jenkins if I can find her.'

Sellers shook his head. 'If the Snowman finds out about this, all three of us'll be giving fire-safety talks in primary schools before the week's out.'

'Let's not shit ourselves before we have to,' said Simon. 'Charlie must know she's put us in an impossible situation. I bet she's back here within the hour. Check the Brown Cow before you set off to the chalets, just in case she's in there. If she is, ring me.'

'Yes, guv,' said Gibbs sarcastically.

'This isn't a joke.' Simon stared at his shoes. The idea that Charlie had been romantically involved with Graham Angilley – a man who was very probably a monster, a sadistic rapist – bothered Simon more than he could understand or explain. He felt almost as if it had happened to him, as if he'd been assaulted by Angilley. And if that was how he felt, he didn't like to think how much worse it must be for Charlie.

A uniformed constable was walking purposefully towards them along the corridor. The conversation ended abruptly, and Simon, Sellers and Gibbs felt the silent conspiracy hanging in the air around them as PC Meakin got closer.

'Sorry to interrupt,' Meakin said, though all he was interrupting was an atmosphere of mute awkwardness. He addressed Simon. 'There's an Yvon Cotchin here to see you or Sergeant Zailer. I've stuck her in interview room two.'

'Another coincidence,' said Gibbs. 'Saves you a trip.'

'Did she say what she wants?' Simon asked Meakin. Behind him he heard Sellers insisting, 'I *was* going to arrange a bloody stag night for you, all right? I *am*.'

'Her friend's disappeared, she said. She's worried about her because when she last saw her, the friend was pretty upset. That's all I know.'

'Cheers, Meakin,' said Simon. 'I'll be there in a minute.' Once the young constable had gone, he turned to Sellers and Gibbs. 'Upset, disappeared – ring any bells?'

'What are you saying?'

'I don't know.' Simon's first thought, on hearing what Meakin had to say, was too ludicrous and paranoid to be worth repeating. Sellers and Gibbs would think he was losing his grip. He decided to play it safe. 'I've no idea,' he said. 'But if I were a betting man, I'd put money on this being something else that isn't a coincidence.'

'Why wouldn't she tell me where she was going?' asked Yvon Cotchin. 'We'd sorted everything out, she wasn't annoyed with me any more, I know she wasn't . . .'

'It's unlikely to be anything you did wrong,' Simon told her. They'd been talking for less than three minutes, and he was already impatient with Cotchin's hand-wringing and lip-biting. She seemed to care more about how her friend's unexplained absence might reflect on her than about the risk of harm to Naomi.

Simon had just heard, second-hand, Naomi Jenkins' theory that Robert Haworth had cooked the food that the audiences watching the staged rapes had eaten. It was possible, he supposed, and a good reason for Haworth to withhold from Jenkins the fact that he'd once been a chef.

What Simon couldn't make sense of, no matter how hard he tried, was why Haworth should want to strike up relationships with both Sandy Freeguard and Naomi Jenkins, knowing his brother had raped them. He thought back to the two recorded interviews between Naomi and Juliet Haworth. He and Charlie had listened to the tapes again, only a few hours ago. *He doesn't see any of his family. Robert's the official black sheep.* But if his family comprised a serial rapist, a slag who sold sex to strangers on the phone, and a National Front-supporting racist thug . . .

Simon felt excitement stir inside him. If Robert Haworth was the black sheep of a rotten family, wouldn't that make him, by any objective ethical assessment, a white sheep? The only good thing to come from a bad family?

Simon was desperate to talk to Charlie. Her scepticism was the acid test for all his theories. Without her, it was as if half his brain was missing. So he was probably wrong, but still . . . what if Robert Haworth had known what his brother Graham was doing to women and decided to seek at least some of those women out and try to make it up to them?

Why didn't he just go to the police? Charlie would have said.

Because some people would never do that, no matter what. Shop a member of your own family to the law? No; too big a betrayal, too public.

The more Simon tried to squash the theory down, the more determined it seemed to sprout wings and take off. If Robert knew about the rapes and felt unable to report them to the police, he'd have felt all the more guilty. Wasn't it possible that he made it his mission to try to compensate Graham's victims in another way?

No, dickhead. Robert Haworth had raped Prue Kelvey. That was beyond question.

'Naomi's not thinking straight at the moment,' Yvon Cotchin said tearfully. 'She could do any crazy thing.'

Her voice returned Simon to the moment. 'She left a note saying she'd be back later,' he said. It was more than Charlie had done. 'That's a good sign. We'll think again if she doesn't turn up soon.'

'This'll sound mad, but . . . I think she might have gone to that village, where Robert grew up.'

'Oxenhope?'

Yvon nodded. 'She'd want to see it. Not for any real purpose, just because it's associated with Robert. That's how obsessed she is.'

'Did Naomi know that Robert Haworth wasn't the name he was born with?' asked Simon.

'What? No. Definitely not. What . . . what did he used to be called?'

Time for a change of subject. 'Yvon, I've got a few questions I'd like to ask you about your work. Is that all right?' He planned to ask them anyway, whatever she said.

'My work? What about it? How's that relevant to Naomi, or Robert?'

'I can't discuss that with you. It's confidential. But take my word for it, your answers will be incredibly useful.'

'All right,' she said, after a slight pause.

'You designed the website for Naomi Jenkins' sundial-making business.'

'Yes.'

'When?'

'Erm . . . I'm not sure.' She fidgeted in her chair. 'Oh! It was September 2001. I remember because I was working on it when I heard about the planes crashing into the World Trade Center. Awful day.' She shuddered.

'When was the website up and running?' asked Simon.

'October 2001. It didn't take me long.'

'You also designed a website for Silver Brae Chalets in Scotland.'

Yvon looked surprised. Her mouth twitched. Simon guessed she was fighting the urge to ask him again what all this was about. 'Yes,' she said.

'Do you know Graham Angilley, the owner? Is that how you got the work?'

'I've never met him. He's a friend of my father's. Is . . . Graham in some kind of trouble?'

'I'm sure he's fine,' said Simon, not caring if Yvon heard the venom in his voice. 'When did you design his website? Do you remember?' Was there a convenient terrorist atrocity that made it stick in your mind? 'Before or after Naomi's?'

'Before,' she replied without hesitation. 'Long before – 1999, 2000. Something like that.'

Disappointment made Simon flinch. Bang went his theory that Graham Angilley had looked at Naomi Jenkins' website to get an idea of the standard of Yvon Cotchin's work. If Simon had been wrong about that, what else might he be wrong about?

'Are you sure? It couldn't have been the other way round, Naomi Jenkins first and then the chalets?'

'No. I did Naomi's long after Graham's. I've got all my old work diaries at home – at Naomi's house. I can show you the exact dates I worked on both, if you like.'

'That'd be helpful,' said Simon. 'I'm also going to need a complete list of all the websites you've designed, since you started. Is that do-able?'

Yvon looked worried. 'None of this has got anything to do with me,' she protested.

'We don't think you've done anything wrong,' said Simon. 'But I need that list.'

'Okay. I've got nothing to hide, it's just . . .'

'I know. Does the name Prue Kelvey mean anything to you?'

'No. Who is she?'

'Sandy Freeguard?'

'No.'

She looked as if she was telling the truth.

'Okay,' said Simon. 'I'm particularly interested in women with businesses, like Naomi Jenkins, who you've designed sites for. Any names you can think of offhand?'

'Yeah, probably,' said Yvon. 'Mary Stackniewski. Donna Bailey.'

'The artist?'

'Yeah. I think those are the only ones you might have heard of. There was a woman who ran a dating agency, another one who made models – she was the daughter of my—'

'Juliet Haworth?' Simon cut her off, feeling the hairs on his arms stand up. Models? It had to be.

'That's Robert's wife.' Yvon looked at him as if he were insane. 'Don't be daft. I could never work for her. Naomi would string me up from the nearest lamp post and shoot me as a traitor—'

'What about Heslehurst, Juliet Heslehurst?' Simon cut her off. 'Pottery models of houses?'

Yvon's eyes were round with amazement. 'Yes,' she said faintly. 'That's the woman who made the models. Hers was the first site I ever did. Is there . . . She was also called Juliet. Is that . . . ?'

'I'm asking the questions. How did you know Juliet Heslehurst?'

'I didn't, not really. Her mother, Joan, used to be my nanny when I was little. Before she had any kids of her own. Our families kept in touch. Joan mentioned to my mum that her daughter needed someone to do her a website . . .'

'So Juliet Heslehurst's website was your first? Before Graham Angilley's?'

'Yes.'

'Did you, by any chance, suggest to Mr Angilley that he look at Juliet Heslehurst's site, to get an idea of the standard of your work?'

Yvon's face had turned red. Sweat beaded her upper lip. 'Yes,' she whispered.

Naomi would string me up from the nearest lamp post. That was the second time Simon had heard the word 'lamp post' in a very short space of time. He'd said it himself, first time round, talking about Gibbs' stag night, the one Sellers had forgotten to arrange. Simon had wondered why Gibbs cared so much – a sane man would want to avoid being stripped and tied up, which seemed to be what happened at these—

Simon's heart screeched to a stop. Then it started with a hefty jolt. Bloody hell, he thought. Bloody, bloody hell.

He excused himself and left the room, his mobile phone already in his hand. A few things were becoming horribly clear; the least important of these was that, from now on, the whole team would have to look back on Chris Gibbs' weeks-long huff as something to be grateful for, however unpleasant it might have been while it lasted.

24

Saturday 8 April

'I'm going to pull over at the next services,' says Charlie Zailer. Then, as an afterthought, 'All right?' Her voice sounds choked. She doesn't look at me, hasn't since we set off. She faces straight ahead as she talks, as if she's using a hands-free mobile phone, speaking to someone far away.

'I'll stay in the car,' I tell her. I want to close myself in, put a metal box around my body so that I'm invisible. This was a mistake. I shouldn't be here. How do I know she's telling the truth about the man and wherever it is we're going?

If I'm going to see him again, it shouldn't be on his territory. It should be at a police station, in a line-up. Panic starts to chew at the corners of my mind. This feels wrong. I ought to tell Sergeant Zailer to stop the car and let me out now, here, on the hard shoulder. It was a bright day when we set off, but we've been driving for an hour, and the sky in this part of the country is light grey with darker grey jagged patches scrawled across it. The wind is hissing, blowing the rain diagonally across the windscreen. I picture myself cold and drenched by the side of the road, and say nothing.

The faint, rhythmic beat of the indicator makes me look up. We pass blue signs with slanted white lines: three, two, one. Motorway language. You once told me you find motorways relaxing, even if the traffic's stalled.

'They have a special rhythm,' you said. 'They *go* some-where.' The intense look in your eyes; was I capable of understanding this thing that was so important to you? 'They're like magic, like a yellow-brick road for adults. And they're beautiful.' I pointed out that most people wouldn't agree. 'Then they're fools,' you said. 'You can keep your listed buildings. There's no sight more impressive than a long, grey strip of motorway stretching into the distance. There's nowhere I'd rather be. Apart from here with you.'

I push the thought from my mind.

Sergeant Zailer drives faster than she should into the service-station car park. I stare at my lap. If I allow myself to look out of the window, I might see a red lorry that looks a bit like yours. If I go inside, I might see a food court that resembles the one at Rawndesley East Services. My breath stops in my throat when it occurs to me that here, too, there might be a Traveltel.

'You should come in, get a coffee, stretch your legs,' Sergeant Zailer says gruffly, climbing out of the car. 'Go to the toilet.' The last few words are faint, carried away by the wind.

'What are you, my mother?'

She shrugs and slams the door. I shut my eyes and wait. Thinking is impossible. I try to point a spotlight at my brain and find it empty. After a few minutes, I hear the car door open. I smell coffee and cigarettes; the combination makes me feel sick. Then I hear Charlie Zailer's voice. 'The man who raped you is called Graham Angilley,' she says. 'He's Robert's brother.'

Bile rises in my throat. Graham Angilley. Where have I heard the name Angilley before? Then it comes to me. 'Silver Brae Chalets,' I manage to say.

'The theatre where you were, where the audience was . . . it wasn't a theatre. It was one of the chalets.'

This makes me open my eyes. 'It *was* a theatre. There was a stage, with curtains.'

'Each of the chalets has its master bedroom on a mezzanine floor. It's like a room without walls, a high square platform that you could easily mistake for a stage. And there are wooden railings around the mezzanine, with curtains, to give the bedroom more privacy.'

As she speaks, I can see it. She's right. That's the detail I couldn't quite remember about the curtains – I knew there was something. They didn't fall down from the ceiling. They *were* attached to a sort of rail. If I hadn't been tied to the bed, if I'd stood up, I'd have been able to peer over the top.

Silver Brae Chalets. In Scotland. A real place, where people go for their holidays, to have fun. Where I wanted to take you, Robert. No wonder you were so shocked and upset when I told you I'd booked it.

'Yvon, my best friend, designed their website,' I say. 'There were no wooden railings between me and the audience. Just a horizontal metal rail, going round three sides of the stage.'

'Maybe each chalet's slightly different,' Sergeant Zailer says. 'Or maybe the one you were in was unfinished.'

'It was. The window I looked through – there was no curtain there. And the skirting boards were still bare wood, not painted yet.' Why has this not occurred to me before?

'What else can you tell me?' Sergeant Zailer asks. 'I know you've been withholding something.'

I stare at my hands in my lap. I'm not ready. How does she know Graham Angilley's name? Has she been to Silver Brae Chalets? Something feels not quite right.

'Fine,' she says. 'Let's talk about the weather, then. Shit, isn't it? I'm surprised you make a living out of sundials, in this country. Anyone ever invents a raindial, they'll make a mint.'

'There's no such thing.'

'Yeah, I know that. I was talking crap.' She lights a cigarette, opening the window a fraction. Cold rain slices in through the rectangular slit, hitting me in the face. 'What do you think of sundials that don't tell the time, ornamental ones?'

'I object to them,' I tell her. 'It doesn't take that much longer to make a proper dial. A sundial that doesn't tell the time isn't a sundial. It's just a piece of junk.'

'They're cheaper than real ones.'

'Because they're rubbish.'

'My boss wants one for our nick. He wants a real one, but the powers-that-be won't let him spend the money.'

'I'll make him one,' I hear myself saying. 'He can pay me whatever he can afford.'

Charlie Zailer looks surprised. 'Why would you do that? Don't say as a favour to me – I won't believe you.'

'I don't know.' Because if I promise to make something for your boss, I will have to survive this trip. If I talk as if I believe I'll survive, then maybe I will. 'What sort does he want?' I ask.

'One that can go on the wall.'

'I'll do it for free if you'll take me to the hospital again to see Robert. I have to see him, and they won't let me in without you.'

'He told you to leave him alone. And he's a rapist. Why do you want to see him?'

She will never guess. Nobody could guess the truth, apart from me. Because I know you so well, Robert. However you feel about me, I *do* know you well.

315

'Juliet Haworth wasn't involved in organising the rapes,' I say. 'Whether they were . . . done for some kind of perverted pleasure or whether money was made out of them . . . whatever. Juliet was nothing to do with it.'

'How do you know that?' Sergeant Zailer takes her eyes off the road, interrogating me with her sharp glare.

'I've got nothing you'd regard as evidence,' I tell her. 'But I'm sure it's true.'

'Right.' She sounds bitter. 'So that pottery model of the chalet, the same chalet you saw through the window while you were being assaulted . . . Juliet just guessed what it looked like, did she? Divine inspiration. Nothing to do with her putting on rape shows with the help of Graham Angilley and her husband, and knowing exactly where they took place.'

'I said she wasn't responsible for the rapes. I never said she hadn't seen that chalet.'

'So . . . you mean Graham Angilley *asked* her to make a model of it? Because he knew its significance even if she didn't?' She smokes furiously as she demolishes what she thinks is my theory. 'But Juliet told us what had happened to you, for fuck's sake! She guessed you'd accused Robert of raping you – she knew all the details. If she wasn't involved, how the hell would she know?'

I can't believe she hasn't got there yet. She's supposed to be a detective. But she doesn't know you, Robert – that's why she's lagging behind. It's why I was lagging behind, the first time I spoke to Juliet in a police interview room. Your wife knew you better than I did at that point.

Not any more.

'Juliet knew what had happened to me because it happened to her too.' Am I saying this aloud? Yes; it seems I am. 'The man, Graham Angilley – he raped her too.'

* * *

'*What?*' Sergeant Zailer pulls over on to the hard shoulder. The screech of the tyres makes me wince.

'Think about it. All the women Graham Angilley raped were successful professional women. Juliet was too, until she had a breakdown. That's why she had one: because she was raped. She was tied to the same bed as I was, on the same stage – mezzanine, whatever. There will have been an audience, men eating and drinking. And while she was tied to that bed, she saw exactly what I saw through the window. She made a model of it. She put it in the display cabinet in her living room.' I stop, fill my lungs with air.

'Go on,' says Sergeant Zailer.

'She didn't know Robert knew what had happened to her, so she had no reason to think the little pottery house with the blue arched door would be familiar to him . . . Like me, she hadn't told anyone what had been done to her. She was too ashamed. It's not easy, to go from being envied and successful to being pitied.'

'But Robert did know, didn't he? And when he met Juliet in the video shop that night, it wasn't a chance meeting.'

'No. Nor when he met me at the service station. He must have followed us both, for weeks, maybe months. And Sandy Freeguard. Didn't you say she crashed her car into his? He was within crashing distance because he was following her too. That was the pattern: his brother raped us, then Robert followed us until he was able to arrange a so-called chance meeting.'

'Why?' Sergeant Zailer leans towards me, as if greater proximity will coax the answer from me. 'Why did he want to meet and start relationships with his brother's victims?'

I don't answer.

'Naomi, you've got to tell me. I could charge you with obstruction.'

'Charge me with high treason if you want. What do I give a shit?'

Charlie Zailer sighs. 'What about Prue Kelvey? She doesn't fit the pattern. Robert raped her, and she saw him before he put the mask on her. He couldn't follow *her* and contrive a meeting, couldn't become *her* boyfriend.'

'Juliet tried to kill Robert because she found out he knew about her rape all along. Probably the only reason she was able to marry him, or even to look him in the face, was because she was sure he didn't know, sure he'd *never* know. In his eyes, her dignity was intact. She wasn't . . . violated and disgusting; she was how she used to be. But Robert *did* know, and Juliet found out, and she realised he'd been lying to her for years, letting her think her secret was safe, and her privacy, but actually all the time . . .' I swallow hard, trying to quell the lurching in my chest. 'She thought he'd been laughing at her behind her back, that the whole relationship was a mockery, him taunting her. His secret knowledge was a way of having power over her, power he could wield at any time, or keep in reserve for as long as he wanted. He didn't need to tell her he knew until he was ready, didn't have to tell her at all if he didn't want to.'

Charlie Zailer frowns. 'Are you saying this is how it was, or how Juliet saw it?'

'How she saw it. I'm explaining why she tried to kill him.'

She nods.

'I won't speak to her again. Juliet. Those interviews – I'm not doing it again.'

Your wife is out of control, Robert. Well, I don't need to tell you that, do I? Talk about stating the obvious. So far she's been content to goad me with her maddening ambiguities. If I talk to her again, she will become more explicit, step up her campaign of hate. She will start to tell me things, and I can't allow that to happen. Next time I come to the hospital, I want to tell you what I know in my heart and soul, not what I've been told. There's a big difference; it's the difference between power and helplessness. I know you'd understand, even if Sergeant Zailer wouldn't.

'How did Juliet find out that Robert knew?' she asks me. 'Do you know that too?' An uncomfortable silence fills the car, one I am determined not to break. 'Naomi, this is no time to clam up! Jesus! How did she know? Why did Robert want to go out with women his brother had attacked? *Why?*' She taps the dashboard with her fingernails. 'You know, everything you've just told me about Juliet could be true of you as well. You didn't know Robert knew about what had happened to you, did you? But he did. Perhaps you're the one who feels he was laughing at you behind your back, wielding some sort of sick power, manipulating you. Perhaps you want revenge, and that's why you want to go to the hospital – to finish off what Juliet started.'

'I want to see Robert because I need to talk to him,' I say. 'I need to explain something to him. Something private that's between me and him.' Just the two of us, Robert, and nobody else. It's what I've always wanted.

25

8/4/06

They arrived as daylight began to fade. Charlie didn't stop where she should have, in the circular gravelled area where chalet guests parked their cars. Instead, she drove up on to the grass, feeling the muffled bump beneath the car. She kept up a steady pressure on the accelerator. There was only one thing in her mind and that was the necessity to keep going, keep looking straight ahead, not allow herself to think too much. How many times had she wondered, about both the victims and the perpetrators of violent crimes, how they had done it, how they had made themselves carry on? Now she understood: the trick was to avoid, at all costs, seeing the full picture, the overview. To avoid seeing yourself.

Charlie slammed her foot down on the brake only when the blue door with the arched top was right in front of the windscreen. Her and Olivia's chalet. Not long ago, she'd leaned against that door, smoking a cigarette and talking to Simon on her mobile phone while Graham waited in her bed. It would be easy to think, And now . . . , but Charlie wasn't going to fall into that trap. Thinking about the past in relation to the present and the future would be enough to make her lose it, and she couldn't risk that. She was here to get the information she needed from Graham and Steph; that was what she had to focus on.

She heard Naomi's ragged breathing as it harmonised

with her own; it reminded her she wasn't alone in the car. 'This is it,' said Naomi. 'The cottage I saw through the window.' She pointed to the chalet beside it, which was bigger than the one Charlie and Olivia had stayed in and had a rectangular, pistachio-coloured front door with matching window frames. 'That's the one I was attacked in. And that's the window.'

Charlie didn't bother asking if she was sure. Naomi was looking around, eyes bright and sharp, as if trying to remember every physical detail of the place for some future test. Charlie wondered how she would feel now if she too had been raped by Graham, instead of what had actually happened. Instead of her going out of her way to flirt with him, to seduce him . . .

A loud banging on the car window made her jump. Knuckles as well as several bangles knocking against the glass, a flash of pink fingernails. Steph.

'Who's she?' Naomi sounded jumpy.

Coming here had been a mistake. Another one. Charlie was in no fit state to interview Steph or to reassure Naomi. I ought to phone Simon, she thought, and then, I can't face it. He'll know. There's no way he won't already know. She pressed the button to open the window. Cold air filled the car. Naomi huddled in her seat, wrapping her arms round her body.

'What the hell do you think you're doing?' Steph demanded. 'You can't park here. You can't drive over the grass like that.'

'Too late,' said Charlie.

Steph sucked on the inside of her glossy upper lip. 'Where's Graham?'

'That's what I was going to ask you.'

'Don't be stupid! I thought he was staying with you. I

thought the two of you were having a nice, romantic weekend together. That's what he told me, anyway. Don't tell me he's got someone else on the go as well. Typical.' She folded her arms.

Charlie didn't think she was acting. 'He's not here, then?'

'As far as I know, he's at your house. What do you want, anyway?'

Charlie felt Naomi's horrified stare branding itself on her skin. She couldn't look at her, kept her eyes fixed on Steph instead. She should have told Naomi about her and Graham, should have known Steph would let it slip. But that would have involved thinking ahead, and even Charlie wasn't self-destructive enough to do that at the moment.

She opened the car door and stepped out into the chilled air. It wasn't raining any more but the grass was wet, and so were the tops of the cars in the car park. The walls of the chalets were streaked with dark, damp patches. Even the air seemed thick with moisture.

'Let's talk in the lodge,' said Charlie. 'For the sake of your guests.'

'About what? I've got nothing to say to you.'

Naomi emerged from the car, pale and solemn. Charlie watched the expression on Steph's face change from one of irritation to one of shock. 'You recognise Naomi?' she said.

'No.' Steph's denial was too quick, too automatic.

'Yeah, you do. Graham raped her, in that building there.' Charlie pointed. 'There was an audience of men, eating dinner. I bet you cooked that dinner, didn't you? Your famous home-cooked meals.

'I don't know what you're on about.' Steph's face was red. She was a bad liar; at least that was something. Charlie didn't think it'd take long to break her.

'She didn't see me,' said Naomi. 'I didn't see her. How could she recognise me?'

'From the photographs Graham took with your phone and sent to his,' said Charlie. She saw Naomi wince and thought that perhaps she'd tried to forget that detail. 'Isn't that right, Steph? I bet I'd find plenty of photos if I had a look round. You're probably stupid enough to keep souvenirs, and Graham's certainly arrogant enough. Where are the pictures of Naomi and all the other women? In the lodge? Shall we go and have a look?'

'You can't look anywhere! You haven't got a warrant, so it's against the law. Get lost, all right? I'm not wasting time talking to one of my husband's many whores!'

Charlie's arm flew out, knocking her to the ground. Steph scrambled up on to her knees and tried to speak, but Charlie grabbed her by the throat.

'You could kill her,' said Naomi quietly.

It was probably meant as a warning. Not as the excellent suggestion it was.

'You know what your husband is, don't you?' Charlie spat at Steph. 'You know about the rapes. You cooked the meals. Probably sold the tickets and did all the admin, like you do for the chalets, the legitimate side of the business.'

'No,' said Steph, gasping for breath.

'Why the change of venue, from one of your chalets to Robert Haworth's lorry? Were you worried someone'd recognise the location? Or did some of the chalet guests hear screams in the night and start asking awkward questions?' Charlie took pleasure in embedding her nails into Steph's flesh.

'Please let me go, please! You're hurting me! I don't know what you're talking about.'

'Did you know Robert had changed his name from Angilley to Haworth?' Charlie positioned her mouth so that it was next to Steph's ear. '*Did you?*' she shouted as loud as she could. It felt good, a necessary release of tension.

'Yes. I can't breathe . . .'

'Why did he change his name?'

'Charlie, for fuck's sake! You're choking her. You'll kill her if you don't watch out.'

Charlie ignored Naomi. She wasn't interested in hearing about how she ought to be behaving. It was too late for that. 'Why did Robert change his name?' she asked again, feeling Steph's throat fluttering in panic beneath the skin of her palm.

'He and Graham had a row. They haven't spoken since. Robert . . . I can't breathe!' Charlie relaxed her hold, but only slightly. 'Robert didn't want anything to do with Graham or the family. Even the name.'

'What caused the row?'

'I don't know.' Steph coughed out the words. 'That's Graham's private business. I don't get involved.'

Charlie kicked her in the stomach. 'Like fuck you don't! How do you think it'd feel to be kicked to death in front of an audience? How much would *you* sell the tickets for? Hey? What about Sandy Freeguard? You recognise that name, don't you? Juliet Heslehurst? Prue Kelvey? Although it was Robert who raped her, not Graham. Why? Why the change, after Graham had raped all the others?'

'I'm not saying anything until I've spoken to Graham.' Steph sobbed. She curled into a ball on the grass, clutching her stomach.

'You're not going to be speaking to him, shit-face. Not today and not for a fucking long time. What, do you think we're going to put the two of you in a cosy little furnished cell together, let you play house?'

'I haven't done anything, I don't know what you're talking about. I haven't done anything wrong, nothing at all!'

Charlie pulled her handbag out of the car and lit a cigarette. 'That must be a nice feeling,' she said. 'To have done nothing at all wrong.'

Steph didn't try to get up. 'What's going to happen to me?' she asked. 'What are you going to do? None of it was my fault. You've seen how Graham treats me.'

'None of what was your fault?' Charlie asked, feeling better for the nicotine.

Steph covered her face with her hands.

Charlie felt like kicking her again, so she did. 'If you want to spend the rest of your life in prison, that's up to you. Keep denying everything. If you want to stay out of jail, though, you've got choices.' Yeah, right. Steph was an idiot if she believed there would be any way out of this for her. If she was involved in arranging the rapes and profiting from them, she'd be going down for a very long time. Charlie had no doubt that both the lodge and Steph and Graham's home were full of pictorial evidence of their crimes. Never in their most extravagant and far-fetched dreams had they expected to get caught. Charlie gleaned all of this from Steph's eyes, from her manner. Graham must have promised her there was no danger, that he had it all under control.

What sort of stupid bitch would believe a man like Graham Angilley?

Steph looked up. 'What choices?' she said, tears and snot dripping down her face.

'Get me a photograph of Graham. And I'll need the keys to that chalet.' She indicated the pistachio-coloured door. 'Naomi needs to identify the man and the place.

After she's done that, we'll go to the lodge and you'll tell me everything I want to know. If you fob me off with even the smallest lie, I'll know, and I'll make sure you rot in the shittiest prison I can find,' Charlie lied confidently. In reality, the police had no control over where prisoners served their sentences. Steph might end up in the new, cushy Category D resort on the other side of Combingham. Everyone in CID knew it as 'The Resort' because it had boarding houses instead of cells, and the inmates' food was rumoured to be reasonable.

Steph staggered across the field towards the lodge. The back of her skirt was soaking. She'd been lying on the wet grass, but Charlie was pretty sure she'd pissed herself as well: the smell gave it away. I ought to feel some compassion for her, thought Charlie. But she didn't. There was not even an ounce of sympathy for Steph inside her.

'What if Graham forced her into it?' said Naomi. 'What if she really doesn't know anything about it?'

'She knows. Nobody forced her into anything. Can't you tell when someone's lying to you?'

Naomi rubbed her hands together and blew on them. 'You and Graham—' she began tentatively.

'We're not going to talk about that,' Charlie cut her off. Naomi couldn't have chosen a worse combination of words than those three if she'd tried.

The lodge door opened and Steph emerged. She began to make her way across the field, steadier on her feet. She'd changed into black tracksuit bottoms and trainers. From a distance, Charlie saw the photograph in Steph's hand, saw Naomi recoil. 'It's only a picture,' she said. 'It can't hurt you.'

'Spare me the therapeutic crap,' Naomi snapped. 'You think it can't hurt me to see his face, after all these years?

What if he comes back? I'm not sure I can do this. Can't we just go?'

Charlie shook her head. 'We're here,' she said, as if that state of affairs were somehow irreversible. That was how it felt. She would always be stuck here, at Silver Brae Chalets, with the wet grass tickling her ankles through her tights.

Steph looked as terrified as she had before. As she approached, she began to speak frantically, too desperate to wait until she got closer. 'I didn't know they were raping the women,' she said. 'Graham told me they were actresses, that the frightened-victim thing was all an act. Like it was when I did it.'

'When you did it?' Charlie echoed. She snatched the photograph out of Steph's hand and passed it to Naomi, who looked at it for a second and passed it straight back. Charlie tried to catch her eye, with no success; Naomi was staring fixedly in the opposite direction, at a bank of trees. Charlie put the photo in her handbag, which she dropped on to the driver's seat of her car. She didn't want to be anywhere near a picture of Graham. Why wasn't Naomi saying anything? Was Graham the one who'd raped her or not?

'Most of the time, I was the victim,' Steph went on, breathless. 'I was the one Graham tied to the bed, I was the one who had to scream and beg and try to struggle free. It was knackering. I had the chalets to see to as well, all the cleaning and the reservations, the confirmations—'

'Shut the fuck up.' Charlie held out her hand. 'Give me the key. Go and wait for me in the lodge. And do *nothing* else, do you hear me? Don't try to ring Graham on his mobile. If you phone anyone, I'll find out. I can get the information from BT, from your mobile service provider – easy. One wrong move and you'll spend the next twenty years in a dirty, stinking cell. You won't see daylight till you're an old woman, and even when you get out, someone'll probably knife you in the street.' If only, Charlie thought. Still, she was enjoying the pretence. 'Women who collaborate with serial rapists tend not to be popular,' she concluded.

Whimpering, Steph handed her the key and stumbled back towards the lodge. 'Well? Is that the man who attacked you?' Charlie asked Naomi.

'Yes.'

'How do I know you're not lying?' *Please be lying.*

Naomi turned to face her and Charlie saw how white her skin had gone, almost translucent. It was as if she'd been bleached by the shock of seeing that face, Graham's face. 'I don't want it to be him,' she said. 'I don't want to say yes. In a way it was easier not to know, but . . . it's him. That's the man who raped me.'

'Let's look at the chalet, get it over with,' said Charlie, walking towards the door with the key between her thumb and forefinger, ready to stab anyone who got in her way. She stopped when she realised Naomi wasn't following her. 'Come on,' she said.

Naomi was staring up at the window. 'Why do I have to go inside?' she said. 'I know it's the place.'

'You might, but I don't,' said Charlie. 'I'm sorry, but you said in your statement that you didn't see the outside of the building you were in. I need you to recognise the inside.' She unlocked the door and walked into darkness. She felt the walls on either side of the door and found a panel of light switches. Most of them were dimmers. She fiddled with them until a few came on. It was just like the chalet she and Olivia had rented, except bigger. Nobody appeared to be staying at the moment: there was no evidence of clothes or suitcases. The place was empty apart from the furniture, immaculately clean. The dark-red curtains on the rail around the mezzanine bedroom were open and Charlie saw a wooden bed. At the top of each of the four bedposts, an acorn had been carved out of the wood.

She heard laboured breathing coming from behind her. When she turned, she saw that Naomi was shaking. She climbed the stairs to the mezzanine, wondering if Graham had chosen the bed precisely because of these protuberances, because of how easy they were to tie rope around. For a second she thought she might throw up.

'Can we get the hell out of here now?' said Naomi, from the bottom of the stairs.

Charlie was about to reply when the lights went out. 'Who's there?' she shouted, at the same time as Naomi shrieked, 'Charlie!'

There was a loud thud, the sound of the chalet's front door slamming shut.

26

Saturday 8 April

It's the worst sort of darkness that surrounds us, the sort that folds you in and makes you feel you might never claw your way back to the light. It only lasts a second. I hear a buzzing sound, and the chalet's interior is visible again. Just. Everything looks grey. A man's voice says, 'Shit.' I see two forms in the dimness – a thick one, and a smaller, narrow one. The broader shape could be yours, Robert. For a moment I convince myself it is and my heart soars. I do not think about DNA matches and the lies you have told me, or the real name you share with your brother, a rapist. Not immediately, anyway. I think about your kisses, and how they felt, how I felt when you told me to go away and leave you alone. The loss of you.

Gradually the room gets brighter. The buzzing was the sound of a dimmer switch. Neither of the two men is you, or Graham Angilley. My shoulders sag as the tension drains from my body. It's DC Sellers and DC Gibbs.

'What the fuck are you playing at?' Charlie yells at them. 'You nearly gave me a heart attack.'

I look at Gibbs, expecting him to react badly to being reprimanded, but he doesn't look as fierce as he did on Wednesday, in my workshop. 'Sorry,' he says. 'I must have leaned against the switch.'

Sellers, the fat one, is angry. 'What are *you* playing at?'

he says. 'Just buggering off without a word to anyone. What were we supposed to tell Proust?'

Charlie doesn't respond.

'Switch your bloody phone on and ring Waterhouse,' says Sellers. 'He's not all right. He's more worried about you than about lying to the Snowman. I've seen men with wives missing in less of a state. If he doesn't hear from you soon, God knows what he might do.'

A small gasp comes from Charlie, as if his words have shocked or upset her.

'Where's Angilley?' says Gibbs.

Charlie looks at me, then back at her two colleagues. 'We'd better talk in private. Naomi, wait here. We'll go outside.' Halfway to the door, she stops. 'Unless you'd rather wait outside,' she says.

I feel three pairs of eyes on me. I don't want to stay here in this place where I was tortured, especially not on my own, but outside I will be unprotected if Graham Angilley suddenly returns. I might be the first person he sees. But Steph said she thought he was at Charlie's house . . . 'Why would Graham Angilley be at your house?' I ask her.

Suspicion begins to swell inside me when I see Gibbs and Sellers looking as embarrassed as Charlie. They know something. 'What's going on?' I try not to sound as if I'm pleading for information, begging to be allowed in. 'Are you and Graham . . . Have you been seeing each other? Are you having sex with him?' As crazy as it sounds, I can't think of any other explanation.

'How?' I yell at her. 'How could you be? Did you know him before you met me? When I gave you that card—'

'This'll have to wait,' Sellers interrupts. 'We need a chat, Sarge.'

Charlie rakes her short hair with her fingers. 'Give us five minutes, Naomi. Please. We'll talk later, okay.'

None of the detectives moves, and I realise that I am being sent outside. As quickly as I can, I walk to the door, which seems a million miles away. I close it behind me. Trying to eavesdrop proves pointless: the walls are too thick, the building too well made. It's like a sealed container; nothing escapes.

It's dark now, but there is a floodlight attached to the wall of one of the chalets. I feel as if I'm right in its beam, attracting the full glare. If Graham Angilley drives up in his car, he will see me immediately. I crouch down, hugging my knees, feeling like a hunted animal.

My breath starts to come in short, sharp bursts. There are too many connections, too many links that are wrong, that shouldn't be there. You shouldn't be the brother of the man who raped me. Yvon should not have had his business card, or designed a website for him. Charlie shouldn't be sleeping with him, but she is, she must be.

Sellers and Gibbs didn't know she was in Scotland. They didn't know she brought me with her. Why did she run off without telling anyone? Why *did* she bring me? As some sort of bait? There was shock on Sellers' face when he looked at her before. Horror, almost. As if he'd never have thought her capable of whatever it is she's done.

It could happen again.

Here I am, in the place where I was once raped, with a woman who has blithely lied to me and to her colleagues. What the hell am I doing? I spring to my feet. I need to move, to replace thought with action before my suspicions turn into full-blown terror.

Charlie's handbag is on the driver's seat of her car. The door is closed, but not locked. I pull it open and unzip the bag, looking for keys. If I were brave, I'd escape on foot, but I'm not much of a runner and this place is miles from anywhere.

No keys inside the purse, in the zipped compartment, anywhere in the bag. Damn. In desperation, I bend down to look in the ignition, knowing I'm not the sort of person who has that kind of good luck. I blink several times, to check it isn't a stress-induced hallucination: the keys are there, a whole bunch. Home, work, car. Perhaps one to a neighbour's house as well. I stare at the dangling bundle of metal, wondering why it doesn't annoy Charlie to have it hanging there as she drives. If it were me, I'd take the car key off the ring and keep it separately.

I throw the handbag on to the passenger seat, climb into the car and start it. The engine is quiet. I drive over the grass to the edge of the field and bump on to the gravel. Within seconds I am driving along the narrow lane away from Silver Brae Chalets. It's a good feeling. Better than standing under Graham Angilley's spotlight, on his property, waiting for him to come and find me.

Which didn't happen because he's at Charlie's house. I've got her keys. I could go and find him. He doesn't know I know where he is, or who he is.

I gasp at the idea that, finally, I have the advantage over him. I don't want to lose it. I won't, can't. I've lost enough already. Now would be a good time to try to remember, in detail, all those revenge fantasies that used to play in my head all day every day until I met you. Which one did I like best: stabbing, shooting, poisoning? Tying the man up and doing to him what he did to me?

I need to ditch Charlie's car as soon as possible, leave it by the side of the road, as soon as I get to a proper road, and hitch a lift. Otherwise it won't be long before I'm stopped by a police car. Believe me, Robert, nothing is going to stop me this time. With or without Charlie, I am coming to that hospital, and if you tell me again to go away and leave you alone, I won't care.

Because I understand now. I know why you said it. You thought I'd been talking to Juliet, didn't you? You assumed it. Or, rather, that she'd been talking to me. Giving me her version of events, ruining everything, telling me all the things you couldn't bear for me to know. And so you gave up.

I told you I loved you, at the hospital. You must have been able to see that I meant it, how much I meant it, from my eyes and from my voice, yet you still gave up. And expected me to do the same, to walk away. Until I can get to the hospital again, you will be certain that I am never coming back.

How could you think that, Robert? Don't you know me at all?

27

8/4/06

'She's taken my fucking car!' Charlie yelled into the darkness.

'You didn't leave the keys in it, did you?' said Sellers, running up behind her.

'Keys, handbag, phone, credit cards. *Jesus!* Don't say it, I don't want to hear it. Don't either of you tell me I shouldn't have brought her with me, or left the car unlocked with my bag inside, all right? In fact, can we steer clear of any discussion of what I should and shouldn't have done? I'm still your sergeant, remember.' Charlie wanted to ask them how much Proust knew, but was unwilling to show weakness. Extreme situations called for a return to the crude playground tactics that had got her through at school: never show you care.

'Sellers, get on your mobile. I want my car back.'

'You'll be lucky, Sarge. You know what Scottish police are like.'

'She won't be in Scotland for long. She's heading for Culver Valley General Hospital and her beloved psychopath, Robert Haworth. Get some uniforms to meet her in the car park. Gibbs, you and me'll talk to Mrs Graham Angilley.' The arrival of Sellers and Gibbs had given Charlie a jolt, and now she felt a bit more like her old self. Enough to do a passable impression, at any rate.

Steph was in the lodge, sitting behind one of the desks,

with a roll of pink toilet paper and a bottle of nail-varnish-remover in front of her, rubbing at the nail of her index finger with the tissue. The skin around her neck was red. She made a point of not looking up. Her face – like her arse, if her husband's word could be relied upon – was sunbed orange, apart from just above and below her eyes, where paler patches of skin remained. She looks like a fucking owl, thought Charlie.

'Stag nights,' she said loudly, slapping her palms down flat on the desk.

Steph's body seemed to contract. 'How did you find out? Who told you that? Was it him?' She jerked her head in Gibbs' direction.

'Is it true?'

'No.'

'You just asked how I found out. Nobody says "found out" about something that isn't true. You'd say, "What makes you think that?" Or are you too dense to understand the difference?'

'My husband only wanted to fuck you because of your job,' said Steph, her voice full of venom. 'He never fancied you. He gets a buzz from taking risks, that's all. Like letting you use our computer the other night, even though he knew you were a cop. If you'd bothered to look, you'd have found all sorts. I told Graham he was daft letting you, but he can't help himself. It's a buzz – that's what he said.' Steph sniggered. 'Do you know what he calls you? The Boob Tube. Because you're skinny and your tits are too big.'

Don't think about it. Don't think about Graham. Or Simon.

'What's on the computer that your husband wouldn't want me to find?' asked Charlie. 'I thought you said the women were all actresses, that it was all consensual and above board? If that were true, Graham would have nothing to fear from the police, would he? You'd better face it, Steph. You're not intelligent enough to be able to lie to me convincingly. You've just contradicted yourself twice, in less than a minute. And I'm not the only person who's considerably sharper than you and who might well want to shaft you. Think about Graham. Don't you reckon he'd love to pin it all on you? Don't you think he could string together a story that's . . . oh, miles better than anything you could come up with? He's got a first from Oxford. You're just his dogsbody.'

Steph looked cornered. Her eyes were roaming uncomfortably, landing on objects around the room for no particular reason.

Her eyes. The skin around them wasn't orange because Steph wore an eye mask when she went on the sunbed, like the masks the rape victims were made to wear. Unlike DS Sam Kombothekra, who claimed never to go to Boots, Steph would know where to buy eye masks in bulk. Did Graham send her on a shopping trip every now and then, to stock up? Charlie knocked the roll of toilet paper and the nail-varnish-remover on to the floor. 'I'll ask you once more,' she said stonily. 'Is it stag nights, your little business?'

'Yeah,' said Steph after a pause. 'And Graham couldn't pin it on me. I'm not a man. I can't rape anybody, can I?'

'He could say you were the brains behind the operation. He could even say you made him do it. He *will* say both those things. It'll be your word against his. I bet you did all the admin, didn't you, kept all the records, like you do for the chalets?'

'But . . . it wouldn't be fair for him to say that,' Steph protested. Charlie had observed, during her years in the police, that everyone felt entitled to just treatment, even the most ruthless and depraved sociopaths. Like many criminals Charlie had met, Steph was horrified by the idea that she might not be dealt with fairly. It was so much easier to break the rules – ethical and legal – if other people continued to follow them.

'So whose idea was it – the business? Live rape stag nights. Inspired, by the way. Well done. I imagine your little shows were popular.'

'It was Graham's idea, all of it.'

'Not Robert Haworth's?' asked Gibbs.

Steph shook her head. 'I never liked it,' she said. 'I knew it was wrong.'

'So you knew the women weren't actresses,' said Charlie. 'You knew they were being raped.'

'No, I thought they were actresses.'

'Then what was wrong?'

'It was wrong anyway, even though the women wanted to do it.'

'Oh, really? Why?'

Steph cast about for something to say. Charlie could almost see the cogs moving inside her head: slow, creaking rotations. 'Those men who came along . . . they might have watched the shows we . . . the shows Graham put on and . . . got the wrong idea. They might have thought it was okay to do that to women.'

'Tell me the fucking truth!' Charlie yelled, grabbing Steph by the hair. 'You knew, didn't you, you shitty little bitch? You knew those women were being raped!'

'*Ow!* Let go of me, you're— All right, I knew!'

Charlie felt the tightness slacken in her hand. She had pulled out a clump of Steph's hair, leaving beads of blood on her scalp. Gibbs watched impassively; he might have been staring at an uneventful rugby match on a television screen for all the difference it would have made to his expression or manner.

Steph began to snivel. 'I'm not part of this, I'm a victim too.' She rubbed the side of her head. 'I didn't want to do it, Graham made me. He said he couldn't risk taking women off the street too often, so I had to act the victim most of the time. Whatever he did to those other women once or twice, he did to me hundreds and thousands of times. Some days I'm so sore I can't even sit down. You can't imagine what that feels like, can you? You've no idea what it's like to be me, so don't —'

'You described yourself as acting before,' said Charlie. 'Graham was your husband. You slept with him anyway. Why not do it in front of an audience and make a bit of cash? A lot of cash, probably.'

'Graham raped me, just like he raped the others,' Steph insisted.

'Earlier, you described your role in the proceedings as "knackering",' said Charlie. 'Not traumatic, horrific, terrifying, humiliating. Knackering. A funny way to talk about being endlessly raped in front of live audiences, isn't it? It sounds much more convincing as a description of taking part in live sex shows, willingly, night after night. That, I can imagine, would be knackering.'

'I didn't do it willingly. I hated it! I said to Graham, give me a bog to clean any day rather than make me do *that*.'

'Then why didn't you ring the police? You could have put a stop to the whole thing with one phone call.'

Steph blinked several times at the outlandishness of this idea. 'I didn't want Graham to get into trouble.'

'Really? Most women would be quite keen for a man who's raped them only once to get into trouble, let alone hundreds of times.'

'No they wouldn't, not when it's their husband!' Steph wiped her wet face with the backs of her hands.

Charlie had to concede she had a point. Was it possible Steph was a reluctant participant? And Robert Haworth too? Could Graham have forced his brother to abduct and rape Prue Kelvey?

'Graham's not a bad person,' said Steph. 'He's just . . . He sees the world in a different way, that's all. In his own way. Women have rape fantasies all the time, don't they? That's what he says. And it's not like he harms them physically.'

'You don't think rape counts as physical harm, you stupid bitch?' said Gibbs.

'No, I don't,' said Steph indignantly. 'Not necessarily. It's just sex, isn't it? Graham would never beat anyone up or make them need to go to hospital.' She looked up at Charlie resentfully. 'Look, Graham had a really terrible childhood. His mum was a slut and a pisshead, and his dad didn't give a toss. They were the poorest family in their village. But it was the making of Graham, he always says that. People who've never had anything bad happen to them, they're the *un*lucky ones, not the lucky ones. They never get to learn what they're made of, what they could do if they were really up against it.'

'Are you quoting him?' asked Charlie.

'I'm just saying, you don't understand him, and I do. After his dad left, his mum got her act together and started a business . . .'

'Yes, a telephone sex business,' said Charlie. 'Enterprising of her.'

'She went from being an amateur whore to being a professional whore, Graham says. He was ashamed of her. But he was pleased about the business in one way, because finally they had some money, and he could escape. He got himself an education and made something of himself.'

'He made a kidnapper and a rapist of himself, that's what he made,' said Gibbs.

'He's a successful businessman,' Steph said proudly. 'Last year he bought me a personalised number plate for my car that cost five grand.' She sighed. 'Loads of businesses have got stuff going on behind the scenes that if everyone knew about it, they'd—'

'How did you advertise?' Gibbs interrupted her pathetic justifications. 'How did you attract customers?'

'Internet chatrooms, mainly. And a lot of word of mouth.' She spoke in a bored drawl. 'Graham takes care of that. Recruitment, he calls it.'

'The audiences – do they make group bookings?'

Charlie nodded at Gibbs' question. It was an important one. She'd let him take over for a bit. Her interest in this was too personal; Gibbs was thinking about the mechanics of the operation.

'Only very occasionally. Once we had a group, with some women in it as well. That was unusual. Normally it's individual bookings, and Graham'd never let women book – the men in the audience wouldn't like it.'

'So how exactly does it work?' asked Gibbs. 'A man who's getting married approaches Graham, wanting one of his speciality stag nights, and then what?'

'Graham finds the other men, to make up a party of anywhere between ten and fifteen.'

'How does he find them?'

'I told you. Mainly through talking to people on the Net. He's in all these . . . porno cyber-communities. He's got loads of contacts.'

'Friends in high places,' Charlie muttered.

'So these men spend their stag nights with people they've never seen before?' asked Gibbs.

'Yeah,' said Steph, as if this should have been obvious. 'Most men can't invite their normal mates along, can they? Chances are their normal mates wouldn't be into that sort of thing, so our customers wouldn't want to let on that they were. Do you see what I mean?'

Charlie nodded, feeling disgust spread through her body like a slow, dull poison.

'Normal men want to spend their stag nights with their mates,' Gibbs said quietly. 'That's the whole point. Not watching a rape, with strangers. That's not a stag night.'

'So Graham drums up ten to fifteen twisted perverts for each rape, and what happens next?' asked Charlie. 'Do the men meet beforehand, get to know each other?'

'No, of course not. They don't want to know each other. They just want to spend one evening with like-minded people they'll never see again. They don't even use their own names. Soon as they book, Graham assigns them a new name, which they use for the whole of that evening. Look, I hope I'm going to get some credit for all the help I'm giving you. You can't say I'm not cooperating now.'

An unpleasant memory broke through the surface of Charlie's thoughts. 'Isn't Graham supposed to be absent-minded, always cocking up the chalet bookings?'

Steph frowned. 'Yes, but I run the chalets. Graham's not passionate about them, not compared with his stag nights. When he really cares about something, he does it properly, one hundred per cent.'

'How admirable,' said Charlie.

Steph appeared to miss the sarcasm. 'Yes,' she agreed. 'He makes sure never to put his customers at risk. He really cares about protecting them, it's his main rule. Always look after the customer, never bite the hand that feeds you.'

'I'm looking forward to telling him that all his customers are going to be charged with being accessories to rape,' said Charlie.

Steph was shaking her head. 'You can't do that,' she said. She was trying to come across as an objective supplier of information, trying to hide the triumph in her voice, but Charlie heard it. 'What I said about the women all being paid actresses – that's the official line. Graham tells everyone who books, if any shit ever hits any fans, the men must all say they fully believed the women were willing participants, that it was all a show, the rape part wasn't real. That's why Graham does the sex and the men only watch, even though most of the time they probably want to join in. It's so they can't be done for anything. You can't prove any of our customers knew the women were being forced to have sex.'

'You've just told us.' Gibbs was unimpressed by her logic. 'We both heard you explain it, very clearly. That's all we need.'

'But . . . it's not written down or anything.' Steph had turned pale.

'Do you really think we can't crack these men? You think they won't talk, give themselves away?' Charlie leaned over the desk. 'There's too many of them, Steph. Some of them will give up and spill whatever beans they've got, because they'll be shit-scared. They'll fall for the same lie you fell for: that talking'll help them stay out of prison.'

Steph's bottom lip trembled. 'Graham'll kill me,' she said. 'He'll blame me, and it's not fair! We were only

343

providing a service, that's all. Entertainment. The men didn't do anything wrong, they didn't touch those women.'

'Did you cook the food?' asked Gibbs. 'The elaborate dinners? Or did Robert Haworth do that? We know he was involved in the rapes, and we know he used to be a chef.'

Charlie hid her surprise. Robert Haworth, a chef?

'I cooked,' said Steph.

'Is that another lie?'

'She's trying to protect Robert because he's Graham's brother,' said Charlie. 'If Graham's sentimental about his customers, imagine how he must feel about his brother.'

'You're wrong there, actually,' Steph gloated. 'Robert and Graham aren't speaking, haven't for years.'

'Why?' Gibbs asked.

'They had a huge row. Robert started going out with . . . one of the women. He told Graham he was going to marry her. And then he did marry her, the stupid bastard.'

'Juliet?' said Charlie. 'Juliet Heslehurst?'

Steph nodded. 'Graham was furious that Robert would even think of going near her, after . . . well, you know. It was such a risk to the business. Graham could have ended up behind bars, and Robert didn't give a toss, just went ahead and married her.' Her lips twitched in anger. 'Graham's way too soft on Robert. I keep telling him, if Robert was my brother, I'd never speak to him again.'

'I thought you said Graham doesn't speak to him,' Charlie reminded her.

'Yeah, but he keeps trying to make up. I'm the go-between, and I'm bloody fed up of passing messages back and forth. He's too soft, my husband. It's Robert who keeps the feud going.' She frowned, deep in thought. 'Graham says he can't give up on him, though. Robert's his kid brother, he's always looked after him. More than their useless parents did, anyway.'

'So Graham was willing to forgive Robert for endangering the business?' said Gibbs.

'Yeah. Family's family to Graham, whatever they do. He was the same with his mum and dad. Robert was the one who cut them off, both of them. Didn't speak a word to them after he left home. Claimed they'd let him down. Well, they had, but . . . then he said the same about Graham, after the row when he started seeing that Juliet woman. As if that was in any way the same!' Old indignation, newly expressed.

'If Graham cares about Robert, that gives you a reason to lie about Robert's involvement in the rapes,' said Charlie.

Steph frowned. 'I'm not saying anything about Robert.'

'He raped Prudence Kelvey,' said Gibbs.

'I don't know what you're on about. I don't know that name. Look, I don't remember most of the women's names. I was busy in the kitchen most of the time.'

'Prue Kelvey was raped in Robert's lorry,' Charlie told her.

'Oh, right. In that case, I wouldn't know. Once there were no meals involved, I kept out of it. Apart from when I was . . . being the victim.'

'Why the change from chalet to lorry?' asked Gibbs.

Steph examined her fingernails.

'Well?'

She sighed, as if the questions were putting her out. 'The chalet business started doing better and better. It got to the point where there were people around, guests, nearly all the time. Graham thought it was too risky – anyone might have seen or heard something. And the lorry was . . . mobile. It was more convenient. For me, especially. I was fed up of all the bloody cooking. I've got enough on my plate without that as well. The only downside is, we can't charge as much now we're offering a package that doesn't include dinner. But we still provide drinks.' Steph's voice was shrill, defensive. 'Champagne – good-quality champagne. So it's not as if we don't offer them anything.'

Charlie decided she'd be quite happy if Steph Angilley were to die, suddenly, of an unforeseen but particularly painful heart attack. Gibbs looked as if he felt the same.

'I hate Robert,' Steph confided tearfully, as if she couldn't keep it in any longer. 'Changing his name like that – the bastard. He only did that to hurt Graham, and it worked. Graham was devastated. He's in a terrible state at the moment, ever since *you* told him Robert was in hospital.'

She spat the words at Charlie, who tried not to flinch as she remembered talking to Simon on her mobile in front of Graham. 'So, what's happened to this Haworth chap?' Graham had asked casually afterwards. And Charlie had told him about Robert, that he was unlikely to live. Graham had looked upset; Charlie remembered thinking it was sweet of him to be concerned.

'Graham really cares about family, and his are all shit,' Steph went on. 'Even his little brother turned out to be a traitor. Who does Robert think he is? He was the one in the wrong, not Graham. It's so unfair! Everyone knows you don't mix business with pleasure, and you certainly don't try to ruin your own brother's business. He did it again as well.'

'What?'

'That Naomi woman you were with before. Robert must have been shagging her, because she tried to book a chalet for the two of them. She pretended she was called Haworth too, but I knew it was her as soon as I heard the name Naomi. Graham was spitting feathers. "Robert's done it again," he said.'

Charlie tried to clear her mind. There was nothing like talking to a very stupid person for bringing on a sort of mental claustrophobia. 'Graham and Robert aren't speaking. Yet you use his lorry for your stag nights.'

'Yeah,' said Steph. 'Graham had his own key cut.'

'You mean to say Robert doesn't know you use the lorry for your stag dos?' Gibbs' voice was incredulous. 'He must notice it's missing some nights. Does Graham pretend he uses the lorry for some other purpose?'

Charlie didn't like the slant of Gibbs' questions. Why was he trying to find a way for Robert Haworth not to be guilty of anything? They *knew* Haworth had raped Prue Kelvey – there was solid, incontrovertible evidence to prove it.

Steph bit her lip, looking wary.

Gibbs tried again. 'If Robert wants nothing to do with Graham, why let him use the lorry? For money? Does Graham hire it from him?'

'I'm not saying anything about Robert, all right?' Steph folded her arms. 'As it is, Graham's going to bloody kill me. If I talk about Robert, he really will murder me. He's very protective of his little brother.'

28

Sunday 9 April

It's after midnight by the time I get to my house. I hitched a lift with a chatty young lorry driver called Terry, and made it back safely. I wasn't nervous about being in a stranger's car. All the worst things that might happen to me already have. I feel immune to danger.

Yvon's car isn't here. She must have gone back to Cambridge, to Ben's. I knew she would, when I left home yesterday without telling her where I was going. Yvon is one of those people who can't be alone. She needs a strong presence in her life, someone to rely on, and my recent behaviour has been too unpredictable. She imagines life with Ben Cotchin will be safer.

The cliché 'Love is blind' should be replaced with a more accurate one: 'Love is unconscious.' Like you, Robert. If you'll pardon the sick joke. Yvon sees everything Ben does, but can't draw the right conclusions. It's her mind that's not working properly, not her eyes.

I go straight to my workshop, unlock the door and pick up the largest of my dummy mallets, weighing it in my palm. I stroke its gold head with my fingers. I've always found dummy mallets satisfying to hold; I like the absence of straight lines. They're the same shape as the pestles some people use for grinding herbs into pastes, except they're made of wood and bronze. With this one in my hand, I could do serious damage, which is what I want to do.

I pick up a length of rope from the floor, under my work table, then some more. I have no idea how much is enough. I'm used to tying up wrapped sundials, not men. In the end, I decide to take all the rope I've got, and a large pair of scissors. I lock up the workshop, go back to my car and drive to Charlie's house.

No one could blame me for what I'm about to do. I'm performing a service, a necessary one. There's no alternative. Graham Angilley attacked us all too long ago – Juliet, me, Sandy Freeguard. Simon Waterhouse told me on Wednesday that the conviction rate for years-old rapes is low, and Charlie said there's no DNA evidence from Sandy Freeguard's attack. Only Prue Kelvey's, and Angilley didn't touch her. It would be his word against mine.

Charlie's house is dark, as it was when Terry the lorry driver – your colleague, as I like to think of him – dropped me off outside it forty-five minutes ago, to collect my car. I wasn't prepared to go inside then, unarmed.

The building looks empty, radiates cold stillness. If your brother Graham is inside, he must be asleep. I take Charlie's keys and, as quietly as I can, try them in the lock one by one. The third one works. I turn it very slowly, then, inch by inch, I push open the front door.

Holding the dummy mallet in my hand, I wait for my eyes to adjust to the darkness. Once they have, I begin to climb the stairs. One step creaks slightly, but not enough to wake someone who's sleeping, oblivious. On the upstairs landing, there are three doors. I assume they lead to two bedrooms and a bathroom. I tiptoe into the bedrooms, one by one. Nobody. I check the bathroom: also empty.

I'm not as frightened as I probably should be. I've slipped back into I-can-do-anything mode. Last time I felt like this, I went to the police station and told a detective that you'd raped me. Thank God I did. It's thanks to me that Juliet's attempt to kill you failed.

I go back downstairs, holding the mallet level with my head in case I need to use it suddenly. I've got the rope over my arm and the strap of my bag round my neck. I open the only door in the hall and find a long, thin lounge with open glass doors in the middle, off which is a small, messy kitchen, with lots of washing-up heaped on one side of the sink.

Satisfied that there's no one in the house, I close the curtains in the lounge and pat the walls near the door until I find the light switch. If Graham Angilley comes back to the house and sees a light on, he'll assume it's Charlie. He'll ring the bell. I'll open the door, but not wide enough for him to see me. Then I'll hide behind it, and when he pushes it all the way open and walks in, I'll smash the dummy mallet down on his head.

I blink, dazzled by the sudden bright glare in the room. I see a lamp and switch that on instead, turning the main light off again. There's a note on the table, next to the base of the lamp. It says, 'Where the hell are you? You didn't leave a key. I've gone to get something to eat and a few stiff drinks. I'll come back later. Ring me on my mobile when you get this message – I'm v. worried. Hope whatever you're doing isn't mad/life-threatening.'

I drop the piece of paper as soon as I've read it. I don't want to hold your brother's handwriting, don't want it to touch my skin. The message puzzles me. Why did Angilley need a key? He must already have been inside the house, in order to put the note on the table. Then it occurs to me that if he wanted to go out, he would need to be able to let himself back in. He is probably somewhere nearby, phoning every so often to see if Charlie has come back. No one's rung since I've been here, though. Why isn't he trying the landline?

And the front door was locked when I arrived. Who locked it, if Angilley has no key?

I pull Charlie's mobile phone out of my handbag. It's switched off. I turn it on, but don't know her pin number, so I can't access any messages Angilley might have left.

I'm v. worried. Hope whatever you're doing isn't mad/ life-threatening.

He cares about her. Pain and bitterness rise inside me like a tidal wave. There's nothing worse than to be confronted with evidence that a person who has nearly destroyed you is capable of being kind to somebody else.

I shiver, telling myself it's not possible. Charlie Zailer cannot be Graham Angilley's lover. I could have spoken to any detective about your disappearance on Monday; I gave her the Silver Brae Chalets card by mistake. And she just happens to be sleeping with your brother?

I don't believe in coincidences.

I hear a car door open and close in the street outside. Then it cuts out. It has to be him. I run to the hall, take up my position by the front door. Dropping the rope on the floor at my feet, I grab the handle, ready to twist it as soon as the bell rings. Just one, soft, small turn should do it.

Then I hear the noise I imagine the door will make when I open it. Except I'm not imagining it; I'm really hearing it. Inside the house – the sound is coming from behind me, where there should be silence. In my shock, I loosen my grip on the dummy mallet and it drops to the floor. I swallow a scream, and bend to pick it up, but I can't see it. My hands get tangled in the coils of rope.

The hall is darker than it was only seconds ago. How can that be? Was the noise I heard the sound of a light bulb dying? No; the lounge door has swung almost shut. Get a grip, I tell myself, but my heartbeat races on, heedless. I need to get back in control.

I hear footsteps, tapping up the path towards the door. I drop down on to my haunches, patting the floor to find the dummy mallet. 'Where is it?' I whisper, desperate. The bell rings. A female voice says, 'Char? Charlie?' I hold my breath. It's not your brother. I haven't a clue what to do now. Who else could it be? Who drops round at one in the morning?

I hear the voice mutter, 'What the fuck sort of welcome is this?' but I don't dare to open the door. My fingers close around the dummy mallet. Should I say something?

'Charlie, open the door, for Christ's sake.'

The woman sounds frantic. She must be the one who wrote the note I found, not Graham Angilley. But the note was in the lounge, on the table. Not on the hall carpet near the letter box, where it should have been . . .

The woman bangs her fists against the stained glass. I leave the mallet on the floor and crawl back into the lounge, pushing the door open with my head. That's when I see him. He's standing, feet wide apart, in the centre of the lounge. Smiling at me.

'Naomi Jenkins, as I live and breathe,' he says.

Panic engulfs me. I try to stand up, but he pulls me towards him, clamping his hand over my mouth. He tastes of soap.

'Ssh,' he says. 'Listen. Can you hear it? Footsteps. Quieter and quieter and . . . there we are! Charlie's little sis is squeezing her fat bot back into her car.'

I hear the engine again. His touch corrodes my skin. I am slipping away from myself.

'There she goes. Bye-bye, Fat Bitch Slim.' Still pressing his hand down over my mouth, he puts his lips against my ear. 'Hello, you,' he whispers.

29

9/4/06

For the first time in his police career, Simon was pleased to see Proust. He was the one who'd called the inspector, told him to come in. Nearly begged him. Anything was better than being alone with his thoughts. There's something wrong with my life if, *in extremis*, I turn to the Snowman, Simon thought. But who else was there? With Charlie gone, he could think of no one whose company would make him feel better. Ringing his folks was out of the question. The minute they got a whiff of any sort of problem, their voices filled with shrill alarm, and Simon had to put his own worries to one side in order to comfort them.

He still thought of Charlie as gone, even though Sellers had phoned to update him. He knew where she was, that Gibbs was with her, that she was safe. He also knew she'd been to bed with Graham Angilley. A serial rapist. Without knowing what he was, who he was. The idea made Simon panic. How could Charlie ever be the same after an experience like that? What ought he to say next time he saw her?

Assuming he ever saw her again. She'd run off without a word to him. Even now, knowing he knew where she was, she hadn't called him. Her phone was in her bag, which Naomi Jenkins had taken, but she could have used Gibbs'.

She's spoken to Sellers and Gibbs. It's only you she doesn't want to speak to.

Well, why the fuck should she? What use had Simon ever

been to Charlie? A few months ago she'd drawn his attention to a song that was playing on his car radio, when they'd been driving to a meeting at Silsford nick. Simon still remembered the lyrics; they were about one person giving another nothing but pain. Charlie had said, 'I didn't know you were a Kaiser Chiefs fan. Or are you playing this song for some other reason?' She'd looked scornful at first, then disappointed when Simon told her it was the radio, not a CD. He hadn't chosen the song, didn't even know it.

Proust's arrival stopped him from thinking about which song he'd choose now. The inspector was pink-eyed and unshaven. 'It's two in the morning, Waterhouse,' he said. 'You interrupted a dream. Now I'll never know how it ends.'

'A good one or a bad one?' Simon was playing for time. Delay the bollocking for as long as possible.

'I don't know. Lizzie and I had just bought a new house and moved into it. It was much bigger than our present one. We arrived tired, and went straight to sleep. I got no further, thanks to you.'

'A bad dream,' said Simon. 'I know how it ends. You realise you've made a terrible mistake buying the new house. But the old one's already sold, to people who love it and are determined to stay. There's no way of getting it back. A nightmare of eternal regret.'

'Charming.' Proust looked cross. 'Thank you so much for that. Since you're feeling chatty, perhaps you could explain why you've woken me up to give me information you could just as easily have given me this afternoon.'

'I didn't know then that Charlie had taken Naomi Jenkins to Scotland with her.'

Proust frowned. 'Why not?'

'I . . . I mustn't have been listening when she told me.'

'Hmm. Hear that, Waterhouse? The sound of thinly veiled scepticism? You and Sergeant Zailer are like Siamese twins. You always know where she is, who she's with, what she had for breakfast. Why not this time?'

Simon said nothing. Oddly, he felt better now that the Snowman was berating him; he felt as if he'd handed something over, something he was glad to be shot of.

'So, let's get this right: the first you knew about Sergeant Zailer taking Jenkins to Scotland with her was Sellers' phone call, is that what you're saying?'

'Yes, sir.'

'And when did you receive this call?'

'Mid-evening.'

'Why not tell me then? You could have saved me the trouble of getting into my pyjamas.'

Simon examined his shoes. At that stage, he'd thought he could ride it out. He'd grown more edgy as the night went on, when Charlie failed to contact him. He'd been expecting her to ring ever since Sellers had, to tell Simon what she wanted him to do. She hadn't, though, and it had suddenly struck him as entirely possible that she never would. In which case, Simon needed to tell Proust enough of the truth to cover himself.

The inspector's eyes narrowed, ready to scrutinise each new lie as it emerged. 'If the sergeant went to this chalet place to arrest the owner and his wife, why didn't she take you with her, and some uniforms? Why take Naomi Jenkins, who is at best a witness and at worst a suspect?'

'Maybe she wanted Jenkins to identify Angilley as the man who assaulted her.'

'Well, that's not the way to do it!' said Proust angrily. 'That's the way to get your car stolen, and your bag. As has become apparent. Why would Sergeant Zailer be so stupid? She put herself and Jenkins at risk, all our hard work—'

'I've just had a call from the police in Scotland,' Simon interrupted him.

'I find that harder to believe than anything I've heard so far. That lot are useless.'

'They've found Charlie's car.'

'Where?'

'Not far from Silver Brae Chalets. About four miles down the road. The handbag was gone, though.'

Proust sighed heavily, rubbing his chin. 'There are so many dubious aspects to this, I hardly know where to begin, Waterhouse. Why would Naomi Jenkins, having gone to Scotland to identify her rapist, suddenly take it into her head to steal a car and run away – start behaving like a criminal, effectively?'

'I don't know, sir,' Simon lied. He couldn't tell the inspector what Sellers had told him: that Naomi didn't trust Charlie any more, that she knew about Charlie's involvement with Graham Angilley because of something Steph had said.

'Speak to Sergeant Zailer,' said Proust impatiently. 'Something must have happened, mustn't it? At the chalets. Sergeant Zailer must know what it is, and so should you, by now. When did you last speak to her?'

'Not since before she left,' Simon admitted.

'What aren't you telling me, Waterhouse?'

'Nothing, sir.'

'If Sergeant Zailer went to Silver Brae Chalets to arrest the Angilleys, why did Sellers and Gibbs also go there, separately? Does it take three of them? One detective with uniform back-up would have been adequate.'

'I'm not sure, sir.'

Proust walked a small circle round Simon. 'Waterhouse, you know me pretty well by now. Wouldn't you say? You must know that if there's one thing I hate more than being lied to, it's being lied to in the middle of the night.'

Silence was the best Simon could do. He wondered if, on one level, he wanted Proust to break him down, force the full story out of him. Charlie and Graham Angilley. Could the Snowman say anything that would make him feel better about that?

'Maybe I ought to ask Naomi Jenkins. She's unlikely to be less helpful than you. What's being done about finding her?'

At last, a question Simon could answer truthfully. 'Some uniforms are at the hospital. Sellers said Charlie's certain that's where Jenkins'll go, to see Robert Haworth.'

'So you and the sergeant are communicating via Sellers. Interesting.' The inspector walked another slow circle round Simon. 'Why does Jenkins want to see Robert Haworth? She knows he raped Prudence Kelvey, doesn't she? Sergeant Zailer told her?'

'Yes. I don't know why she wants to see him, but apparently she does. A lot.'

'Waterhouse, it's two in the perishing morning!' Proust tapped his watch. 'She'd be there by now, if that was where she was going. Sergeant Zailer must be wrong. Have we got anyone outside Jenkins' house?'

Shit. 'No, sir.'

'Of course we haven't. Silly of me.' The voice had thinned; the words were projected at Simon like lead pellets. 'Get someone there as soon as possible. If she's not there, try Yvon Cotchin's ex-husband's house. Then Jenkins' parents'. I'm astonished to hear myself saying all this, Waterhouse.' As if afraid he'd been too subtle in his disapproval, Proust yelled, 'What's the matter with you? You shouldn't need a sleep-befuddled old man like me to tell you the basics!'

'I've been busy, sir.' *Everyone else is in fucking Scotland. Sir.* 'Charlie said Jenkins'd go straight to the hospital. Since she was the last of us to speak to her, I assumed she knew what she was talking about.'

'Find Jenkins and find her quickly! I want to know why she absconded. I was never happy with her alibi for the period during which Robert Haworth must have been attacked. Her best friend's word is all we've got, and that same friend designed Graham Angilley's website!'

'You never said you had a problem with the alibi, sir,' Simon muttered.

'I'm saying so now, aren't I? I've got a problem with this whole confounded mess, Waterhouse! Circles within circles, that's what it is. We're chasing our tails! Look at that big, black blob.' He pointed at the whiteboard on the wall of the CID room, on which Charlie had written, in black marker pen, the names of everybody involved in the case, with arrows between them wherever there was a connection. Proust was right; there were more connections than one might expect. Charlie's diagram now resembled a morbidly obese spider – a huge black mass of lines, arrows, circles, loops. The shape of chaos. 'Have you ever *seen* anything so unsatisfactory?' Proust demanded. 'Because I haven't!'

Speaking of unsatisfactory, thought Simon. 'Juliet Haworth's stopped talking, sir.'

'Did she ever start?'

'No, I mean stopped altogether. I've tried twice, and both times she was completely silent. I knew it'd happen. The closer she thinks we are to the truth, the less she's going to say. There's enough evidence to convict her, but . . .'

'But it's not good enough,' Proust finished Simon's sentence. 'Much as I'd like a conviction here to satisfy the higher-ups, I want to know what went on. I want to see a clear picture, Waterhouse.'

'Me too, sir. It's getting clearer. We know Angilley selected his victims from websites, at least two from sites designed by Yvon Cotchin.'

'What about Tanya, the waitress from Cardiff who killed herself, the one who couldn't spell? Did she have a website?'

'She's the exception,' Simon conceded. 'We can explain the audiences at the rapes – Angilley was selling hard-core stag nights. I've found references to his operation in Internet chatrooms already. That's what I've been doing . . .'

'Instead of talking to your sergeant, or trying to find Naomi Jenkins,' Proust said pointedly. 'Or telling me the truth about what's really going on in your peculiar mind and your even more peculiar life, Waterhouse. If you'll pardon my bluntness.'

Simon froze. This was among the more hurtful things he'd had said to him over the years. Charlie would have said, 'Peculiar, as far as the Snowman's concerned, is any man who doesn't have a bread-baking, sock-darning wifie at home.' Simon could hear her voice clearly in his mind, but it wasn't the same as having her with him.

His life *was* peculiar. He didn't have a girlfriend, had no real friends apart from Charlie.

'Sellers has picked up a stack of evidence from Silver Brae Chalets,' he went on. 'Angilley had it all neatly filed, as if it were completely legitimate: contact numbers for dozens of men, and a list of twenty-three women's names – past victims and future ones, by the look of it. Some names with dates and ticks beside them, some without. Sellers has Googled all the women – they've all either got their own websites or a page on a company one. They're all professional—'

The telephone in front of Simon began to ring. He picked it up. 'DC Waterhouse, CID,' he said automatically. It wasn't going to be Charlie: she'd have rung his mobile.

'Simon? Thank fucking God!'

His heart soared. It wasn't Charlie. But it sounded a bit like her. 'Olivia?'

'I lost your mobile number and I've spent the past hour being pissed around, first by an electronic imbecile and then by a human one. Never mind. Look, I'm worried about Charlie. Can you send a police car round to her house?'

Simon's nerves buzzed as he said to Proust, 'Get some uniforms to blue-light it round to Charlie's place.' He'd never given the Snowman an order before.

Proust picked up a phone on the adjacent desk.

'What's happened?' Simon asked Olivia.

'Charlie left a message for me today – well, yesterday, I suppose, except I haven't been to sleep yet. She told me to go round to her house. She said the key'd be in its usual place, and to let myself in if she wasn't back yet.'

'And?' Simon knew about the key Charlie left underneath her wheelie-bin. She'd left it there for him on the odd occasion. He'd remonstrated with her; what was the point of being a detective if you left your key in the first place any burglar would look? 'I haven't got the mental energy to think of a better hiding place,' she'd said wearily.

'I got there at about eight,' said Olivia. 'Charlie wasn't there, and neither was the key. I stuck a note through the letter box, telling her to ring me. I went to the pub, had something to eat and a couple of drinks, read my book, didn't hear anything. Eventually I got really worried and went back to the house. She still wasn't back. I sat in my car and waited for her, basically. Normally I'd have sacked it and gone home, but the message she'd left me . . . she sounded really upset. She as good as told me something bad had happened.'

'And?' Simon tried hard to keep his voice steady. *Get to the fucking point.*

'I fell asleep in my car. When I woke up, a light was on in Charlie's lounge and the curtains were closed. Before, they'd been open. I assumed she was back, so I went and rang the bell, ready to have a go at her for not phoning me as soon as she got in and saw my note. But no one answered the door. I know someone was in there, I saw movements in the hall. In fact, I'm sure it was two people. One of them must have been Charlie, but then why didn't she let me in? You'll probably think I'm being neurotic, but I know something's not right.'

'Charlie's in Scotland,' Simon told her. *And Graham Angilley isn't.* 'She can't be in her house.'

'Are you sure?'

'Positive. It was a last-minute thing.'

'Has she gone back to Silver Brae Chalets?' asked Olivia, sounding more like the journalist that she was. 'You rang and asked me all those questions about Graham Angilley . . . Why the fuck didn't Charlie tell me, if she was going to see him again, instead of letting me turn up at her house like an idiot?' There was a pause. 'Do you know what she's so upset about?'

'I've got to go, Olivia.' Simon wanted to get off the phone, wanted to get round to Charlie's house himself. Proust already had his coat on.

'Simon? Don't put the phone down! If it's not Charlie in the house, then who is it?'

'Olivia—'

'I could drive back there, smash a window and find out for myself! I'm only five minutes away.'

'Don't do that. Olivia, do you hear me? I can't explain now, but I think there's a dangerous, violent man in Charlie's house. Keep well away. Promise me.' His failure to protect Charlie made him all the more determined to protect her sister. 'Promise me, Olivia.'

She sighed. 'All right, then. But ring me as soon as you can. I want to know what's going on.'

So did Proust. He raised an eyebrow as Simon put the phone down. 'A dangerous, violent man?'

Simon nodded, feeling his skin heat up. 'Graham Angilley.' He was already heading for the door, patting his jacket in search of his car keys. Proust followed; Simon was surprised to discover that the inspector – normally so slow and deliberate – could run faster than he could.

Both men were thinking the same thing: Naomi Jenkins had Charlie's handbag, had the keys to her house. If Olivia was right about having seen two people, Naomi could be inside the house with Angilley. They had to get there, fast.

The Snowman waited until they were in the car, driving at double the speed limit, before saying, 'It's just a small thing, a tiny detail, but why is Graham Angilley in Sergeant Zailer's house? How does he know where she lives?'

Simon kept his eyes on the road. He didn't answer.

When Proust next spoke, his tone was quietly courteous, his lips thin and white. 'I wonder how many people are going to be getting their marching orders, once all this is over,' he mused.

Simon clung to the steering wheel as if it were all he had in the world.

30

Sunday 9 April

Graham Angilley stands over me, holding the scissors I brought with me from home. He cuts at the air in front of my face. The blades make a metallic slicing sound. In his other hand, he holds my dummy mallet.

'How considerate of you to come well equipped,' he says.

There is only one thought running through my head: he cannot win. That can't be how the story ends, with me being stupid enough to come here, knowing there was a good chance he'd be here, carrying with me everything he needs to humiliate and defeat me. I try not to think about my own recklessness. I must have been crazy to think I could overpower him. But I can't dwell on that. Three years ago I allowed myself to feel powerless in his presence and that's what I was: utterly helpless. This time I must do everything differently.

Starting with showing no fear. I will not cower or beg. I haven't so far, not when he held the scissors to my throat and not while he tied me to one of the two straight-backed wooden chairs in Charlie's kitchen. I was silent, and tried to keep my face blank, free of expression.

'It's just like old times, isn't it?' he said. 'Except you've got your clothes on. For the moment.'

My hands are bound together behind the chair, and each of my feet is tied to one of the back legs. The strain on my thigh muscles is becoming worse than uncomfortable.

364

Angilley closes the scissors and puts them down on the kitchen table. He rolls the dummy mallet in both hands.

'Well, well,' he says. 'What have we here? A long conical object with a blunt, round end. I give up. Is it some sort of sex toy? A big bronze dildo?'

'Why don't you sit on it and find out?' I say, hoping he'll think I'm not scared.

He grins. 'Fighting back this time, are you? You do right, as we Yorkshire folk sometimes say. I like a bit of variety.'

'Is that why you do the same thing over and over again: tie up women and rape them? You even say the same thing: "Do you want to warm up before the show?" What a ridiculous line.' I force myself to laugh. Whatever I say to him, whether I'm defiant or timid, will make no difference to what he does to me. He knows how he wants this to finish. No words of mine will affect him either way, because he takes nothing to heart. Realising this enables me to speak freely. 'You might think you're adventurous, but you'd be lost without your stupid routine. That stays the same, whoever the woman is, whether it's Juliet, me, Sandy Freeguard . . .'

The skin round his eyes crinkles as his frown becomes a twisted smile. 'How do you know about Sandy Freeguard? From Charlie Zailer, I bet.'

'Or from Robert,' I suggest.

'Nice try. Charlie told you.' Angilley sniffs the air. 'Yes, I thought I detected the unmistakable odour of female solidarity and mutual empowerment. Do the two of you make patchwork quilts together in your spare time? You must be pretty close if you've got her house keys. A bit unprofessional of her, I'd say. Not as bad as doing the deed of darkness with yours truly, though. That's the sarge's most serious faux pas to date.'

I try to shift my position to make my legs more comfortable, but it doesn't work. My feet are starting to tingle; soon they'll be numb.

'You do look sexy when you wriggle and writhe like that. Do it again.'

'Fuck off.'

He puts the dummy mallet down on the table. 'There'll be plenty of time to use this later,' he says. My insides lurch. I have to keep him talking.

'Tell me about Prue Kelvey,' I say.

He picks up the scissors and walks slowly towards me. A scream rises in my throat. It takes all my willpower to subdue it. If I show even the tiniest bit of fear, I won't be able to pretend after that. My act has to be constant, impervious. He lifts the collar of my shirt and tells me to lean my head forward. Then he starts to cut, all the way round the back of my neck. I feel the cold metal of the scissors against my skin.

He throws the collar into my lap once he's cut it off. 'How about you answer my questions first? How did my brother end up nearly dead in hospital? The good sarge would only tell me so much. Did you put him there, or did Juliet?' He sounds less flippant now. As if he cares.

I look at his eyes, wondering if it's some kind of trick. Letting me see that this matters to him is like handing me a weapon. But maybe he thinks there is nothing I can do to him. He's tied me to a chair to make sure of that.

'It's a long story,' I say. 'My legs are hurting and I can't feel my feet. Why don't you untie me?'

'I always do eventually, don't I?' Angilley says flirtatiously. 'What's the hurry? I should point out that if my little brother dies and if I find out that it was you who tried to murder him, I *will* kill you.' He cuts the top button off my shirt.

'Shall we just have sex and get it over with?' I suggest, feeling my heart pound in my mouth. 'There's no need for foreplay.'

The man looks irritated, briefly. Then his smooth smile reappears.

'Robert isn't going to die,' I tell him.

He puts the scissors down on the table. 'How do you know?'

'I've been to the hospital.'

After a pause, he says, 'And? There's no point being enigmatic and mysterious with me, Naomi. Don't forget, I know you inside out.' He winks. 'You've been to the hospital *and* . . . ?'

'You don't want Robert to die, and I don't want Robert to die. We're on the same side, whatever happened between us in the past. Why don't you untie me?'

'Not a chance, old beanie. So, who does want Robert to die, then?' the man asks. 'Somebody seems to.'

'Juliet,' I tell him.

'Why? Because he was taking a dip into you behind her back?'

I shake my head. 'She's known about that for months.'

He picks up the scissors again. 'My patience was wearing thin when this conversation started,' he says. 'Now it's Karen Carpenter anorexic. So why don't you be a good girl and tell me what I want to know?' He snips off another button.

'Leave my clothes alone,' I snap, as panic rears inside me. 'Untie me and I'll take you to see Robert in hospital.'

'You'll take me? Why, thank you, Fairy Godmother.'

'The only way you'll get to see him is with me,' I say,

making it up as I go along. 'He's not allowed any visitors, but I could get you in. The ward staff know me. I've been in to see him with Charlie.'

'Stop boasting before you embarrass yourself. I've seen Robert today, as it happens. Just a couple of hours ago.' The man laughs at my shock, which I've obviously failed to hide. 'Yes, that's right. I got into the intensive care unit all by myself, like a big boy. It was a piece of piss. There's a keypad outside the ward door with letters and numbers on it. All I had to do was watch a couple of doctors going in, and memorise the code they were good enough to tap in right in front of me. It makes me laugh, actually.' He puts down the scissors, pulls the other kitchen chair away from the table and sits down beside me. 'The trappings of vigilance and security – keypads and alarm codes and the like – all they do is make people *less* vigilant. In the old days, ward sisters and doctors probably kept beady eyes peeled for unsavoury elements like *moi*. But there's no need, not any more. Now that there's a digital panel on the door and a code – a *code*, no less! – everyone can wander around with their heads in the clouds, like sheep on Valium, trusting some paltry appliance to take care of safety for them. All it took was a quick tap-tap and I was in, slipping through the door in a cloud of invisible drug-resistant superbugs.'

'How is Robert?'

Your brother chuckles. 'Do you love him? Is this a love sort of thing? It is, isn't it?'

'How is he? Tell me.'

'Well . . . can I be tactful and say he's a good listener?'

'But he's still alive?'

'Oh, yes. He's a little better, actually. The nurse I was flirting with told me. He's no longer – what did she call it? –

intubated. I should explain, in case you went to a sink school – no more tubes. He's breathing on his own. And the old heartbeat was chugging away. I watched it on the screen. The green line went up and down and up and down . . . I tell you what: real hospital's nothing like a TV hospital drama, is it? I was quite disappointed. I was in Robert's room for ten minutes or so, and I encountered not one single nurse or doctor who was determined to interfere in our personal business. There was no stern sister instructing me to confront my unresolved issues. I felt a little bit neglected.'

He has forgotten about the scissors for the time being. I decide to try a more direct approach. 'Graham, I want to go and see Robert. I need to see him. He's your brother, and I know you care about him, however flippant you are about it. Please will you untie me so that I can go to the hospital?'

'I'm more concerned about myself than I am about either you or Robert,' he says, smiling apologetically. 'What's going to happen to me? I'll be arrested, probably, and you'll tell the police I did all sorts of unmentionable things to you. Won't you?'

'No,' I lie. 'Listen, I know for a fact that the police have got no forensic evidence against you. No DNA. Charlie told me.'

'Excellent.' Angilley rubs his hands together. There is something inclusive about his pleasure, as if he expects me to share it.

'If you let me go, I swear on my life I'll tell the police that you weren't the man who attacked me. There's no way you'd be convicted of anything.'

'Hm.' He rubs his chin thoughtfully. 'What about Sergeant Charlie? What have you already said to her? I know women and their big mouths. Intimately, remember?'

My brain is buzzing with the strain of trying to think faster than I can. He can't have spoken to Steph or else he would know that Charlie knows a lot more about his involvement in the rapes than I could have told her. 'She trusts you,' I say. 'She thinks you're her boyfriend.'

'Sweet. But like all great romances, ours can't last. It's only a matter of time before Charlie finds out Robert's real name and works out that I'm his brother. And then she'll wonder why I haven't told her. I thought the game was up when you let yourself in, actually. I assumed you were Charlie, and hid behind the lounge door. It was only when you started creeping around and I snuck a peek that I realised it was you. If the Boob Tube had found me in her house when I wasn't supposed to be there, I dare say we'd have had a big bust-up.'

'What were you doing? Why were you here when Charlie wasn't?'

'I wanted to see if she'd brought any work home with her, anything to do with the attempted murder of my little brother. I want to know who to blame.'

I cannot feel my feet at all any more, can't ignore the shooting pains in my legs and back. 'Look, if I say you weren't the man who raped me, the police can't touch you.'

Angilley frowns. 'Raped? Isn't that putting it a bit strongly?'

'Will you untie me? Please?'

'What about Sandy Freeguard?'

'She doesn't know who you are, and I won't tell her. Untie me.'

'I might. If you tell me why Juliet tried to kill Robert.'

I hesitate. Eventually, I say, 'He told her he was leaving her for me.' I do not need to go into detail about how you told Juliet, the precise words you chose. It must have taken you a long time to explain everything. The abbreviated version's good enough for your brother. 'Now you tell me about Prue Kelvey,' I say.

'What about her? She was one of my leading ladies, like you.' He picks up the scissors again and cuts the last two buttons off my shirt. It falls open. 'You can't go to the hospital like that, with your boobs hanging out. Most unseemly.' His voice hardens. 'How do you know about Prue Kelvey?' Slowly, he closes the scissors around my bra strap, cutting it on one side.

'You didn't have sex with her. Robert did. Why? Did you make him?'

' "Made" is putting it a bit strongly. I encouraged him. Or rather, I asked my wife to pass on a message of encouragement. Robert and I weren't speaking, and I wanted to put things right. Prue Kelvey was my peace offering. Robert accepted, and I was thrilled. I thought he'd enjoy it. Sadly, he didn't, and I ended up regretting my generosity. And things were made worse instead of put right.' Angilley sighs. 'Robert's my kid brother. I wanted him to be part of things, properly involved. He was there at the beginning, on my stag night, when I first had the idea for the business. We went to Wales for the weekend, to Cardiff, just me and Robert. We ended up pissed in a grotty little Indian restaurant, which was a bit of an anticlimax. Until I had the inspired idea of giving the mousy waitress a night to remember. It was just us and her, I was drunk – it seemed the obvious thing to do. I made sure Robert also had his turn with her. And from that acorn of experience grew the great oak of a very successful business. I've single-handedly revolutionised stag nights in this country.'

'Stag nights,' I repeat vaguely, feeling cold and numb. The word 'acorn' rings in my head. I close my eyes and see bedposts with wooden acorns at the top. I feel light-headed, as if I might faint.

'I knew you'd understand,' says the man. 'You've got a business head on your shoulders, just like I have, just like my dear mama had. She made a fortune simply by being her slutty self – the woman was quite brilliant. I do admire successful women.' He begins to cut my trousers, starting with a hole at the knee. 'Peekaboo,' he says, grinning at me. 'Hello, Mr Knee.'

'You've got to untie me,' I tell him. 'I feel as if my back's going to break.'

'My mum was the one who told me your big secret.'

'What secret?'

'Yours plural, not singular. Women. You all have forced-sex fantasies. I enable you to act out those fantasies. I give you what you daren't admit to wanting. Not that I'm any kind of altruist; I won't pretend I am. I'm lucky. Not many people enjoy their work like I do. Though it's been a hard slog too, mainly thanks to Robert. After our Welsh wait-ress, when it came to setting up on a more professional basis, it was hard to persuade him to pull his weight. I became the male lead, permanently. It's a bugger persuad-ing my brother to do something if his heart's not in it. He's forever getting on his high horse about one thing or another. All he'd agree to do was give our leading ladies a lift home after they'd performed. He drove you home.' Watching my face, he begins to smile. 'You didn't know that, did you? Yes, it was Robert who drove you safely back to your car. Course, you wouldn't have seen him because you had a mask over your eyes.'

'You wanted him to play more of a role, so you forced him to rape Prue Kelvey. Did you blackmail him, was that it?'

Angilley smiles, shaking his head. 'You seem to have me down as some kind of tyrant,' he says. 'I'm a mild old soul, me. Robert didn't enjoy his night with Ms Kelvey, and I regretted facilitating it. Since that night, he and I haven't exchanged a word.' He shakes his head. 'Robert insisted on Prue-dential wearing her eye mask throughout the performance, which was no good for the punters. Some of them complained, including the groom-to-be, and I had to give them some money back. They all like to see the eyes – windows to the soul and all that.'

'Why did he make her keep the mask on?' I ask, testing him.

'Who the fuck knows?' He cuts a larger hole in the other leg of my trousers, at the knee. 'That's usually the answer where Robert's concerned. Scared of her recognising him, maybe? Robert's a pessimist. He might have panicked about bumping into her again one day.'

I nod, satisfied that your brother knows nothing. 'Why choose women with websites? Why not take random women off the street?'

'Because, my dear nosey Naomi, it's so much more frightening for the women if they feel they've been chosen. Didn't you wonder why you? And how I knew all those things about you? Sinister; much worse than being plucked off the street, anonymous. No, it's the personal angle that puts the fear in the eyes, and the fear in the eyes, as my punters constantly tell me, is crucial.'

I smile coldly at him. 'The personal angle. Sounds good. And you're right, it does make it worse. I bet you wish you'd thought of it yourself, don't you?'

Angilley stiffens. 'Enough talking,' he says. He crouches down by the side of my chair and begins to cut the leg of my trousers, from the bottom up.

'Bit low, isn't it? To plagiarise other people's ideas and pass them off as your own?'

'If you say so. Now, we mustn't forget the long conical object you so kindly brought, and all its possible uses . . . There!' One leg of my trousers has gone, is in pieces on the floor. Sharp fear silences me. I can't breathe.

'Whatever Robert's told you, he doesn't love you or care about you.' Angilley looks pleased with himself. 'I'm the one he cares about. Why do you think he goes out of his way to meet my leading ladies after the show and make them fall in love with him?'

'Why do you think he does?' I manage to ask.

'Simple: one-upmanship. I'm a success, Robert's a failure. 'Twas ever thus, as they say in corny BBC adaptations. Our mum gave him a hard time after our dad fucked off. Dad never really took to Robert, and Mum treated him like the bogeyman once Dad had gone. Whereas I could do no wrong; I was Golden Boy. Robert's always wanted, secretly, to beat me. To prove he's better. That's how he does it: he seeks out the women who were, shall we say, reluctant to do the deed with me, and charms them or manipulates them until they're gagging to do it with him.'

I stare at him, stunned and horrified by his arrogance. 'You can't honestly believe that,' I say.

He smiles, and begins to cut downward from the waistband of my trousers. 'If you're not lying, if Juliet really *did* try to kill Robert, I'm afraid you don't stand a chance. If he didn't prefer her before, he will now. My little bro's a masochist. He's always had a pash for women who treat him like crud. Dear Mama's legacy, I fear. The more she punished him, the more devoted he was. He cut her off eventually – manly pride and all. And he's been looking for a replacement ever since, though I don't think he realises it.

I only know all this from reading my wife's bubble-head magazines.'

I feel the scissors inside my underwear, smooth and cool against my skin. My mind goes blank and instinct takes over. With all my strength, I propel my body to the left, unbalancing the chair. It's a matter of four or five seconds, no more. How can so few seconds contain so many distinct incidents? Your brother looks up as the chair and I fall towards him, as his wrist is bent back. He pulls his arm free and it jerks towards his body, almost as a reflex. As the chair crashes down on him, I see him staring at the open scissors in his hand. I feel the sickening thud as the chair hits his arm, pushing his hand towards his face.

He screams. Blood is spurting, splashing my face, but I can't see where it comes from. The chair crashes down on Graham Angilley. Instead of being upright, I'm now on a slant, the slope of his prone, shaking body. I hear him wailing, groaning, but I cannot see his face, even when I turn my head as far as I can. I try to shout for help, but I'm panting too hard to make myself heard.

I couldn't see blood before, but now I can. The red creeps across the blue checked linoleum. I take a deep breath and scream for help, drawing out the sound for as long as I can. At first it's words, then it turns into pure howling, the high-pitched release of pain.

I hear a loud crash, feet pounding down the hall. I carry on screaming. I see Simon Waterhouse and a bald man behind him, and I carry on screaming. Because no one will ever help me properly, or enough. Not these men who've burst in, not Yvon, not Charlie, not anyone. I will never escape. That's why I have to keep making this noise.

31

Monday 10 April

I will not go away. I will never leave you alone. I'm standing outside the door to the intensive care unit, and I sense your presence, like something heavy in the air. I could almost believe, if I didn't know better, that the hushed, solemn atmosphere in the hospital today is on account of us. Staff, visitors and outpatients walk past me with their heads bowed.

I was here yesterday, but I couldn't come and see you then. Simon Waterhouse insisted on staying with me the whole time. While the doctors checked me over, he waited outside the examination room. I think you'd approve of his patience and thoroughness; they're two qualities you also have. He drove me home, once he'd satisfied himself that the experts thought I was fit to leave. There was nothing physically wrong with me, I kept telling him, apart from the pain in my legs and arms from being tied up.

Yesterday I was nowhere near the intensive care unit. Which is lucky. It makes today easier.

I type the code into the keypad, the one I have just watched a doctor use: CY1789. The trick that worked for your brother has worked for me as well. The door buzzes, and when I push it, it opens easily. I am on your ward. Straight away, I realise that physically getting into the unit is only part of the challenge. I now need to look as if I belong here, as if I take for granted my presence on this corridor. Graham must have done this too, must have been aware that to look as if he was sneaking around would have been fatal.

Holding my head high, I walk quickly and confidently past the nurses' station towards your room, glad I had the presence of mind this morning to put on my only smart suit. I left my handbag at home; instead, I'm carrying a brown leather zipped case that I hope makes me look official. I smile at everybody I pass – a warm, busy smile that says, 'I'm sure you all know who I am. I belong here; I've been before and will come again.' And I will, Robert, whether you want me to or not. I won't be able to keep away.

The wooden door to your room has a square window. When I came here with Charlie, the curtain was open, but it's closed now. I reach for the door handle and walk into the room without looking around to see who's watching me. Without hesitation.

Two young nurses are in your room. One is washing your face and neck with a sponge. *Shit*. Shock wipes the smile off my face. 'Sorry,' says the other nurse, who is putting some fluid in a bag attached to one of the machines. She has mistaken my fear for anger. I am older than her and expensively dressed; she assumes I'm senior hospital personnel.

Her colleague, the one with the sponge in her hand, is less deferential. She says, 'Who are you?'

This is easier now that you're in front of me. You're a man in a bed, immobile. Your eyes are closed, your skin pale. I stare at your face and realise how separate we are. We could so easily be nothing to do with one another. Everything about you – your thoughts, feelings, the network of internal organs that keeps your body going – it's all packed inside your skin.

For a moment it strikes me as odd that another person, sealed and self-contained as you are in your casing of flesh, has got under my skin to such an extent. If a surgeon cut you open, he would find all the different parts of you. If he cut me open, he'd find the same thing. You have almost replaced me, Robert, inside my own self. How did I allow that to happen?

'This is Robert Haworth, is that right?' I say, aiming to sound like someone who has every right not to be patient but is being patient nonetheless.

'Yes. Are you from CID?'

'Not quite,' I say. I hold up my leather case, to suggest it contains important documents. 'I'm the family liaison officer. I'm working with the police. Sergeant Zailer said it'd be okay to come and see Robert now.' Thank God for Simon Waterhouse. He mentioned the possibility of engaging a family liaison officer to look after me, on the way back from the hospital yesterday. It's a bit late for that, I felt like saying.

The nurses nod. 'We're finished anyway,' one says.

'Great.' I flash her a busy, efficient smile. Neither of them questions why a family liaison officer would need to spend time with an unconscious man. The title I gave myself was enough for them. It sounded right, suggested procedures in place and guidelines diligently drawn up, clear aims and objectives. No need for the nurses to be on their guard.

Once they're gone, I walk over to you and stroke your forehead, which is still damp from the sponge. Touching you now is an odd experience. Your skin is just skin, like mine, like anybody else's. What makes you so special? I know your heart is still beating, but I'm more interested in what your brain is doing. That's the bit of you that makes you different from other people.

Robert Angilley.

The scream is still there, the one that started yesterday. But at the moment I'm making sure no one can hear it apart from me.

'Hello, Robert. I'm back.'

It's crazy, but I wait for a response, watch your face for signs of movement.

'Your brother's lost an eye. Graham. I've seen him again. It wasn't as bad as the first time.' There's too much to say. I don't know where to start. 'He's in hospital too. Not this one. Another one. It was because of me that he was hurt. I didn't do it deliberately. It just happened.'

I imagine that I see your eyelids flicker. Probably because I've been staring so intently. We see what we want to see.

'I know everything, Robert. Nobody told me. Well, some things I found out, from the police, from talking to Juliet. But I worked out the most important bits on my own. And ever since, all I've been able to think about is coming here to tell you. You might live or you might die, but either way, I want you to know I've beaten you. I have, Robert, though you had the advantage over me for so long. You were the one with all the information, who could decide whether to reveal it or not.'

I bend to kiss your lips. I expect them to be cold, but they're not. They're warm. I back away. 'I can do and say whatever I want to you now, can't I? You've got no control. It's all up to me. I'm the one with the information, and all the power. I'm the one who's going to be doing the revealing, and you've got no choice but to lie there and listen to me. It's the opposite of how it was with Juliet.'

Another flicker of your eyelid, barely noticeable.

'I know Graham raped her too. And you found her and looked after her, married her, made her trust you and need you. Just like you did with me. It must be easy to make a woman fall for you when you know so much about her, so much she doesn't know you know. Easy to say all the right things. It worked so well with Juliet, didn't it? And then you wanted to see if it would again. With Sandy Freeguard.'

My legs start to shake. I sit down in the chair beside your bed. 'Sandy wasn't quite as good as Juliet, though. For your purposes. You must have been disappointed, after such a good start – her falling for your knight-in-shining-armour act. Why wouldn't she? You know how to make us feel safe and looked after. But Sandy wasn't like Juliet, or me. She didn't shrink into herself and make it her life's work to hide her sordid little secret. She told the police, joined support groups, dealt with the rape better than anyone could have expected. It didn't occur to her to feel ashamed, or try to conceal anything. Your brother's the one who should be ashamed. Sandy Freeguard realised that long before I did, long before Juliet did.'

The anger I feel is unlike any I've known before. It's cold, meticulous. I wonder if this sort of icy fury, the sort you can control and mould, is the same thing as evil. If it is, then there's evil inside me for the first time in my life.

'How much did Sandy Freeguard talk to you about what your brother did to her? A lot, probably. It must have been the main thing on her mind. She was a talker, and you were her loving, caring boyfriend.'

I lean in closer. 'How infuriating for you. What a waste of all your efforts. Your sick little game only worked with women who buried the experience, went into hiding. People like me and Juliet, who were terrified of anybody knowing, because of what the world might think about us. That was the kick you got, wasn't it? Marrying Juliet, knowing she had no idea that you knew. Watching her make a fool of herself day after day, loving and trusting the brother of the man who'd raped her, who'd profited from raping her. Thinking that, however awful she felt, however shattered she was inside, at least she'd succeeded in concealing her defeat from the world, and now she had you, and things were starting to improve. You must have known all that was in her mind. You relished your secret knowledge, didn't you? Gloated privately about how wrong she was, how far from the real truth. I can see the two of you at home, in your lounge, watching television, eating dinner. Fucking. And all the time, every second you were together, you knew you could destroy her entire world at any moment, if you chose to, by telling her you knew about the rape, that it was the only reason you were ever interested in her. And it wasn't only Graham who'd made money out of it. You did too. You were in business together. You knew you could tell Juliet that any time you wanted. The ultimate power trip.'

I stand up, walk over to the window. A man in a green boiler suit and protective goggles is trimming the small round bushes in the courtyard outside your room, using a motorised blade. The droning sound stops every so often, then starts again.

'It's one of the most effective ways of ruining someone's life – showing them, suddenly, that their interpretation of the world, everything they think they understand and believe to be true, everything that matters to them, is based on a lie, a cruel, sadistic trick. Maybe it's the most effective way to destroy another human being. You must have thought so. I know what you're like, Robert; only the best will do.'

You say nothing. I am trying to provoke somebody who's unconscious.

'I hope you're impressed,' I say. 'You might have misled me successfully, but there were side effects that you didn't foresee. You can't give someone a year of your life and let them love you in the way I did without giving some of yourself to that other person. And you gave me enough to be sure I'm right about this. Now I'm the one who knows things about you, things you'd never have imagined I'd be able to figure out. But I have, because our relationship was real as well as fake.'

Your eyelids twitch; this time I know I haven't imagined it. The phrase 'rapid eye movement' comes to mind. Doesn't it happen when you're deeply asleep? Perhaps you're having a bad dream. What would that mean, for someone like you, whose chosen way of life is more horrific than most people's nightmares?

'You raped Prue Kelvey, although you didn't really want to. Graham wanted you to, so you did, but you didn't enjoy it, did you? Not like Graham enjoyed raping women – he loved it. He said you weren't interested in the waitress either, on his stag night, though you raped her too, egged on by your brother. It was a sort of experiment, wasn't it – doing what Graham did, just from time to time? To prove to yourself that your way was superior, in a different league.'

I am terrified of your eyes opening. I need to be able to finish, and I'm not sure I could with you looking at me. Answering me.

'I know you made Prue Kelvey wear a mask over her eyes while you were forcing yourself on her. Graham thinks you did it because you were scared of her seeing your face, scared she might meet you again one day and recognise you. I knew he was wrong when he said that. But I was also wrong. Until I walked into this room and saw you today, I thought you'd made Prue Kelvey keep her mask on so that she didn't see your face. So you could do to her what you did to Juliet and Sandy, and me: engineer a meeting, become her boyfriend, her saviour. And then wreck her life, bring it all crashing down.'

I shake my head, wondering how I could have believed this. 'Of course it wasn't that. The order of events would have been all wrong. I know your tidy mind, Robert. You had to be the saviour first – really *be* a saviour – and then become the destroyer. That's why Graham's victims were perfect. It wouldn't have worked at all for you, would it, with a woman you'd already raped yourself?'

I swallow hard and continue. 'You made Prue Kelvey wear a mask when you were raping her because you couldn't bear to see the *lack* of recognition in her eyes. Her terror was nothing to do with you as an individual – you were just some nameless attacker. You couldn't stand that thought, could you? You felt insignificant – as if you might as well have been anyone. She didn't even know your name, though you and Graham knew hers, had chosen her specifically from all the women you might have picked. Which made her more special than you, and that drove you insane. You needed it to be more personal. You wanted to be important to the women, wanted it to matter to them that you were you. Not some anonymous rapist, interchangeable with your brother.'

I stand up, get as far away from you as I can in this small room. When I next speak, my voice is hoarse, as if there's sandpaper in my throat. 'You and Graham aren't interchangeable at all. You wanted to hurt women more than he did. Raping them was enough for him, but not for you. I'm not surprised you wanted people to notice how unique you are. There's nobody in the world like you, Robert.

'You told me about hurting distance, remember? There was a limit to how much you could hurt Prue Kelvey, and that waitress on Graham's stag night, because they didn't know you. Everyone knows there are brutal, violent people in the world, like there are hurricanes and earthquakes. If we don't know these monsters personally, we can think of them as being almost like natural disasters – when they devastate our lives, we don't take it personally. It's just random. They haven't known us and loved us, been close to us. We tell ourselves that they don't know the good, sensitive, vulnerable people we truly are. If they did, they wouldn't be able to hurt us in the way they have. The damage might be terrible, but it isn't really about us. It could have happened to anyone. You told me all this yourself, and you were right.'

My breath mists the windowpane. I draw a heart with my index finger, then rub it out. 'I know from personal experience, Robert. It makes it so much easier if you can put some distance between you and your attacker. Your brother knew my name, when he forced me into his car at knifepoint, but he didn't know *me*. I knew it wasn't about me. That was a consolation.' The inside of my mouth feels like leather. The air in your room is warm and dry. I can't open the window. There's a lock on it and it won't budge.

'Graham pretended it was his idea to choose women who had websites as your victims, so that you could taunt them with what you knew about them. The personal angle – more fear and hurt in their eyes, as they wondered why they, of all women, had been chosen. Graham told me all about it, and was happy to take all the credit. But it was your idea, wasn't it, Robert? After Graham's stag night, you were frustrated. Probably angry. You felt as if that waitress had got off scot-free, didn't you? It felt like a wasted opportunity because, however much Graham had enjoyed himself, you knew the waitress would already have started to console herself with the idea that she was simply a victim of bad luck, in the wrong place at the wrong time.'

I wipe away tears. 'You suggested an amendment to Graham's business plan: instead of strangers, you suggested choosing particular women, letting them know you knew who they were and what they did. Letting them know they'd been hand-picked. Graham liked the idea, but he's more easily satisfied than you. You still weren't happy. It's your name you want known; no one else's is important. But you could hardly suggest to Graham that the two of you introduce yourselves to the women you planned to rape, build up a relationship with them and *then* rape them, could you? Graham didn't want to be caught.'

But he has been, and that's partly thanks to me. I try to remember that I am not only a victim of you and your brother. I am also, or could also be, a winner. Depending on what I do now.

I carry on talking to your closed eyes. 'You didn't worry about getting caught, did you? You were confident you could destroy your victims so completely that they'd pose no threat. You thought your method was foolproof. Shall I tell you about your method?' I laugh, a hard, rusty cackle from the back of my throat. 'First you get close to us, you get within hurting distance. You make us love you, and need you, so that our whole world is Robert, Robert, Robert. God, you're brilliant at that part of it! So loving, so romantic. You're the perfect husband or lover – whatever the role you're playing, you put all your energy and enthusiasm into it. If we didn't believe you were the perfect soul mate, it wouldn't hurt as much when we found out the truth, would it?'

I grab the edge of your top pillow and yank it out from under your head, holding it in both hands. 'That's the part you look forward to most. The hurting. The big shock when you reveal who you really are. You told me yourself.'

I fall silent as I remember your exact words: *I've thought about leaving her for so long. Planning it, looking forward to it. It's turned into this . . . legendary thing in my mind. The grand finale.*

'Yvon was wrong to think you'd never leave Juliet for me,' I say. 'You would have done, eventually. That was always part of your plan. But you wanted to draw out the thrill of anticipation, extend it for as long as possible, before moving on to your next victim. We were Graham's victims first, then yours. I bet you saw Graham as some kind of support act – you knew that you were the one who was really going to destroy us: Juliet, Sandy Freeguard. Though you saw that Sandy Freeguard would be very hard to destroy, so you moved on to another name on the list – mine.'

I squeeze the pillow in my hands, digging my fingernails into it. The fabric springs back. I cannot leave a mark, however hard I press, cannot transmit my agony to this inanimate object.

'You pride yourself on having nerves of steel,' I say, 'but deep down you're a coward, and a hypocrite. Much as you despise your brother, you don't cut all ties, do you? You still let him use your lorry for his rape nights. You even raped Prue Kelvey to keep him happy, keep him onside. Because there's one thing Graham's got that you desperately need – his list of victims' names. So that you can make them your victims too.

'All the time you were married to Juliet, you knew one day you'd hit her with the truth. The Wednesday before last

– that was the day you chose. You were supposed to be meeting me the next day at the Traveltel. It would have been the thirtieth of March, the anniversary of the day your brother raped me. How perfect, from your point of view. You knew that if you told me you'd left Juliet to start a new life with me, I would think of that date as having been vindicated, cleansed. I'd have been even more sure that we were destined to be together, that you were my saviour. Because there's no such thing as a coincidence, right?

'You didn't turn up, but if you had, if your plan had worked, you'd have had a suitcase with you. You'd have told me you'd left Juliet and asked if you could come home with me. Can you guess what I would have said?'

I laugh bitterly. Tears fall on my hand, on the pillow. I'm crying hard, but I'm not upset. I'm angry, so angry that the pressure in my head is squeezing moisture out of my eyes.

'What did you say to Juliet? How did you break the news? If I'm right – and I'm sure I am – you probably waited until the two of you were in bed. Did you climb on top of her, ignoring her protests that she was tired? She must have been confused. You were always so gentle with her – what was going on? Suddenly you weren't gentle any more. She didn't recognise you as the Robert she knew and loved, the man she'd married. You raped her, like you'd always known you would one day, like you'd always planned to. Except it was so much better than with Prue Kelvey, because you were within hurting distance. You saw the terrible pain in Juliet's eyes and you knew it was all for you.

'And raping her in itself wouldn't have been enough for you either – not when you could make it even worse for her. You wanted her to connect this ordeal with the other one, the night in Graham's chalet.' I shake the pillow in front of your inert features. 'You see how much I know? Aren't you impressed? It was important to you that Juliet should realise the full horror of what you'd done to her, how badly you'd betrayed and deceived her. So how did you do it? I bet you said what Graham said, didn't you? "Do you want to warm up before the show?" Or something along those lines. That will have been the best moment for you, seeing her eyes widen in shock, seeing the incomprehension on her face. And what then? Apart from rape. Did you tell her you were leaving her for me, another of your brother's victims? Did you tell her everything at that point, including that you planned to spend the next few years wrecking my life in exactly the way you'd wrecked hers: first marrying me and making me idyllically happy, then demolishing it all, once you'd lined up another of Graham's casualties to take my place?'

My whole body is shaking, sweating. I put my face close to yours. 'I don't think so,' I answer my own question. 'You'll have wanted her to think she was the only one you'd done it to. You wouldn't allow her the comfort of knowing she wasn't alone in her victimhood. No, you just told her you were leaving her for another woman. That's all you said about me. But you told Juliet everything else – that the man who raped her was your brother, and all about the family business. Every little detail made it worse for her and better for you.

'Except you made a mistake, didn't you? A fucking big one, as it turns out, because look at you now. You thought Juliet would crumble when she knew the truth. You thought you'd be able to walk out of that horrible house, leaving behind a quivering wreck of a wife, far too weak to go to the police or do anything about the new information you'd given her. She didn't report the first rape, did she?

Because she was too ashamed. You were counting on her being too ashamed to report the second. Who'd have believed her, anyway? Suddenly she's claiming to have been raped not once but twice, the second time by her devoted husband? If she'd told anyone, you would have looked baffled and expressed concern about her sanity.'

I walk up and down your room, folding and unfolding the pillow. 'I know what it's like to make plans and have them destroyed, Robert. I understand, I really do. I'm a planner too. And you'd been so thorough, thought of every detail. God, it must have been annoying when your revelation changed Juliet in a way you'd never anticipated. She became stronger, not weaker. She didn't collapse in a helpless heap. She picked up a stone doorstop and bashed your head in with it. Didn't even call an ambulance afterwards, just let you lie there bleeding. Dying. I can't say I blame her.'

My throat is burning. I can't talk for much longer. I also can't stop yet. This is what I've been looking forward to: telling you everything, getting it all out of me. 'You're too caught up in your own thoughts, in your own little world,' I say. 'Well, you've not got much choice now, I suppose. But I mean before. Because you're such a narcissist, you miscalculated. Juliet had already fallen apart once. She'd had a nervous breakdown. She was insecure and timid for all the years you were married to her. The only way was up, Robert – why didn't you see that? Why didn't it occur to you that human beings are actually quite resilient, especially ones like Juliet, and me, who've come from loving families and secure backgrounds. When you showed Juliet the twisted creature you really are, it was a big enough shock to send everything flying in her brain. Everything rearranged itself. Seeing that her rescuer was actually her enemy made her fight back in a way that nothing else probably could have.'

Your eyelids move.

'Is that your way of asking me how I know all this? I know because the same happened to me. When I worked out the truth, put it all together, I realised how stupid I'd been to believe another person could save me. For the first time since your brother raped me, I wanted to fight back, on my own. Other people trick you and lie to you, and the ones who are supposed to love you do it the most – that's what Juliet thinks now. That's how she sees the world. You've turned her into a monster too, one who doesn't care about anything any more, not even herself.'

I laugh. 'You know, she could have told me everything she knew about you, but she didn't. Instead, she used it to taunt me. Even though she knows what a grotesque, sick pervert you are, she still hates me for trying to steal her husband – the kind, sensitive one. You might find that weird. I don't. Two Roberts exist in my head, just as they do in hers. That's probably the worst thing you've done to us both. You've left us mourning the loss of a man who never existed. Even knowing that, we still love him.'

I look down at the pillow in my hands. When I first reached for it, my intention was to smother you. To succeed where Juliet failed. I'm glad she didn't kill you. Now I can. You deserve it. Anyone would agree you deserve to die, apart from the naïve and the misguided, those who believe killing is always wrong.

But if I end your life now, your suffering is almost over. It will only last a few more seconds. Whereas if I don't, if I walk out of this room and leave you alive, you'll have to lie there and think about everything I've said, about how I won and you lost, in spite of your best efforts. That'll be torture for you. Assuming you've heard everything I've said.

The trouble, now as before, is that I have no way of knowing what you're thinking, Robert. You can see how much you've hurt me. I've kind of given the game away on that front. Maybe that's what you'll concentrate on, if I leave you breathing in this room. Maybe you're the winner, immune from punishment in your cocooned state, and I'm destroyed, utterly destroyed, even more so because I haven't faced up to it yet.

I want to say one last thing to you before I either end your life or allow it to continue, a few words I prepared in my head before I came here. I chose them as carefully as I choose the mottos for my sundials. I whisper them in your ear, like a blessing, or a magic spell: 'You're the worst person I've ever known, Robert. And the worst person I'll ever know.' Saying this aloud underlines something in my mind: that the worst is over.

And now I need to decide.

32

13/4/06

'I don't think he wants to give you a hard time,' said Olivia. 'I think he's genuinely worried about you. You should ring him. You'll have to speak to him eventually.'

Bright sunlight glowed through the closed curtains. Charlie wished she'd bought thicker ones, wondered how much it would cost to have black-out lining added. She shook her head. Her plan – a far better one than Olivia's – was to go nowhere near the phone. Simon had left lots of messages that she didn't want to listen to. Besides, Olivia was wrong: Charlie would not necessarily have to speak to Proust eventually. Or Simon. She could hand in her notice. Then she'd never need to face either of them again.

Olivia sat down beside her on the sofa. 'I can't stay here for ever, Char. I've got work to do and a life to get on with. And so have you. This is no good, lying around in your pyjamas, smoking all day. Why don't you go and get dressed, have a nice hot bath? Brush your teeth.'

The doorbell rang. Charlie huddled on the sofa, pulling her dressing gown tight around her body. 'It'll be Simon,' she said. 'Don't let him in. Tell him I'm sleeping.'

Olivia gave her a stern look and went to answer the door. She couldn't understand why Charlie wasn't happier about Simon's relentless pursuit of her, why he had suddenly become the person she least wanted to see. Charlie was unwilling to demean herself by explaining. She knew she'd go to pieces as soon as he opened his mouth to speak. Whatever he said would be wrong. If his attempts to make her feel better were subtle and indirect, Charlie would put it down to embarrassment, which would add to her shame. If he was explicit, she would have to have a conversation with him – the man who'd been rejecting her love ever since they'd met – about Graham Angilley, the serial rapist she'd fallen for on the rebound . . . No, there was only so much degradation a person could take.

Charlie heard the front door close. Olivia reappeared in the lounge. 'It's not Simon. Ah!' She pointed an accusing finger at Charlie. 'You're disappointed, and don't deny it. It's Naomi Jenkins.'

'No. Tell her no.'

'She's got something for you.'

'I don't want it.'

'I've told her you need five minutes to get ready. So why don't you go and throw on some clothes, make yourself presentable? Otherwise I'll just let her in and she can see you in your tea-stained dressing gown and shapeless pyjamas.'

'If you do that, I'll . . .'

'What? What will you do?' Olivia's nostrils flared. 'Simon I'd have sent away, but not her.' She nodded in the direction of the hall. 'Stop feeling sorry for yourself for a minute and think about what she's been through. Think about what she went through only a few days ago, right here in this house, never mind the rest of it. Tied up, *again*. Nearly raped, again.'

'You don't have to tell me,' said Charlie quickly. She didn't want to think about what Proust and Simon had found in her kitchen: Graham's detached left eye, sliced neatly in two, staring up at them from a pool of blood.

'I think I do,' Olivia disagreed. 'Because you seem to think you're the only one who's ever had anything bad happen to her.'

'I don't think that!' said Charlie angrily.

'Do you think it's easy for me, knowing I can't ever have children?'

Charlie tutted quietly, turning away. 'What's that got to do with anything?'

'Any man I meet, any man I start a relationship with that's even vaguely serious, I've got to break the bad news – imagine dropping that bombshell on a first date. You have no idea how many blokes I never see again, after I tell them. It really hurts, but I keep the pain to myself because I'm a stoic, and I believe in stiff upper lips . . .'

'A stoic? You?' Charlie laughed.

'I am,' Olivia insisted. 'About serious things, I am. Just because I moan when my local deli runs out of venison and chilli pâté, that means nothing!' She sighed. 'You're lucky, Char. Simon knows about you and Graham . . .'

'Shut up!'

'. . . and he knows it wasn't your fault. No one blames you.'

'All right, I'll see Naomi.' Anything to stop Olivia talking about Simon and Graham. Charlie stood up, stubbing out her cigarette in the ashtray on the table, which was already full of butts. They shifted and rearranged themselves – a writhing heap of fat, orangey-brown maggots – as a new one pressed down on the pile. How disgusting, thought Charlie, perversely pleased by the sight.

Upstairs, she washed, brushed her hair and teeth, and put on the first clothes she saw when she opened her wardrobe: jeans with frayed ends and a lilac-and-turquoise rugby shirt with a white collar. When she came back downstairs, the front door was open, and Naomi Jenkins and Olivia were both outside. Naomi looked more relaxed than Charlie had ever seen her, but older as well. There were lines on her face that weren't there two weeks ago.

Charlie struggled to smile, and Naomi did her best to respond. This was what Charlie had wanted to avoid: the twisted, awkward greeting, acknowledging shared experience and pain that could never be forgotten.

'Look,' said Olivia. She appeared to be pointing at the front wall of the house, beneath the lounge window.

Charlie pushed her feet into a pair of trainers that she'd discarded days ago by the bottom of the stairs, and went outside. Propped against the front wall was a sundial, a flat rectangle of grey stone, about four feet by three, and two inches deep. The gnomon was a solid iron triangle with a round lump, the shape of a large ball bearing, halfway along its top edge. The motto was in Latin, spelled out in gold letters: *Docet umbra*. At the very top of the dial, in the centre, was the bottom half of a sun. Its downward-slanting rays were the lines that represented the hours and half-hours: the time lines. Another line – a horizontal curve, the shape of a tilted smile – cut across these and ran all the way along the dial, from its left edge to its right.

'I said I'd make one for your boss,' said Naomi. 'Here it is. You can have it, there's no charge.'

Charlie was shaking her head. 'I won't be back at work for a while.' *If ever.* 'Take it into the police station, ask for Inspector Proust . . .'

'No. I've brought it here because I wanted to give it to you. It's important to me.' Naomi was trying to catch Charlie's eye.

'Thank you,' said Olivia pointedly. 'It's very kind of you.'

Charlie was convinced her sister was behaving well with the sole aim of making her seem even more ungracious by comparison. 'Thanks,' she mumbled.

There was a heavy pause. Then Naomi said, 'Simon Waterhouse told me you had no idea about Graham. When you got involved with him.'

'I don't want to talk about that.'

'You shouldn't punish yourself for something that wasn't your fault. I did for years, and it got me nowhere.'

'Goodbye, Naomi.' Charlie turned to go back inside. If Olivia wanted to, she could bring the bloody sundial in. Charlie didn't care. Proust had probably forgotten by now that he'd ever wanted one.

'Wait. How's Robert?'

'The same,' said Olivia, after Charlie failed to answer. 'They keep trying to bring him round, but nothing so far. He's still having epileptic fits, but not as often.'

'If he does regain consciousness, he'll be facing a long list of charges,' said Charlie. 'It's clear from what we found at Silver Brae Chalets that he was very much involved in the stag-night business. He did a lot of the driving and took half the profits.' Olivia would have told Naomi all this if Charlie hadn't got her version in first. Olivia was the one who had spoken to Simon; Charlie had heard it all second-hand. She didn't want Naomi to know the extent to which she'd relinquished her grip on her life. 'Robert likes impersonal, bland places, doesn't he? Service stations, the Traveltel, hospital? Just as well. Prison makes your average service station seem like the Ritz.'

'He deserves whatever he gets,' said Naomi, turning to Olivia when Charlie refused to look at her. 'So does Graham. And his wife.'

'They've both been refused bail—' said Olivia.

'All right, for fuck's sake, that'll do!' Charlie cut her sister off.

'Simon Waterhouse also said that Juliet hasn't spoken for several days,' said Naomi.

Charlie looked up this time. Nodded. She didn't like to think of Juliet Haworth sitting silently in a cell. Charlie would have felt better if Juliet were still making demands, taunting everybody she came into contact with. Juliet would also be going to prison for a long time, perhaps as long as Graham Angilley. It didn't seem right.

'What haven't you told me?' Charlie asked Naomi. 'Juliet tried to kill Robert because she found out he'd colluded with her rapist – I know that much. What I still don't know is, why did Robert deliberately befriend the women Graham had attacked?' She felt herself getting sucked back in, and resented it. Naomi Jenkins had been playing games with her from the start, and Charlie wasn't prepared to lose any more games.

Naomi frowned. 'I'll tell you when it's over,' she said. 'It's not over yet.'

'What do you mean?' asked Olivia. Charlie wished her sister would keep quiet, or, ideally, go back into the house. Where hopefully she might remember that she was an arts journalist and not a police officer.

'There's a date line on the sundial,' said Naomi, pointing.

Charlie looked again at the rectangular slab propped against her wall.

'On the ninth of August, Robert's birthday, the shadow of the nodus will follow that line exactly, follow the curve all the way along. This is the nodus, here.' Naomi rubbed the small metal sphere with her thumb.

Suspicion flared inside Charlie. 'Why would you want to

mark Robert's birthday on a sundial and ask me to give it to my inspector?'

'Because that's when it began,' said Naomi. 'On the day Robert was born. The ninth of August,' she repeated the date. 'Remember to look, if it's a sunny day.'

She turned to leave with a small wave. Charlie and Olivia watched as she got into her car and drove away.

33

Thursday 4 May

It will get better. I will get better. One day I will stand here and be able to breathe easily. One day I will feel brave enough to come here without Yvon. I will say the words 'room eleven' in another context – perhaps about another hotel, a luxurious one on a beautiful island – and not think of this square room with its scratched double-glazed windows and chipped skirting boards. Or the pushed-together twin beds with their horrible orange gym-mat mattresses, or this building that looks like a shabby university hall of residence or a cheap conference centre.

Yvon sits on the sofa, picking at the small bobbles on the cushions, while I stare out at the car park the Traveltel shares with Rawndesley East Services.

'Don't be cross with me,' I say.

'I'm not.'

'I know you think it's bad for me, being here, but you're wrong. I need this place to lose its significance. If I never came again, it'd always haunt me.'

'The haunting would fade over time,' Yvon obligingly contributes her lines to this by-now-familiar argument. 'This Thursday-night pilgrimage of ours is keeping your memories alive.'

'I have to do it, Yvon. Until I get bored, until coming here's a chore. It's like what people say about falling off a horse and being scared: you have to get straight back on.'

She puts her head in her hands. 'It's so *un*like that, I don't know where to begin trying to explain it to you.'

'Shall we have a cup of tea?' I pick up the kettle with the peeling label and take it into the bathroom to fill it with water. At a safe distance from Yvon, I say, 'Maybe I'll stay here tonight. You don't have to.'

'No way.' She appears in the doorway. 'I'm not letting you do that. And I don't believe this is what you say it is.'

'What do you mean?'

'You know what Robert is, what he did, but you're still pining for him, aren't you? That's why you want to be here. Where were you this afternoon? When I rang? You were out and you didn't answer your mobile.'

I look away, out of the window. There is a blue lorry pulling into the car park, black letters painted on its side. 'I told you: I was sawing in my workshop. I didn't hear my phone.'

'I don't believe you. I think you were in the hospital, sitting by Robert's bedside. And it's not the first time. There've been other times I've not been able to get hold of you recently . . .'

'Intensive care's a locked unit,' I tell her. 'You can't just walk in. Yvon, I hate Robert. I hate him in the way you can only hate someone if you once loved them.'

'I hated Ben that way once, and now look at us,' she says, her voice full of scorn for us both.

'It was your choice to give him another chance.'

'And it'll be yours to stay with Robert, if and when he wakes up. Despite everything. You'll forgive him, the two of you'll get married, you'll go and visit him every week in prison . . .'

'Yvon, I can't believe you're saying this.'

'Don't do it, Naomi.'

A ringing sound comes from my jacket, which I slung down on the bed when Yvon and I first arrived. I pull my phone out of the pocket, thinking about love, about hurting distance. Thanks to my conversation with your brother in Charlie Zailer's kitchen, I understand you better than I did before. I worked out for myself that you wanted to hurt women, and that you needed them to worship you first in order to magnify the hurt so that it was unbearable, but it wasn't only about that, was it? Your psychosis is like a – what are those things called? That's right: a palindrome. It works in reverse as well. Love and pain are inextricably linked in your mind – Graham made me see that. You believed that only if you injured and abused women would they ever truly love you. *Dear Mama's legacy*, Graham said. However much you might have loved your mother before she turned on you, you loved her more afterwards, didn't you? When your father left and she made you suffer, it was your anguish that forced you to acknowledge the strength of that love.

'Naomi?'

For a moment I mistake this man's voice for yours. Only because of where I am.

'It's Simon Waterhouse. I thought you'd want to know. Robert Haworth died this afternoon.'

'Good,' I say, without hesitation, and not only for Yvon's benefit. I mean it. 'What happened?'

'Nobody's sure yet. There'll be a post-mortem, but . . . well, to put it simply, it looks like he just stopped breathing. It sometimes happens, after bad brain bleeds. The swollen brain can't send messages to the respiratory system in the way that it needs to. I'm sorry.'

'I'm not,' I tell him. 'I'm only sorry that the hospital staff think he died a natural, peaceful death. He didn't deserve that.' It would be easy to tell myself you were a damaged person, sick, as much a victim as your victims. I refuse to do that. Instead, I will think of you as evil. I have to draw a line, Robert.

You are dead. I'm talking – directing my thoughts – to nobody. Your memories and justifications, they're all gone. I don't feel elated. It's more the sensation of crossing something off a list and feeling lighter. Now there's only one more thing to cross off, and when that's done, this will be over. Maybe then I'll be able to stop coming here. Maybe room eleven has become the headquarters of my operation, until close of business.

That's assuming Charlie Zailer cares enough about closing our business to start thinking about that sundial I gave her.

As if he is reading my mind, Simon Waterhouse asks, 'Have you – I'm sorry to ask you this, but have you spoken to Sergeant Zailer recently? There's no reason why you should have, it's just . . .' His voice tails off.

I am tempted to ask him if he's seen the sundial. Perhaps Charlie's sister took it in and gave it to the inspector who wanted it. I would like, one day, to walk past Spilling Police Station and see it there, on the wall. I wonder if I should mention anything about the dial to Simon Waterhouse. I decide not to. 'I've tried,' I tell him, 'but I don't think Charlie wants to speak to anyone at the moment. Apart from Olivia.'

'It's okay,' he says. His descending voice tells me very clearly that it isn't.

34

19/5/06

Charlie sat at a window table in Mario's – a small, loud, Italian café in Spilling's market square – so that she could watch the street. She'd see Proust before he came in, which would give her time to arrange her features. Into what? She didn't really know.

This wasn't the first time she'd left the house since coming back from Scotland – Olivia had made her walk round the block and to the corner shop every few days, claiming it would be good for her – but it was the first time she'd been out alone, to a proper place, to meet someone. Even if that someone was only the Snowman.

Naomi Jenkins' sundial was leaning against the wall of the café, attracting bemused glances, and some admiring ones, from waitresses and other customers. Charlie wished she'd wrapped it, but it was too late now. Still, at least it was the dial everyone was looking at and not her. She dreaded the day when someone in the road would point at her and yell, 'Hey's it's that woman copper, the one who screwed that rapist.' Charlie had decided to grow her hair, to avoid being recognised. When it was longer, she might dye it blond.

Proust was in front of her; she'd forgotten to look out for him. Most of the time, she thought, the real world might as well not exist. She barely heard the CD of famous opera arias that was deafening everybody else in Mario's, or the

403

flamboyant owner's loud, tuneless vocal accompaniment from behind the counter. Charlie's universe had been reduced to a few agonising thoughts that repeated endlessly in her mind: why did I have to meet Graham Angilley? Why was I stupid enough to fall for him? Why has my name been all over the papers and the news while he's protected by anonymity? Why is life so fucking unfair?

'Morning, Charlie,' said the inspector awkwardly. He was carrying a large paperback book, the one about sundials that Simon had bought for him. He'd never called Charlie by her first name before. 'What's that?'

'A sundial, sir.'

'You don't need to call me sir,' said Proust. 'We're in a café,' he added, as if it were an explanation.

'It's yours for free. Even Superintendent Barrow can't object to that.'

Proust looked disgruntled. 'Free? Did Naomi Jenkins make it?'

'Yes.'

'I don't like the motto. *Docet umbra*: the shadow informs. It's too pedestrian.'

'Is that what it means?' Of course. Charlie should have guessed the words were significant.

'When are you coming back?' Proust asked.

'I don't know if I am.'

'You have to ride it out. The quicker you put it behind you, the sooner everyone'll forget.'

'Really? If one of my colleagues slept with a famous serial rapist, I don't think I'd forget about it.'

'All right, perhaps people won't forget,' said Proust impatiently, as if this were a mere detail. 'But you're a good officer and you did nothing wrong.' Giles Proust, determined to remain upbeat? This was a first.

'So why the official inquiry?' said Charlie.

'That wasn't my decision. Look, it'll be over before you know it. Between you and me, it's just a formality, and . . . you have my full support.'

'Thank you, sir.'

'And . . . everyone else . . . also wants to . . .' Evidently the Snowman didn't know how to broach the subject of Simon. He fiddled with the cuffs of his shirt, then picked up the laminated menu and examined it studiously.

'What's Simon Waterhouse told you to say?' asked Charlie.

'Why won't you see him? The man's beside himself.'

'I can't.'

'You could speak to him on the telephone.'

'No.' Every time Simon's name was mentioned, Charlie felt her composure start to unravel.

'Email?' Proust sighed. 'Come back to work, Sergeant. The first few days might be awkward, but after that . . .'

'Not awkward. A nightmare. And after that, the next few days'll be a nightmare. Every day will be a nightmare, until I retire. And even then—' Charlie stopped, realising her voice had started to shake.

Proust said, 'I can't do without you, you know.'

'You might have to.'

'Well, I can't!' She'd made him angry.

A young blonde waitress with a tattoo of a butterfly on her shoulder approached their table. 'Can I get you anything?' she asked. 'Tea, coffee, sandwich?'

'Do you have green tea?' asked Proust. When the answer was no, he produced a paper-wrapped tea bag from his jacket pocket.

Charlie couldn't help smiling as the waitress walked away, carrying the little packet at a distance from her body as if it were a tiny, ticking bomb. 'You brought one with you?'

'You insisted on meeting here and I feared the worst. She'll put milk and sugar in it, no doubt.' Proust turned his attention back to Charlie. 'Why did you ask me to bring this?' He patted the book on the table.

'I want you to look up a date for me: The ninth of August. When we were talking about Gibbs' wedding present, you said something about the date line on a sundial: that it represents two days of every year, not just one. That's right, isn't it?'

Proust's eyes shot towards the large slab of stone and metal that was propped against the wall. He looked at it for a few seconds, then looked back at Charlie. 'Yes. Each date has a twin, as it were, at some other time of the year. On those two days, the declination of the sun is exactly the same.'

'If one of those dates is the ninth of August, what's the other? What's the twin?'

Proust picked up his book and consulted the index. He turned to the relevant page. Stared at it for a long time. 'The fourth of May.'

Charlie's heart flipped over in her chest. She'd been right. Her crazy idea hadn't been crazy at all.

'The day Robert Haworth died,' said Proust, his tone matter-of-fact. 'What's the significance of the ninth of August?'

'Robert Haworth's birthday,' Charlie told him. What had Naomi said? *Because that's when it began.*

It's not over yet. She'd said that as well. But now it was. Robert Haworth was dead. His birthday was twinned with the date of his death, joined for ever, on the date line of this sundial in front of Charlie.

Docet umbra: the shadow informs.

'Naomi made this before Robert died,' said Charlie.

'Naturally, of respiratory failure,' Proust reminded her. 'That was the verdict at the inquest.'

His green tea arrived. Without milk or sugar.

'I think it'll look very handsome on the wall of our nick.' The Snowman sniffed his drink cautiously, then took a sip. 'And, given my colossal workload, I might well be too busy to notice, on the fourth of May next year, if the shadow of the nodus is on the date line. And even if I'm not too busy and I do remember to look, the day might be overcast. If there's no sun, there are no shadows.'

Does that mean, Charlie wondered, that if there are plenty of shadows, there must be a source of light somewhere?

'There's precious little man-made justice in this world,' said Proust. 'I like to think of Robert Haworth's death as a piece of natural justice. His body gave up the struggle, Sergeant. Mother Nature corrected one of her mistakes, that's all.'

Charlie bit her lip. 'With a little help,' she mumbled.

'True enough. Juliet Haworth almost certainly contributed to the outcome.'

'And she's going to go down because of that. Is that fair, sir?'

'She attacked Haworth in the heat of the moment. She'll be treated sympathetically.' Proust sighed. 'Come back to your team, Charlie. You won't change my mind about anything to do with work in a crowded, noisy café. I can't think properly with *La Traviata* screeching in the background.'

'I'll think about it.'

The inspector nodded. 'That'll do for now.' He leaned

over and ran his fingers across the sundial's smooth stone surface. 'I'd chosen my motto, you know, for the sundial I wanted. Before Superintendent Barrow put his foot down. *Depresso resurgo.*'

'Sounds a bit depressing,' said Charlie.

'It isn't. You don't know what it means.'

How could she not ask, with him sitting there like a schoolboy who'd done his homework, so evidently eager to tell her? 'Well?'

Proust gulped down the remains of his tea. 'I set, then rise again, Sergeant,' he said, keeping his eyes on Charlie as he lifted the wet bag out of the cup with his spoon. He held it up, a gesture of triumph. 'I set, then rise again.'

Acknowledgements

I am extremely grateful to the following people, all of whom helped a great deal: Peter Straus, Rowan Routh, Carolyn Mays, Kate Howard, Karen Geary, Ariane Galy, the whole team at Hodder, Lisanne Radice, Mark and Cal Pannone, Jenny Geras, Adèle Geras, Norman Geras, Chris Gribble, Tom Palmer, James Nash, Ray French, Guy Martland, Harriet James, John Davis, Wendy Wootton, Tony Faulkner, Suzie Crookes, Susan Richardson and Dan Jones.

A chilling standalone novel from
the queen of psychological crime…

SOPHIE
HANNAH

a game for all
the family

Justine thought she knew who she was, until someone seemed to know better . . .

After escaping London and a career that nearly destroyed her, Justine plans to spend
her days doing as little as possible in her beautiful new home.

But soon after the move, her daughter starts to withdraw when her new best friend,
George, is unfairly expelled from school. Justine begs the head teacher to reconsider,
only to be told that nobody's been expelled – there is, and was, no George.

Then the anonymous calls start: a stranger, making threats that suggest she
and Justine share a guilty secret. And then the caller starts talking about
three graves – two big and one small, to fit a child . . .

COMING SOON

the narrow bed

Linzi Birrell and Rhian Douglas: murdered.

Angela McCabe and Josh Norbury: murdered.

A killer the police have dubbed Billy Dead Mates is murdering pairs of best friends, one by one. Just before each murder, he sends his victim a small white book . . .

Three regional police forces are working together to identify and catch Billy. For five months, they've been failing. Then a fifth victim, scared by what she's seen and heard on the news, comes forward to seek help. Unlike Billy's first four victims, she isn't dead. Yet . . .

February 2016

She's only been gone two hours.

Her husband David was meant to be looking after their two-week-old daughter. But when Alice Fancourt walks into the nursery, her terrifying ordeal begins, for Alice insists the baby in the cot is a stranger she's never seen before.

With an increasingly hostile and menacing David swearing she must either be mad or lying, how can Alice make the police believe her before it's too late?

Sally is watching the news with her husband when she hears a name she ought not to recognise: Mark Bretherick.

SOPHIE
HANNAH

the point of rescue

It began with an affair.
And ended in murder.

'Addictive'
MARIE CLAIRE

'Irresistible'
GUARDIAN

Last year, a work trip Sally had planned was cancelled at the last minute. Desperate for a break from her busy life juggling work and a young family, Sally didn't tell her husband that the trip had fallen through. Instead, she booked a week off work and treated herself to a secret holiday.

All she wanted was a bit of peace – some time to herself – but it didn't work out that way. Because Sally met a man. Mark Bretherick. All the details are the same: where he lives, his job, his wife Geraldine and daughter Lucy. Except that the man on the news is a man Sally has never seen before. And Geraldine and Lucy Bretherick are both dead . . .

Ruth Bussey knows what it means to be in the wrong and to be wronged.

SOPHIE
HANNAH

the other half lives

Why would anyone confess to a
murder that never happened?

'Utterly gripping'   'Thrilling'
THE TIMES   SUNDAY TELEGRAPH

She once did something she regrets, and her punishment nearly destroyed her. Now Ruth is rebuilding her life, and has found a love she doesn't believe she deserves: Aidan Seed.

Aidan is also troubled by a past he hates to talk about, until one day he decides he must confide in Ruth. He tells her that years ago he killed someone: a woman called Mary Trelease.

Ruth is confused. She's certain she's heard the name before, and when she realises why it sounds familiar, her fear and confusion deepen — because the Mary Trelease that Ruth knows is very much alive . . .

TV producer Fliss Benson receives an anonymous card at work.

OVER ONE MILLION COPIES SOLD IN THE UK ALONE

SOPHIE HANNAH

a room swept white

Murder begins at home...

'Terrifying'   'Beautifully written'
HEAT   *DAILY EXPRESS*

The card has sixteen numbers on it, arranged in four rows of four — numbers that mean nothing to her.

On the same day, Fliss finds out she's going to be working on a documentary about miscarriages of justice involving cot-death mothers wrongly accused of murder. The documentary will focus on three women: Helen Yardley, Sarah Jaggard and Rachel Hines. All three women are now free, and the doctor who did her best to send them to prison for life, child protection zealot Dr Judith Duffy, is under investigation for misconduct.

For reasons she has shared with nobody, this is the last project Fliss wants to be working on. And then Helen Yardley is found dead at her home, and in her pocket is a card with sixteen numbers on it, arranged in four rows of four . . .

It's 1.15 a.m.
Connie Bowskill should be asleep.

SOPHIE
HANNAH

lasting damage

Don't go into the other
woman's house...

'Jaw-droppingly
assured'
DAILY EXPRESS

'A first-class
whodunnit'
SCOTSMAN

Instead, she's logging on to a property website in search of a particular house: 11 Bentley Grove, Cambridge. She knows it's for sale; she saw the estate agent's board in the front garden less than six hours ago.

Soon Connie is clicking on the 'Virtual Tour' button, keen to see the inside of 11 Bentley Grove and put her mind at rest once and for all. She finds herself looking at a scene from a nightmare: in the living room, in the middle of the carpet, there's a woman lying face down in a huge pool of blood. In shock, Connie wakes her husband Kit. But when Kit sits down at the computer to take a look, he sees no dead body, only a pristine beige carpet in a perfectly ordinary room . . .

When Amber Hewerdine consults a hypnotherapist, she doesn't expect that anything much will change.

She doesn't expect it to help with her chronic insomnia . . .

She doesn't expect to hear herself, under hypnosis, saying words that mean nothing to her: 'Kind, cruel, kind of cruel' – words she has seen somewhere before, if only she could remember where . . .

She doesn't expect to be arrested two hours later, as a result of having spoken those words out loud, in connection with the brutal murder of Katharine Allen, a woman she's never heard of . . .

An overnight plane delay is bad. Having to share your hotel room with a stranger is worse.

But that's only the beginning of Gaby Struthers' problems.

Gaby has never met Lauren Cookson. So how does Lauren know so much about her? How does she know that the love of Gaby's life has been accused of murder? Why is she telling her that he is innocent?

And why is she so terrified of Gaby?

A Q&A with Sophie Hannah

What inspired you to begin writing?

I always read obsessively as a child and I loved mystery stories and rhyming poetry in particular. Love of reading, and the escape books provided from real life, were my main inspirations. As soon as I could write, I started to invent my own characters, stories and poems. It was my main hobby throughout my childhood. I neglected first my school work and later my university work in order to be able to concentrate on it!

Which authors are your biggest inspirations?

Agatha Christie and Ruth Rendell on the crime front, for sure. My approach to plotting comes from Agatha, and my interest in psychological dysfunction comes straight from Ruth, I think. And, of the newer generation, I love the work of Tana French and Belinda Bauer.

What is the best piece of advice you could give to an aspiring writer?

Always write the thing you most want to write, and make sure it's something you're emotionally invested in or, ideally, completely obsessed with. Don't write something to please others — write from your own passion.

Why was crime fiction the genre that got you to move from writing poetry to writing novels?

I didn't move from poetry to mystery novels, it's just that my novels weren't good enough to get published when I first started trying to write crime fiction aged 17. My not-very-good attempts didn't get published, while at the same time my poetry was being published and praised all over the place, so I just assumed I was better at poetry. For ten years I wrote only poetry, but then when I had my first baby, I had the idea for *Little Face* — a crime story about a woman who's certain her baby has been swapped for another baby and nobody believes her. I couldn't get the idea out of my mind, so I decided to give the mystery genre one last go. Luckily, *Little Face* got published, became a bestseller, and I've been writing crime fiction ever since.

How does your experience as a poet affect the way you write novels?

I actually think there's an important connection between the two genres. In both, structure is fundamental, and I'm obsessed with structure in any piece of writing. Whether it's a poem or a crime novel, every single piece needs to be in the exact right position in relation to every other piece, or else the whole thing risks being flabby and shapeless. Also, both my poems and my novels are about people and their relationships to each other, so there's some overlap in terms of content.

How do you come up with the core mystery that each novel is centred around?

Sometimes I start with a twist or solution or motive for murder that I love, and I then work backwards to create the opening mystery. But when I do start with the mystery, it's always a question I can't immediately answer, a puzzle with apparently no solution. Often it's an apparently impossible scenario, and yet it seems to be happening. It has to be something I find compelling and intriguing, so that I'm desperate to solve the mystery myself. That way I know the reader is more likely to be intrigued and in suspense too. Most of my inspirations come from everyday life – I take something I've observed and then add to it, or build on it, to make something completely unusual that seems to defy explanation. Then the challenge for me is to come up with a satisfying solution to the puzzle.

How much planning goes into plotting every twist and turn of your novels?

Lots! I am a dedicated planner. I have to be, because of the sort of impossible scenarios that I create. If I didn't know the solution I was working my way towards, I'd find it impossible to write the book, so I construct a scene-by-scene plan of the whole novel before I start. I might change the odd detail as I go along – once I even changed the identity of the murderer! But it's very comforting to have a plan to work from. I regard it as the equivalent of an architect's drawing of a house – you need to look at the whole thing in miniature before starting to make it, or else you have no way of knowing whether the whole thing is likely to fall down!

Why do you choose to create mystery through psychological means rather than through violence?

I don't think there's anything inherently interesting or intriguing about violence. Most violence isn't at all mysterious – someone hits someone else because they're feeling angry in that moment, for example, and so it doesn't really interest me. However, people and their psychological dysfunctions and their warped behaviours create endless possibilities for mystery. It's the 'why' of violence and crime that interests me, assuming the 'why' is unusual enough.

Why are you drawn to exploring the dysfunctional aspects of ordinary people?

I believe we all have our dysfunctional, weird attributes. I think much harm and misery is a result of people failing to understand what makes others tick. There's a terrible problem of psychological illiteracy in our society, which results in people being judgemental and writing others off as evil instead of trying to understand.

Is it difficult to write such psychologically tortured characters that you may not be able to identify with?

No. I can identify with all my characters, even those who do things I would never do. Any human being, placed under intolerable pressure or subjected to great psychological pain and trauma, could do a terrible thing. It wouldn't mean they were necessarily a terrible person.

Stay up to date with Sophie Hannah.

🐦 @sophiehannahCB1

f /SophieHannahAuthor

www.sophiehannah.com